There Ain't No Do-Overs

By Gordon Amick

319 Press LLC

Copyright © 2024 by Gordon Amick

Published in the United States by 319 Press LLC

P.O. Box 341117
Austin, Tx 78734
www.319press.com

All rights reserved. No part of this book may be reproduced in any form or by any electronic or mechanical means including information storage and retrieval systems, without permission in writing from the author. The only exception is by a reviewer, who may quote short excerpts in a review.

This is a work of fiction. Names, characters, places, and incidents either are products of the author's imagination or are used fictitiously. Any resemblance to actual persons, living or dead, events, or locales is entirely coincidental.

ISBN 9798990895904 (ebook)
ISBN 9798990895911 (Paperback)
ISBN 9798990895928 (Hardcover)

Gordon Amick | gordonamick.com

Cover design by HJ Studios

To the Amicks
for teaching me about
loyalty, strength, and perseverance
Jay, Rob, Brenda
Iris, BJ, D

Chapter 1

Newcomers were big news in the tiny Texas town of Hamilton, and the Saturday Alex Patterson moved into the old Webber house in early 2018, the rumor mill ran wild. Hamilton was far off the beaten path; an hour south of Dallas and an hour west of the Baptist homeland of Waco, and the predominantly conservative locals grew suspicious of anything new or different.

As soon as real estate agent and resident busybody Cynthia Coker spread the word that she had sold the house to a single, long-haired stranger in his late thirties, the town was abuzz. Cynthia was skilled at embellishing, so the first wave of gossip painted their new neighbor as a sketchy character, perhaps a burnout from Dallas. "Although," she was quick to add, "he's a bit overweight, but tall and quite handsome." Before the ink was dry on the contract, she called local housewife, businesswoman, and fellow gossipmonger Irma Buchanan to broadcast the latest.

"He smelled like a brewery," Cynthia said. "And, Lord, the man looked like he hadn't bathed in a week. Although, I couldn't hardly tell where the smell was comin' from the way he was puffin' on that cigarette. 'Course, if he'd put on some decent clothes, cut that ridiculous hair and shave, he'd be nice looking."

"He actually bought the house?" Irma asked.

"Paid cash. Said he'd be movin' in as soon as possible. 'Course he didn't say where he was livin' now. I asked, but he said was he was some sort of musician and somethin' about bein' on the road. His driver's license said Los Angeles, California, but if I'd a just met him on the street, I'd think he was a beggar. I didn't really care 'cause after two years on the market I was finally selling Carl Webber's house."

"Have you told Darlene and Ruth Ann?" Irma inquired, asking about the two senior sisters who had lived across the street from the Webbers for decades.

Cynthia smirked, not being terribly fond of those two. "I'll let 'em find out on their own."

"On their own" meant only an hour as Irma called the sisters, defying Cynthia. Life in Hamilton was slow, but gossip moved at light speed. A few days later, sisters Darlene Viriglio and Ruth Ann Waterman would see whether Cynthia's reports were accurate when they heard a commotion on their usually tranquil street and peeked out from behind the curtain of their front parlor window to find an actual moving van parked at the old Webber place.

"Get your binoculars," Darlene called to Ruth Ann. "He's here!" and both sisters nestled into their loveseat for an afternoon of spying—one with binoculars, the other through squinted eyes, watching their new neighbor pull a stack of boxes from his slightly banged-up pickup truck. The movers carried additional boxes and furniture before carefully unloading a grand piano. "I guess Irma was right," Darlene remarked. "Said Cynthia said he was some sorta musician. Must be a piana player."

Both sisters were well beyond retirement age but had the vibrancy of women twenty years their junior. Darlene was tall with a sturdy build; most polite southerners would say she was 'big-boned'. Ruth Ann was much smaller, almost petite. Each had a full head of gray hair and maintained their appearances, always wearing clean, pressed clothes. Ruth Ann was more self-conscious about her appearance and would apply a full face of makeup before leaving the house, while Darlene preferred a casual look, often going makeup-free and wearing sneakers. As different as they were, Darlene and Ruth Ann never missed an opportunity to pass along good gossip.

The sisters covertly watched as the movers struggled with the legless, heavy piano while their new neighbor jumped around making animated gestures at what was clearly his prized possession.

"He sure is pitchin' a fit," Darlene the elder sister said, lowering the binoculars.

Ruth Ann squinted and leaned forward. "Why's a nice lookin' young man bein' all persnickety like that 'bout a piano? I hope he ain't one of them gays."

"Oh Lord. Antoinette'd have a fit bein' ignored by a bunch a handsome men comin' and goin'."

"'Course he might fix up that dumpy-lookin' lawn that Carl never took care of, rest his soul," Ruth Ann added. "I wouldn't mind that, unless he starts addin' a bunch a them gaudy statutes like we seen on that TV show 'bout that fella in Austin."

Once the movers had eased the piano inside and closed the door, Darlene picked up the phone and updated their circle with the latest on their new neighbor.

The sisters didn't have any *best* friends, other than one another—as their mama taught them—, but they'd maintained the same tight group of ladies for decades.

The first call was to Sarah Livingston, a widow Darlene talked with daily. "I seen him," Darlene started with an enthusiastic tone. "He's a looker."

"Cynthia said he looked like a bum," Sarah said.

"Pfft. Cynthia don't see nothin' but money. He don't look rich, but who dresses up to work in the hot sun, other 'n Cynthia?"

"Tell her about him jumpin' around," Ruth Ann prodded from nearby.

"Ruthie thinks he might be gay."

"I didn't say that. Said I hope he ain't."

Darlene waved her away, slightly annoyed.

"Uh oh," Sarah said. "They like throwin' parties. Folks'll be comin' and goin' from there at all hours."

"I don't know 'bout that," Darlene said. "He's nice lookin', but that don't mean he's gay. 'Sides, what do I care?"

"What'd Toni say?"

"Ain't told her yet."

"Who?" Ruth Ann asked, again drawing an irritated wave from Darlene.

"What a shame," Sarah said. "A nice-lookin' man moves in and her bein' single."

"Listen," Darlene snapped. "That's her business. My daughter don't have to go chasin' ever fella that comes along."

"I know, but she's been through a lot, and she's such a sweet girl."

"She'll figure it out, so just let her be. You know she don't like folks bein' in her business."

"I know. So, tell me more about this new fella."

Darlene knew little but passed on the tidbits—the piano, his good looks, the furniture—she'd observed from the parlor.

Ruth Ann peered out the window at Alex's house a few times, engaging her suspicious mind. "I wonder why he moved here, of all places," she asked herself out loud. "There's gotta be somethin' wrong with him."

Darlene pulled the phone away from her ear. "What are you babblin' about?"

"Why would a handsome young fella move here? Maybe he's done somethin' wrong, and he's tryin' to get away from it."

Darlene stared at her sister for a moment before putting the phone back to her ear. "Listen, I gotta start dinner and Ruthie's ramblin' on about there bein' somethin' wrong."

"Is she okay?"

"She's fine. She's just talkin' herself into believin' this fella done somethin' wrong."

"Like what?"

Darlene chuckled. "Who knows? Ruthie thinks ever'one's up to somethin'. I'll call you later."

Darlene checked the window for any activity across the street but all was quiet. Before starting dinner, she made a quick call to her daughter.

"So, the fella moved in across the street."

"Wonder why he moved here?" Toni pondered. "Ain't nothin' here."

"Maybe he's got kin."

"We know everyone goin' way back."

"There's somethin' wrong with him," Ruth Ann chimed in from across the room.

"What'd she say?"

"Oh, you know Ruthie. She don't trust nobody."

"What's her problem with the new guy?"

"She thinks he's a little fruity."

"Really? Why?"

"Hell, I don't know. You ask her." Darlene handed the phone to Ruth Ann.

"Listen," Ruth Ann started. "I never said he was gay. But he's a nice-lookin' young man with a piano, and Cynthia said he's single. Now, what does that tell ya?"

"Not much," Toni said. "There's a lotta single piano players out there. Don't mean he's gay."

"A man that age with enough money to buy a house? Why ain't he been snatched up by now?"

"Maybe he's divorced."

Ruth Ann paused, having not considered such an obvious possibility. "Then where's the young'uns?"

"Maybe he ain't got none or they're with the ex-wife," Toni said. "Maybe that's why he moved here, to get away from her. Maybe he ran out on his kids."

"Well!" Ruth Ann said contemptuously. "He better not've."

Toni chuckled. "We don't know nothin'. He could be a single guy without kids or an ex-wife who moved to Hamilton. Although, I can't imagine why."

"Hmph," Ruth Ann said, holding on to her suspicions. "I'd ask Cynthia, but—"

"She'll make somethin' up," Darlene called out. She took the phone from Ruth Ann. "Listen," Darlene said. "Cynthia's just gonna spout a bunch a nonsense. I'll go over there and find out for myself."

"Mom, leave him alone. At least till he gets moved in."

"I ain't goin' right now."

"Give him a couple a days to get settled."

"Well, I don't want Cynthia fillin' ever'one's head with a bunch a foolishness."

"Everyone knows not to believe her."

"What'd she say?" Ruth Ann asked.

Darlene ignored Ruth Ann. "Listen, baby, I need to start dinner."

"Tell her to join us," Ruth Ann suggested.

Toni heard her and said, "Thanks, but I'm seein' Andy later."

"Alright, sweetheart. I'll see you tomorrow."

She hung up the phone and said, "She ain't comin'. She's seein' Andy later."

"That Andy's a nice boy."

"Don't matter. Antoinette ain't all that crazy 'bout him."

"You don't know that. She's been seeing him over a year."

Darlene shook her head. "She likes goin' around with him, but it ain't serious."

Ruth Ann seemed disappointed. "What'd she say when you told her about this new fella?"

"Said we oughta leave him alone till he gets settled."

Ruth Ann peered out the window. "We oughta find out more about him 'fore we go traipsing over there."

"Pfft. How we gonna do that without meetin' him first?"

"Well?" she pondered, not finding a suitable answer. "I don't trust him."

While the stew cooked, Darlene called a few friends to report on what she'd observed across the street. Finally, dinner was ready, and the sisters sat down to eat.

"When's Toni comin' tomorrow?" Ruth Ann asked.

"She didn't say exactly. You already know she only works half-day on Friday, so I 'spect she'll be here after lunch."

"Remind me to pick up a few extra things at the market."

"Write 'em down," Darlene ordered. "I don't want you blamin' me if I forget."

"I ain't payin' for another delivery from Winkley's. He charged me an extra five dollars just to bring us two measly sacks of groceries."

"Write it down so you get ever'thing you need tomorrow."

"Maybe we should get a car."

"Ain't no way. You drive like an old lady, and I ain't gettin' in a car with you. Plus, cars need gas and insurance. Neither of us has had a license in more 'n three years, so we'd have to take a test, and I ain't messin' with that nonsense."

"It sure would be nice if we didn't have to bother Toni every time we need to go somewhere."

"She don't mind. 'Sides, where else you wanna go? Church on Sunday and the market on Friday, that's it. Ever where else we can walk."

"I don't like walkin'. 'Specially with my hip."

"It ain't so bad we need a car."

Ruth Ann paused her eating and stared off. "I miss takin' drives with Arthur."

"So, find you a new fella," Darlene said with a sly grin.

Ruth Ann smiled nostalgically and shook her head. "He was the only man I'll ever love."

"You ain't gotta find someone you love. Just someone who can drive."

"Stop it," Ruth Ann said, not fond of Darlene's teasing. "Before Arthur passed, I said I'd see him in Heaven."

"It's been five years. I don't think he'd mind you spendin' time with one of the men from the church."

"That just wouldn't be right."

"Maybe he's up there in Heaven with someone."

Ruth Ann flashed a quick glare at her sister before turning away and putting on a sly expression of her own. "Maybe Joe's up there with Lorraine Keller."

"Don't start with me," Darlene warned. "Joe had better taste than some hussy like Lorraine Keller."

Ruth Ann smiled at getting a rise out of her sister. "You started it."

"Well, I'm endin' it."

"Remind me to get eggs tomorrow," Ruth Ann said.

"Write it down."

As word spread that the new guy was moving in, the curious locals drove by the house, trying not to appear too obvious as they slowed to a crawl, hoping to catch a glimpse of Hamilton's newest resident.

Chapter 2

The sanctuary of the First Christian Church of Hamilton comfortably accommodated three hundred worshippers, but there was limited space for Sunday school classes.

After the morning worship service, the congregants were divided up by age—infants, youth, young adults, and adults—and sent to four small classrooms for refreshments before being led through a lesson on the Bible. Because of the limited space, as the story goes, a small, faithful group of senior ladies held their own "Bible study" at the Superbowl Bowling Alley two doors down from the church.

Of the twelve senior ladies in the congregation, nine regularly attended Sunday school. They ranged in age from 64-year-old Dorothy McArthur to 83-year-old Bertha Hutchins. Darlene and Ruth Ann were among the more aged at 79 and 76, respectively. Sarah and Irma, both 75, were closely followed by Cynthia Coker who had been 69 for the past four years. Miss Virginia and Rebecca Mathis, the quietest of the group, were in their early 70s.

The regular nine—along with Ernie, the bowling alley owner—strolled down the sidewalk from the church to the Superbowl with a lively discussion underway.

"I ain't sayin' Pastor Brown does it ever week," Darlene said to Dorothy. "But he don't let too many meetin's pass without harpin' on givin' money."

"He only mentioned it at the end," Dorothy said. "He mostly talked about how we oughta serve the less fortunate, like how Jesus washed people's feet."

"'Cept he started with talkin' 'bout servin' but ended with passin' the plate. Now, I don't mind givin', but Pastor used to preach about the rewards of Heaven and such. Now, ever'thing comes down to askin' for money."

"It's like that everywhere," Irma said. "I think Pastor's tryin' to remind us not to get all caught up in chasin' material things."

Darlene chuckled. "Who can afford material things if we give all our money to him, 'cept Cynthia?"

Everyone looked at Cynthia, expecting a retort. "Hmph," she said with a smirk. "Ain't nothin' wrong with wantin' nice things."

Darlene and Cynthia exchanged jabs any time they were in the same room. The war between them went back decades to an unknown origin. The other ladies tried to remain neutral, but Cynthia had a knack for provoking them too.

Darlene was about to fire another shot at Cynthia, but Ruth Ann brought up the hot topic of Hamilton's newest resident. "Did anyone see the new fella at the service?"

"I ain't ever seen him," Irma said. "What's he look like?"

"He wasn't there," Cynthia stated.

"He's a looker," Darlene said.

"Who can tell?" Ruth Ann remarked. "With all that hair and dirty clothes."

As the comments flew, Ernie stepped ahead of the ladies and unlocked the door. He always attended church before opening the bowling alley lounge for the senior ladies, granting them a full hour to themselves. In Texas, it's illegal to sell alcohol on Sunday before noon, so Ernie made sure the ladies maintained a certain amount of discretion, even though everyone in town knew about the Senior Lady Sundays.

Ernie held the door open as the ladies filed past him, greeting and thanking him between the quips and comments.

"Good mornin', Ms. Ruth Ann," Ernie said, singling her out with a smile and a slight bow as she passed by.

Irma was on the heels of the sisters, eagerly asking, "What'd Toni think of him?"

"She won't want nothin' to do with him," Ruth Ann quickly answered before giving Ernie a shy smile, saying, "Mornin' Ernie. Thank ya."

"She's never been good at pickin' winners anyway," Cynthia sniped.

Darlene turned sharply, having heard fighting words. She glared at Cynthia strutting past her on a victory lap. "Don't you start bad mouthin' my Antoinette. It ain't like you got perfect kids."

Cynthia ignored the insult, having gotten the rise out of Darlene she'd hoped for. She led the way to the lounge, keeping a few steps ahead of her foe.

The ladies plopped down into plastic chairs surrounding a wobbly table, as the chatter continued.

The best-looking of the group, Sarah Livingston strolled in last, jingling keys in the air. Despite her youthful appearance, she remained single after losing her husband in an accident a few years earlier.

"Refreshments?" she called out as she sauntered past the group. She'd been the de facto bartender/host for years, drawing from her time in Dallas as a socialite. Sarah rarely shared her private struggles, but Darlene was always there for her when her late husband Woody was at his worst, listening, taking care of her, and never letting her give up on life, even though she was in a hopeless situation. Darlene was the only one who knew how truly horrific her life had been.

Sarah entered the storage room and opened a roll-up door that connected it to the lounge via a bar. Dorothy and Irma followed her to retrieve the chips and napkins.

Sarah held up a bottle of cheap whiskey and called out, "Darlene, the usual?"

Darlene pulled a small flask from her giant purse and headed to the bar. "Here," she said, handing the flask to Sarah. "Use this. I can't drink that swill Ernie buys." She patted Sarah on the hand, then ambled back to her seat.

The ladies relaxed as several kicked off their shoes.

Cynthia stood nearby. While she'd lived in Hamilton her entire life and was an integral link in the gossip chain, she was the least popular among the senior ladies. Quick to criticize, Cynthia was always looking down her nose. The group tolerated her, and often took her remarks with a grain of salt. Cynthia acknowledged how she frequently irritated people, but she saw her unpopularity as a result of being better than everyone else. If the Sunday meeting wasn't such a goldmine for gossip, she probably wouldn't attend.

With everyone served, Sarah joined the circle for the predominant topic of the day; the new man in town.

"Dar, you still think he's gay?" Sarah asked, taking her seat next to Darlene.

"Never said he was. That was Ruthie. I said I hope he ain't."

"You worried about wild parties goin' on all night?"

"Ain't that. I seen him and I might like a shot at him myself." She raised her glass high as the group burst into a roaring laugh. Even Cynthia couldn't hold back a chuckle.

"Darlene!" Ruth Ann scolded, being the more proper of the two. "You don't even know this man. What if he's married? He's half your age."

"He ain't married," Darlene said dismissively.

"You don't know that."

"Aw hell, Ruthie. I'm almost a huner'd. Ain't no point in savin' myself."

"You're seventy-nine," Ruth Ann said disdainfully.

Sarah laughed and broke the tension between the sisters, saying, "Y'all said he didn't have much—cheap furniture and an old pickup. And we know that house ain't much. He must play piano since he is so particular about it."

"Why move to Hamilton?" Irma asked. "We ain't got no night clubs or concert halls. And it's miles to the nearest airport."

"No idea," Darlene answered. "Maybe he got a great deal." She turned to Cynthia. "What'd he pay for Carl's house?"

Cynthia unfolded her arms and held a smug expression while appearing to search her brain for an answer she knew off the top of her head. "Well... Let me see..."

"Get on with it," Darlene barked.

Cynthia smirked, having again gotten under Darlene's skin. "He got it for next to nothin'," Before Darlene could demand to know the exact price, Dorothy quizzed Cynthia. "What'd he say about why he moved here?"

"Said he was looking for a change."

"A change from what?" Dorothy pressed.

Cynthia shrugged. "He got it cheap, but ninety-thousand doesn't buy much of a house."

"I heard that two-story over on Bell went for ninety-five thousand a couple a years ago," Dorothy remarked.

"Toni looked at that place when got back from Dallas," Cynthia said. "'Course she had to pass on it 'cause she was still married."

"What's that got to do with anything?" Darlene snapped.

"Nothin'. But no one's gonna loan money to a woman goin' through a divorce."

"Pfft," Darlene retorted. "Antoinette's got her own money. She coulda done what she wanted."

"I heard Andy Pharris is thinkin' about poppin' the question," Dorothy said.

The room rustled from this fresh piece of news.

"Says who?" Darlene asked.

"I like Andy," Irma said. "He helps me and Otis with the ranch. He's a good hard worker."

"Not like that ex-husband of hers," Cynthia taunted, folding her arms.

"Listen," Ruth Ann chimed in ahead of Darlene. "You hush up about Toni."

Cynthia shook her head, appearing innocuous. "I like Toni, but I was talking about her choice of husbands."

Irma stood and said, "You don't think Andy's good enough for her?" Irma's intimidating physical presence caused Cynthia to take a step back.

"Andy's alright. His daddy likes to drink a little too much."

Irma, Darlene, and Ruth Ann were about to unload when Sarah, the peacemaker, steered the discussion away from Cynthia. "Has anyone stopped by to meet the new guy?"

"I think we oughta wait," Ruth Ann said.

"For what?" Dorothy asked.

"Ruthie thinks he's hiding from the law," Darlene kidded.

"I didn't say that."

While collecting the empty glasses, Sarah said, "We still don't know what kinda musician he is. Hell, I got a piano, but I sure can't play it." She walked behind the bar and poured Darlene a refill from her flask, then mixed a weak cocktail for Dorothy along with a fresh glass of tea for Ruth Ann.

"Whatever he is," Dorothy said, rising to help Sarah, "I still wonder why he moved here? How old did you say he was?"

"Darlene thinks he's in his forties," Ruth Ann said. "It's hard to tell with all that hair, but I'd say he's more like thirty-five."

"That's awful young to move to boring old Hamilton," said Irma.

"Perhaps that's the point," Cynthia said, her polite tone drawing quizzical looks. "Perhaps he's an overworked, famous person trying to get away from everything." The group went silent, pondering the idea.

"If he's famous, then he's rich," Sarah said. "Why buy Carl Webber's dumpy little house?"

"He paid cash," Cynthia added. "So he didn't have to show any tax returns or financial statements."

"I seen him," Ruth Ann said. "He's nice looking, but he don't look famous. 'Course, he coulda lost his money gamblin' or buyin' drugs."

"He is nice looking," Darlene added with a mischievous smile, drawing a quick chuckle from the group but a sharp glare from Ruth Ann. "The rest don't matter. Not to me, anyway."

"Somethin's not quite right," Ruth Ann reiterated. "And I don't trust him."

"Pfft. You don't trust no one. He ain't done nothin' to you."

"Not yet," Ruth Ann fired back.

"I'm with Miss Ruth Ann on this one," said Miss Virginia, the only black woman in the group. She was born and raised in Hamilton, and worked most of her adult life cleaning houses for the handful of upscale families around Hamilton. She'd spent her entire life in the white world, never married or had kids. Now at seventy-one, the ladies considered her just another member of the group. "Remember that woman over in Granite who took that fella in? He killed that poor woman."

"That ain't the same," said Darlene. "That man was a serial killer."

Another silence hit the group until Sarah called from behind the bar. "Ernie's getting ready to open. Anybody need another one before I lock this?" When no one responded, she removed any evidence of illegal drinking, then pulled the metal panel down and secured the bar.

Irma shook her head. "I don't think this new fella's a serial killer. The guy in Granite showed up with just a suitcase. But I am curious about what he's doin' here."

With their hour at an end, the group began gathering themselves up to leave.

Rebecca Mathis, a quiet, retired clerk for the county, looked at Darlene and smiled. She was painfully shy around strangers and thus spent most of her life toiling away, silently working. "Listen Dar, if you've got him in your sights, you make him earn it, as the kids today say. Don't give it up till he tells you his story."

Darlene laughed as she stood and struck a pose. "How could he resist?"

The other ladies joined in the laughter as the group headed towards the door, with some unable to walk straight. As a rule, those who were unstable received assistance until they were out of the public view, sometimes needing a ride home. Since most of the group were experienced drinkers, a slight wobble now and then was not concerning.

The senior ladies' Sunday school ritual had been a tradition for many years. This was just another Sunday.

Toni picked the sisters up outside the Superbowl after attending the adult's Sunday school class at the church.

After church and Sunday school, Ruth Ann normally took a nap while Darlene busied herself with chores around the house, visiting with friends, and finding ways to occupy her time. She wasn't fond of being idle.

Chapter 3

Alex walked through the cluttered rooms of his new house, holding a beer and a cigarette. Everything he owned except his record collection and musical equipment was cheap, damaged, out of date, or all three. He wondered why he'd gone to the trouble of moving it all the way from Los Angeles instead of donating it to Goodwill or tossing it in the trash. Alex had made good money as a musician, but his perpetual traveling had kept him from considering anything permanent or long term. Consequently, he owned few valuable belongings but had sufficient cash to buy the house.

As he plodded from room to room, pushing boxes aside, he reflected on how, weeks before he'd turned thirty-nine, he had a calendar full of gigs, money in the bank, and a wide circle of acquaintances. Life wasn't bad, but it added up to nothing. He glanced around the disorganized room and exhaled a cloud of melancholy wrapped in cigarette smoke.

"Well, here we are," he said to no one, raising his beer and toasting himself ironically. How had life as a professional musician—something Alex had loved for many years—become so full of drudgery and disappointment? He stared at a calendar tacked to the wall listing his upcoming gigs and felt nothing but dread. Each date would be an unending night of uninspired playing. He'd always enjoyed playing every song all night long. Now, his only desire was to leave the stage and go home. He couldn't bear the thought of living the rest of his life like that. *A year and a half,* he thought, marking the beginning of his depression. Eighteen months of anguish and still unable or unwilling to face the truth that had plunged him into darkness. Once again, he forced the unresolved conflict from his mind, cleared the boxes from around the piano, and waited for Chuck, the piano tuner to arrive.

With thirty years of experience, Chuck was the sole piano tuner in Hamilton. He was immediately enthralled with Alex's piano and meticulously tuned each string. Upon finishing, he looked at Alex. "Do you mind if I play?"

"Knock yourself out."

Chuck smiled and launched into a classical piece.

"Mr. Patterson, I've tuned and played a thousand pianos over my lifetime, but I've never found one that comes close to this one. Where did you find it?"

Alex smiled. "Years ago, I was dating this incredibly talented artist. She was painting a mural for a wealthy couple who were renovating their Bel Air mansion. The contractor was nearly finished with the interior when the wife changed her mind about the rosewood piano.

Someone convinced her that *real* pianos are ebony, so she instructed her designer to get rid of the rosewood and order an ebony one."

"Unbelievable," Chuck said. "I hate to ask what you paid."

"That's where the story gets interesting. While working on her mural, my girlfriend overheard the contractor's complaints about the last-minute change and the piano dilemma, and said she knew someone who may want it. She was thinking about me. The contractor suggested she cut a deal with the owner and get it out of there. Otherwise, shipping it back to the dealer would've been a colossal pain in the ass, and expensive. So, my girlfriend calls me and tells me about it. I was on hiatus for a week with a touring band, so I showed up at this ridiculous mansion thinking how stupid am I for even thinking I could buy this rare Yamaha grand. I didn't have any real money, and I wasn't even sure the piano would fit in my tiny apartment."

He sipped his beer and lit another cigarette. "So, my girlfriend lets me in the house and I start playing this incredible piano. Oh man, I was in love. I had to have it… until I faced reality. This is a high-end, six-foot grand. It had to be crazy expensive. Thousands. *Tens* of thousands."

Chuck nodded. "Without a doubt."

"So, I'm sitting there playing, knowing it would be the last time I'd ever hear this piano. Lost in the music, I glanced up at a stunning woman staring at me from a few feet away. 'Please don't stop,' she says. I wasn't sure who she was, but I figured it was her piano, so I kept playing. When I finished, she put her hands together as if she was praying. I thought she was going to cry. 'That's the most beautiful thing I've ever heard,' she tells me. She continued gushing over my playing, and trust me, I'm a sideman, so I'm really not that good as a soloist. I figured maybe she's nuts, as she asked me to play again and again. I was still playing when the contractor returned. He was not happy.

"The piano had to go immediately because the ebony one would arrive in a few hours. The woman, who I learned was the owner, was staring at the piano. 'Oh, I wish this piano went with the room,' she says. 'It sounds *so* beautiful.' She put her hand on my arm and said her name was Susanne. 'Promise me you'll come play the new one,' she said. I said I'd come back anytime she wanted. Just to be invited back flattered me. According to my girlfriend, Susanne and her husband were big shots in the art world, and their house was unbelievably massive. Although I never play for free, I couldn't resist saying yes, especially at that point. After closing the keylid, I got up and thanked her for letting me play, and she asked me where I was going. 'I'm heading home,' I said. 'What about the piano?' she asked. 'What about it? I can't afford it.' It took her a second, but she said, 'Can you get it moved by tomorrow?' 'Moved where?' I asked. She laughed and said, 'Home with you, of course!'"

"No shit!" Chuck blurted.

"No shit. She said, and these are her words, 'If you can get it out of here, take it and we'll figure out the money later, or maybe never.' *Maybe never.* The best *never* I've ever heard. The contractor was stunned, but he had a house to finish, so he said, 'Get to it.' Man, I jumped into action, calling everyone I knew. Luckily, I found a few friends to help. After that, I stopped by Susanne's house every week for months whenever I was in town to play her seven-foot ebony Steinway."

"Wow."

"It was a great gig, even though it didn't pay, except for the free grand. She offered me a job for some parties, but it's not my thing. Like I said, I'm not a soloist."

"She must've hated seeing you move away."

Alex released a deep sigh. "She never knew I left. She passed away about two years ago."

"I'm sorry to hear that."

"Yeah, thanks. She'd been fighting cancer for a long time. By the end, she was really sick. It was terrible seeing her like that. I'd stop by and play for as long as she wanted. She was a great lady."

"That's sad."

"I got to know her husband a little. He was gone a lot, but said my playing made a big difference for Susanne." Alex stared at the piano. "This piano is very special."

After Chuck left, Alex returned to the piano and sat on the bench. He played a single chord, then a second. He let the sound ring out and stared into space while the sound faded. He pulled his hands back and sat in silence. Telling Chuck about Susanne reminded him of how painful her passing had been, and how much he used to love playing.

I miss that, he thought, remembering the sincere contentment on Susanne's face every time he played. Now her memory evoked bittersweet emotions.

He pulled a cigarette from his shirt pocket and walked out the back door onto the patio. While his light brown hair blew in the wind, he looked around the modest back yard with patchy, dried-out grass and no trees. It was depressing. The yard was a symbol of his lonely, stark life. What was once vibrant and flourishing now lay desolate and barren. Even the magnificent piano inside seemed like an empty treasure chest. He could make beautiful music, but without inspiration, it was simply dictation.

Before going to bed, he halfheartedly packed a bag for a week on the road.

The following morning Alex locked up his house and drove to Dallas to board a tour bus for a five-night run playing gigs in Texas, Colorado, and California.

* * *

The sisters kept Alex's house under surveillance, unaware he was out of town. Ruth Ann pulled back the curtains and watched from the kitchen window.

"Maybe he's over there takin' drugs," she said.

Darlene sat at the kitchen table adding a little Jack Daniel's to her tea. "Doubt it."

"Why do you insist on always disagreein' with me? No matter what I say, you pick the other side. You're only doin' it to rile me."

Darlene smiled and raised her teacup, as if to toast. "Ain't it fun?"

"No. It's not!"

"Oh relax. I'm just funnin' with ya. And that fella across the street ain't done nothin' to you. Leave him be."

"Don't tell me to relax. What about that man in Granite? No one worried about him till he killed that woman."

"Pfft. Listen, if that fella comes over here and starts trouble, I still got Joe's Winchester."

Ruth Ann snickered. "You ain't ever even held a gun. You'd miss, and he'd kill you for sure."

Darlene waved her away. "You're bein' ridiculous."

"*I'm* bein' ridiculous? You thinkin' you can use a shotgun is ridiculous." She peered out the window again. "That fella's been there near a week and no one's talked to him. He's up to somethin'."

Darlene joined Ruth Ann at the window and said, "He ain't up to nothin'. He's probably mad 'cause no one's stopped by to welcome him."

Ruth Ann turned to Darlene, shocked. "Welcome *him*? We don't know a thing about him, and he ain't had nothin' to do with anyone in Hamilton, and I don't think he wants to."

"It still ain't right not to welcome him to the neighborhood."

"You go right on ahead."

"How 'bout we invite him over for a home-cooked meal?"

"Here?" Ruth Ann shrieked.

"Relax. He ain't gonna do nothin'. And I 'spect he needs a good meal."

Ruth Ann shook her head, thinking out loud. "Somethin' ain't right about him."

The doorbell rang and Darlene got up to answer. "That's Sarah. She and I are goin' for a drive. I'll be back later."

* * *

Sarah, like many others, discretely confided in Darlene, especially after the *accident* that took Sarah's husband a decade earlier. The official police report stated that Woody Livingston fell down the stairs and broke his neck, but the actual story was told in whispers about how, after decades of being beaten, Sarah finally defended herself against Woody's last act of violence. Devastated by what she'd been forced to do, Sarah withdrew from all social interaction. It was only through her close relationship with Darlene that she was able to regain her life.

Sarah pulled away from the house and said, "I appreciate you goin' with me." Darlene nodded, and after a long silence, Sarah asked, "You didn't tell anyone, did you?"

"Ain't no one else's business."

"I know. Thanks anyway. It's probably nothin'. Doc Weatherly said it's probably a fat deposit or a cyst." Sarah tried to appear brave, but Darlene detected fear in her voice.

Soon, they were in Dr. Weatherly's exam room, Sarah shivering in a surgical gown with a scared look on her face. Darlene stood beside her saying, "It ain't nothin' till you know better. You ain't doin' yourself no good worryin'."

"I'm shakin' 'cause it's cold in here."

Darlene took her hand. "Even if they find somethin's wrong, you'll get a couple a shots or some pills, then it's on with your life."

Sarah nodded, trying to appear confident, but when the doctor entered, she squeezed Darlene's hand.

An hour later, they were back in the car, driving home. "It's gonna be a long three days," Sarah said disquietly.

"Only if you let it. It'll go by faster 'n you think."

"I hope so. It's just hard goin' through this alone. I ain't wishin' for Woody, but I miss havin' someone at home."

"Listen, hon. You ain't alone, and you can come stay with me and Ruthie anytime, for as long as you like."

"I appreciate it. But I'll be fine."

"How 'bout I stay with you tonight?"

Sarah thought for a moment and nodded. "I'd like that."

"Stop off at my house and I'll tell Ruthie you and me's goin' out on the town, and not to wait up."

Sarah laughed, and for the first time in several days, her fear seemed manageable.

That night, Darlene sat with Sarah, often in silence, but her presence gave Sarah comfort. By the next day, Sarah was back to her old brave self. She pulled up in front of Darlene's house to let her out. "Thanks for stayin' with me."

"Anytime. But next time pick up some whiskey 'fore I get there."

Chapter 4

In a spacious dance hall just outside Denver, Colorado, The Caribou Station Band played to a full house with Alex off to one side of the stage playing keyboards.

Despite the exuberant crowd, Alex tuned in to his own thoughts.

Three more songs and we're done. Back on the bus. Two nights in L.A., then home. He took a drink from a cocktail perched next to his keyboards. Alex had been drinking heavily, but the angst of being on the road, along with depression, negated the effects of the alcohol, forcing him to experience every moment with utter clarity. *Home*, he again thought, imagining his empty house and feeling alone. *This gig sucks, but it's just as lonely at home.* He thought of Ananya, the love of his life. *I wish she was gonna be there when I got home.* He sighed and reached for a cigarette but caught himself, remembering there was no smoking on stage. *I've got to get out of this shit.* The next song started. *Two left.*

* * *

After three days of no activity, the sisters' curiosity about the new neighbor waned. With nothing to share on the gossip line, their attention returned to the everyday routines.

Sarah got the test results back from Doc Weatherly and immediately called Darlene.

"Doc called. Said it's just a common fat deposit. I ain't even gotta go back."

"Don't get no better than that."

"Amen. And thanks for goin' with me and bein' there."

"Pfft. You'd a done the same for me."

"See ya Sunday?"

"Count on it."

Darlene hung up the phone and Ruth Ann said, "Who was that?"

"Sarah. She was tellin' me about a friend. You made a shoppin' list yet? Antoinette's gonna be here any minute."

Toni worked as a medical billing clerk. She worked remotely on occasion, but the office closed early on Friday, so she worked half-days, then drove Darlene and Ruth Ann to the market. She pulled into the driveway, and the sisters piled into her truck.

"Remind me to cash a check," Ruth Ann said.

Darlene shook her head. "You say the same thing ever Friday."

"I need something for the offering on Sunday."

"Y'all seen the new guy?" Toni asked while driving.

"Not in a couple a days," Darlene said. "He moved in and left."

"Or he's over there doin' somethin'," Ruth Ann added.

"He ain't doin' nothin'. He ain't there. We ain't seen no lights on and his trucks gone. He ain't there."

"So, Cynthia's the only one who's met him?" Toni asked.

Darlene chuckled. "Maybe that's why he left. He thinks ever'one in Hamilton's like Cynthia."

"C'mon, Mom. Cynthia's not that bad."

"She ain't that good either."

"She said he paid cash for the house," Ruth Ann said. "Maybe he got some money from his folks."

Darlene glanced quickly at her sister. "Maybe he one of them gang members from California and he's settin' up shop here."

"He better not!" Ruth Ann shrieked, drawing laughter from Darlene.

"Mom, stop."

"I'm just funnin'."

"So, he didn't tell anyone he was leavin' or how long he'd be gone?" Toni asked.

"Ain't nobody talked to him."

"Hmm. That's weird," Toni said.

"I'm tellin' you he's up to something," Ruth Ann reiterated.

After shopping, Toni helped unload and put away the groceries. She looked out the window at Alex's house several times. "Wonder where he is?"

"Ain't none a our business," Darlene said.

Toni laughed. "Look who's talkin'. You ain't gonna tell me you're not curious?"

"'Course I am, but I ain't gonna get all beside myself 'cause of it. He'll show up eventually."

After Toni left and Ruth Ann lay down for her afternoon nap, Darlene fixed herself a small glass of whiskey, peering out at Alex's house a few times. "Hmm," she questioned softly.

Several curious locals drove by Alex's house on Saturday, and the sisters couldn't help but glance across the street now and then at the dark house.

* * *

Alex quietly returned home in the middle of the night Monday. He slept through much of the next day, recovering from the constant drinking, smoking, and lack of sleep.

Late Tuesday afternoon he showered, put himself together and headed for Gibson's General Store for provisions. As he traversed the aisles, filling his shopping list, he stopped at the sound of a nearby voice.

"Ain't you the guy who moved into the house on Blanton?"

Alex turned to face an attractive woman wearing jeans, boots, and a T-shirt. She had long brown hair pulled back, and striking eyes fixed on him, but it was her voice—sweet but confident—that caught Alex's attention. Plus, her heavy southern drawl piqued his musical ear.

She extended her manicured hand. "I'm Antoinette Conroe, but everybody calls me Toni. It's nice to finally meet the mystery man everyone's been talkin' about."

Enamored and stupefied that she knew who he was, Alex's blank stare created an odd silence in the middle of the noisy store. "Oh," he said, snapping out of his trance and taking her hand. "Alex Patterson. How do you know where I live?"

Enjoying the intrigue she held over him, Toni smiled. Her green eyes lit up, fanning the spark she'd set off in

Alex. "My mom and aunt live across the street from you. I'm surprised they hadn't stopped by to welcome you to the neighborhood. You're all they talk about these days."

"I left town right after moving in. I wouldn't have been there even if they had." They locked eyes until the moment turned awkward.

"Where'd you move from?"

"L.A."

"Hmm," she said quizzically. "Well, welcome to Hamilton, although I don't know why anyone'd move here. 'Specially from Los Angeles."

"L.A.'s alright, but what's wrong with Hamilton?" He didn't care about the answer, he just wanted the conversation to continue.

"Nothin's wrong. Hamilton's just a nothin' little town."

"But you live here?"

"I grew up here, but I moved to Dallas after I got married. I just moved back."

Married, Alex's mind repeated, disappointed.

"Oh... There must be something that brought you and your husband back."

She hesitated, not ready to disclose her divorce. "There ain't much here, but... Let's just say this ain't L.A."

"I guess not, but maybe you can point me toward some of the local attractions."

She chuckled. "There ain't no local attractions, 'cept the fair and the rodeo."

"The Hamilton Arts Fair?" he asked excitedly.

Puzzled, Toni replied, "Yeah, so?"

"I first heard about Hamilton from a girl I dated in L.A. She used to come here from Dallas."

"Okay, too much information."

Alex smiled at being derided. "I know. Besides the fair, what else do you do for fun?"

"Not much. We usually drive to Abilene or Waco. Sometimes Dallas." She studied him through a long pause, uncertain of what to make of him. He was friendly and handsome, and definitely out of place in Hamilton. She felt a connection with him, yet remained guarded due to her history with men. "But hey, it's nice to meet you," she said, turning to walk away.

"You too," he said, trying to think of a clever way to see her again. "Do you live with your mom?" He immediately wanted to kick himself for asking such an insulting question—*a strong, thirty-something, married woman living at home.*

She snickered. "I got a place 'cross town." She sauntered away but glanced back, flashing a sweet smile. "I'll see ya 'round."

He continued staring until she disappeared around the corner, thinking, *I've got a place, not we've got a place. She's got to be divorced or separated. Her mother lives across the street, so I'll see her again.* In that moment, Alex felt a renewed hope that perhaps he could find someone who wasn't just another passing fling. Reveling in his first small-town encounter, he shifted his attention back to shopping, smiling at the passing shoppers.

After checking out, Alex steered his overflowing cart out the door and across the parking lot. As he filled his truck, a jacked-up, four-wheel-drive pickup pulled up with blacked-out windows.

The driver lowered the window, revealing Toni behind the wheel. "Listen," she said. "I didn't mean to give you the wrong idea. Hamilton ain't a bad place. I just get tired of it."

"I understand. I've been sick of living somewhere, too."

"It's hard to imagine someone wantin' to move here, but…" She hesitated before adopting a thoughtful posture with her chin resting on her hand. "I gotta ask. Why'd you move to Hamilton? I mean, I get that maybe L.A.'s too big, but why nothin' little Hamilton?"

It was a question he didn't have a simple answer for so he turned it into a joke. "Hamilton? I thought this was Houston."

She smirked and shook her head, remaining coy and careful not to reveal her budding attraction. She flashed a polite smile. "See ya."

He watched as Toni's truck turned the corner and went out of sight.

Once Alex disappeared from her rearview mirror, Toni called her mother to say she'd met the new guy.

"What?" Darlene asked. "Where?"

"I just left him at Gibson's."

"What'd you think of him?"

"He's nice. Looks like a musician with the long hair and all. He said he'd been travelin', which is why y'all ain't seen him."

"Is he married?"

"You know he ain't married. Cynthia already told y'all everything about him."

"Yeah, but she don't tell it like it is. Did you tell him who you were? Did you ask him what he's doin' in Hamilton? Was he—"

"Mom, stop. This is why I don't tell you everything. You always give me the third degree."

"I ain't givin' you nothin' of the kind. You knew me and Ruthie was curious. It ain't ever'day we get a new neighbor."

"Well, I told you everything I know."

"Did he tell you why he moved to Hamilton?"

"I asked, but he just made some dumb joke."

"What else did he say?"

"Not much. I told him he was crazy for movin' to boring ol' Hamilton."

"But he was nice?"

"I guess. Nice eyes."

"But he didn't say why he moved?"

Toni smirked, frustrated by her mother's repeated questions. "We only talked for a second."

"Did you offer to show him around?"

"Mom," she protested. "There ain't nothin' to show him, and I ain't gonna just throw myself at him."

"I didn't mean it like that. Did he say where he moved from? Does he have young'uns? Is he married?"

Toni laughed. "Seriously, Mom. You keep askin' that. I didn't see a ring, but I'm just as clueless as you. Like I said, I introduced myself, said my mom and aunt live across the street, and that's about it. You're just gonna have to march yourself over there and ask him yourself."

"I guess me and Ruthie'll go over and introduce ourselves, now that we know he's back in town."

"Lemme know how it goes," Toni said, interested in knowing more about Alex but deliberately sounding aloof.

"Love you, sweetheart."

"Love you, Mom."

After they hung up, Darlene relayed the information to Ruth Ann and suggested they take the initiative and welcome Alex to the neighborhood.

Ruth Ann peered out the kitchen window. "Who moves into a house then leaves two days later?"

"A travelin' musician," Darlene said, crossing the kitchen to fix herself a small glass of whiskey. She took a sip and peered out the window. "But he's home now."

"We ain't got nothin' for a house warmin' gift."

"Why don't you make him a cake?"

"I don't know if I got eggs."

Darlene returned to her seat near the space heater, sipping her whiskey. It was early March and a late winter chill was drifting through their drafty house.

Ruth Ann found her cake recipe and began scribbling on a piece of scratch paper.

"What're you doin'?" Darlene asked.

"Makin' a list."

"We ain't goin' to the market for another three days."

"Ain't for shoppin'. I'm makin' sure I got everything I need to make a cake."

Darlene watched as her younger sister puttered around the kitchen, opening and closing the cupboard, refrigerator, and drawers over and over while checking her recipe.

Darlene called Antoinette back.

"Sweetheart, are you workin' tomorrow?"

"Mom, I work every day. Why?"

"Ruthies gonna be makin' a cake for that new fella, and I don't wanna sit around while she messes up the kitchen. Can you come get me tomorrow so I don't have to get my blood pressure up fussin' at her?"

Toni wanted to join them when they delivered the cake—eager to get a glimpse inside Alex's house—but didn't want her mother to think she was interested in him.

"I'm workin' tomorrow, but I guess I can pick up some stuff to enter into the computer later at home."

Chapter 5

The following morning, Toni took Darlene for shopping and lunch, while Ruth Ann got busy making the cake.

Ruth Ann hadn't done a lot of baking in recent years, so the kitchen quickly descended into chaos. Each step: cracking eggs, mixing in flour and sugar, and making the icing, added to the mess. She had every intention of cleaning up each spill as it occurred, but with her focus on finishing the cake, she ignored the growing problem. It wasn't long before the kitchen looked like a tornado had struck. There were mixing bowls, pans, and utensils everywhere, along with flour and sugar spilled across the counters and floor. In the middle of the disaster, Ruth Ann stood at the counter icing a German chocolate cake.

Darlene entered from outside with Toni on her heels. "Holy mother of God, Ruthie!" she exclaimed, stunned by the sight of the wrecked kitchen. "What in the world happened?"

Ruth Ann casually turned at the sound of her name. "Hey Dar," she said cheerfully. "Hello Toni."

While Darlene remained paralyzed in the doorway, Toni slipped past her into the room. "Hey Aunt Ruthie. That's a nice-looking cake."

Ruth Ann smiled. "It's for Mr. Patterson. We're going to take it to him and introduce ourselves."

"Yeah?" Toni answered, surreptitiously excited about seeing Alex.

"Shut that door," Ruth Ann barked at her sister. "You're lettin' in flies."

Darlene shut the door and looked around, derisively snorting. "This happens ever'time. I ain't cleanin' up this mess." She stormed through the kitchen to the den.

"I'll help you clean up," Toni said.

"Thank you, dear."

Ruth Ann placed the finished cake under a plastic Tupperware dome she'd bought in the 1970s and set it in the refrigerator. She and Toni started cleaning up.

"When're you gonna take it to him?" Toni asked.

"Hadn't thought about it."

"She's lyin'," Darlene chimed in from the adjoining room.

"Don't pay her no mind."

Toni shook her head, smiling.

"You said he was nice?" Ruth Ann asked.

"Seemed so," Toni said.

Darlene appeared in the doorway. "Thought you just introduced yourself," she snarked.

"Let her be," Ruth Ann said, coming to Toni's defense.

"Both a y'all are just as interested as I am," Darlene said. "So don't act like ya ain't." She turned to Ruth Ann. "When're we gonna take him that cake?"

"Now you wanna take credit for *my* cake? You're too good to help me make it or clean up, but here you are rarin' to go deliver it." She waved her sister away, adding a contemptuous hiss.

Darlene glanced at the sink and shook her head at the mound of dirty dishes. "How in the world does one person make this much mess?" She found a clean towel to dry her glass, then poured a small refill.

"Maybe next time you'll help and I'll show you."

"I'd rather eat razor blades."

"I got some."

Toni intervened. "Let's finish cleanin' the kitchen, then take the cake over."

"It'd go faster if you'd help," Ruth Ann jabbed at her sister.

"It'd go faster if you'd quit bakin'," Darlene fired back.

"Stop. Mom, she's right. It'll go faster if you help or got out of the way."

Darlene begrudgingly put down her glass and picked up a broom.

After a few tense moments of silence, Ruth Ann said, "What'd he buy at Gibson's?"

"Half the store," Toni said with a chuckle.

"We ain't seen him up close, but Cynthia said he's nice lookin'."

Toni didn't want to offer too much opinion and risk a full-blown interrogation, so she said, "He's alright, I guess. Kinda tall with nice eyes."

"So, you like him?" Ruth Ann asked.

"I just met him."

"Well, don't go jumpin' into somethin,'" Darlene said.

"Let her be," Ruth Ann said. "It's been long enough."

"That ain't what I was talkin' about," Darlene said, turning to Toni. "You've got plenty of time to get to know him, if you're interested."

"Thanks for givin' me permission," Toni chided, "But I'm seein' Andy."

"Pfft," Darlene snorted. "I like Andy just fine, but he ain't the one for you."

"How do you know?"

"I seen how you look at him."

"I've only been divorced from Virgil for a year."

"Y'all split up two years ago. That's when I'd start countin'. And ain't nothin' wrong with seein' any fella that asks."

"I don't wanna date someone just to date, 'specially someone I'd never marry, like Grady Pearson."

Darlene chuckled. "You'd spend your whole life in the kitchen tryin' to keep Grady Pearson fed." They laughed, adding to the lighter mood. "Don't let what happened with Virgil stop you from findin' the right man."

"Mom," she said, becoming agitated. "We've been through this ten million times. It's my decision."

"I know, sweetheart, but you're still my baby and I worry about you."

"I love you too. But it's my decision."

After an hour of cleaning, Ruth Ann pulled the cake out of the refrigerator, took a quick look under the dome, and said, "Y'all ready?"

* * *

Toni hid her excitement as she and the sisters stood at Alex's front door. She rang the doorbell, waited a few minutes, then rang it again.

"I don't think he's here," Toni said, disappointed.

"There's a car in the driveway," Ruth Ann noted.

"Alex drives a pickup," Toni replied.

All three ladies appeared puzzled by the car but quickly returned their attention to Alex's front door.

"Maybe he's sleepin'," Darlene offered.

"It ain't even suppertime," Ruth Ann said. "Who sleeps in broad daylight?"

"You do," answered Darlene.

The door clacked with the sound of locks being released and swung open. Before them stood a curvy, disheveled young woman wearing little more than a long T-shirt. "Yeah?" she tersely asked.

Darlene initially raised her eyebrows, bemused by the unexpected woman. "Well, howdy. I'm Darlene Viriglio. This is my sister Ruth Ann and my daughter Antoinette. We live across the street and came by to welcome y'all to the neighborhood."

Ruth Ann smiled and held the cake out.

The annoyed woman glanced at the offering and the ladies. "He's sleeping, but hang on." She shut the door.

Darlene chuckled. "I guess he ain't gay."

Toni was not amused. Her low opinion of men surfaced; brought back to the day she confirmed her ex-husband had been cheating on her. Torn between disappointment and outrage, she stepped back, ready to leave. Her infatuation with Alex vanished, and she felt a certain shame for allowing a stranger to hurt her.

Ruth Ann turned sharply to her sister. "Well, I never. That little girl needs to learn some manners."

"We was the ones who showed up uninvited," Darlene reminded.

"I don't care. You don't answer the door half naked and talk to no one like that, 'specially your neighbors. She coulda said pleased to meet you, or you've come at a bad time, but she obviously don't know pea turkey about manners."

The three women remained speechless until a minute later when the door opened and Alex appeared wearing a bathrobe. He wasn't as out of sorts as the young woman, but looked as though he'd been woken up. "Can I help you?"

Ruth Ann smiled and held up the cake.

"Welcome to the neighborhood," Darlene blurted.

He smiled and took the cake. "Thank you…"

"Darlene Viriglio. I live across the street in that white house with the shutters—number 4402—with my sister Ruth Ann Waterman here."

Alex shook hands with each sister and said, "Thank you, Darlene and Ruth Ann. This is so nice. I haven't met many people yet."

"This is my daughter, Antoinette. She goes by Toni, but y'all already met."

She smiled as her attraction resurfaced, dampening the sting. "Nice to see you again, Alex."

"Yes," Alex said. "We've met. How's it going?" He glanced down at his robe and bare feet. "Forgive my appearance. I was up all night. I'd ask you in, but my place is a complete wreck."

"That's all right," Darlene said. "Can I call you Alex?"

"Please."

"Alex, we didn't come to stay. We brought you my sister's famous German chocolate cake, and to say welcome, so… Welcome!"

Toni and Ruth Ann leaned sideways to get a better view into the house, intrigued by the young woman and her actions.

Toni stepped forward and said, "We're sorry to bother you." They all turned to leave.

"Listen," Alex said, clearing his throat. "Tomorrow's Thursday. How about I come by in the afternoon and return your container? We can chat."

Darlene lit up. She loved company. "That'd be wonderful. How 'bout two o'clock?"

Alex smiled and nodded. "Two it is."

As they walked away, he called out, "Thanks again for the cake."

Darlene waved. "See you at two, Alex."

Alex closed the door while the ladies strolled across the street.

"I'm gonna have to go to the store," Ruth Ann said. "We're out of tea and coffee."

"So, we'll serve him whiskey," Darlene replied as they reached the porch.

"I'm not servin' him hard liquor," Ruth Ann replied with a chuckle. "Shame on you."

They laughed and filed through the door.

"Give him a shot of penicillin," Toni whispered, entering last and shooting a glare at the extra car in the driveway. "Aunt Ruthie, I gotta work tomorrow. You think Sarah or Irma can take you shoppin'?"

"Certainly, dear."

That evening, while Toni fixed dinner, the sisters sat around the kitchen table.

"That Alex seems like a polite young fella," Darlene said.

"I hope he likes the cake."

"I'm sure his little girlfriend will," Toni sniped from the stove.

Darlene smiled at Toni's jealousy. "Maybe she's his sister," she teased.

Toni spun around. "Mom! Seriously?"

"Leave her be."

Darlene smiled. "Listen, you don't know nothin' 'bout either one. She might be some passin' thing."

"Passin' thing," Toni repeated with contempt. "He *is* a man." She hated being interested in Alex, especially after witnessing his taste in women.

"Now don't go gettin' your feathers all ruffled," Darlene said. "You ain't got no claim on him. What he does is his business."

Toni sighed. "I just wish men weren't such pigs."

"Honey, they ain't all pigs. Andy's not. Your daddy wasn't."

"I know, but it seems like everyone I meet is either married, cheatin', gay, or sleepin' with every young thing that breathes."

"Maybe Alex is different."

"I doubt it."

Ruth Ann began setting the table. "I'm not so sure about him, either. But maybe that girl was a friend."

"Some friend. She was half naked. You said it yourself."

"That don't mean they ain't just friends," Ruth Ann said. "But the way she acted don't speak too well for him."

"Exactly," Toni snapped.

"Listen, y'all are paintin' Alex with an empty brush. You don't know nothin'. Y'all sound like Cynthia Coker."

"What am I s'posed to think?" Toni questioned. "He comes to the door wearin' a bathrobe after some *woman* answers the door barely dressed and lookin' all rumpled."

"You oughta join us tomorrow and we'll all find out," Darlene suggested.

Toni shook her head. "I gotta work, and I'm havin' supper with Andy."

"He can wait."

"It's his daddy's birthday. I gotta be there."

Darlene shrugged. "I guess you're gonna have to wait to find out."

Toni chuckled. "For about five minutes after he leaves. That's how long it'll take you to call me with all the details."

Ruth Ann snickered while Darlene delivered her standard, "Pfft."

Chapter 6

Alex placed the cake on the kitchen counter and fished out a cigarette. He felt arms slip around him from behind as Desiree, the young woman who'd answered his door, pressed her body against him.

"Did you get rid of the Geritols?"

Alex grimaced, disapproving of her rude comment, and feeling a little irritated that Desiree was the first impression the neighbors had gotten. He slipped out of her arms and lifted the cover off the cake. He sampled the icing.

"Wow! This is great. No one has ever done something like this for me."

"That's what old ladies do," she callously remarked. "Your mother never made you a birthday cake?" She plucked the cigarette from his hand and started smoking it then pulled a beer from the refrigerator. "Where're we going for dinner? I mean, is there any place *to* go in this town?"

Alex studied Desiree. He'd met her two days earlier at the gig in Dallas. She was beautiful and alluring, but all he felt was regret that she was there. It was a familiar feeling. Too many times he'd meet a beautiful woman while drinking in bar or at a gig, only to discover that initial spark wasn't real, leading to an agonizing and sometimes ugly breakup.

His attention shifted to the cake as he thought fondly about the sisters and Toni. Pulling a bottle of water from the refrigerator, he remarked, "I got a cake for my birthday, but no one's ever welcomed me like this."

Desiree wrapped her arms around him and placed the cigarette between his lips. As he inhaled, she said, "I know how to welcome you." She rubbed against him, inviting him to fondle her. But as easily as Alex was enticed into going through the motions, he quickly lost interest. *Déjà vu*, he thought.

Irritated, Desiree took a step back. "What's going on with you? You've hardly touched me since I got here." Alex shrugged, and she again slipped her arms around him, but he stepped back. "What the hell? Is this how you treat me? I drove two hours in the middle of the night because you wanted me to."

"I'm sorry. I've just got a lot on my mind."

"Why don't you let me take your mind off it?" She ran her nails across his chest. He tried to engage with her, but couldn't muster any excitement. He stepped back and she snorted, "Really?"

"I'm sorry."

Her frustration was close to boiling over but she silently watched as he pulled a knife from the drawer and cut the cake.

"You want a piece?"

She shrugged and curtly said, "I guess."

After sampling the cake, she dragged her index finger through the icing and fed it to Alex. "Give you any ideas?" she seductively asked. She reloaded her finger and raised it to Alex's mouth but pulled it back, teasing him. "Uh-uh," she said, holding her finger away while kissing him. She leaned back from the kiss long enough to feed him the finger full of icing then returned to passionately kissing him. "You just needed something sweet." She took his hand and led him toward the bedroom, but Alex released.

"Hang on," he said, returning to the counter where he covered the cake and put it in the refrigerator. He again smiled at the sisters' act of kindness. Then he flashed on Toni, remembering their first encounter at Gibson's. He found her intriguing. His thoughts were interrupted when Desiree tugged at his arm. "I probably should take a shower," Alex said. "I'm still pretty grungy from the gig."

Desiree's eyes lit up. "Ooo, that sounds good." She started peeling off what few clothes she had on. "Then maybe we can go back to Dallas and hit the West End tonight. You can stay at my place. I might even let you sleep—eventually." Now naked, she again started caressing him. "C'mon, let's get you cleaned up." She took a step back and smiled, giving him a moment to ogle her.

Alex stared at her perfect body and thought of her willingness to do anything he wanted, but felt nothing. *What's wrong with me?* he wondered.

With Alex standing there looking dumbfounded, she said, "You like?"

Instinctively, Alex nodded, but he had no desire to follow through. He took a step back and said, "Let me get a beer."

"Don't take too long," she said, heading into the bathroom and turning on the shower.

Alex stood in the kitchen holding a beer hearing the water running in the bathroom. *What am I doing?* There was no doubt he could have his way with Desiree, but his thoughts jumped ahead to what would happen after the shower; he'd want her gone more than he already wanted.

He downed half a can of beer in one gulp then went to the living room, took a seat, and waited.

"Hurry up, Alex. I need to you…" she giggled, "wash my back… and my front, and everything in between." She laughed, but Alex didn't move.

He finished his beer, and it wasn't long before Desiree appeared, her hair wet and body wrapped in a towel. "What the hell. I thought we were gonna have some fun. Aren't you going to join me?"

Alex rose and she immediately closed in on him, losing the towel along the way. She wrapped her arms around him and started undressing him, but he stopped her. "I'm sorry," he said. "I've got a couple of things that are bugging me, and I need to take care of them," he lied.

"Are you okay?"

"I'm fine."

"But we're still going to my place, right?"

"I can't. It's a two-hour drive there and back and I have to be here for lunch tomorrow."

"With the Geritols? Gimme a break. What happened to the party animal I met two nights ago?"

He somberly shook his head. "I don't know."

"You invite me here for some fun and now you're just gonna blow me off?"

"I'm not blowing you off, but maybe now's not a good time for us."

"What the hell's that mean?"

"It means I need time to figure things out."

"So you are blowing me off." She stared into his eyes until he failed to disagree. "I get it," she said as her anger began overflowing. She got dressed then stormed through the house gathering up her belongings. "Don't bother calling me again."

"I'm sorry."

"You're pathetic. I thought you were a rocker who knew how to party, not some old fart like your neighbors." She grabbed her purse and abruptly stopped to glare at him. Through the silence, her expression softened, and she started crying. She put her arms around his neck, lowering her head. "I'm sorry, Alex."

"It's not your fault."

Alex led her to the driveway and loaded her into the driver's seat. He stood next to her window. "I don't have to leave," she said meekly.

"I know, and I'm sorry. But this is my problem. I need to work it out."

"Fine!" she snapped, quickly firing up the car. Burning rubber, she backed out of the driveway and raced away.

Alex felt terrible for hurting Desiree, but he was glad she was gone.

Inside the sisters' house, Darlene turned sharply at the sound of Desiree ripping down the street. "You hear that?"

Ruth Ann glanced out the window in time to see Desiree's tail lights at the end of the street. "Looks like Miss Manners left in a huff," she said with a slight smirk.

* * *

The following day, Sarah dropped Ruth Ann off from their trip to the market. She helped put the groceries away while the sisters began setting up for Alex's arrival.

Ruth Ann planned a classy afternoon serving tea and snacks instead of whiskey and pizza, as Darlene had suggested.

Rummaging through the grocery sacks, Darlene asked, "Where's the Jack?"

Sarah pulled a bottle of whiskey and set it in front of Darlene. "We didn't forget you, Dar."

"'Preciate it." She briefly considered taking a shot, but ultimately stored the bottle in the cupboard.

"I don't want you drinkin' while Alex is here," Ruth Ann said.

"Why not? He's a big boy."

"It ain't proper drinkin' hard liquor in the middle of the day, and I don't want him gettin' the wrong idea."

"Pfft. What's the harm in an old lady sippin' on a few fingers now and then?"

"'Cause it ain't just a few fingers and it ain't just now and then. I don't want you actin' up."

Darlene smiled, spotting an opportunity to yank Ruthie's chain. "Wonder if Alex likes his whiskey straight."

"We ain't servin' hard liquor!" Ruth Ann barked. She slapped a box with tea on the counter. "Sarah, dear, can you put on a kettle of water?"

"My pleasure," Sarah said. "Should I also make a batch of iced tea?"

"That's a good idea, dear."

"I'm guessin' he's a drinkin' man," Darlene started, "based on that gal he had over. He might be disappointed with tea."

"Well, he can just be disappointed. I ain't servin' no hard liquor."

Darlene got a kick out of her sister's angry tone. "You know I don't like drinkin' alone."

Ruth Ann realized she was being needled, so she fired back. "Since when?"

"You sure you don't wanna join us?" Darlene asked Sarah.

"You know I'd love to Dar but I think it's best I bow out and let y'all get acquainted."

"It's up to you."

"Maybe next time. Do you need any more help?"

"Nah, but thanks," Darlene said, turning to Ruth Ann. "I'll get the tea set."

"I'll get it," Ruth Ann said. "It probably needs a quick wash."

Social gatherings were Ruth Ann's domain, so Darlene was happy to stay out of the way.

Before leaving, Sarah said, "I expect a full report."

Chapter 7

Alex knocked on the sister's door a few minutes after noon. He was wearing his best jeans and a colorful shirt that resembled a dashiki. He'd used a little gel to pull back and tame his hair.

Ruth Ann opened the door and Alex immediately handed her the cake dome. "The cake was great," he said. "Thank you."

"You're welcome," she said, turning for the kitchen. "Let me put this away."

Darlene appeared and led Alex to the living room. "Please, have a seat."

Alex sat on the couch while Darlene took the adjacent chair. Ruth Ann returned to pour the tea.

"Don't you look nice, Alex," Darlene commented.

Alex smiled. "I was going to wear my bathrobe but you've already seen that."

Ruth Ann was startled by his casual familiarity, but tittered politely. Darlene laughed, immediately connecting with his sarcasm.

"We heard you was a musician or somethin'. Is that what you wear when you perform?" Darlene asked.

Alex glanced at his shirt and jeans. "Sometimes. I usually wear whatever I want, as long as I stand out from the crowd."

"How long you been a musician?" Darlene asked.

"For the last twenty years."

"Do you sing?"

"Only in the shower. I'm a keyboard player."

"What's the name of your band?"

"I don't play in just one band. I'm what's known as a sideman. Sometimes I play in the same band for a few months or a year, but usually it's temporary because I'm filling for someone who's sick or quits."

"How'd you ever get started doin' that?"

"Now Darlene," Ruth Ann interrupted. "He didn't come here just to play twenty questions." She pointed to the tray of food. "Alex, would you like a snack?"

"Thank you. Just the two of you live here?"

Darlene nodded. "Joe, my late husband, and I bought this house in 1971. He passed in '03, so I lived here alone till Ruthie's husband passed 'bout five years ago."

"I'm sorry to hear about your husbands. And Toni, she's your daughter?" he asked Darlene.

"Yep. She lives over off Bell, but she grew up here in this house."

"She said she lived in Dallas for a while."

"When she was married."

Alex felt a flutter hearing the word *was*. He was curious about Toni, but didn't want to appear too interested. "Dallas is nice."

"Where're you from?" Darlene asked.

"Originally, I'm from Columbus, Ohio, but I've moved around a lot."

"Was your daddy in the service?"

"No. My parents divorced when I was young, so I moved with my mom to Oregon. From there, we moved to California, then back to Oregon, where I finished high school."

"So, you moved to Hamilton from Oregon?" Darlene continued.

Alex chuckled, "Oh no, I've moved a dozen times since high school."

"So, you're kind of a drifter," Darlene said in jest.

"Darlene!" Ruth Ann scolded. "That ain't a nice thing to say."

"I don't mean nothin' by it."

Alex smiled, not at all offended. "I feel like a nomad. After high school, I moved to Los Angeles before moving to Nashville five years later. I spent three years there, followed by a couple of years in New York, and the last ten in L.A."

"Mercy," Darlene said. "You must like movin'."

Alex smiled. "I'm usually on the road performing, but this is my first actual move in a while."

Darlene shook her head. "Well, this sure ain't L.A."

"No. But living in big cities gets old."

"So, what're you gonna do here in Hamilton?" Darlene asked. "There ain't no concert halls. 'Course Dallas ain't far."

Alex wasn't sure how to respond. It was a question he'd been struggling with for many months. He munched on some crackers and gave a slight shrug. "I'm not exactly sure."

"Bein' a musician sounds excitin'," Darlene said. "I'd love travelin' and performin'."

"I used to love traveling, but I got tired of waking up in a strange bed or on a bus."

"Sounds like a hoot to me. A different city ever night. Drivin' through the countryside. I'd take it." Darlene pondered for a moment as her thoughts spilled out. "I'd take it in a heartbeat."

"Darlene was a dancer," Ruth Ann said.

Alex shifted forward in his chair. "Really?"

"Oh," she sighed. "Not really. That was a long time ago. I was a young girl, and it wasn't nothin'."

"So, what happened?"

"I was pretty good at ballet, but my teacher said dancers live in New York."

"So, what'd you do?"

"Nothin'."

Alex studied her through the long pause.

Ruth Ann rose to heat more water. "'S'cuse me."

"Nothing?" Alex asked.

Darlene sighed. "Nah. I was gettin' too big. Years later, me and Joe talked about movin' somewhere, but he didn't wanna leave Hamilton. He was a little older 'n me and we both wanted young'uns."

"So you had Toni?"

"Not right off."

"But eventually you got what you wanted." She furrowed her brow, as if questioning his remark. "You'd rather have been a professional dancer than raising kids and grandkids?"

"Listen, I love my Antoinette. She's my miracle baby, but she ain't got no kids, and thank the good Lord."

Alex wondered what made Toni a miracle baby, but asking seemed inappropriate.

"What would you do differently if given a second chance?"

As she considered the question, Darlene was struck by how comfortable she felt talking with Alex. "I don't know. I was almost thirty before havin' young'uns, so I mighta liked livin' in New York 'fore that. I don't know with all them people. Seems kinda foolish when I think about it now, but when I was young, I mighta."

Alex turned quiet.

"Somethin' wrong?" Darlene asked.

He sighed as his expression lost some of its spark. "No. But I've had similar thoughts. I pursued a career and never married or had kids. I wonder sometimes if I missed out. Now, I'm too old."

"Too old to what? To have kids? Pfft."

Alex chuckled. "Thanks, but even if I'm not too old, I lost the only…" he stopped himself before divulging his deepest regret. "I haven't found the right girl."

"What about that young lady who answered your door?" Alex smiled at Darlene's sly grin just as Ruth Ann reentered the room.

"What are we talkin' about?"

"That young woman who answered Alex's door."

"Darlene!" Ruth Ann scolded. "That's personal."

Alex smiled at Darlene's lack of remorse. "It's okay," he said. "She's just a friend."

Darlene flipped an eyebrow as her smile grew. She immediately recognized Alex as a good sport and was thrilled to have a partner for teasing Ruthie. "Seemed like y'all was mighty friendly."

"Shoot, Darlene!" Ruth Ann again snapped before turning to Alex. "You gotta forgive my sister. She don't always think 'fore she speaks." She gave her sister another visual reprimand.

"It's not a problem," Alex said, smiling at the skirmish between the sisters. He glanced around the room. "I like your house. You said Toni grew up here?"

Darlene nodded. "Yep."

"And you've lived in Hamilton all your life?"

"Me and Ruthie have."

"Where's the house you grew up in?"

"'Bout six blocks that way." Darlene pointed. "Daddy was the postmaster and Momma taught school."

"That's pretty cool. What grade did she teach?"

"All of 'em. When we was young, there was only one class."

"How many kids were in your graduating class?"

Darlene glanced at Ruth Ann. "There was three in mine and what, five in yours?"

Ruth Ann nodded. "Most of 'em are still here."

Alex smiled, imagining such a simple time. "And Toni grew up here then moved to Dallas. How long ago was that?"

"How'd you know that?" Darlene suspiciously asked. Toni's failed marriage wasn't something Toni or Darlene discussed publicly, and certainly not with strangers.

"You told me earlier, and she told me when we first met at Gibson's."

"She don't normally talk about that. You musta said somethin' that made it alright."

Ruth Ann made a contemptuous snort. "She don't always make the right decision."

"Ain't on her," Darlene snapped at Ruth Ann, then turned to Alex. "My Antoinette's a sweet girl, but she picked the wrong man to marry."

Alex waited for her to continue, but she left the thought unfinished, piquing Alex's interest.

"So, it didn't work out?" he prodded.

Darlene leaned forward. "Alex, let's just say we're glad she's back."

Alex hoped to learn more about Toni, but was afraid to pry. Hamilton was a close-knit community and he was an outsider. He proceeded with caution, trying to sound aloof.

"So, she's here to stay? I mean, she seemed to say Hamilton's too small for her."

"This is home to her," Darlene said. She could tell Alex was interested in Antoinette.

Ruth Ann left with the empty teapot.

"Hmm," Alex pondered. "But no grandkids?"

Darlene smiled. "It's a blessin'. Not ever'one's meant to have young'uns."

"That I understand. I might be a decent husband, but I wouldn't have been a good father in my youth. I was gone all the time."

"Then you shouldn't've had young'uns."

"I didn't."

"That's good."

Ruth Ann returned. "What are we talkin' about?"

"Talkin' about why Alex ain't got no young'uns?" Darlene was grinning with anticipation.

"For Heaven's sakes! Darlene, leave the man alone." Darlene and Alex shared the laugh. Ruth Ann smirked at her sister then smiled at Alex. "When's your next performance?"

"I leave in a few days for a handful of dates in Dallas, Denver, Vegas, and Kansas City."

"That sounds exciting," Ruth Ann said.

"It's not. I committed to playing the dates last year, but I'd get out of them If I could."

Ruth Ann gave him a puzzled look. "Why? You're a musician. That's what you do."

Alex hesitated. "To tell you the truth, I'm probably going to quit playing."

The ladies stared at him, perplexed. "Why would you quit?" Ruth Ann asked.

"I've been doing this a long time, and I guess I'm just tired of being on the road."

"What're you gonna do?" Darlene asked.

"I'm not sure. I'd like to write and publish songs, which I can do from anywhere."

"Do you write a lotta songs?"

He frowned. "Lately, I've written nothing." He immediately wished he hadn't revealed his private struggle. "But I'll figure it out," he quickly added while looking at his watch and rising. "Listen, I don't want to overstay my welcome."

"Nonsense," Darlene barked. "Sit back down. Ruthie, put some water on and bring me my whiskey."

Ruth Ann rose, but Alex raised his hand. "Thank you, no. I should go. I've barely slept in the past few days."

The ladies led him to the entryway. "Thanks again for having me over, and for the cake."

"You're welcome, Alex," Ruth Ann said. "Come by anytime." She stepped away, leaving Alex and Darlene at the door.

Darlene patted him on the arm with a smile. "I'm glad you stopped by, and I think you'll figure out what to do."

"Thank you. I hope you're right."

At midnight, Alex was wandering around his backyard with a beer and a cigarette. He paced, puffed, and drank, stopped and stared for a time, then paced again. The conversation with the sisters replayed in his head. Their questions filled his thoughts. *Why would you quit?* The past eighteen months swirled around in his mind, leaving him with no single answer. *I love playing,* he thought. *I used to.* His memories turned from performing to waking up next to the woman of his dreams. He sighed. *It's just not the same without her.* He walked inside and sat at the piano. He played a few chords and stopped.

"There's just nothing there," he muttered to himself. He stared at the keys, wondering if the music would ever return.

Chapter 8

With Alex frequently traveling, it was difficult for the residents of Hamilton to get to know him, adding to the rumor mill. Some reported seeing him walking around town, while curious sorts drove by his house, observing him mowing the lawn.

Darlene spotted him working on his car and sauntered over.

"Hey there, stranger," she said, crossing the street.

Alex emerged from under the hood, wiping grease off his hands, ready for a handshake. "Hey. How've you been?" he asked.

"I should ask you. Ain't seen much of ya lately."

"I've been in and out a lot, and keeping musician hours; sleeping all day and up all night."

"Ain't heard any partyin' at night?"

He chuckled. "No, that's not really my thing. I'm usually up watching TV or trying to write something."

"Havin' any luck?"

"With writing?"

She nodded. "I'd love to hear somethin'."

He frowned. "So would I." He felt the frustration of writer's block but wasn't willing to talk about it. "At least there's always something to watch with streaming."

"I don't know what that is, but you oughta get out and meet folks."

"I should, but I haven't figured out where everyone hangs out."

"Well, me and Ruthie go to church Sunday and Wednesday. You're welcome to join us."

"Thanks. I'm not a big churchgoer, and like I said, I'm usually sleeping Sunday morning."

"Well, shame on you."

"I know. But you grew up here. What did you do for fun as a kid?"

She laughed. "It's been a while since I was runnin' the streets. Wasn't like it is today. We didn't go 'round lookin' for things to do."

"Surely you had fun."

"'Course we did. But when we was young we had things to do. And by the time folks was your age they was married with young'uns to take care of."

"Okay, so what did you and your late husband do for fun?"

She paused to consider the question. "Oh, sometimes me and Joe'd go visitin' or folks'd come visit us."

"What about movies or parties or going out to eat? I'm sure you never went out drinking, but were there any nightclubs back then?"

She chuckled. "There was a couple, but churchgoin' folks never went to places like that."

"Is that why there's no clubs here, no one went?"

She shook her head. "They had to close when the county went dry 'bout twenty, thirty years ago."

"Dry, like you can't sell alcohol?"

She nodded.

"But you can buy it at a liquor store?" he noted.

She gave a sly smile. "Truth is, Alex, folks around here'll tell you good Christians don't touch alcohol, but when it came time to outlaw it, most folks had a slightly different idea."

Alex was intrigued by Darlene's unusual inflection. "So, good Christians don't drink, so they can't be seen at a nightclub, but it's okay to sell in a store?"

"Pretty much. They made a law that says any place that sells alcohol has to make most their money off somethin' else."

"So restaurants can sell it because they make most of their money off food."

"'Xactly. You know, I ain't ashamed to admit to sippin' on a few fingers now and then, but lotsa folks ain't so keen on it."

Alex smiled. "Now, don't be offended, but why should you never go fishing with only one Baptist?"

She gave him a suspicious squint. "Why?"

"Because he'll drink all the beer."

She laughed riotously, "Alex, I'm gonna use that one, 'cause that's how it is, and it ain't just Baptists."

"It's only a joke. I don't want to offend anyone."

"Pfft. If they can't take it, to hell with 'em."

"No pun intended?"

"What? Oh." She laughed again then smirked.

"But back to the issue of meeting people. If there's no clubs and most people are married, where do the rest go for fun, or even to meet people?"

"You oughta ask Antoinette where she and Andy go."

"Is that her boyfriend?" Alex asked, hating to see Darlene nod.

"They been datin' a while, but Antoinette can fill you in on the goin's-on in Hamilton."

Alex nodded, happy to have a reason to talk to Toni. "Next time I see her."

"Keep an eye out for her pickup truck and come on over."

"I can't just drop in unannounced. That's bad manners," he said in jest.

"Shoot, Alex. Neighbors can stop by whenever they want."

"Really? I thought it was a major faux pas to just show up."

"Well I don't know what that word means, but you can come on over any time you like."

"For a couple of fingers?" he asked with a huge grin.

"'Specially for that. Just not after eight o'clock 'cause me and Ruthie's normally in bed by then."

"Wow, night owls."

"Wisenheimer." She turned to leave. "Don't be a stranger, Alex."

Alex smiled, always feeling lifted by conversation with Darlene.

* * *

The next day, Toni and Andy were at Gibson's shopping when she spotted Alex. His long hair, ripped jeans, and hip jacket stood out.

"I'll be right back," Toni said, planning to slip away from Andy for a quick conversation with Alex. Andy was occupied with browsing the merchandise but Toni's anxious tone caught his attention. He glanced at her, noticing an eager look that didn't match the one she'd been wearing. As she started walking away, Andy spotted Alex and hurried to catch up.

As Toni approached Alex, his eyes opened wide while his smile revealed a little too much enthusiasm. Toni reached out for what Alex hoped would be a hug but Andy arrived just in time to snatch her hand back before she could act.

"Hey there," Toni said, sounding overly eager, triggering Andy to flash a look of ire at Alex.

"How've you been?" Alex replied.

"Mom said you've been avoidin' everyone."

He noticed her wily grin. "No she didn't."

Toni's smile grew but quickly retreated when Andy tightened his grip and pulled her slightly behind him, placing him eye-to-eye with Alex. He gave Alex an icy nod and grudgingly said, "Andy Pharris."

"Alex. Nice to meet you."

A quick handshake, then Andy threw an arm around Toni's shoulder as an obvious declaration of ownership.

"Toni said some guy from California moved in." He gave Alex a contemptuous up-and-down look. "Ain't a lotta… Californians here."

Message received, Alex thought. He'd met plenty of insecure boyfriends.

"No, I guess not," Alex said matter-of-factly.

The two men were about the same height, with Alex being slightly taller. Andy was thin and wiry while Alex was more filled out, bordering on overweight. Being shorter, even wearing cowboy boots, Andy stood as tall as he could to match eyes with Alex.

After an uncomfortable silence, Toni said, "Mom said you been lookin' for somethin' to do, at night I mean."

"I'm gone a lot, but yeah."

She laughed. "I told ya, ain't nothin' to do in Hamilton."

"What about mud bogging or cow tipping?" he joked, having Googled some stereotypes of Southern entertainment.

Andy scoffed at Alex's ignorance, but Toni recognized his humor. She smiled, thinking about how a snarky remark like that would tickle her mother.

"Don't forget pig wrestlin' and cow chip tossin'."

Both Toni and Alex enjoyed the bantering, but Andy was fuming. "We gotta go," Andy snapped, tugging Toni's arm and slowly pulling her away.

"Ain't nothin' to do at night," Toni quickly remarked. "'Cept the fair and rodeo startin' this weekend."

"Great. Where?"

"Downtown. You can't miss it."

Toni suddenly stopped as Andy's tugging reached her limit. She glared at him. "Hang on a sec." She turned to Alex and said. "Starts Saturday mornin' and runs three weekends. Mom and Aunt Ruthie usually go early on Saturday."

"Cool," Alex said. "Maybe I'll see you there."

Andy gingerly pulled her hand, and she slowly backed away from Alex. She gave a slight wave and turned to Andy with an irritated expression. Alex couldn't hear exactly what she said, but Andy was getting an earful.

Chapter 9

Every May, Hamilton hosted an arts fair that attracted vendors and shoppers from all over the country. For three consecutive weekends, the city closed off two blocks of downtown and lined the center of Main Street with dozens of booths butted up against one another. Visitors filed down one side, rounded a corner, then walked up the other side. Thousands came to eat, drink, and peruse the artwork, jewelry, woodwork, and literature. Several locals exhibited their work, but many aspiring artists and craftsmen from around Texas also displayed their work. This was Hamilton's biggest claim to fame and the highlight of the year.

Alex was looking forward to the fair, seeing it as an excellent opportunity to meet and interact with the locals.

Darlene and Ruth Ann always attended the first Saturday morning when the crowds were smaller. Neither enjoyed keeping up with the prime-time crowd, nor did they appreciate being jostled around because of their slower stride. As Darlene put it, "I'll go as fast as I go. Y'all can go around."

Not long after the sisters and Toni kicked off their slow stroll, they stopped at one of the first booths when a painting caught Ruth Ann's attention. As she dug through her purse to pay for the piece, Toni stepped away to chat with an old friend from high school.

Once Ruth Ann had her purchase in hand, Darlene hooked her arm around Ruth Ann's arm and said, "Let's get this show on the road." They wandered around the corner, leaving Toni to catch up.

Toni noticed the sisters leaving her sight and told her friend, "Good seein' you." She make a few quick steps, and while turning the corner, collided with Alex, who had just arrived and was merging into the flow of traffic.

"Whoa," Toni said, startled and unaware of who she'd hit. "Sorry." She looked up and saw who it was. "Oh, hey," she said indifferently.

"You trying to run me down?" he asked in jest.

"If I was, you'd be on the ground." She was smiling but Alex wasn't sure if she was joking.

"Good to know. Where's —"

"Alex!" Darlene interrupted. "Where've you been?" She looked past him. "You here alone?"

He nodded and gave a slight shrug.

"Come on," she said, taking his arm without giving him a choice. "You're with us."

Darlene strolled along proudly with Alex as her escort. Ruth Ann and Toni followed a few steps back.

Alex glanced back at Toni. She flashed a quick smirk, but shook her head and smiled. She was pleased with how her mother had taken to Alex.

They wandered from booth to booth, chatting, eating, and shopping.

While the sisters were admiring the handcrafted woodwork at one booth, Alex stepped back to strike up a conversation with Toni.

"Great weather," he said, glancing up at the blue sky. "What do you guys got planned for later?"

She smiled; sensing Alex was fishing for an opening to ask her out. She was interested, but instinctively shut him down. "Me and Andy, my boyfriend, are probably gonna do somethin'."

Alex had met many women who deliberately mentioned their boyfriend to thwart an interested guy from pursuing further. He smiled. "Oh, yeah," he said, pretending to forget she had a boyfriend. "Where is Andy?"

She smirked, suspecting he was toying with her. "He's busy."

Alex said, "Tell him I said hey." He smiled, fully aware that Andy didn't like him.

"He'll be sorry he missed you," she quipped with a sardonic smile. Alex grinned, then returned his attention to Darlene.

Along the route, they ran into Esma Beth Anderson, the organist at Darlene's church.

"Well, hello there, Miss Darlene," Esma Beth said, noticing Alex on her arm. "And who's this handsome man?"

Dalene smiled and placed her free hand on Alex's arm. "This is my friend and neighbor, Alex Patterson. He moved into Carl Webber's house a few months ago."

"Very nice to meet you, Mr. Patterson. Welcome to Hamilton. Will we be seeing you at the service tomorrow morning?"

Alex smiled. "I'm not normally up early on Sunday."

"Shame on you," Esma Beth said with a sweet smile.

"Alex, Esma Beth's 'bout the best organist in Texas, so y'all have somethin' in common."

Esma Beth gave Alex an inquisitive look. "Are you an organist?"

"I play keyboards, mostly piano and synthesizer."

"Alex is a professional musician."

"That's wonderful. I'd love to hear you play sometime."

"Likewise. I'm not much of a soloist, but I do love big church organs."

"Well, ours isn't large, but the Lord has blessed us with a very nice one. Our doors are always open, so visit anytime."

"I might take you up on that." He stepped back to leave before she could press him further on why he didn't attend church.

Esma Beth smiled and said, "Darlene, you behave yourself and bring him with you tomorrow."

Darlene nodded, and she and Alex started toward the next booth. "She don't like no one skippin' church."

"I could tell." He didn't want to engage in a conversation about attending church since he hadn't been in decades.

Darlene tugged Alex toward an elderly couple dressed in western wear standing away from the flowing crowd.

"Alex," Darlene said. "This here's Buford and Ada McCaleb." Alex reached out to shake the firm, weathered grip of Buford. The feeble-looking man's strength surprised him.

"Howdy there, Alex," Buford said with a hearty voice.

"Darlene has told us all about you," Ada added with a pleasant smile.

"Uh oh," Alex said. "I hope it wasn't bad."

As the aging couple chuckled, Darlene said, "Buford's great-great granddaddy was one of the first folks to settle in Hamilton."

"I looked at a house over off McCaleb Lane," Alex said.

"They named that after my great grandpa Jefferson around the turn of the century."

Darlene turned to Alex. "Buford's family's been supplyin' beef to the tri-county since, well, as long as I've been around."

"So, is your ranch on McCaleb Lane? I saw a lot of cattle out there."

Buford proudly replied, "We usually run 'bout a thousand head dependin' on the season. 'Course, my son and grandson handle all the work now."

"I heard that Texans never retire," Alex joked.

Buford chuckled and glanced at Ada. "I still manage to get out occasionally, but the boss here don't like me wanderin' too far."

Ada gripped Buford's arm and said, "He knows who to listen to."

Darlene stepped back, signaling to Alex it was time to move on. "It's very nice to meet you," Alex said.

"Stop by the ranch sometime. We'll show you around."

"Thank you."

Once they were out of earshot, Darlene said, "Don't tell no one, but Buford's about the most charitable man in the county."

"That's a secret?"

"He don't want folk askin' him for money, but he gives lots of it to the school and the church. Does it anonymously." She stopped and turned to Toni and Ruth Ann. "How 'bout gettin' some barbeque at Whitman's?"

Toni pointed. "Mom, they've got a booth right over there."

Toni led the way to an area where the food vendors shared several picnic tables. They ordered sandwiches and sat. Toni took a seat next to Alex while the sisters sat across from them.

"Are you havin' a good time?" Ruth Ann asked Alex.

He nodded. "I'm surprised at the number of people."

"And it's still early," Toni said.

"Are you only coming today?" he asked Toni, hoping to see her again.

Alex's veiled attempt at spending time with Toni was flattering, but she was spoken for.

"I ain't comin' back," Darlene declared. "These outta towners get ta pushin' ever'one around. It's a wonder no one gets knocked down."

"Probably not," Toni said regretfully. "I've seen everything already."

Disappointed, Alex nodded. "Let me know if your plans change. I hate wandering around alone, like a tourist."

"You are a tourist," she kidded.

"I'm a local," he proudly corrected.

Ruth Ann tapped Alex on the arm. "Alex, we've had artists come here and become famous. Like Windberg." She held up the sack with the painting she'd purchased. "I love his work."

Interrupting the conversation, a middle-aged man wearing dress slacks and a button-down shirt appeared. "Good afternoon, ladies." The man looked out of place among the locals. Most wore jeans and cotton work shirts.

"Larry," Darlene said, unenthusiastically.

"You must be Alex," the man said, reaching out to shake Alex's hand. Alex was leery, hearing Darlene's lukewarm greeting. "I'm Larry Westin, owner and editor of the *Hamilton Gazette*."

Alex rose and shook his hand. "Nice to meet you."

"I heard you're a musician."

Alex nodded.

"Tell me Alex, are you doing anything here in Hamilton like teaching music or repairing instruments?"

"No. Not really."

Larry handed him a business card. "Well, if you do, call me. We're running an advertising special for new accounts. We've increased circulation over thirty percent this year, and our online traffic has nearly doubled in the same period. So, if you're looking to extend your reach, we offer some of the most competitive rates."

Alex glanced at the business card. "Thank you. I'll keep that in mind."

Larry turned to the ladies. "I'm sure you all read the seniors column this month."

Toni looked away, ignoring him, while Ruth Ann stuffed her face, making it conveniently impossible to reply. Darlene realized it was up to her to say something so he'd leave.

"I thought it was alright," she said. "Seems like you coulda saved a whole page the way Veronica rambled on about Jesenia's restaurant. She coulda just said she liked it."

"Yes, well," Larry said, fumbling. "Not all contributors possess the same writing flair. But listen, your turn is coming up soon."

Darlene shrugged. "I can wait if someone wants to take my turn."

Larry flashed the fake smile of a salesman. "Oh, you know you love it." He glanced at the crowd and spoke quickly, as if he were late for an important engagement. "Hey, I gotta run. Alex, nice to meet you, and think about how the Gazette can help you attract new business." He hurried into the crowd, much to the trio's relief.

"I don't like him," Toni said.

"Oh, he's just a salesman," Darlene said.

"A slimy one."

"Why's he so dressed up?" Alex asked.

"'Cause he's got a high opinion of hisself," Ruth Ann said.

Alex looked at Toni. "Why don't you like him?"

"He grew up here," Toni said. "But moved to Houston to work on some big newspaper. If you ask him, he'd say he ran the whole operation, but he was probably just an errand boy. I don't like him 'cause he's full a sh… He'd sell his own mother."

"How big is his paper?"

"Not as big as his imagination," Darlene said, rising to throw her trash away, but Alex grabbed the tray along with Toni and Ruth Ann's. "Thank ya Alex," she said, stretching her arms and yawning. "I'm 'bout spent."

"Y'all 'bout ready to get outta here?" Toni asked.

"I wanna look at them painted flower pots, but it's on the way out," Ruth Ann said.

Darlene and Ruth Ann quickly browsed the flower pot booth while Toni went to get the truck. Soon, Alex was escorting the sisters toward the parking lot.

Inside the last booth, Alex spotted an exotic-looking young woman with black hair and olive skin talking to a middle-aged man surrounded by stacks of the same book. He immediately thought of Ananya, the love of his life. She, too, was an olive-skinned beauty. It had been eighteen months since he'd last seen Ananya, but very few days passed without him thinking about her. When the girl inside the booth made eye contact with Alex, he felt a jolt of excitement, like a shock of electricity. He was stunned until Darlene pull his arm, snapping him back to reality.

"I need to sit down," Darlene said. "My dogs are killin' me."

The sisters sat on a bench, giving Alex a vantage point whereby he see could see when Toni arrived at the pick-up spot. Sneaking glances at the sexy woman, Alex reflected on the life he'd had with Ananya. He replayed the memory of one special New Year's morning with Ananya peacefully sleeping with her head on his chest, their reflection in a dresser mirror across the room. *If I could freeze time,* he remembered wishing.

Flooded with emotion, Alex was torn between the desire to rush to the booth and meet a new Ananya and the inclination to run away from the painful reality that she wasn't his lost love.

He sighed and looked away, spotting Toni climbing out of her truck in the distance. He started walking the sisters to Toni's truck as his melancholy flashbacks began fading. "Alright, let's get this done," he muttered.

"What?" Ruth Ann asked.

"Nothing."

"I can't thank you enough," Toni said as Alex loaded them into the back seat. Her remark struck Alex, breaking his fixation on the past. Toni's voice reminded him of their first meeting in the general store. He felt that same attraction.

"My pleasure," Alex replied. "I enjoyed it."

"Come on by later," Darlene said. "We'll have us a snort." Her comment drew a swat from her sister. "But wait till after five. I need a nap."

"See ya later, Alex," Toni said. Her lilting tone sent another spark of interest through him.

Alex shut the door and watched them drive away. Toni had again captured his imagination, until he remembered the exotic beauty. He made a beeline for the booth, but she was gone.

Chapter 10

The only person in the booth was the middle-aged man who'd been talking to the beautiful, young woman. Alex glanced around, wondering where she'd gone.

"Baneta will be back shortly," the man announced.

"Who?"

"You know who."

Alex tried to appear nonchalant. He picked up a book from the stacks and read the title aloud. "*Understanding the Belief Systems of Ancient and Modern Man.* What's it about?" he asked while scanning the area for a young woman named Baneta.

"Sir, I don't want to waste your time."

The response caught Alex off guard. "What? Believe me, you can't waste my time."

"No?"

"These days, all I have is time." His words trailed off as his eyes again wandered.

The man reached out to shake hands. "Dr. Pradeep Sharma."

"Alex."

"Alex, why would you say all you have is time?"

Somewhat disinterested, Alex shrugged. "I'm between careers, so I have more time on my hands than normal."

Dr. Sharma gave him a puzzled look. "Between careers, not between jobs?"

"I'm a musician, but I'd like to earn a living in the studio rather than performing live."

"Most artists such as yourself pursue a calling with what they do. Look around." He directed Alex's attention to the various booths. "Many here—writers, painters, and craftsmen—have come to share their work with others."

"And to make money," Alex cynically added.

Dr. Sharma nodded. "Tell me Alex, do you play music for the money?"

"I don't do it for free."

"If you had more money than you could spend, would you play for free? Or would you give up playing and enjoy spending your money?"

Alex smiled, intrigued by the question. "I'd buy some stuff and have some fun, but I wouldn't quit playing." His own words immediately struck him. *I wouldn't quit.*

"Exactly. Alex, you feel a calling."

Alex chuckled. "You make it sound like a religious experience."

"It is, and it is why I can say are the first person today who truly needs my book."

Alex guffawed. "Yeah, I'm sure."

"Please don't dismiss what I am saying. The calling of an artist is no different from a clergyman."

"That's a stretch."

Dr. Sharma picked up his book. "Alex, many people seek understanding of the human spirit, the universe, and the passage of time. They may not say it like that, but we all have a conscience and a finite amount of time on Earth. This book is about belief systems. Everyone believes in *something*, and understanding your beliefs is the first step to finding your way through time. And time, as you mentioned, is all you've got."

The discussion was starting to rub salt in Alex's mental wound. Time had become his enemy. Time at the piano—his one love—had become endlessly and inescapably frustrating. Hearing himself admit he'd never quit—this thing he both loved and now hated—amplified the interminable paradox. "Yeah, I know," he said dismissively, flipping through a few pages, trying to block out the problems. "I'll think about it."

Dr. Sharma stepped away to attend to a potential customer.

As Alex absently turned a few pages, he kept hearing the same words in his head. *I wouldn't quit. Dammit!* he mentally shouted, frustrated that he couldn't escape the nagging conundrum. He closed his eyes and gripped the book, staging an internal tantrum.

"Can I help you?" a soft voice said, interrupting his inner tirade. He opened his eyes and there she was. She was breathtaking.

He set the book down and stammered, "Hi... Uh..." Caught off guard, he almost called her Ananya.

"Baneta," she said.

"I knew that."

"How do you, like, know my name?" She acted flirty but somewhat mysterious. She was beautiful and likely of Indian descent, like Ananya, but that's where the similarities ended.

"I'm Alex, and you remind me of someone I used to know. And Mr. Book, over there, told me your name."

Her face lit up as she laughed. "Mr. Book. That's funny. You're funny, Alex."

"So… do you work for him?"

"He, like, married my mom, so as long as I help with these stupid fairs, he pays for my college."

College? That's young, he thought.

"Do I, like, remind you of someone good?" she asked, placing her hand on his, causing him to wince and pull back. Her eyes widened as she smiled. "I don't bite." His thoughts vacillated between cherished memories and the tumultuous present. Suddenly he flashed on Desiree angrily driving away. Baneta was no longer Ananya, but rather a desirable and perhaps disposable bedmate.

"Baneta," Dr. Sharma's voice rang out. "There are other customers waiting."

She rolled her eyes then smiled at Alex. "I hate to say it, but this really is, like, a good book."

"He said it's about what people believe in."

"Totally. It's about all these, like, weird religions." She flipped to a certain page. "Like these people in Africa who believe this woman appears and, like, abducts people then holds them until they agree to, like, give up sex."

"What?" he said, spinning the book around so he could read.

She laughed. "There's some crazy stuff out there."

"Mami Wata," he said.

"What?"

He pointed to the page she'd opened to. "That's the abducting woman's name."

"Crazy, huh?"

"Totally. Maybe I'll come back later and pick up a copy."

"Really?" she said, sounding disappointed.

"What?"

She put on a convincing pout. "You're not gonna, like, buy one now?"

Alex was always a sucker for a pretty girl, especially one showing interest in him. "I don't know. Maybe."

She looked at his hand, noticing no wedding ring. "Buy it for your girlfriend. Where is she?"

"What are you talking about?"

She coyly smiled. "I saw you earlier with her and, like, two old ladies."

Alex was put off by her being so forward, so he had a little fun. His expression turned dead serious. "Oh her? She's one of six."

"Six!"

He grinned. "Just kidding. She's a friend."

Baneta turned up the charm, but Dr. Sharma returned. "You're back," he said. "And still not buying a book, right?"

"I might."

The doctor chortled and waved his hand. He moved to the back of the booth and began unpacking more books for the counter.

Alex gazed at Baneta, finding her attractive but too young. Still, her smile had ignited his primal desire.

"You need this book," she said. "I can tell."

"You think so?" he asked, feigning an inquiring expression.

"Oh, totally."

He looked into those hypnotizing green eyes. *I'm an idiot*, he thought, wrestling with his sexual attraction for her. Everything beyond her looks was wrong, but the loneliness he'd been desperately trying to fill overruled his rational thinking. "Hmm," he murmured, trying to convince himself she would be more than just another one-night stand. He couldn't completely close the door on her despite his rational side shouting, *Desiree!*

She leaned across the counter and whispered. "Maybe we can, like, get together later."

"Hmm. Maybe," he said, thinking *no freakin' way!*

She again put her hand on his. "The sooner we, like, sell all these books, the sooner I can do whatever I want." She flashed a seductive look that finally toppled Alex.

He handed her a twenty-dollar bill. "What the hell?" he added resignedly.

She laughed. "Thank you so much."

Dr. Sharma rushed over. "I can't believe it. Baneta, you can sell anything. Thank you, sir. I hope you enjoy my book."

Baneta turned to address another man, who was also giving her dreamy eyes. She ignored Alex's exit. Slowly walking away, he realized he'd been played. He expected her to at least give him a longing goodbye stare, but she never looked at him again. He glanced at the unwanted book in his hands.

Disappointed with himself he muttered, "Great. Twenty bucks wasted." He made one last glance back, seeing Baneta working her next victim.

At home, he set the book on the kitchen table and reflected on the encounter. *I could've gotten her.* A thought that made him smile. *I probably dodged a bullet. A 21-year-old hustler with a 40-year-old dreamer?* He shook his head. *Better a failed dreamer than a broke fool.*

Chapter 11

After the fair, Alex moped around the house until he remembered Darlene's invitation to stop by. Shortly after his arrival, Ruth Ann excused herself, saying the fair had worn her out.

Alex and Darlene sat at the kitchen table, her with a glass of whiskey and him with a beer.

"Thanks for letting me tag along today," Alex said. "Everyone I met made me feel welcome."

"We call that Southern hospitality, and we was glad to see ya."

"Toni said not much happens after the fair ends. I don't think she's too sure about me."

"Sure 'bout what? She don't hardly know you."

"I think she got the wrong idea when Desiree answered the door."

Darlene smiled and raised her eyebrows. "We was all surprised, but hell Alex, it ain't for us to say what you do."

Embarrassed, Alex said, "Even though Desiree's from Dallas, she acts like the people I know in L.A.; a high opinion of herself and a low opinion of everyone who's not rich, famous, or well-connected."

Darlene laughed. "We got one like that, Cynthia Coker."

"The real estate agent who sold me the house?"

"You just described her to a T."

"That's funny, but now that I think about it, she did ask a lot of personal questions."

"That's Cynthia. Antoinette ain't like that."

"Well, I dodged most of that Cynthia woman's questions, but Toni seems pretty down to earth, but wary of me."

"She don't naturally warm up to strangers, but she's a sweet girl. Y'all got a lot in common. She likes the big city and music."

"What about musicians? There's a big difference, you know." He grinned.

"Wisenheimer." She took a sip of whiskey. "There ain't a lotta single folks in Hamilton."

"Well, my dating history isn't all that good. The girls I meet usually aren't looking for anything long term. And, even if they are, most aren't really my type."

"You got a type, Alex?"

"Let's just say that girls who want to party all the time aren't my type."

"Like that number who answered your door?"

He chuckled. "She wanted me to drive to Dallas and party all night."

"Hmph. Young folks ain't like they was in my day. You ain't gonna find that in Hamilton."

"Good. I'm too old for that, and I never really enjoyed it."

"Have you ever had a serious girlfriend?"

Alex sighed. "A few, one in particular, but that was a while ago."

"Are you lookin' to settle down?"

"I wouldn't mind finding someone to spend time with."

"Next time you and I get together, I'll invite Antoinette."

"I don't think Andy would approve."

"How do you know 'bout Andy?"

"I met him at the grocery store. He's not too fond of me either."

"Andy's alright. Antoinette's been goin' around with him for a while, but it ain't serious."

"In that case, definitely invite her next time. Just don't invite that real estate woman."

"Oh, Lord."

Both chuckled as Alex stood up and finished the rest of his beer. "Listen, I should get going. It's getting late."

"No, it ain't," she barked, grabbing his arm. He sat back down. "There's another fridge in the garage with a six-pack. Go fetch it and fix me about two fingers of whiskey." She stood up. "Aw hell, I'll get the liquor."

"I don't need another beer, but I can hang around for a bit. Remember, I'm used to sleeping in the daytime."

Darlene nodded and sat back down. "Me too. Say, how long you been playin' the piana?"

"I took lessons as a kid but didn't get serious about it until I was in college. What about you? Did you have a career?"

"I had a job. My dad worked for the post office but he was sickly and couldn't always work. The post office paid his medical bills, but we didn't have much money to live on, so it was up to me and Ruthie to help out."

"What about your mom?"

"She passed when I was in the sixth grade."

"Wow, that had to be tough."

"Folks always say that, but that's just how it was. We didn't know no different."

"Was she sick?"

"No. She went to bed one night and never woke up. Doctor said her heart quit."

Alex shook his head, trying to imagine what that was like. "How different was life back then compared to today?"

"Not a *lot* different, but there weren't many jobs."

"So what'd you do?"

"After Momma died, I did odd jobs—muckin' out stalls and washin' dishes—till I was 'bout fifteen and started workin' for the telephone company."

Intrigued, Alex said, "I've seen old pictures where a woman sat plugging wires into a board. Is that what you did?"

She laughed. "I ain't *that* old Alex. I started out cleanin' the office—moppin', sweepin', takin' out the trash—but it wasn't long 'fore I started doin' what they called directory assistance. Folks'd call and ask for someone's number and I'd give it to 'em."

"Did Ruth Ann work there too?"

"She was a hostess a few days a week till she married Arthur Waterman the summer after graduation. He helped in his daddy's shop fixin' tractors and farmin' equipment."

"So she was taken care of."

"They didn't have much, but no one did. Eventually, Arthur took over for his daddy."

"Did they have any children?"

Darlene shook her head. "I don't think Arthur wanted young'uns."

"It's hard to imagine life in Hamilton back then. How long did you work for the phone company?"

"Fourteen years."

"So you were in your late twenties and married by then, I assume?"

"Me and Joe got married in '66. I was 25."

Alex looked puzzled. "So you waited to have Toni?"

"Not exactly," Darlene said, rising to refill her small glass of whiskey. "We had a son 'fore Antoinette." She returned to her seat and spoke in a more somber tone. "Joey was born in '71. By then, I was almost 30." She took a solid drink of whiskey.

Her pensive mood gave him pause. "Where's he?"

"He passed."

"I'm sorry," Alex said, fearing he'd opened a wound.

She spoke in a low, quiet voice. "Life is what God gives you, Alex, and what you do with it." She stared blankly for a moment before purposefully lifting her tone. "But listen to me, I'm just ramblin' on 'bout myself. I wanna know more about you, Mr. Alex Patterson."

He smiled. "I'm a simple man just passing time."

"Pfft. You're good at pushing manure." They both laughed. "Alex, I still don't get it. You got a lot goin' for you and you ain't that old. Why's a fella who loves playin' music, travelin', chasin' girls like that young number who answered your door..."

He smiled.

"Why give all that up for a small town like Hamilton?"

"That's a long, boring story you don't really want to hear."

"I wouldn't've asked."

He took a deep breath and slowly exhaled. "The music business is hard. At some point, everyone thinks about giving up. I promised myself that if I quit, I'd escape to the farthest place from the cities of my failures. One night, while drinking with friends, I shared my plan. They found a map and figured out which city was farthest from L.A., Seattle, New York, and Nashville. There were several choices, but Hamilton was the winner."

"That's the biggest load of manure I ever heard."

Alex tried to maintain a straight face. "That was about five years ago. I never forgot it."

"You're tellin' me you moved here just so you could avoid them other cities? That don't make sense, and I don't believe a word of it."

He smiled. "You asked how I ended up in Hamilton."

"Hogwash. There ain't nothin' to do in Hamilton other 'n Sunday church and bowlin'."

"I'm not much of a churchgoer, but I like bowling."

"For the rest of your life? If you don't mind me askin', what're you gonna do for money?"

"That's part of why I moved here. I considered moving to Austin because they have a good music scene, but it's really expensive to live there. It's a lot cheaper here.

I don't have enough money to last forever, so I'll have to figure it out before I run out of money."

"Figure out what?"

He observed Darlene's stare as she fixated on every sound he made, every move, every nuance. "You don't miss much," he said. She raised her eyebrows and shook her head. "Maybe I *do* need a beer. You want a refill?"

"I'm fine," she said as he left for the garage and returned with three beers. He placed two in the fridge and opened the third. "Now tell me what you're tryin' to figure out."

He wandered over to the window, shaking his head, wrestling with the words. "It's hard to explain."

"Try me."

"Okay. Like you said, I used to love playing, partying and chasing girls, but it's not the same." He took a big drink of beer and zoned out for a moment, hearing Dr. Sharma's words: *Time is all you have.* "I feel like I've been wasting my life."

"Doin' what you love ain't a waste of time. And neither is bringin' joy to people by makin' music." She paused when a thought struck her. "What're you playin' music for in the first place?"

"That's a good question. Once I learned how to play anything I heard, I immediately started composing my own material, which was like a drug. I'd practice and write all day every day because it was the greatest feeling in the world." His nostalgic smile faded and his voice softened. "But it's not like that anymore. That *something* I'd always felt, that addictive joy… It's gone."

"It sounds to me like you're goin' through a dry spell."

"For eighteen months?"

"You ever try doin' somethin' else?"

"Music is the only life I know."

"Life ain't only 'bout playin' music."

"It is for me. Plus, I don't have a family, or any other activities or hobbies. What's left?"

"God."

"Yeah, I'm just not sure that's the answer for me."

"Just 'cause you don't go to church don't mean God ain't the answer. Some folks find Him in other ways. Try readin' that book you bought at the fair."

He gave her a quizzical look. "How did you know I bought a book?"

She laughed. "'Cause every man in town buys a book."

"What?"

"I seen you eyein' that young lady. That fella with her, Dr. Sharma, has a booth every year and always puts some young number there to flirt with the men. I'd bet dollars to doughnuts you couldn't resist."

He laughed, but felt embarrassed. "I can't believe she played me."

Darlene grinned. "You and every man in town."

"And Dr. Sharma does it every year?"

She nodded.

"I knew it when I was walking away. Makes me want to throw that book in the trash."

"Don't fret. His books ain't bad. He's one a them self-help guru types. He's a real smart man, and he ain't a fool when it comes to sellin' books. Try readin' what he wrote. Maybe him usin' that pretty young lady is another one of life lessons he threw in for free."

Alex smiled at her light-hearted jab. "That doctor asked me if I'd play if I had all the money in the world."

"And you said you would," Darlene stated.

"How'd you know?"

"No one spends all them years learnin' to play without lovin' it."

"I do, and Dr. Sharma said artists create so they can share their art with the world."

"Ain't that why you do it?"

He nodded. "Mostly. I wanted a career that had meaning, not like business."

"And now playin's become meaningless."

He nodded.

"Alex, no one can make you feel somethin'. But when you play music, you're lettin' what God gave you come out for all to see and hear. You might be havin' a bad day or the best one ever, but whatever comes out is a gift from God."

Alex considered her words. "I get what you're saying about feeling inspired or blessed or whatever you call it, but lately it feels like nothing."

"God don't always make life sunshine and rainbows, Alex. Sometimes he knocks you down so you'll fight to get back up."

"It sure isn't fun."

She chuckled. "I bet when you first started playin' the piana, it wasn't always fun, but you kept fightin' and look where it got ya."

"What doesn't kill you…"

She nodded. "Makes you stronger. And remember Alex, if it was easy, everyone'd do it. You got somethin' special, but that don't always mean smooth sailin'."

"No, I guess not." He stood and downed his beer. "I need to go home."

She walked him to the kitchen door.

"Thanks for listening."

She patted his forearm and said, "Anytime, dear."

He let himself out and walked across the street.

He picked up the book from the kitchen table. Just as he was about to toss it in the trash, he remembered Darlene's words; *his books ain't bad*. He took the book into the master bathroom and set it beside his toilet. "Seems appropriate."

Chapter 12

On Sunday morning, Ernie held the door while the Sunday ladies filed in to the Superbowl. "Mornin' Miss Ruth Ann," he said.

"Morning Ernie," Ruth Ann replied.

While everyone found a seat—except Cynthia, who remained standing—Sarah made her way to the liquor room and assumed the role of bartender.

"Let me help you," Irma said, following Sarah and grabbing the chips and snack bowls. Irma, the toughest and largest of the group, had grown up with three older brothers who pushed her around like one of the boys. She learned to push back at a young age.

With the fair in town, the discussion quickly took off.

Ruth Ann happily stated, "I bought a wonderful painting by Dalhart Windberg."

"I saw his booth," Dorothy said. "You know he lives right outside Austin? I love his landscapes."

"Ruthie's picture ain't like his normal stuff," Darlene said. "It's..." She stopped, noticing Ruth Ann glaring at her. "So go on and tell 'em."

"Thank you," Ruth Ann sniped at Darlene before addressing the group. "It looks like a photograph, but it's a painting of a hamburger on a plate with French fries and a soda pop on a gingham tablecloth. It looks just like the one me and Arthur had."

"We all had that tablecloth," Sarah said, setting a drink in front of Darlene. "I got there late, but I saw y'all with the new guy at Toni's truck."

Darlene took a sip and said, "We introduced him to Buford and Ada, and Esma Beth."

"Then that Larry Westin showed up," Ruth Ann complained.

The ladies let out a collective moan.

"Lemme guess," said Irma. "He tried to sell Alex some advertisin'."

"Well, that ain't no big stretch," Darlene said.

Miss Virginia plucked a few nuts from the snack bowl. "What'd Alex think of the fair?" she asked.

"Said he liked it. He dropped by last night to chat."

"Really?" Sarah said with great surprise. "What'd he say?"

"Said he liked meetin' some a the locals."

"I'da thought a big city musician like him woulda been bored."

"I think he's lonely, so me and him talk."

"What do y'all talk about?" Irma asked.

"Oh, we just sit around shootin' the bull. He likes drinkin' beer and y'all know I don't like drinkin' alone."

"Since when?" Ruth Ann quickly remarked, getting in a rare jab at her sister. "And by the way," she added with hint of irritation. "Next time he comes over, he oughta know when it's time to leave." She gave her sister a slight glare before addressing the group. "Ain't right keepin' me awake to all hours drinkin' and chattin' with my sister."

"Pfft," Darlene said. "Shut your door next time, Miss Busybody."

"I wasn't bein' a busybody," she snapped. "Just makin' sure you're alright."

"I ain't even gonna respond to that," Darlene said.

"I'm with Ruth Ann," said Cynthia. "There's something not right about that Mr. Patterson."

"Pfft. Somethin' ain't right with you," Darlene cracked, drawing a few chuckles.

Everyone looked at Cynthia, waiting for her reply. "Well, then tell me why a handsome single man spent all that time with you, but when your daughter practically threw herself at him, he did nothin'?"

"Bein' nice ain't the same thing as throwin' yourself at a man," Sarah quipped at to Cynthia. "Not everyone's as easy as you."

The group laughed while Cynthia snorted derisively.

Darlene added, "Antoinette don't throw herself at no man."

Miss Virginia said, "I'm kinda with Cynthia on this. I saw Toni talkin' to the new guy outside Gibson's. She looked awful friendly. And a couple a folks said they saw 'em yesterday at the fair."

"They was just talkin' outside Gibson's," Darlene said. "And at the fair, Antoinette and Alex was with me and Ruthie. So don't none a y'all go spreadin' nonsense 'bout my daughter."

Cynthia sauntered closer and spoke with an exaggerated inflection. "Word is, Toni gave your Mr. Patterson every opportunity to, well... as they say... spend a little alone time with him."

"You're makin' that up," Ruth Ann barked.

"Antoinette was bein' neighborly," Darlene added. "But she's a lady."

"Hmph," Cynthia snorted. "With a fella like Alex? A musician from the big city? Stands to reason Toni'd take notice. Single woman pushin' forty, needin' a man?"

Outraged and feeling mocked, Darlene popped up from her chair and took a step toward Cynthia. "You need to shut your mouth, little girl. You only come here to stir up trouble. Why don't you run along 'fore you test my last nerve."

As Cynthia stepped back, she defiantly said, "I don't need your permission, and I can't help it if the truth hurts."

Irma stepped between them with hands up. "Both y'all need to stop."

After a tense moment, Darlene sat back down while Cynthia folded her arms and leaned against a pole.

Sarah took another drink order and shifted the focus. "Well, it's no wonder why the ladies like him. He's cute."

"Dar, did he tell you why he moved to Hamilton?" Irma asked.

"Tell 'em what he told you," Ruth Ann urged, directing everyone's attention at Darlene.

"Dar, are you holdin' out on us?" Sarah asked, sipping on a drink of her own.

"He said he was tired of the big city."

"That ain't all he said," prodded Ruth Ann.

"Give," Sarah said.

"Listen, he tried to fill me with a bunch a nonsense 'bout playin' not bein' fun anymore. Said he was quittin'."

"Who quits workin' at forty and moves to Hamilton?" Irma asked. "Especially a musician?"

"And a successful one," Darlene added.

"How do you know he's successful?" Irma said.

Darlene took a sip of whiskey and said, "He talked about tourin' and makin' albums, so he must be successful. And, he had money to buy a house. But I don't believe him 'bout movin' here 'cause he ain't havin' fun playin'."

"Me neither," Sarah said. "There's somethin' else goin' on. Maybe he's mixed up in somethin'."

"Like what?" Irma asked.

"I don't know. Maybe his health is failin'."

"Looked healthy to me," Miss Virginia said.

"Wonder if he's tryin' to get away from an ex-wife or something like that," Sarah wondered.

"You said some young girl answered the door when y'all first met him," Dorothy said. "Who was she?"

"That's his private business," Ruth Ann said.

Darlene flashed a wry smile. "He wasn't too proud of her. I think she was just a port in the storm." Ruth Ann snorted at Darlene's choice of words.

"Sure pissed Toni off," Cynthia chimed.

"What're you mouthin' off about?" Darlene asked, as if daring Cynthia to say something disrespectful.

"She told me."

"That's a lie," Darlene fired back. "She don't hardly talk to you."

"Shows what you know. Toni and I talk all the time." Darlene couldn't believe Toni would communicate with the enemy, but made a mental note to question Toni about it immediately after Sunday school. Darlene waved her arm, dismissing Cynthia's comment. "She called Alex a womanizing man-whore."

"She don't talk like that," Darlene insisted. "And I don't appreciate you disrespectin' my daughter, 'specially without her bein' here to defend herself. I'll thank you to hush."

Before things escalated, Ernie flicked the lights, letting the ladies know it was time to go.

Darlene rose and pulled Ruth Ann up. "C'mon. I ain't gonna listen to this nonsense." They said a quick goodbye to everyone but Cynthia before storming out.

Toni was waiting outside to drive the sisters home, something she did every Sunday. Darlene waited until they were driving away to question Toni.

"Cynthia said you was complainin' 'bout Alex."

"Please," Toni hissed. "She asked me what I thought, and I said he was alright."

"When was this?"

"I ran into her outside the market. Jeez, Mom. I swear everything I say gets broadcasted."

"That's what you get for talkin' to Cynthia."

"It was two sentences!"

"She said y'all talk."

"When I see her. I ain't gonna be rude."

"I would. She said you was makin' snide remarks 'bout Alex. Said you threw yourself at him at the fair."

"What? That's BS. You were there."

"Sweetheart," Darlene said, "I ain't tryin' to rile you, but you know Cynthia likes to spread it on thick."

"I wish y'all'd leave me outta your discussions."

Darlene nodded. "I try, but when that Cynthia starts stirrin' the pot, it gets my blood pressure up."

"I gotta watch what I say around her."

"Say nothin'. That's what I'd do."

"Wouldn't matter," Toni said. "She's gonna make up BS no matter what."

"Well," Darlene said. "She's probably just spoutin' nonsense around me tryin to get my goat. If you ain't hearin' about it in your Sunday school group, she probably ain't tellin' the world, like she likes to do."

"Sounds like it worked," Toni replied.

"What worked?" Darlene asked.

"Cynthia tryin' to get a rise outta you. It worked." Toni's remark drew a smile from Ruth Ann. Darlene had always enjoyed teasing Ruth Ann just to make her angry, so anytime someone turned the tables on Darlene; something Ruth Ann rarely accomplished herself, she found it entertaining.

Toni pulled into the sisters' driveway and helped them out of the truck. She glanced over at Alex's house. The lights were on and the driveway empty of strange cars. Still, she wondered if he was in there alone. She decided to find out.

Chapter 13

Alex stepped out of the bathroom carrying *Understanding the Belief Systems of Ancient and Modern Man*. Darlene's favorable opinion of the author intrigued him.

While seated at the kitchen table, he read page after page, captivated by the various ideologies discussed in the book. He'd been to church and occasionally preached to by zealots. He'd even performed with a Jewish band, but had no exposure to Eastern and African teachings. Alex was so engrossed with the material he almost missed hearing the doorbell.

He opened the front door to the unhappy face of Toni. He was excited to see her but surprised she'd violated the traditional norm by showing up unannounced. "Hey," he said casually. "What are you all dressed up for?"

"I just came from church. Sorry I didn't call first, but I need to get somethin' off my chest. You alone?" She glanced beyond him into the house.

He nodded and stepped aside, inviting her in.

Once inside, she folded her arms and said, "Folks been talkin'."

"Okay. Who? And about what?"

"Everyone. Mom, Aunt Ruthie, Cynthia, Irma, everyone. Even Andy accused me of havin' a thing for you, which I most definitely do *not*."

He smiled and nonchalantly said, "Okay," while thinking *she doth protest too much*.

"They're also sayin' I was mad about that day we brought you the cake 'cause you was with that girl. Which I wasn't. I barely know you and I don't care what you do or who you sleep with."

He nodded, expressionless, but inside he was almost giddy. *She's really fired up*, he thought, excited about being the reason. There was something about her fiery personality that Alex found attractive.

"Got it," he said, starting toward the kitchen. "You want something to drink?"

Alex's nonchalance confused and irritated Toni. "No. Thank you. Are you listenin' to me? This is serious."

"I'm listening." He fixed himself a glass of tea and sat at the kitchen table. "I don't understand why it's such a big deal."

She gasped. "Because this is a small town, and everyone knows everyone's business."

"So?"

"So, they got the idea you and I are doin' somethin'."

"Why do you care? Like you said, we barely know one another."

"'Cause I don't like folks talkin' behind my back. And I certainly don't want 'em thinkin' you and I are a couple or somethin'." Alex chuckled once, but stopped at the sight of her angry expression. "You think this is funny?" she said, her eyes narrowing.

"No, I mean, kind of. What's the big deal? We're both adults. Let them talk or tell them the truth. Who cares? Surely your boyfriend believes you?"

"'Course he does." The mention of Andy threw her off balance. "It ain't that simple. Folks already got the wrong idea. If I ignore what they say, they'll say we're tryin' to hide somethin'."

He laughed despite her glaring expression. "Seriously? This is ridiculous. It's like high school. There's no way to win. If you say nothing, they'll say we're together, and if you tell them otherwise, they'll still think we're together."

"Which we ain't."

His eyes opened wide. "What will they think of your truck parked in front of my house? The horror!"

"It's not funny, Alex. And besides, my truck's parked at Mom's."

"Oh, my God! Is she going to show up with a shotgun?"

Toni tightened her lips, shifted her weight, and put a hand on her hip. "This ain't a joke."

"Okay, then what do you suggest we do?"

"I don't know, but if you hear folks talkin', I want you to know it ain't comin' from me."

"Noted. But remember, I don't know anyone here, so I don't know who I'm going to hear talking, other than your mom and aunt."

She stared at him, unable to refute his observation. Her anger was losing steam, but she wasn't ready to give in. As the silence lingered, Alex casually focused on his book. "Have you read this?" He lifted it up so she could read the title.

Preoccupied with her own thoughts, she missed the question. "No. Look, I don't know what's makin' people talk about you, but it pisses me off when they talk about me."

He nodded, noting her softening tone. "Makes sense."

As her anger subsided, their eyes momentarily locked, and she began feeling foolish for becoming so outraged. She deliberately looked away, absently staring at the book while the moment passed. "So, what's it about?"

"Religions from around the world."

"Hmm, really? I thought you didn't go to church."

"I don't, but this is pretty interesting."

"Good. You could probably use some religion."

"Maybe. I got it at the fair. The—"

"Oh, my God!" she interrupted. "You bought this from that pimp who comes here every year!" She plopped down and yanked the book away from him. She looked at the cover, then shoved it back in front of him. "I should've known you'd buy one. What'd she promise?"

With a smile on his face, he knew he was busted. "What're you talking about?"

She laughed. "You know exactly what I'm talkin' about. What did his little *assistant* offer you? A quickie behind the booth?" Toni's entire demeanor changed. She was suddenly the same playful woman he'd first met at Gibson's.

His smile grew. "She offered to drive me to church on Sunday morning."

Her laugh increased as she light-heartedly said, "I'm sure she did. You're such an idiot." She shook her head, seeing *Mr. Cool* Alex—bigshot California musician—in a new light. Like any average guy, he'd been manipulated by a woman. She found it both entertaining and disappointing that he fell for nothing more than a pretty face.

He flipped the page and said, "I am. But believe it or not, this book has some interesting stuff."

"Yeah. That's why you bought it." She smirked. "Men just can't resist pretty young girls who throw themselves at 'em."

"Either way, it's interesting."

"Seriously? Mom reads books on religion, but what in the world would you find interesting?"

"All of it. He compares religions and belief systems from all over the world. There are some wild ideas out there."

She leaned over for a closer look. "Like what?"

He was titillated by her proximity, causing a quick rise in the temperature. Alex took in her perfume, which had a sweet, intoxicating aroma. Equally aroused, she deliberately slowed her breathing, hoping to conceal the pounding that was growing in her chest. The chemistry between them was approaching a boiling point when Toni stepped back, letting some cool air flow between them. It was enough to avert an explosion. The entire episode lasted only a minute, but left an impact neither would soon forget.

Alex acted as if nothing had happened. He flipped to a certain page and said, "Like Jainism. The Jains place the life of animals above humans. But it says women must be reincarnated as men."

"Uh huh," she replied, still a bit flustered. "Wait, what?"

"You have to come back as a man before your soul can be free."

"That don't sound right. But I wouldn't mind bein' a man."

He chuckled. "Yeah?"

Like old friends, the conversation suddenly felt comfortable and relaxed.

"You guys got it easy. No babies, no complicated plumbin', no BS about missin' out on *havin'* babies. You can sleep with a woman one day and forget her the next."

"And you envy that?"

"Maybe not envy, but it's easier than never hearin' from some jerk who said he'd call."

He gave a conceding nod. "You'd be okay with coming back as a man?"

"I ain't comin' back, but if I did, yeah."

"How do you know you're not coming back?"

"The Bible says the believers go to Heaven."

"What if Jainism is right and reincarnation is real?"

"It ain't."

"But what if it is?"

"I don't know. I believe what the Bible says; believers go to Heaven. You think you're comin' back?"

"I don't know, but it's interesting to think about."

"What're you comin' back as?"

He closed the book and leaned back. "I don't know. I'm still trying to figure out what to do with the rest of this life, but I don't think we come back as something different."

"So, you're comin' back as Alex Patterson?"

"I'll probably have a different name but the same soul."

"What's the point? You'll be the same person with a different name? Why come back?"

"To fix what I did wrong."

"Oh?"

Lost in thought, he spoke while gazing into the distance, his mind replaying the last conversation he had with the love of his live. "Everyone makes mistakes."

She stared at him curiously. "What was your big mistake?"

He rose, dumped the rest of his tea in the sink, and pulled a beer from the refrigerator. "You want one?" She shook her head no. "C'mon," he said, motioning for her to follow him. They walked into the backyard where he lit a cigarette. He took a slow drag and a sip of beer. "This book has really got me thinking."

"'Bout what?"

"The mistakes I've made."

"So? Like you said, everyone makes mistakes."

"But actions have consequences."

It struck Toni that Alex wasn't making jokes. She thought about their impassioned moment earlier and hoped he'd reveal more about himself. "What are you talkin' about?"

He took a moment to organize his thoughts. "I've met lots of people and had lots of opportunities."

"Like what?"

"I've had relationships that could've worked, and I've turned down bands that could've made it big."

"But they didn't, right, the bands I mean? What about the serious relationships? What happened there?" She was again hoping he'd open up about his personal life.

Alex wasn't ready to talk about Ananya, so he steered the conversation around the question, giving her a pensive glance. "How would your life be different if you never got married?"

"I wanted to get married. But if you're askin' what if I'd a married someone else, I don't know."

"Hmm," he mumbled, still thinking about his failures. "Life is about the decisions you make. And if you make the wrong ones, you live with the consequences. I mean, I've dated lots of girls, but I never got married."

"Be glad you ain't a girl. All you hear is, 'When're you gettin' married?' 'Specially once you graduate high school."

"But you liked being married, I assume?"

She was reluctant to discuss her marriage, but Alex's vulnerability seemed to draw her out. "Yeah, I guess. We had some good times." As she reflected on her life with Virgil, her thoughts inadvertently spilled out. "Until he cheated."

"He cheated?"

"I don't wanna talk about it."

"I'm sorry. Sounds like he was a bigger idiot than me for buying that book."

"No doubt," she said. In the ensuing silence, she considered what her life would've been like without the cheater. *Better*, she initially thought, but then she remembered how lonely she'd been since her divorce. "Life ain't perfect," he muttered.

"What if you could go back and do things differently?"

"You're goin' to that comin'-back stuff again?"

He smiled nostalgically. "I'd do a lot of things differently."

His unusual expression intrigued her. "Like what?"

He was about to speak, but stood up, looked away, and took a draw from the cigarette. "Oh, no. I'm not telling you that."

"Oh, c'mon. You know I'm divorced, and I'm sure Mom blabbed a few other things about me. I don't know nothin' 'bout you."

"You know I'm a musician. You know I'm what you'd call a heathen since I don't go to church."

"I never said that."

"I know. But your mom didn't tell me much about you, just that she wasn't fond of your husband."

"*Ex*-husband."

Alex waited for her to reveal more about the man she'd married; anything he could draw from to understand what she was attracted to, but she disclosed nothing.

"So, tell me what you done wrong," Toni said.

He smiled and sipped his beer. "I need some food. You wanna grab a bite somewhere?"

She checked her watch as a ruse. "Thanks, but I got plans. And I already told you, folks think somethin's goin' on between you and me. Goin' *anywhere* together would be gas to the fire."

He nodded. "Some other time?"

"Maybe." Thoughts of Andy crept in, adding guilt to her feelings of attraction for Alex. "I gotta go."

He led her back through the house and across the street to her truck.

He glanced around suspiciously then smiled. "Should I hold up a sign that says nothing happened?"

She smirk and shook her head. "Laugh now, but you'll see."

"I'm just kidding."

Toni got in her truck and rolled down the window. She handed him a piece of paper with her phone number.

"Does this mean we can be seen together in public?"

She rolled her eyes, smiled, and drove away. She hadn't made it a block when Darlene called saying she'd seen her leaving Alex's house.

"Mom, we was just talkin'."

Toni filled Darlene in on most of what was said, finishing with, "There ain't nothin' goin' on so I'd appreciate it if you wouldn't parade it all over town that me and Alex talked."

Darlene agreed, always respecting Toni's wishes.

Chapter 14

The following afternoon, Darlene spotted Alex mowing his lawn. She invited him over for a cold drink.

Alex had barely made it through the door when she remarked, "Heard you riled Toni up."

He didn't realize Darlene was fishing for details about he and Toni's conversation. "Not me. She was mad at the rumor mill." His thoughts drifted to that moment when Toni mesmerized him with her closeness. He almost smiled, but snapped back to reality at the sound of Darlene's voice.

"She don't like bein' talked about."

"That's for sure. I bet she hated everyone talking about her husband cheating."

"She told you 'bout that?"

"Not about the gossip. I just assumed. But she did tell me her husband cheated. I don't think she meant to."

Darlene shook her head. "Broke her heart."

"I can deal with a lot of things, but not cheating. I used to date a lot of women at once, but when I commit, I don't cheat."

"Amen."

"I bet she let him have it."

Darlene gave a serious nod. "If you test her, she can be spirited."

"She gave me an earful, but we had a good talk."

"You plannin' on seein' her?"

Alex gave Darlene a sly smile. "Now you know I don't like to gossip."

"Pfft," she said with a chuckle. "I'll just ask her."

Alex laughed. "I don't know about seein' her, but we might hang out. Plus, she's seeing that guy Andy."

"That ain't serious, and I think y'all'd be good for one another. She probably misses the big city, so y'all got somethin' to talk about."

"We'll see." He glanced toward the window and sighed. "I better finish my yard work. I'm going out of town this weekend. It's my last gig for a while."

"You don't sound too excited."

"About the yard work or the gig?"

"Either."

"Nobody likes yard work, but I'm kind of torn on the gig. I've worked hard every year to fill up my calendar, so it's a little unsettling to see it so empty."

"I told ya, Alex. You're just in a rut and you're gonna kick yourself for lettin' the well run dry."

"Maybe. But I like the slow pace of Hamilton. Maybe I'll find something to do here that I like better."

"What else can you do?"

He chuckled. "Not much, but I have a college degree."

"Fat lotta good that'll do ya here. Folks in Hamilton are farmers and ranchers."

"Not everyone. What's Toni do?"

"She does medical billin'. She wanted to be a nurse but there ain't no nursin' schools here. She's been talkin' 'bout takin' some correspondence classes."

"So there's jobs other than farming and ranching. I've seen banks, schools, government offices, restaurants, and a bunch of businesses besides manual labor."

"Yeah, I s'pose. Any of 'em strike ya?"

He shook his head and rose to leave. "Not really."

"There you go. I'd keep at least one foot firmly planted in playin' music."

"I'll see how I feel after this next gig."

"Where're you goin'?"

"Colorado, Vegas, and L.A. I'll probably be home sometime Saturday."

"Come visit with me when you get back."

"Will do."

* * *

After work on Tuesday, Toni loaded everyone into her truck for a quick store run. "You shoulda gotten ever'thing on Friday," Darlene chided her sister.

"I told you they was out of bread," Ruth Ann said.

"Mom, you know they always run outta stuff when the fair's goin' on."

Ruth Ann tapped Toni on the shoulder. "Toni, dear, I need to stop by the bank to cash a check."

"I done told you a thousand times," Darlene said. "You can cash it at the market. What do you need cash for, anyway?"

"For the offerin' tomorrow."

Darlene opened her purse and checked her cash. "Get a few extra dollars for me."

After the short drive, Toni parked and helped the ladies climb down from the jacked-up pickup. She grabbed a shopping cart and led the sisters inside.

"Why don't we get us a brisket and make Alex a home-cooked meal for when he gets home," Darlene suggested.

"When's get getting back?" Ruth Ann asked.

"He said late Saturday, I think. We can invite him over for after Sunday school." She turned to Toni. "You got his number, don't you?" Toni nodded. "Well, send him one of them messages and see if he's interested. You're gonna be there too?"

Toni was careful not to seem too eager to see Alex. "Andy mentioned doin' somethin'."

"That'll wait."

"Mom, I can't just blow Andy off. He might've made plans."

"He ain't planned nothin' that can't wait. Go on ahead and invite Alex."

"Let her be," Ruth Ann said. "Maybe she don't wanna. And it ain't right to cancel on Andy like that."

"Pfft. Andy ain't put a ring on her finger so he don't get a say." She patted Toni on the shoulder. "Go on. Worst thing he can do is say no."

While the sisters argued over which produce to select, Toni typed a simple text message to Alex.

- *Hey, it's Toni. Mom and Aunt Ruthie want you to come to lunch on Sunday. Interested?*

She considered joining them for lunch to get to know Alex better, but being under the microscope of her mother and aunt was not ideal. The options of dining with Alex, taking in a movie, or visiting the fair were also unappealing due to the prying eyes of the town.

While the trio continued adding to the shopping cart, Toni's phone pinged. The sisters didn't notice the sound, but Toni's excitement rose. She glanced at Alex's response.

"Alex said yes to lunch on Sunday."

Darlene spun around with a big smile. "Alright! Well, let's see. We'll get a brisket and some potatoes. Ruthie, you can make a peach cobbler. Or, I know—"

"Mom, it's just Alex. We don't need to overdo it."

"With the way he lives, anything home-cooked would be an improvement," Ruth Ann said.

Darlene was almost giddy while Ruth Ann remained guarded. Toni seemed indifferent, but Darlene could tell her daughter was thrilled.

After checking out, they had barely made it to the truck when Darlene eagerly started quizzing Toni.

"You told him you was comin', didn't ya?"

She shook her head. "I don't think I oughta be there."

"What? Why not? You like Alex, I mean from ever'thing you know."

"Yeah, but I'm seein' Andy, and I don't think he'd approve."

"He don't own you."

"No, but I already told him I'd do somethin' with him."

"Have lunch with us and Alex, then go out with Andy Sunday night."

"That might work," Toni said, wistfully.

Darlene clapped her hands once. "There you go! I know Alex'd like gettin' to know you."

"Mom, stop! You're gettin' way ahead of yourself. I agree Alex seems nice, but so was Virgil for the first five years."

"Not all men are donkeys."

"No, just the ones I attract."

"Alex ain't like Virgil. First time you brought him home he was wearin' them red boots and thought he was somethin' special."

"You don't know Alex ain't the same," Ruth Ann said. "We know he likes the ladies. He might not be all high and mighty like Virgil, but I bet he's a cheater."

Toni sighed, imagining the worst in Alex. "I ain't ready for that."

They arrived at the sisters' house and began unpacking the groceries.

"It's just lunch," Darlene said. "But I ain't gonna drag you to the table."

"She oughta wait," Ruth Ann said.

"For what?"

"Till we know a little more about Alex. He might bring home another young girl. For all we know, he's got girlfriends in every city."

"Hogwash. If he was like that, he'd have girls comin' and goin' all the time. We ain't seen but the one."

"That's still one," noted Toni.

"She coulda been just a friend."

"Sure looked like more than a friend to me," Ruth Ann cautioned.

"Listen," Toni said. "Alex is a friendly guy, and if he wants to have a bunch of girlfriends, that's his business. But I don't wanna be one of 'em."

"Pfft. Y'all got him figured for somethin' when you don't know nothin'. Both y'all oughta stop thinkin' like Cynthia Coker and see what kinda fella Alex really is."

"I like Alex," Ruth Ann said. "But bein' from California and that… that woman who answered the door… I don't trust him."

"It ain't just his girlfriends," Toni said. "He bought that dumb book at the fair."

Darlene snickered. "I done gave him a hard time 'bout that."

"That young assistant sure turned his head, and that book's been givin' him a bunch a crazy ideas. He tried tellin' me he was gonna come back."

"From where?" Darlene asked.

"He thinks he's gonna die then come back to life."

"Now what kinda nonsense is that?"

"I told you. There's somethin' wrong with him," Ruth Ann reiterated.

"He went on and on 'bout makin' mistakes and gettin' a second chance. I didn't understand, but he said somethin' 'bout fixin' what he done wrong."

"California folks are just plain weird," Ruth Ann declared.

"That's kinda kooky, but ever'one has things in their past they'd like to fix. I think y'all are misunderstandin' what he's sayin'."

"I don't know, Mom. He was sayin' some pretty far out there stuff. You know he don't go to church."

"Lotta folks don't go to church," Darlene reminded. "Judge not lest ye be judged."

"I know, Mom, and I ain't tryin' to judge him." She wished Alex was the exception to her past suitors, including Andy. She couldn't admit that while she loved

Virgil, she'd married him because she was expected to get married. Virgil was like all the men she'd dated; average, predictable, small town, convenient. Andy was no different. In all her experiences, she had never encountered that knock-your-socks-off kind of love that only seemed to happen in fairy tales. She wondered whether Alex, with his free-spirited persona, could be that man. She'd entertain the fantasy, but wasn't ready to let down her guard.

With the groceries stored away, Ruth Ann started preparing lunch. "Toni, honey, are you going to join us?"

"I gotta get home and start a load of laundry." She grabbed her purse.

Darlene met her at the door and kissed her cheek. "Love you, baby."

"Love you, Mom."

Chapter 15

Thursday morning, Toni was working at the clinic when Andy called to invite her to dinner.

When Andy arrived at seven to pick her up, Toni immediately noticed he was wearing slacks and a nice button-down, not his normal faded jeans and wrinkled shirt. He only dressed up for church and funerals.

"You look nice," Toni remarked. "Where are we goin'?"

"You'll see."

During the drive, Andy was unusually quiet, adding to Toni's concern.

They drove out Highway 36 to the Circle-T Resort, an upscale country club with one of the few fine-dining restaurants in town. Andy was a beer and barbecue kind of guy, and in the year they'd been dating, he had only taken her to a nice restaurant once, for her birthday.

He escorted her into the elegant restaurant where they were seated at a quiet table for two. With each passing moment, Toni became increasingly curious. *He ain't talkin' and he ain't ever brought me here*, she thought.

Andy's nervous expression began changing into a goofy grin, like a child with a secret trying to get out. "What's goin' on, Andy?"

"Can't I just take my girlfriend to a nice restaurant?"

You never have before, she wanted to say. "Sure, but it ain't my birthday?"

The waiter took their drink order, with Andy ordering a beer and Toni opting for water.

"You said you wanna talk to me about somethin'," she said with an inquisitive head tilt.

"You know I just got back from Dallas."

"Your uncle's funeral," she replied.

"He was fifty-five."

She nodded.

"And him dyin' got me thinkin' about how short life is. He was a healthy guy who had a heart attack outta nowhere."

She suddenly feared Andy was sick. "Andy, what's goin' on?"

"Toni," he said, briefly glancing down before locking eyes with her. "Me and you been seein' one another for a year now. And I kinda see us as bein' exclusive." He paused, expecting her to agree, but Toni's heart started pounding, sensing where this was going; *being exclusive* was a prelude to being engaged. She remained silent long enough for him to continue without her affirmation.

"When I saw how you acted around that guy, Alex… And hearin' y'all was hangin' out, I felt sick, like I was losin' you."

"Where'd you hear we was *hangin' out*?" she asked defensively.

"From lotsa people. It doesn't matter."

She smirked and spoke sharply. "Well, they're wrong. I told you. Alex is just a friend."

Andy waited for Toni's angst to subside. He again gazed deeply into her eyes. "You and me go back to junior high."

"Ms. Adams' Spanish class."

He smiled. "We've been friends for over twenty years, and—."

The waiter interrupted to take their orders. Toni knew what was coming and welcomed the interruption.

When the waiter left, Andy continued. "From the beginning, I knew Virgil wasn't right for you, and I shoulda said somethin'."

"Wouldn'ta mattered. That was my mistake to make."

"Now I feel like it's the same thing with Alex."

She pursed her lips. "Alex is a friend, nothin' more."

"Maybe so, but I'm here to make sure it stays that way." He looked like he was about to burst at the seams with anticipation.

"Okay, I don't know how you're gonna do that." *Please don't propose*, she wished.

"By marryin' you."

Crap.

Andy stood up, pulled a ring box from his pocket, and knelt in front of her. He opened the box and said, "Toni, will you marry me?"

Her gaze shifted from the ring to Andy's eager expression. It was a long moment.

"Wow, Andy. I don't know what to say."

The restaurant patrons watched, and Andy had alerted the staff to bring champagne when she said yes. They observed from a distance, waiting for a sign like an elated hug, but he remained on one knee and she remained seated.

Toni was painfully aware of all the eyes watching her. It was among the most uncomfortable moments of her life.

His goofy grin was in full bloom. "Say yes."

Flustered, she fanned herself. "I didn't expect this."

"I know, but why wait? Life's too short. C'mon. Say yes."

She waited as long as she could. "Andy, we got a good thing goin', and I really like you and all, but I just got out of a marriage. I ain't sayin' no, but I don't know if I'm ready to get married again. Can I think about it?"

Those five words crushed him. He took a deep breath, wanting to crawl away and die. But since she didn't say no, he clung to a tiny glimmer of hope.

"Take all the time you need." He suddenly felt foolish down on one knee, so he closed the box and returned to his seat.

The restaurant staff realized things didn't go as planned, so they hurried the entrées out while Toni and Andy suffered through an awkward silence that made the minutes pass like hours. Neither knew what to say.

They ate in near silence, exchanging small talk that did nothing to lessen the tension.

After a quiet ride home, Andy pulled up in front of her apartment, opened her car door then tried to hurry back to the driver's seat, but she caught his arm and pulled him into an embrace.

"Hey," she said, forcing him to look her in the eye. "Thank you." She gave him a long, passionate kiss. "Call me later."

She walked inside and he drove away.

Toni paced around the living room, deep in thought. It was doubtful she'd say yes, but she needed to talk to someone. She grabbed her keys and dialed the phone on the way out the door.

"Hey Mom. You gonna be up for a while?"

Toni's voice immediately signaled to Darlene that something was amiss.

"'Course. You alright?"

"I'm fine. I'll see you in a few minutes."

Despite wanting to greet Toni with 'What's wrong?' Darlene acted nonchalant, like it was any other day. She made it a point to appear busy wiping down the kitchen counters when Toni arrived.

Toni glanced around. "Where's Aunt Ruthie?"

Darlene casually replied, "She's in bed." After the phone call, Darlene asked Ruth Ann to make herself scarce in case Toni didn't want her to hear. Ruth Ann sat quietly in her bedroom near the door, listening.

"You wanna snack?" Darlene asked, opening the refrigerator.

"No, I'm good." She took a seat at the table and flatly said, "Andy asked me to marry him."

Darlene's eyes widened. "Well, how 'bout that." She closed the refrigerator door and reached out for a hug, but Toni wasn't smiling. "What's wrong?"

"Mom, I care about Andy a lot. I mean, he's a great guy…"

"But you don't love him."

Toni's eyes filled with tears. "It ain't that easy. I loved Virgil, and look what happened."

"Apples and oranges, sweetheart. You married him 'cause you loved him. He cheated 'cause he's a…" She searched for a strong word but settled on, "he's a cheater. You lovin' him don't have nothin' to do with him cheatin'."

Toni sniffled back her emotions. "I know, but I don't have to be in love to get married."

Darlene shook her head. "It ain't gonna last without it. You'd have an easier time stayin' married to Virgil."

"That's crazy. I'd never be with a cheater."

"If you loved him, you might."

"Never!"

Darlene chuckled. "Love's a funny thing. There's a lotta women who stay with cheaters. But there ain't many who stay when they ain't in love."

Toni thought about the painful end to her marriage. "I'd never stay with a cheater."

"Maybe it ain't the right time for you to get married. That don't mean you won't marry him when you're ready."

"That ain't fair to Andy. If I say no, he'll break up with me."

"And if you say yes, you'd marry a man you don't love."

Toni stood up and started pacing around. "You're sayin' I shouldn't marry him?"

"Sweetheart, it's your decision. It don't matter what I think. You gotta live with him."

"I'm thirty-six years old. This might be my last chance. And I can forget about kids."

"Do you want young'uns?" Darlene knew the answer, but wanted to help Toni find her own answers.

"I don't know. I didn't, but I can't say definitely never."

Darlene prepared a small glass of whiskey for each of them. "Maybe you oughta think about what you *wanna* do instead of what you don't want. You been talkin' 'bout goin' back to school and travelin'."

"Andy likes travelin' and I think he wants kids." She stared blankly while her thoughts swirled.

"What about Alex?" Darlene asked.

"What? What about him?"

"I'm sure Andy heard you was spendin' time with Alex."

"We ain't been *spendin'* time, other 'n a walk through the fair with you and Aunt Ruthie, and a few text messages. So what?"

"Andy mighta proposed 'cause he's jealous?"

"Maybe. So?"

"You don't wanna marry a man who's only tryin' to keep you from someone else."

Toni wanted to disagree, but replayed the proposal. "He mentioned Alex."

"Was he mad about you seein' Alex?"

"I'm not *seein'* Alex," she protested. "He's a friend—maybe not even that. He's just your neighbor."

Darlene smiled. "Listen to yourself."

"What?"

"You're gettin' all riled up."

"'Cause you're actin' like there's somethin' goin' on between me and Alex, and there ain't!"

"I know, dear. I don't mean to pick at ya. I'm just tryin' to get you thinkin' 'bout ever'thing."

"Well, Alex ain't a part of this. Like I told you, I don't wanna man like Alex—always gone, and datin' a bunch a girls."

"I don't know that Alex is datin' anyone, but there ain't no guarantee any man'll remain faithful."

"Daddy did."

Darlene chuckled and took another sip of whiskey. "He knew better. But your daddy also had an eye for the ladies. More 'n once I caught him makin' eyes."

"No way."

Darlene smiled. "Listen, I told him he could look all he wanted, but the day he wanted more would be the last day he could come home to me."

Toni smiled. "I get it. Men are gonna look around."

"As long as it ends at lookin'."

"Alex would definitely go beyond lookin'."

"You don't know that. He said he don't cheat once he commits. Some men are like that. They date ever'thing that moves till they find the one, then they never even look around."

"I thought Virgil was like that." She took a big sip. "Maybe it's not Andy. Maybe I can't trust another man."

"Listen, sweetheart, life's a gamble. You can't control what anyone does. You gotta pick your own road and follow it. Sometimes, you're gonna pick the wrong one, like Virgil. But then you pick another one and try again, a little wiser."

"I wish there was an obvious path to choose."

"Sometimes there is. But sometimes the obvious one turns out to be the wrong one."

"Great. So no matter what I do, I'm screwed."

"You don't know till you try. You gotta learn from ever'thing you do. That way, you don't keep repeatin' the same mistake."

"So you think I should marry Andy?"

Darlene shook her head and carried the empty glasses to the sink. "What I think don't matter."

Ruth Ann decided it was time for Toni to get a second opinion. She entered the room and shuffled over to the cupboard. "Toni, dear, I thought you were out with Andy?"

"I was, but..." she instinctively paused, accustomed to hiding her personal problems. "But Andy asked me to marry him."

Ruth Ann put on a convincing performance, appearing genuinely surprised. "Oh, my. That's wonderful! You could have a June wedding, although we'd need to start planning immediately. I'll make the cake, and I'm sure Mr. Barton'll do the flowers."

"I don't think I'm gonna say yes."

"What?" Ruth Ann remarked, again feigning ignorance. "Andy's such a nice young man. Why wouldn't you wanna marry him?"

"She don't need a reason," Darlene said.

"You hush," Ruth Ann snapped at her sister before turning to Toni. "Now listen, Andy'd make a fine husband."

"Let her be," Darlene said. "It's her decision." She looked at Toni. "Don't listen to her, or anyone."

"*You* let her be," Ruth Ann fired back. "Bein' married's more than just bein' in love. It's havin' a good friend. It don't have to be some whirlwind romance. Look at Irma and Otis. They've been together over forty years."

"She don't want what Irma's got, so don't go fillin' her head with a bunch a nonsense. You know as well as anyone Irma ain't happy with Otis. She's just too old and set in her ways to change. That ain't Antoinette."

"That's what I mean," Ruth Ann said. "She's married to a man she don't even like 'cause that's better than bein' alone."

"No, it ain't," Darlene barked.

Toni raised her hands. "Stop! I appreciate what you're sayin'—both a y'all—but like Mom said, this is my decision." She sighed. "Let's talk about somethin' else 'fore I gotta go so y'all can go to bed."

Ruth Ann fixed herself a glass of warm milk while the conversation was light except for the occasional snipe. "If my sister had a lick a sense, she'd tell you to marry him."

"Anyone can tell you what to do when they don't know what they're talkin' about," Darlene said.

Soon, Toni hugged both sisters, thanked them for their input, and left.

Chapter 16

Andy took Toni out Saturday night for an answer. They hadn't talked in the two days since the proposal.

They drove to City Lake, a small secluded place that was popular with young lovers.

Toni stepped out of the car saying, "I haven't been here since high school."

Hand in hand, they strolled leisurely along the shoreline.

"How was your week?" he casually asked.

Her words flowed faster than normal. "Busy. I been learnin' this years' billin' codes. There's a ton a new ones."

They continued on in silence until Andy abruptly stopped and faced her. "I couldn't stop thinkin' about you the last couple a days. It's been torture."

"I missed you too," she lied.

"You know what I'm talking about. What's your answer?"

Unable to find the right words, she bought some time by tossing a rock into the lake. She knew the answer was no, but didn't know if it was no for now, no always, or no to marriage to anyone. While meandering around, searching for another rock, she nonchalantly asked, "Why can't we continue doin' what we're doin'?"

His head slumped. "I guess that's a no."

"It's not no. It's not yet." She felt his pain and disappointment. "Look, Andy, I ain't ready to get married, and I might never be ready."

He sighed, "I understand."

"Hey!" she said, drawing his attention. "I don't wanna stop seein' you."

"Whatever." Andy turned and starting slogging toward the car.

"Don't be like that," she said, following him.

His tone turned angry. "Like what? Like a man who had his heart ripped out?"

She snatched his hand and interlocked their fingers, stopping him from walking away. "Like someone who's forgettin' this is hard for me, too."

He pried his hand free and said, "It's pretty damn easy to say yes or no." His eyes were fiery and his breathing heavy.

"Andy, don't do this."

"Do what? Face the fact that you're just gonna string me along?"

"You know I wouldn't do that."

"No, actually, I don't know that." She tried to retake his hand, but he yanked it away.

Despite knowing he was hurt, acting like a child lowered her opinion of him.

"Andy!"

He angrily returned to the car and got in without first opening her door.

Fearing he might drive off without her, she quickly jumped in the passenger seat. Seeing Andy's true colors, Toni quickly went from irritated to mad. *If he'd a left me...* she fumed.

They rode in silence until she said, "You're bein' an ass."

"Uh huh," he replied curtly, driving dangerously fast.

"Andy, seriously. If you're gonna to act like this, let's just end it now."

They reached her apartment building, and he slammed on the brakes. "Fine. We're done. Get out."

She grabbed his arm, hoping he'd come to his senses. "Is that what you really want?"

He yanked his arm away. "If you ain't gonna marry me, yeah. Go!"

"Fine!" She opened her door and stepped out. Despite her anger, she felt a sense of relief that he'd revealed his true self.

He spun his tires the instant she closed the door. She flashed on Virgil and how he deceived her for years. "Assholes!" she blurted.

Toni immediately knew their blow-up would become the lead story on the gossip channel. The next day being Sunday, there would certainly be whispers among the congregants, which heightened her aggravation. She was already considering skipping church altogether.

There was little hope Andy would keep the breakup to himself—postponing the inevitable broadcast—because

Andy was a momma's boy. Madelyn Pharris, Andy's mother, would know the entire story— at least Andy's side of it—within the hour. The news would spread like wildfire.

Toni called her mother to begin damage control.

"Well, we broke up."

Not surprised, Darlene said, "Sweetheart, I'm sorry. Do you wanna come over and talk about it?"

"I wanna talk, but I'm home, so I'm fine."

Toni relayed the basic details to Darlene. "And I thought he'd understand, but he just acted like an idiot. I ain't ever seen him like that. I guess all men got a shitty side."

"Ain't just men. Folks do things they don't normally do when they're hurt."

"Yeah," she said sharply. "But that don't give him the right to leave me on the side of the road."

Darlene smiled at Toni's exaggeration, happy to be the one she vented to. "'Course not."

"And now he and his momma are gonna go blabbin' all over town 'bout what a terrible person I am."

Darlene cringed, knowing Toni was right, but tried to put it in perspective. "You can't stop folks from talkin'. And ever'one's been through a bad breakup. Andy and his momma might say some ugly things 'bout you, but folks 'round here know better."

She sighed, imagining the inevitable gossip she hated being the subject of.

"I just wish they'd let it go. It's between me and Andy, not the whole damn town."

Darlene could almost hear Cynthia Coker lighting up the phone lines with wild remarks about the breakup. She didn't mind the chatter, but had zero tolerance for anything disrespectful toward Antoinette.

"Listen, you'll get through this. And I'll make sure folks get the real story."

"Mom, you don't have to defend me," Toni said, thankful that her mother was always in her corner.

"You're my daughter and I love you. I ain't *gotta* do nothin', but I'd fight the devil himself if he tries messin' with my family."

Toni chuckled, wiping the moisture from her eyes. "I love you too, Mom." The day's stress was catching up with her. She needed to cry a little, get angry a few more times, then sleep and start fresh tomorrow.

"You pickin' us up in the mornin'?"

"'Course."

"You ain't skippin' the service are ya?"

"I thought about it, but I ain't missed many and I ain't about to start."

"Good for you."

"But I might skip Sunday school. Andy's sister's usually there and some a Andy's friends might try me. I'd kinda like to avoid that for now."

"You're welcome to join me and Ruthie at the bowlin' alley."

Toni laughed. "And listen to the likes of Cynthia Coker? No thanks."

Darlene chuckled, pleased to hear the resolute spirit in her daughter. "I don't blame ya. Get some sleep."

"Thanks Mom. I love you."

"I love you too."

* * *

The following morning, the Sunday senior ladies filed into the Superbowl and got comfortable.

Sarah set a glass of tea in front of Ruth Ann and said, "Did y'all hear the youth choir's goin' to Glorietta next summer?"

"There's only twenty of 'em," Ruth Ann said. "I hope they ain't drivin' that old bus."

"That heap wouldn't make it to Abilene," Darlene said.

The door to the lounge swung open and Cynthia Coker came rushing in breathless.

"Any y'all talk to Toni?" she hollered, drawing all eyes to her.

Darlene tried to undermine what she knew was coming. "Yeah, we know. Andy proposed. That's old news." She turned to the group. "Is Pastor gonna start a fundraiser for the choir?"

Sarah said, "I heard he's gonna—"

"She said no!" Cynthia shouted.

"No way," Irma said.

"Really?" Sarah asked.

"That ain't exactly how it went," Darlene said, spinning her chair around to face Cynthia.

"I just talked to Madelyn Pharris. That's why I was late. She said Andy called her last night after they broke up."

Everyone turned to Darlene. "Antoinette gave me the whole story. Turns out she told Andy she wasn't ready to marry anyone but wanted to keep datin'. Andy didn't like that and acted like a donkey, so they broke up. End a story."

"Andy acted up?" Irma repeated. "That don't sound like him, and he's crazy about her."

"Got it straight from Antoinette," Darlene stated confidently. "And y'all know no one likes not gettin' their way. Andy ain't no different."

Miss Virginia said, "I heard Toni was out with that new fella, Alex."

Cynthia nodded. "That's why Andy dumped her."

Darlene slapped the table. "Now that ain't true, and you know it."

Ruth Ann put her hand on Darlene's shoulder, trying to calm her. "Don't pay her no nevermind."

"Andy's a momma's boy," Sarah said. "But I can't see him breakin' up with Toni."

"Madelyn said he did it last night."

"I just told you," Darlene said, exasperated. "Antoinette tried to keep things goin' but when she didn't say she'd marry him, he got all huffy and they ended things."

"My niece isn't ready to get married," Ruth Ann politely added.

"I also heard she was out with Alex," Rebecca McKnight, one of the quieter regulars, said.

"Aw hell!" Darlene barked. "Ain't none a y'all listenin'? Alex and Antoinette was walking with me and Ruthie at the fair. Ain't nothin' wrong with that."

"If that's the only time they were together," Cynthia jabbed, implying a scandalous relationship between Alex and Toni.

"My Antoinette ain't like that, and you know it."

Ruth Ann squinted at Cynthia, saying, "And don't you go draggin' her name through the dirt, missy."

"Ever'one knows my Antoinette's as loyal as the day is long. Ain't no way she'd go 'round with another man while she's with Andy."

Sarah agreed. "Toni wouldn't do that."

"If she was interested in Alex, she'd end it with Andy first," Irma said.

"Damn right," Darlene grumbled.

"Well," Cynthia said, not backing down. "Madelyn said Andy broke it off 'cause of Alex."

"Just 'cause that's what Andy told his momma don't make it true. And he ain't gonna tell Madelyn he's jealous of Alex. Even if he did, Antoinette don't have nothin' to do with that."

"All I know is the wedding's off," Cynthia stated unabashedly.

Darlene nodded. "But it ain't 'cause Antoinette done somethin' wrong." She pointed an angry finger at Cynthia. "You need to get your facts right 'fore spreadin' lies about my daughter."

"I'm just repeating what Madelyn told me."

"That's sad," Miss Virginia lamented. "They're such a nice couple."

"Better to break up now than end up in a bad marriage," Sarah said.

"Amen," Irma concurred.

Darlene quietly sipped her whiskey while waiting for another crass remark from Cynthia. However, Ruth Ann changed the subject, hoping to improve her sister's disposition.

"Irma, are you showing next month at the rodeo?"

"Two bulls," she answered with pride. "Fattenin' 'em up right now," As part of her and Otis's sizable cattle ranch, Irma raised several show animals.

"You think you can beat Buford this year?" Miss Virginia asked.

Irma nodded. "He's won three years runnin' but this year's mine."

Out of respect for Darlene, the topic of Toni and Andy remained suspended.

Darlene and Ruth Ann left early to prepare for lunch with Alex.

Toni had in fact skipped Sunday school but still picked the sisters up from the bowling alley.

Darlene was still filled with indignation when she climbed in the truck. However, she tempered it, knowing if she repeated everything Cynthia had said, it would only upset Toni. "You was right about the gossip."

Toni spoke through a clenched jaw. "How bad was it?"

"Not bad. Cynthia tried stirrin' things up with a bunch a BS, but I straightened her out."

"Good," Toni said, relaxing a bit. "What about the rest?"

Darlene waved her hand. "Oh, they didn't think much of it. They was sorry y'all broke up but didn't pay no nevermind to Cynthia's nonsense."

"You know," Toni said. "Sometimes Cynthia acts like she's my friend, like everything's cool, but then she stabs me in the back."

"She likes playin' both sides," Darlene said. "'Specially if there's a pot to stir."

"That's not very a Christian thing to do," Ruth Ann commented.

"You talked to Andy at all?" Darlene asked.

"I texted him, but he ain't answered."

"Dear," Ruth Ann said. "I know everything's all messed up right now, but do you still wanna date him?"

Toni grunted. "Are you kiddin' me? The way he acted last night?"

"You're better off," Darlene said. "I like Andy, but you don't need someone actin' like that."

They pulled into the sisters' driveway and Toni helped them out of her truck.

"You should work things out with Andy," Ruth Ann suggested. "He's such a nice young man."

"Let it be," Darlene said.

"I don't want him hatin' me, but I don't want someone behavin' like a child. I've known him a long time, and we always got along."

"You got along 'cause you ain't never told him 'no'," Darlene said.

Toni pulled out her phone as they started for the door. "I don't like what he done, but I'm gonna at least try to clear the air."

"What about lunch? Alex'll be here in an hour."

"Tell Alex I'm sorry. I gotta deal with this."

Darlene was disappointed. She'd become very fond of Alex and hoped Toni would get to know him better. She wasn't playing matchmaker, but thought they'd naturally bond the more time they spent together.

"And Mom…" Toni said, pausing to capture her mother's complete attention. "Don't tell Alex about me and Andy. I mean, I don't care, but it ain't really his business."

Darlene nodded. "I won't."

Chapter 17

Alex knocked on the sisters' door at one o'clock sharp. Darlene answered with, "Welcome back, stranger." She led him to the dining room where Ruth Ann was putting food on the table.

"Hello Alex. How was California?"

"It was good."

"I want to hear all about it but you'll have to excuse me while I finish in the kitchen."

"Do you need any help?"

"Oh no, thank you. Please, have a seat."

"You wanna quick snort?" Darlene offered.

He shook his head. "I need to detox from last week."

Darlene excused herself, returning with a pan of brisket. Ruth Ann followed and everyone sat.

"Where's Toni?" Alex asked.

Ruth Ann flashed a nervous look at her sister. "She had a last-minute emergency," Darlene said. "She said tell you she's sorry she couldn't make it."

Ruth Ann's glance at her sister told Alex there was something they weren't telling him.

"Alex, would you like to say grace?" Ruth Ann offered.

He'd played in Christian bands where saying grace was common, but had never led the prayer. "Oh. I'd rather one of you would, please."

Everyone bowed and closed their eyes as Ruth Ann began. "Father in Heaven, we thank you for this bounty we are about to receive, the blessings you bestow upon us, and your mercy. We thank you for bringing Alex into our lives and we ask that you watch over him in all his travels. In Jesus' name, Amen."

"Amen," Darlene and Alex repeated.

Ruth Ann pointed to the pan in the middle of the table. "Try the brisket and tell me if it's dry."

Alex loaded his plate with brisket, potatoes, green beans, squash, and a roll. "It smells great. My taste buds won't know what hit them." He took a bite and closed his eyes. "Oh man, this is incredible."

"It ain't dry?"

"It's perfect."

Ruth Ann smiled, her opinion of Alex improving.

"Now, tell us about California," Darlene said.

The food was so delicious, Alex had a hard time not talking with his mouth full.

"Do you always eat like this?"

"We don't normally make a brisket, but Ruthie usually makes chicken, potatoes, vegetables, and rolls."

"Feel free to invite me over anytime."

"I told you," Ruth Ann said to her sister.

Alex looked at one, then the other, waiting to hear what she meant. Darlene smiled. "My sister thought with all that junky food you probably eat when you're travelin', we coulda served boiled mule and you'd like it."

"I've never had boiled mule, but this certainly beats fast food. I have to admit though, when I'm on the road, we usually eat at decent restaurants. But they don't compare to this. I haven't had home cooking since… I can't remember when."

"So, back to your trip," Darlene said. "Did you have a nice time?"

"I did. We played light jazz and R&B in mostly packed nightclubs."

Darlene smiled. "That sounds like such fun. I don't know why anyone'd give that up."

"For the first time in a while, I had the same thought. The band was good, the crowd was great, and I actually enjoyed the last night."

"So, you're goin' back to playin' full time?"

"I don't know. Probably not."

"Why not? 'Specially if you had fun."

"I only enjoyed the last night at the Troubadour."

"You can't always expect good days with any kind a work. You take the good with the bad, and it sounds like it don't take a lotta good for you to get over the bad."

"It was fun," he said, reloading his plate. "This food is amazing. I hope you don't mind me stuffing myself."

"Please," Ruth Ann encouraged. "It's nice cooking for someone other than Darlene and Toni."

"Don't you cook for church functions?"

"Sometimes, but I usually just make one dish, not a whole meal."

"Did y'all stay in a hotel?" Darlene asked.

"We picked up a tour bus in Colorado and lived on it for three days, then I flew out of L.A. late last night."

"When did you sleep?"

"I got a few hours on the plane. It was a direct flight."

"You must be wore out," Ruth Ann said.

"It'll catch up with me later today and I'll crash. Although I'll probably stay up late and sleep all day tomorrow."

"I couldn't live like that," Ruth Ann remarked.

"You get used to it, but I'm looking forward to being home for a while."

"You're gonna get bored sittin' 'round Hamilton," Darlene said.

"I need to work on my house, and I might make a trip down to Austin to check out the scene."

Darlene nodded. "I told you you'd miss it."

"I'll miss the great nights, but even those aren't perfect."

"Nothin's perfect, Alex."

"I know, but partying every night is only fun with the right people."

"You like the folks in the band, don't you?"

"Some are fun, others are wild, and some are full of themselves. We went to a party after the gig, but I only knew the band."

"So, you met some new folks?" Darlene asked.

He shrugged. "They weren't really my kind of people. Imagine an entire room filled with Cynthia Cokers."

Both sisters moaned, "Oh Lord."

"Hmph," Darlene grunted. "I couldn't a got outta there fast enough."

Alex smiled. "Exactly. I can handle them in small doses, but a whole room and an entire night got old fast."

"It woulda for me."

"Mmm. Lawd," Ruth Ann muttered.

"That's why it's nice to be back in Hamilton where there's only one Cynthia."

"And she can be one too many," Ruth Ann quipped.

"But you had fun playin', and that's all that matters."

He nodded.

"Good for you. But you don't wanna go back to the big city?"

"It's weird how I've only lived here a few months, but it feels like home."

"Maybe you're just gettin' old," Darlene kidded.

"Darlene!" Ruth Ann scolded.

"I'm just funnin'."

"She's not wrong. I felt old when everyone wanted to party all night and I wanted to go to bed."

Darlene raised her glass, as if to toast. "Amen."

Talk of being on the road and coming home reminded Alex of his lonely house across the street, turning his thoughts to Toni. He wanted to know more about her, but wasn't comfortable cajoling information from the sisters.

"Apart from the grass growing, what other noteworthy events took place in Hamilton during my absence?"

"Well," Darlene ruminated. "The president stopped by, but he didn't stay long, just needed some advice."

Alex smiled. "And you straightened him out?"

"Like an arrow."

"Since I couldn't find the Hamilton Gazette in L.A., what's been going on aside from the president's visit?"

"The Gazette's got a website," Darlene remarked with a sly smile.

"Okay, you got me, but I forgot to check it."

"Well, Alex, It's been pretty quiet other 'n…" Darlene paused at the glower coming from Ruth Ann; a clear signal not to mention Toni and Andy. "Don't go lookin' at me like that," Darlene snapped at her sister.

Alex watched the exchange, curious about what they were hiding from him.

Ruth Ann's expression remained pinched, ready to reprimand her sister at the mere mention of Toni and Andy's situation.

Darlene waved her sister away and turned to Alex. "Don't pay her no nevermind, Alex. It was pretty quiet while you was gone. Although Toni told us about some nonsense you was sayin' about comin' back after dyin'?"

Alex smiled. "You shouldn't have told me to read that book I bought at the fair."

"She said you was gettin' some mighty peculiar ideas."

He nodded. "There's some strange beliefs out there, but I've thought about reincarnation before."

"Hmph," Ruth Ann grunted, dismissing any ideology other than Christianity.

"Like them folks that put a dot on their forehead?" Darlene asked.

"I'm not sure who believes what, but there's certainly something living inside all of us that's not physical."

"It's called your soul," Darlene said.

"Your soul, your conscience, your spirit, whatever you call it. I don't think it goes away when you die."

"It goes to Heaven!" Ruth Ann adamantly stated.

Her firm tone warned Alex to tread lightly, especially when discussing religion with a pair of devout Southern ladies. "And that's probably what happens—"

"Not *probably*," Darlene interrupted. "Without a doubt."

Alex raised his hands in mock surrender. "I have no problem with that. But doesn't the Bible mention angels and spirits visiting people on Earth? And wasn't Jesus in Heaven for a few days before coming back?"

"That's right," Darlene said. "But them are exceptions. Christians go to Heaven to stay."

"Well, I'm not well-versed in the Bible, but I wonder if that… sprit or… soul in all of us lives on in more ways than just in Heaven."

"Nonsense," Darlene said firmly.

Alex smiled. "Listen, I've got an active imagination that helps me be creative. I could be totally wrong, but I enjoy thinking about things."

"Well, I think you ain't gettin' enough sleep and it's makin' you dream up nonsense."

His smile grew. "Maybe that book messed up my thinking," he said in jest.

"Maybe it did," Darlene agreed, sensing Alex was being playful. She gave him an impish nod. "Maybe after you get a good night's sleep you'll start thinkin' normal again. Then, you can catch up on all the goin's on around Hamilton by readin' all them Gazette newspapers."

Alex laughed, hoping to change the subject that felt tense. He leaned back and put his hands on his stomach. "I might need a couple of days before I can move again. I ate way too much."

"You ain't had Ruthie's peach cobbler."

"Man, I'm stuffed. I don't know if I can." Ruth Ann scooped out a portion for Alex and without hesitation, he dug in. "Oh, man. This is great."

"Why thank you, Alex," Ruth Ann said. "You'll have to take some home with you."

"I guess I can forget about losing weight."

Darlene waved him off. "Shoot, Alex. You can always lose weight later."

"But I can't always get Ruth Ann's peach cobbler?"

"That's right. Listen, I'd love to hear you play the piana sometime."

"You know, I rarely play as a soloist, but for you, I'll make an exception. I'll need a few days to catch up on sleep and decide what to play, then we can make an afternoon of it."

"Sounds like a plan," Darlene said. "Maybe you can order one of them gourmet meals you get delivered."

Alex grinned. "Pizza and whiskey."

"You supply the pizza and I'll bring the whiskey." Darlene's remark drew a glare from her sister.

"You'll of course join us," he said to Ruth Ann.

"I don't know, Alex. Not that I don't enjoy your company, and I'd love to hear you play, but whiskey and pizza aren't my favorite things."

Alex shot a quick wink at Darlene before saying, "I can get some tequila if you prefer."

Darlene burst out laughing.

Ruth Ann chuckled politely, realizing he was teasing her. "Shame on you."

"How about I serve iced tea?"

"You don't need to go to any trouble on my account."

"But don't cancel the whiskey," Darlene said.

Alex laughed. "I wouldn't think of it. Let's plan on Thursday evening, say seven o'clock."

"That works for me."

"Thank you, Alex," Ruth Ann said. "We'll be there."

"Bring Toni if she's available."

"I'll tell her we're gettin' a private concert."

"Sounds great." He stood up from the table. "But I gotta lie down. I ate too much."

Ruth Ann jumped up and said, "Let me pack up some leftovers to go home with you."

"Okay, but if I can't fit through the door, you're gonna have to come over and help me."

"Shoot," Ruth Ann said, smiling as she left to find the containers.

After the sisters cleared the table, they walked Alex to the door, each holding a sack of leftovers. "Thank you so much," Alex said. "This was the best meal I've had in years."

"You're welcome," Ruth Ann said, handing him a sack and stepping back. "We'll see you Thursday."

"Don't tump over crossin' the street with all that extra weight," Darlene teased.

"I'll try not to, but keep an eye out."

Chapter 18

When Toni left work, she found Andy standing next to his car. He'd been ignoring her calls and texts for days.

"Hey," she said, coolly. "What're you doin' here?"

"We need to talk." He opened the passenger door and extended an arm.

"'Bout what?" she asked, wary of getting in a car with him. "You made it pretty clear it was your way or the highway."

"Get in," he said, sounding somewhat defeated.

She folded her arms. "Just say what you gotta say."

He took a deep breath and a long pause. "You hurt me..." he started. She let the silence linger, unwilling to help him play the victim. "And I'm sorry I got mad, but I've always loved you, and I never thought you'd lead me on."

"I didn't lead you—"

"I'm not finished!" he snapped. She took a step back and refolded her arms. "When I heard you'd left Virgil, I felt my heart beat for the first time in a long time. I was glad it happened 'cause it meant I might get a second chance." His voice quivering, he whispered, "If I could do it all over, I wouldn't have let you go. But I can't go through this again." He faced her with tears in his eyes. "I can't waste the rest of my life waiting for you. And even if I did, I'd always be your second choice."

After his snap, she curtly asked, "So, where does that leave us?"

"I wanna marry you, but I ain't gonna wait."

"Mmm hmm."

"I ain't sittin' around while you throw yourself at Alex."

"Seriously?" Her tone was sharp as she shifted her weight and put her hands on her hips.

"Carolyn said you two was mighty friendly."

"Carolyn Wagner?" she asked contemptuously, her outrage increasing.

Andy nodded.

"You say you wanna marry me, then accuse me a throwin' myself at Alex?" She paused as her jaw clenched. "And now you're listenin' to *Carolyn Wagner*?"

"Look, I tell you everything. Not like..." he caught himself before launching more accusations. "And Carolyn wasn't the only one. Victoria Olsen said you was makin' a fool outta me."

"Victoria Olsen?"

"She's a friend."

"How good a friend?"

"Ain't nothin' goin' on. Like I said, I tell you everything. Me and Victoria mostly just talked about you."

"Victoria Olsen doesn't *just talk* with any man."

"Okay, so we kissed a little, but it didn't mean nothin'. I was confused and angry. I'm sorry."

Toni was livid. "Three days ago, you ask me to marry you. But *I'm* cheatin' on you, so you kiss the biggest slut in town, which I doubt was all y'all did?" She started toward her truck. "You ain't gotta wait around for me no more. We're done."

He tried to catch her hand, but she was too quick. "Wait. Lemme explain. Toni, it ain't like that. We just talked. Me and Victoria's been friends as long as you and me."

Toni was filled with anger and regret that she had opened herself up, *knowing* that her relationship with Andy had ended two days before. Seething, she got in the truck, rolled down the window, and waited.

Andy stood beside her door. "You got this all wrong. Victoria means nothin' to me."

Toni's eyes filled with fiery tears. "You, of all people, know what I went through with Virgil. Now, you wanna use the same bullshit lies he used?" Just as she was about to unleash an angry rant, something inside her switched off, and she shut down completely. "Goodbye Andy." She started the truck.

"I'm sorry. It wasn't my intention to hurt you. I love you and I wanna marry you."

"That ain't ever gonna happen." She dropped the truck in gear and sped away, never looking back.

* * *

During the short drive home, she initially decided not to call her mother. Her anger and hurt were undeniable, but surprisingly, she was feeling better. *Mom was right. I never loved him,* she thought. Within a few minutes, she changed her mind and called Darlene.

"Mom, you busy?"

"'Course not. What'ya got?"

She replayed the confrontation with Andy and added, "You was right. I didn't love him."

"Sweetheart, I'm sorry."

"I'm not. Andy was a nice guy… was. But even if he hadn't turned into a jerk, it wouldn't a mattered."

"It still breaks my heart when someone mistreats you."

"Thanks, Mom. But I'm fine. In fact, I'm better now than when we was datin'."

"What're you gonna do now?"

"I don't know. Nothin' probably."

"What about Alex?"

"Mom, don't start. I just got outta one relationship."

"I know, but y'all get along and I think Alex is interested."

Toni enjoyed hearing that Alex was interested, but said, "No Mom, I ain't ready to see no one."

Darlene didn't believe her, but didn't push. "I understand. Listen, you comin' over for dinner?"

"Not tonight. I'm gonna kick back at home."

"Alright. If you change your mind. And sweetheart, I *am* sorry about you and Andy. I know you liked him."

"Liked. Not loved. But thanks Mom. I'll talk to you tomorrow."

After reflecting on the past year with Andy, Toni felt like she was finally turning around on a dead-end road. She climbed into bed, looking forward to a fresh start.

* * *

Tuesday night, the Hamilton hotline lit up. Cynthia started the ball rolling after listening to Madelyn Pharris rant about how Toni had broken her baby's heart. Cynthia's first call was to Dorothy.

"You won't believe what Madelyn told me. Andy tried everything to make up with Toni, but she all but threw dirt in his face."

"Oh, that's awful."

"It gets worse. Toni accused Andy of cheating on *her*. Can you believe that?"

Cynthia continued tailoring the facts to paint the picture she wanted, and within hours, the story made it from Dorothy to Irma to Sarah, who finally called Darlene.

"Dar," Sarah said. "Irma just told me about Toni breakin' up with Andy."

"That was a couple a days ago. Ain't nothin' new."

"She said Andy went to Toni's work to patch things up."

"It wasn't nothin'. Antoinette heard him out. They talked and called it quits."

"That ain't how I heard it."

Expecting to hear nonsense, Darlene fought the urge to snap at her friend. "Lemme guess, this all started with Cynthia Coker."

"I think so. Irma said Andy tried to makeup with Toni but she wouldn't even listen. Said she accused him of all kinds of things and told him to stay away from her."

"Now, that don't sound like Antoinette, does it?"

"Not really. That's why I called. Irma said Dorothy told her Andy was thinkin' 'bout leavin' town."

Darlene chuckled. "Now *that* sounds like somethin' Cynthia made up. Listen, I talked to Antoinette last night after it all happened, so I know what happened."

"And?"

Darlene didn't want to spread gossip about her daughter, but the truth needed telling. "Andy said he still wanted to marry Antoinette, but then admitted he'd been spendin' time with Victoria Olsen."

"Victoria Olsen!" Sarah exclaimed.

"Now, I don't know 'xactly what he was doin' with Victoria, but Antoinette was plenty mad."

"I don't blame her. Victoria Olsen's got quite the reputation."

"I don't know about that, but Antoinette didn't like Andy spendin' time with any single gals. And like I said, I don't know the particulars, but it was enough to break Antoinette's trust."

"After what Virgil did, I can see why. That's awful, Dar. You tell Toni I'm sorry they broke up."

"I will, and you tell the likes of Cynthia Coker to stop spreadin' nonsense about my daughter. She ain't done nothin' wrong and what happened between her and Andy ain't nobody's business."

"I will. I knew there was more to the story."

"There always is when the Mouth of the South starts stirrin' the pot."

"I'll make sure everyone hears the truth."

"I 'preciate that, but I wish folks'd just let it be. You know how Antoinette hates bein' talked about."

"I know. So, what about her and Alex?"

Darlene inhaled sharply. "Don't start," she warned. "Let's let Antoinette keep her private life private."

"I'm sorry. You're right."

"Thank ya Sarah. Now go straighten out them gossip mongers 'fore this whole thing turns into a pack a lies."

* * *

Over the next two days, Alex practiced the thirty-minute set of songs he'd chosen to play for his new friends.

Late Wednesday, he discovered he needed a few supplies, so he made a quick trip to the market.

As he walked up and down the aisles, his long hair and distinctive dress drew stares.

While most shied away, a young woman he recognized approached him. "I'm Kristi Lynn Martin. I work at Whitman's. You're Alex, aren't you?"

He nodded. "Nice to meet you."

"I saw you and Toni at the fair. Too bad about her and Andy."

"Thank you. Wait… what happened to Toni and Andy?"

Kristi Lynn felt uneasy as she noticed the onlookers tuning into their conversation. "Oh, nothin' really. Come by Whitman's sometime."

"Thank you."

"Bye, Alex." She bounced away as he stood there befuddled. He shook it off and continued shopping, but couldn't stop wondering what had happened between Toni and Andy.

Chapter 19

On Thursday evening, Alex ordered the pizza from a place he had found online soon after he moved to Hamilton, then started a little last-minute cleaning. The house was clean by his standards, as a bachelor, but filthy by most others. He shoved the dirty dishes into the dishwasher and quickly dragged a broom across the kitchen.

While the sisters crossed the street, he paid the pizza delivery kid. He spotted a bottle of Jack Daniel's in the crook of Darlene's arm.

"Whiskey and pizza," he called out as they approached. "That's how the Irish-Italians celebrated."

"If they didn't, they shoulda," Darlene replied.

"Follow me," he said, leading them to the living room. "You'll have to forgive the mess."

"Pfft," Darlene said. "I'd worry if it was clean."

"It's nice to see you Alex," Ruth Ann said.

The sisters sat on the couch while Alex set the pizza on the coffee table. Leaving the room briefly, he reappeared with paper towels, glasses, and a pitcher of iced tea.

"You ain't drinkin'?" Darlene asked.

"I'm still detoxing."

She put the lid on the whiskey, looking disappointed. "I ain't gonna drink alone."

Alex grabbed an extra glass and said, "Where are my manners?"

Darlene poured them each a small amount of whiskey and raised her drink. "Here's to pizza and whiskey."

Alex laughed and poured everyone a glass of tea before sitting in the recliner and grabbing a slice of pizza. "I think you'll like the tea," he said to Ruth Ann. "It a secret recipe from a friend of mine. She told me it's why she sings like a bird."

Ruth Ann cautiously tasted it, then took a big drink. "Alex, this is wonderful. Is that ginger?"

"I'll never tell. She swore me to secrecy. But maybe if you're nice to me, I'll let you in on the secret formula."

Ruth Ann smiled. "I ain't makin' no promises." She laughed and relaxed, leaning forward and sliding a slice of pizza onto her plate.

"I guess Toni's working late?"

"She said she'd try to make it," Darlene said.

"I ran into the girl from Whitman's who said something happened between Toni and Andy. Is everything okay? Not that it's any of my business."

Ruth Ann glared at her sister, but Darlene waved her hand and said, "Aw hell, Ruthie, ever'one in town knows." She turned to Alex. "She and Andy broke up."

Alex hid his excitement and somberly nodded. "Oh, that's a bummer." He had many questions about when and how to ask her out, but none felt appropriate.

Darlene shrugged. "She'll get over it."

Ruth Ann make a slightly derisive snort. "I don't think we oughta be paradin' her private business all over town."

"Pfft," Darlene responded. "It ain't news. You know how gossip flies 'round town. You can't hardly sneeze without someone puttin' ya on death's doorstep."

Alex laughed and rose when the doorbell rang. He looked through the peephole and smiled. He opened the door and asked, "Have you got an invitation?"

Startled, Toni said, "What? Ha ha," she added sarcastically.

"Everyone's in the living room pounding down whiskey and pizza." Toni smirked and Alex led her to the living room, where she took a seat on the couch between the sisters.

"You want some tea?" Alex asked.

"Is there liquor in it?"

Ruth Ann froze with a sudden look of concern.

"Only about a half-bottle of rum." Ruth Ann's eyes widened as she observed her nearly empty second glass. Alex waited a moment before laughing. "Just kidding. There's absolutely no alcohol in there." Darlene raised her whiskey glass to toast Alex for a good joke. She enjoyed seeing Ruth Ann squirm.

"Good," Toni said, "'Cause I gotta be at work early tomorrow."

"Have some pie," offered Alex.

"I thought we were having pizza," Toni said, trying to keep a straight face.

Alex spotted her attempt at humor and said, "Weak." She gave him a sour face.

"When're you gonna play for us?" Darlene asked.

"I guess now's as good a time as any." He sat at the piano and said, "Now, I don't take requests."

The ladies chuckled as Alex started the first piece. It was a medley of songs he'd played the previous week on the road. While it was mostly rhythm rather than melody, the combination of Alex's playing and the sound of the piano left the ladies awestruck. After nearly twenty minutes of playing, the trio erupted in applause.

"That was beautiful," Ruth Ann gushed.

Alex smiled and bowed.

Amazed, Darlene said, "Alex, you can't ever quit. I ain't ever heard nothing like that. God gave you somethin' you was meant to share."

"Keep playin'," Toni said. "Please."

"Let's hear another," Darlene called out.

"I only have one song left. I hope you like it."

He played a ballad he'd written years earlier when he fell in love with Ananya. He'd completed the music, but had never found the right words. It was his favorite composition, though he rarely played it for anyone.

When he finished, the room filled with stunned silence. The ladies were near tears. "Wow," Toni finally said, followed by applause from the trio.

Alex smiled, humbled by their obvious love for the song. "Thanks. I wrote that a long time ago."

"That's the most beautiful thing I ever heard," Darlene proclaimed.

Alex's smile grew. "Thank you."

"I mean it. You gotta record that so ever'one can hear it."

"I'd buy it," said Ruth Ann.

Toni said, "Seriously, Alex. You gotta record it."

"I've thought about it, but I've never been able to write good lyrics."

"It don't need words," Darlene said.

"Thank you."

Toni gazed at Alex like a smitten teenager. "I had no idea you were that good."

Alex wasn't comfortable alone in the spotlight, so he joked, "Thanks, but did you think I was just a hack?"

"No... I mean, I thought you were probably good, but man, I love that song."

"Alex," Ruth Ann asked humbly, "Will you play that again? Please."

"Yes, yes!" Toni and Darlene chanted.

"How can I say no?" He played it once more as the tears flowed.

"I could listen to that over and over," Darlene said with an unsteady voice. "Thank you, Alex."

"You're welcome."

They continued gushing over Alex's playing, despite his attempts to change the subject. They would never look at him the same way again, which was a double-edged sword for Alex. He was extremely flattered, but ill at ease being placed on a pedestal.

Before long, Toni looked at her watch and said, "I hate to say it. I gotta get up early."

Alex escorted her to the door and said, "Thanks for coming." He smiled at her enamored expression.

"Thanks for invitin' me."

"Stop by anytime."

Closing the door, he thought, That went well. We should go out.

He returned to the living room and Ruth Ann stood. "We should go too."

Alex looked at his watch and said, "It's early."

Ruth Ann said, "I told Dorothy I'd call her tonight so we could talk about her granddaughter's weddin' dress. I don't wanna wait too late."

"Hang on a second," Alex said, rushing to the kitchen and returning with a piece of paper.

Alex looked at Darlene and said, "A quick snort for the road?"

Darlene sat forward. "I ain't gonna say no to that. Ruthie, you go on ahead."

Alex escorted Ruth Ann to the door and handed her the piece of paper. "This is the recipe for the tea."

"Oh, thank you."

"You sure you have to go? I still have some of your peach cobbler I can heat up."

"Oh, no thank you Alex. You've done plenty. I just can't get over how beautifully you play."

"Thanks, but if you keep going, my head won't fit through the door."

She playfully swatted his shoulder. "You're a character." As she walked out, Alex kept a watchful eye to ensure she safely crossed the street.

He returned to Darlene and filled their glasses.

"Alex, ain't no way you can quit."

He took a sip of whiskey. "I'm glad you enjoyed my playing but there's more to it than thirty minutes in my living room."

"I don't know 'bout that, but you don't get to playin' like that 'less you got a gift. And if God gives you somethin', He means for you to use it."

"I've been using it for twenty years. Maybe it's time for me to find something else to use."

"It ain't up to you."

"Funny you say that. Ever since I decided to stop playing, I get call after call pulling me back in."

"There ya go."

"For now, I'm just going to take it as it happens. I wanted to write more and travel less, but it hasn't gone as planned. I sit at the piano, searching for ideas, but I end up rehashing old ideas or drawing blank."

"You can't succeed without first failin'."

"Then I should be super successful. I've spent a million hours failing."

"In my day, folks'd sell magazine subscriptions door-to-door. The ones who failed quit after knockin' on nine doors without selling a thing. But if they'd a knocked on one more door, maybe they'd a sold somethin'. And ever ten doors after that, they'd a sold another. You don't know how many times you gotta fail 'fore you succeed. Failin's necessary."

"I understand the analogy, but how does a songwriter find the right door?"

"I don't know, but I ain't ever heard nothin' as beautiful as what you played. If you got *that* in ya, there's more. You just gotta find it."

"Easier said than done." He took a bigger sip of whiskey, unable to dispute her logic, but eager to change the subject. "I'll keep you posted. I'm glad you and Ruth Ann came over."

"All you had to do was ask."

"I was surprised to see Toni."

"You invited her."

"I know, but after she warned me about people talking behind her back, I thought she'd keep her distance. She clearly doesn't like being talked about."

"No, she don't. But she also don't hide just 'cause folks are talkin'."

"I still want to know what happened between her and Andy."

"Like I said, they broke up."

"But you won't tell me anything more?"

"You said it yourself. She don't like folks talkin' about her."

"If I ask her, will she tell me?"

Darlene shrugged. "That's 'tween you and her."

"Maybe I'll ask."

"Alright," she said, raising her glass. "I could tell she liked hearin' you play. We all did."

He poured her a few fingers more with a smiled. "Thank you."

"I'll say it again. You got a gift, Alex. And God don't like it when you don't use His gifts."

"He told you that?"

"Don't fun me about God, Alex."

"Sorry."

"The Bible says, as ever man God has given riches and wealth, He has also empowered him to eat from them and to receive his reward and rejoice in his labor."

"But I'm not rich."

"He ain't talkin 'bout money. You're rich with talent. That's God's gift to you."

He nodded. "I do feel lucky to have what I have."

"You was put on this Earth to use that gift to serve others. That means you gotta keep on playin' or writin', or whatever God tells you to do."

"I don't exactly talk to Him, but I get what you're saying."

"Alex, I ain't gonna start preachin'. You're a grown man who makes up his own mind, but I believe in the Bible. And I believe God's got a plan for all of us, whether or not you know it."

"I wish He'd send me a copy of my plan, because I can't figure it out."

"All you can do is pray." She stood up. "And with that, it's time for me to mosey on home."

"You sure? I enjoy having someone smart to talk to."

"Shoot. I just use common sense and read the Word."

"I like what you have to say, plus you brought whiskey."

She picked up the bottle and nodded. "And I'm takin' it with me."

He let her out the door and watched her cross the street. She turned and waved before disappearing inside.

* * *

The following day, Alex texted Toni.
- *Hey. I'm looking for an excuse to get out of the house. How about lunch?*

She replied:
- *Can't. Too much work. Some other time.*

While Toni was 'over' Andy and moving on, she wanted some time to herself. She also wanted to avoid feeding the gossip mill by being seen in public with another guy, especially Alex.

Alex wanted to see if something more developed between himself and Toni, but it seemed too soon after her breakup to press things. After she declined his invitation to lunch, Alex left the ball in her court, focusing his attention on the bigger problems; his career and future.

The stream of offers to perform remained steady, but without the inspiration he'd lost, playing would continue being a slow, painful death.

Chapter 20

For several days straight, Alex concentrated on writing music. Having no success, he took a break and stepped outside where he spotted Darlene dragging her trash cans in from the curb. He hurried over and said, "Here, let me do that for you."

"Well thank ya, Alex. You wanna come in for a minute? Ruthie made some of that tea y'all like."

He sat at the kitchen table while Darlene poured him a glass. "How's everything going?" he asked.

"Oh, 'bout usual. Gotta find someone to cut that dang branch that keeps rubbin' against the house."

"I can do it. The previous owner left some tools in the garage." He ran across the street, retrieved a saw, and solved the problem within a few minutes.

"Alex, I 'preciate you doin' that. We had us a yardman, but he's too busy to fiddle with small stuff."

"Call me anytime. As long as you supply the beer."

Darlene chuckled. "You got a deal. C'mon, let me get you that beer." He followed her inside as she continued, "You're pretty handy fella, ain't ya?"

"I've done a lot of odd jobs. That's what you do when you're a poor musician. If you don't have a gig, you do what it takes to pay the rent. I've hauled equipment for other bands, set up light shows, unclogged toilets, painted, cleaned carpets, and plenty of other menial jobs."

"A job's a job," Darlene said.

"You said you were an operator. What else did you do?"

"Oh, not a lot. I used to volunteer on weekends at the hospital."

"Bet that was fun," Alex joked.

She shook her head, turning somber. "Back then, young men was comin' home from Vietnam. They was really strugglin'. I was a little older 'n the candy stripers, so it was my job to sit with 'em in case they wanted to talk."

The room fell silent before Alex remarked, "I'm surprised you didn't pursue nursing, having seen all that."

"I thought about it, but I was already married and workin' for the phone company. Wasn't time to go to school."

"If you had it to do it over again, would you become a nurse, or maybe a doctor?"

"I like what I done with my life, so I don't know that I'd a done anything different. I liked bein' a shoulder for them boys to cry on, but I don't think I coulda done it for long."

Alex nodded "I loved music as a kid and everyone told me I should do something in music, but I was worried it would lose its appeal if it became a job."

"And that's what you been bellyachin' about. You think it's a job and you wanna quit."

"It's not what it used to be."

"That's called life, Alex. Folk who have young'uns love havin' a baby, but after a few weeks of changin' diapers and gettin' up at all hours to feed 'em, it ain't no fun."

"But they get through it."

She nodded. "And look what they get."

"No more dirty diapers."

She laughed. "You get somethin' you can't put a price on. There ain't nothin' in this world that compares to my Antoinette."

"Hmm," he pondered. "When I listen to the songs I've written, I feel a sense of satisfaction."

"And it don't matter what anyone else thinks."

"No, not really."

"Love don't always make sense, but it lasts forever."

"Not for everyone."

"That ain't so. You still love the songs you wrote?"

"Yeah, but what about people who get divorced? Their love ended."

"Then they wasn't in love from the start."

"You think Toni didn't love the guy she married?"

"I think she still loves him."

"How can you say that? He cheated on her."

"That don't mean she don't love him. She might hate what he done and never forgive him, but if she loved him when she married him, she loves him now."

"That's hard to imagine, but what about this other guy, Andy? Does she love him?"

Darlene smiled. "Now Alex, I see what you're doin' there. You've been askin' me about that time and again, and I ain't answered. And I still ain't answerin'. You already know they broke up, but if you wanna know more, you're gonna have to ask her yourself."

"I heard it was a nasty breakup."

She gave him a firm look. "Alex, don't start fibbin'."

He smiled. "You can't blame me for trying."

"I don't."

After talking a few more minutes, Alex said, "If you need anything else fixed, call me. Just not too early in the morning." He tossed his empty can in the trash. "And, thanks for letting me hang out."

"Anytime."

* * *

Alex and Darlene chatted every few days, usually in the yard or on the street when they crossed paths. Sometimes they sat at Darlene's kitchen table and talked over a beer for Alex and a couple of fingers of whiskey for Darlene.

One afternoon they idled away the hours at the kitchen table exchanging small talk.

As evening approached, Darlene hadn't started drinking, but Alex, having pounded down his third beer, was antsy and rose to get a fresh one.

"Alex, I ain't one to judge, and lord knows I like sippin' on a few fingers of Jack, but it seems like you been bendin' your elbow more 'n normal lately. You alright?"

His speech wasn't slurring, but the way his thoughts bounced around worried Darlene. "I'm just frustrated from trying to write new music. I guess I've been drinking more than normal."

"You ain't gonna find the answer in a bottle."

"No, I know, but when your mind is stuck on something, or in my case nothing, alcohol helps unstick it."

"You know that ain't true."

"Says who?"

She smirked. "Are you unstuck?"

He set his beer on the table. "Touche." He looked at his open can. "Being drunk's not the same. But writing feels like staring into a giant black hole of nothing." He sighed and wandered toward the window.

"Alex, life's a journey. But it ain't always down the road you want, and you don't get a say in how things turn out. My husband, Joe, worked his whole life as a mechanic. He wanted his own shop, but ever'time he got ready to open up, somethin' got in the way. One time, he got close. He had the money and a fella outta Dallas willin' to work for him. Right before signin' the lease on a shop near Bell, he hurt his back and couldn't work. By the time he was healed, he had to start all over. You see, Alex, all you can do is try, and keep tryin'."

He stared out the window. "Uh huh."

"Listen to me," she said, drawing his attention to her. "Life's got its ups and downs, and you get what you get. Some folks get ever'thing, and others get nothin'."

He began thinking out loud. "I used to look forward to sitting at the piano. I always found something new and exciting to play." He sighed deeply. "That seems like a long time ago." He shook his head. "I blew it. I need a do-over."

He stumbled across the room toward the refrigerator, but Darlene intercepted him and maneuvered him toward the table. "Sit down, Alex, 'fore you hurt yourself. You're makin' me nervous." He sat, and she rose. She pulled a pitcher of water from the refrigerator, poured a glass, and set it in front of him. "Time out." She sat down with her own glass of water. "How, pray tell, do you think you blew it?"

"I was supposed to do something... something memorable; write a great song, maybe a film score ... something. I was supposed to get married. It was all like a... like a calling."

"A calling? From God?"

He thought for a moment. "Yeah, I guess."

"God told you that you'd do somethin' memorable?"

"Not specifically, but I always felt like I had something special that was supposed to be shared with the world. Like a song that people would remember."

"Okay, if that's true, why in the world would you quit tryin'?"

"Because maybe I'm not meant to be an artist."

"Pfft. You sure ain't gonna do nothin' if all you do is feel sorry for yourself, like you been doin' for weeks now." Her words sounded harsh, but he took them to heart, knowing she sugarcoated nothing. "God gave you a gift, and it ain't gone. You're just tryin' to fit God's plan into your schedule. Inspiration ain't somethin' you can buy at the store or read in a book. And it ain't somethin' you just decide to turn on. Alex, I think all them famous people drink so much and do drugs 'cause they ain't inspired when they wanna be, so they go searchin' for somethin' that can't be found in a bottle. And, just 'cause you got a lotta talent, don't guarantee you're gonna find it when you want it either. You might think you missed your callin', but unless you're dead, you ain't missed nothin'."

"I need a do-over."

"That's nonsense. There ain't no do-overs."

"Okay, so call it a second chance."

"Alright, then get one."

"Get what?"

"A second chance. Didn't nobody give you the first chance. You done all the practicin' and learnin' so you could have a career. Sounds to me like a second chance is up to you."

"I did get myself here…" his words trailed off as he wrestled with his thoughts. "I mean, I'd love another shot, but I need a great song."

While he spoke, Darlene stretched her arms out and bent her fingers a few times before slowly walking to the cupboard to retrieve a prescription bottle.

"You okay?"

She nodded. "I get a little stiff sometimes." She continued talking while ambling back to her chair. "Alex, God's gift ain't got limits. If He gave it to you, it's unlimited, like love. If you stop lovin' or creatin' or tryin', that's your decision, but the blessin's don't run out."

"See, I think God lets people wreck their lives. If we're free to accept or reject God, then we're also free to screw up our lives."

"That ain't right. You can't pick one side only and say it's the whole story. It was you who decided to quit and only you can change that. If you can wreck your life, then you can also fix it."

"Fix it by getting a do-over."

Darlene shook her head. "Antoinette said you was gettin' a bunch a crazy ideas from that book."

Alex's ears perked up when she mentioned Toni. "What else did she say?"

"Don't matter. Listen, God's got a plan, and that's all there is to it. Sometimes He gives you a challenge and sometimes He gives you a reward. But this nonsense about comin' back is nothin' but horse manure. If you believe you coulda done better, your life ain't over, so go do better."

"Why can't God's plan include a do-over?"

"'Cause it don't work like that. It don't matter what you done wrong, or what you coulda done better. God forgives you. He put you on this Earth to make mistakes, then repent."

"And if you don't repent?"

"Well, Alex, then you're gonna have to answer to God for that."

"And He's gonna send me to hell?" When she didn't say no, he continued. "See, this is where I have a question. With all the stuff that happens in life, hardships, loss, failure, wars, sickness, and so on, I can't believe God would send people to hell because they didn't figure out what He wanted them to do."

"For the wages of sin is death, Alex. That's what the Bible says."

"I understand there are people who are evil to the core, but I believe most are inherently good. And not everyone finds their way in life. Some need a second chance. A do-over."

"That ain't in the Bible."

"The Bible says believers go to Heaven, but it also says they don't go until the second coming. That means when we die, we don't go to Heaven right away. It could be a thousand years. It's possible that some of us keep coming back until we get it right."

"Pfft. That's nonsense. You die and you go to Heaven."

"I'm no expert on scripture, but ask your pastor why the Bible says believers will see Heaven at the second coming. That means they haven't gone there yet. Ask him."

"Listen, Alex, I like you fine, but don't challenge me with the Bible. I know what it says." Her tone was serious, but not threatening.

"I'm sorry. No disrespect intended. But the Bible talks about Christians going to Heaven *after* the second coming. I'm curious about what happens between death and Heaven."

"The Bible says the believers go to Heaven. Period."

"Right, but when?"

Darlene was tired and not feeling well. "I don't have all the answers, Alex, but I trust God has a plan. I'm gonna ask my preacher about that other nonsense."

Both smiled, but Alex could tell Darlene needed rest. He rose to leave.

"I appreciate you listening to me."

"Anytime."

"Let me know what the preacher says."

"Count on it."

Chapter 21

After a good night's sleep, Darlene insisted Toni drive her to see Reverend Brown.

"Why do you need to see the preacher?" Toni asked.

"I got a few questions for him and I can't ever get him on the phone."

"I only got an hour for lunch. Is it gonna take longer than that?"

"It'll only take a sec."

Toni parked out front while Darlene ambled in as fast as she could. She found Pastor Brown in his small, cluttered office. He stood and came to greet her halfway across the room.

"Good afternoon, Miss Darlene. It's so nice to see you. Please, sit down."

"Thank ya, pastor." She sat in a chair by the desk.

The portly reverend sat behind his desk wearing a friendly smile. "Now, what brings you by?"

"Pastor, a friend of mine tried to tell me that Christians don't go straight to Heaven when they die. I found some scripture that says the believers who've died are asleep and will rise in the second comin'. That'd mean some folks been sleepin' for more 'n two thousand years. 1 Kings 2 says David, Solomon, and Jeroboam rested with their fathers, not their *Heavenly* father. Then, in Thessalonians, it says the dead in Christ shall rise first. My friend also said some nonsense 'bout comin' back to Earth and usin' that time for a do-over. I told him that was hogwash, but I said I'd ask you."

"Miss Darlene, your friend poses a common question. The Bible teaches that death is like sleeping, as you read in 1 Kings. The absence of any reference to consciousness implies the believer is peacefully resting or sleeping in their grave. Removing the soul or person from that state and placing them back on earth is not part of God's word. Several religions subscribe to such beliefs, but those are the pagan-ish ideologies of the Far East. We learn from II Corinthians; to be absent from the body is to be present with the Lord. In Luke 23, Jesus tells a repentant criminal; Today you will be with Me in Paradise. Now, there are different interpretations of God's word, but rest assured, believers go to Heaven."

"But it might be a thousand years after you die?" Darlene questioned.

"Perhaps, but time would pass in an instant. 2 Peter 3:8 says; with the Lord, one day is like a thousand years, and a thousand years are like a day. You see…"

While Pastor Brown continued citing scriptures that supported his belief, Darlene let her mind wander, considering the implications of not going directly to Heaven. It was a revelation she didn't expect, and it made her think over her entire conversation with Alex.

After the pastor finished a lengthy explanation, Darlene stood. "Thank you, Pastor. This has been very enlightenin'."

"You are quite welcome. It is always a pleasure spending time with God's faithful." He waddled around the desk. "How's Miss Antoinette doing these days? I understand she and young Mr. Pharris had a parting of the ways, if you will."

"She's fine, Pastor, and thank ya for askin'. She and Andy decided they wasn't right for one another. You know how that is."

"Yes, well, you tell her I always enjoy seeing her shining face on Sunday morning. And let her know my door is always open if she wants to talk. You know, relationships can be difficult—"

"Pastor," Darlene interrupted. "I'm sorry to cut you off, but Antoinette's outside waitin' to drive me home, and she's only got an hour for lunch."

The pastor smiled. "No need to apologize." He led Darlene to the door. "I will see you all on Sunday."

On the ride home, Darlene stared out the window deep in thought. "Mom, you're awful quiet."

She snapped out of it. "Huh? Oh, yeah. I was thinkin' 'bout what the reverend said."

"'Bout what?"

"He said we don't go to Heaven when we die."

"What!" Toni shrieked, swerving to miss another car.

"Sorry, sweetheart. That ain't what I meant. We still go to Heaven, but Preacher said it could be a thousand years after we die. Said dyin's like sleepin'. I don't rightly understand 'xactly *when* we go, but it might not be right away."

"What does that mean?"

"It means Alex could be right, like he read in that book."

"What? I told you he was gettin' a bunch a crazy ideas."

"Maybe they ain't all that crazy."

Toni glanced at her mother. "Mom, seriously? No."

"I didn't believe it neither, but hearin' the preacher say folks is kinda like sleepin' when they're dead made me wonder. If we've been here more 'n two thousand years, that's a lotta sleepin' folks, and if you go back to Adam and Eve, that's a lotta souls."

"Mom, seriously. People don't come back as birds and cows, like the Hindu's think."

"'Course not..." She stared out the window, letting her mind run wild. Pondering the time between death and Heaven sparked a flurry of fresh thoughts. *Could you blink and a thousand years pass? Could you be with the Lord, but not in Heaven? If the body's gone, where's the soul—on Earth like a ghost?* Her faith and core beliefs weren't in question, but the mechanics of the afterlife and how it starts after death filled her imagination with wonder.

"You gotta quit hangin' out with Alex. He tried givin' me that same BS, and I told him when you die, you go to Heaven."

"That's what I always thought, but the Bible ain't clear on when we go."

"You don't seriously believe you come back?"

"I don't think your soul gets put in another body, but I ain't positive. Preacher said when you pass, you join the Lord, but then he said it's like restin' or sleepin', so even he ain't sure what happens."

"As long as we end up in Heaven," Toni said.

"Amen."

Chapter 22

Late that afternoon, Darlene sat at the kitchen table with a pad of paper and a pencil. It was her turn to write a column for the *Hamilton Gazette*, a twenty-page weekly newspaper that was delivered to most of the addresses in town, as well as published online. Larry Westin, the owner of the *Gazette*, subsidized the paper with his own money, and expected that it would become profitable someday. Larry recognized the importance of Hamilton's aging population and used the column to engage the aged and keep them subscribed. Twice a month, a different senior citizen wrote a short column called the 'Senior Bulletin'. Some authors reviewed the latest specials at the diner, while others promoted upcoming events like church fundraisers or the rodeo. The column had a small group of loyal readers, and occasionally scored a bigger audience when an author penned something especially interesting or entertaining, such as the time Dorothy Macintyre wrote about the dangers of outdoor grilling after her husband poured lighter fluid on an open fire and nearly burned down their house.

In the days following their discussion, when Alex suggested believers don't go directly to Heaven, Darlene could think of little else. She dismissed his idea of reincarnation as pure nonsense, but couldn't stop wondering about how time passed after death and before a soul reached Heaven. She pored over scripture and explored her own thoughts in search of clarity.

When she sat down to write the column, she let her unresolved thoughts flow onto the paper, which helped guide her toward *some* resolution. She sat for hours writing and reviewing, only to crumple up the paper and start over, much like Alex and his attempts at writing songs. As her understanding and opinion of the issue came into view, she realized the answer wasn't clear to anyone; not the preacher, Biblical scholars, or the believers such as herself who had studied the Bible for years. She began what would become the final version with the premise that all roads lead to Heaven, whether souls arrived there immediately after death, at the second coming, or after having led multiple lives on Earth.

While Larry asked for only one full page, Darlene's first draft filled three. Over and over she wrote and rewrote, working into the early morning hours until it was perfect and only one typed page long.

The following morning, Ruth Ann was up early and found the finished copy on the kitchen counter. After reading it twice, she almost stormed into Darlene's room to scold her for writing such a sacrilegious column. Christians in Hamilton believed in the traditional teachings of the Bible and did not tolerate any deviation. The mere idea of reincarnation or life after death outside of Heaven bordered on blasphemy. When Darlene arrived an hour later, Ruth Ann had calmed down but still had concerns. Darlene was barely in the room when Ruth Ann held up the paper.

"You can't give this to Larry."

Darlene paused on her way to the coffeepot. "Why not?"

"'Cause it's nonsense."

"Pfft."

Ruth Ann rattled the paper in the air. "I'm serious. This is a bunch a hooey like them California nuts would say."

"It ain't none of the kind. 'Sides, it's my column and I can write whatever I want."

"Well, you better hope Larry don't print it."

"He'll print it."

"No, he won't. He knows folks around here don't wanna read baloney like this."

Darlene snatched the paper from her hand. "This ain't baloney. I wrote what I thought, and if you'd a bothered readin' it, you'd see it says right there that I don't know any more 'n anyone else. I said folks oughta think about things different from the way they been thinkin' their whole life."

"Hmph," Ruth Ann snorted, knowing Darlene had her heels dug in. "Well, don't come cryin' to me when everyone starts whisperin' behind your back."

"They can whisper all they want." She looked at the paper and nodded. "I ain't changin' one word."

Miffed, Ruth Ann quietly retired to her room.

As lunch approached, Darlene noticed Alex pulling into his driveway. She stuck her head out the kitchen door and waved him over. Excited, she hurried him into the kitchen and handed him the final draft.

"I want you to look at this 'fore I give it to Larry."

Alex glanced at the paper. "What am I looking at? And who's Larry?"

"Larry's the fella you met at the fair. He owns the Hamilton Gazette. Ever month, one of the seniors writes a column for the paper. It ain't a big deal, but it's my turn, so this is what I wrote."

"He's the guy who tried to sell me advertising?"

"That's him."

Alex carefully read every word.

The Road to Heaven by Darlene Viriglio

```
    A young man down on his luck said
to me, "I messed up my life and I
need a do-over." "What do you mean a
do-over?" I asked. He said he wanted
a second chance at life so he could
avoid the mistakes that had put him
on the wrong path. I told him, "Life
doesn't work like that. You live
your life according to God's laws
and He rewards you with eternal life
in Heaven. End of story." The young
man insisted that the Bible says
when a man dies, he doesn't go
straight to Heaven. I said that's
nonsense, but his words got me
thinking.
```

The Bible says believers will spend eternity in Heaven. But the time between dying and going to Heaven isn't so clear. I always believed *Luke 23:43 … 'Truly I tell you, today you will be with me in paradise',* meant you went to be with the Lord the moment you died, but Daniel 12:2 says, *'And many of those who sleep in the dust of the Earth shall awake, some to everlasting life.'* And 1 Kings 2:10 says, *'Then David slept with his fathers and was buried in the city of David.'* Does that mean everyone who has passed is *sleeping* as the scripture implies?

The answer is no one knows. Some religions believe your eternal soul is returned to Earth for what the young man called a do-over. Perhaps, when a man or woman misses knowing God during their lifetime, they are given another opportunity. Maybe you keep coming back until you meet and accept the Father before proceeding on to Heaven.

Many live an unrepentant life of sin. They may be good souls who never knew the Heavenly Father, or hardship or the evils of their fellow man destroyed their faith at a very young age. What happens to children who pass before they can comprehend God? Should they die without knowing Him? I don't know.

> My friends, I can only say that we will be in Heaven someday with the Father. And the path to Heaven may only be through your one life on Earth. But since no one truly knows, no one can say that is the only path there is. Would a compassionate, loving and forgiving God only grant us one way to inherit His kingdom? Or are there many roads to Heaven?
> ~DV

When Alex finished reading, he looked up, astonished.

"This is incredible."

Darlene blushed. "It was you who gave me the idea."

"I'm surprised you wrote this. Seemed like you were mad at me for what I said."

"I was. I thought you was talkin' nonsense, but after I talked to the pastor, I did a little research of my own."

He smiled, again glancing at the article. "Well, this is great."

"Toni's comin' to drive me to Larry's. Should I let him publish it?"

"Absolutely! You're going to blow everyone away."

"Ain't a lotta folks gonna read it, anyway. There might be ten or twenty in all."

"Wow, double digits."

She snickered. "Wisenheimer."

They turned at the sound of Toni's truck rumbling into the driveway. Alex escorted Darlene outside as Toni was walking toward the door.

It was the first time Alex had seen her since texting her about lunch. He was excited to see her but expected a somewhat cool reception, thinking she would continue keeping him at arm's length until she was ready to date again. Surprisingly, Toni was smiling and in a good mood.

"Hey Alex. You over here hasslin' my mom?" she kidded.

"She asked to borrow my rock-climbing equipment."

Toni shook her head. "Always the wise guy."

Alex opened Darlene's door and held his arm out to assist her with the climb into the truck. "Good luck with the article. I think it's great."

Toni climbed into the driver's seat and rolled down the window. "See ya, Alex."

During the short drive to Larry's house, Darlene looked over her article.

"I heard Alex say the article's great. What's it about?"

"I called it 'The Road to Heaven'."

"That sounds interesting...." Toni suddenly remembered a conversation she'd had with a friend. "I forgot to tell you. Melissa Davenport got a job in Abilene. She asked me to help her move." Darlene didn't respond because she was focused on her article. "Did you hear me?"

Darlene looked up. "Yes, dear. That's nice."

"She's goin' to work for some advertisin' agency."

"Mmm hmm," Darlene mumbled.

Toni rambled on about Melissa, never returning to the discussion about Darlene's column.

They arrived at Larry Westin's house, a spacious two-story where he and his wife lived upstairs while the first floor served as headquarters for the *Hamilton Gazette*.

Marilyn, Larry's wife, greeted them on her way out.

"Larry's in his office," she remarked and pointed before continuing out the door.

Curious about the Westin home, Toni followed Darlene through the front door. Darlene continued to Larry's office—a converted den—while Toni perused the pictures on the wall. There were photos of Larry with several famous people, awards he'd won, and framed versions of previous editions.

Darlene found Larry sitting at his desk, leaning back with the phone to his ear. When Darlene entered, he clicked off and leaned forward, reaching for Darlene's page.

"Great. Let's see what you've got. Please, have a seat." Darlene gave Larry the article and sat across from his desk. He read the title aloud. "'The Road to Heaven'?" He gave her an odd look. "I was expecting another review of the arts fair."

"I thought I'd write about somethin' different this time."

He silently read the text, then looked up with wide eyes. "This is amazing."

"Thank you."

He read it again. "Darlene, you know this is gonna upset some people."

"You sound like my sister."

"You're endorsing reincarnation."

"No, I ain't, but so what?"

"I love it." He grew more excited with each passing moment. "This will really engage my readers."

Darlene felt relieved seeing Larry's enthusiasm. After Ruth Ann's warning, Darlene had reservations about how the locals would react.

Larry began transcribing her words into the computer. "I'm putting this on the front page."

Surprised, Darlene said, "Mercy!"

Darlene's outburst caught Toni's attention. She stuck her head in the office. "You ready, Mom?"

Darlene rose from her chair, and Larry hurried over to help her up. "Darlene, this is a game-changer."

"What's goin' on?" Toni asked.

Larry eagerly held up the article. "This is what's going on."

Toni took the paper from Larry and skimmed it. "Mom, what're you doin'? A lotta folks ain't gonna like this. 'Specially the Sunday ladies."

"Pfft," Darlene snorted. "What do them old biddies know?" It surprised Toni to hear her mother dismiss the friends she'd known for over half a century. "If they don't like it, they can lump it." She turned for the door.

Thoughtlessly, Larry remarked, "Popularity is overrated."

Toni glared at him. "You should know."

Larry considered firing back a spiteful remark, but his day was going too well to bother. With a smile, he lightheartedly said, "Say what you want. This piece shows great insight. I know the readers will enjoy having a spirited discussion."

"What do you care if everyone turns against her? You know how they talk and pick sides. Mom's gonna look like a kook just so you can sell advertisin'."

Larry shrugged, still smiling. "Listen, you can hate me, but this is something special."

Toni turned to her mother. "Mom, do you really want a bunch a BS 'cause a this?"

Darlene waved Toni off and started for the door. "I can take care of myself." She nodded at Larry and walked out.

Toni glowered at Larry. "This ain't over."

Toni continued voicing her disapproval all the way into Darlene's driveway.

"Listen, I don't need your approval," Darlene finally said. "'Sides, Alex liked it."

"Alex? Seriously? Mom, he don't know what it's like around here. He don't understand about all the BS talk that goes on." She paused, her expression turning suspicious. "Did Alex tell you what to write?"

Insulted, Darlene said, "I ain't gonna dignify that with a response. You go on now and don't come back till you learn some manners."

Toni waited until Darlene went inside before storming across the street to Alex's front door.

Chapter 23

Toni pounded on Alex's door several times.
 Alex answered, wearing shorts but no shirt.
 "Hey," he said, winded. "Sorry, I didn't hear the door. I was stacking boxes in the closet." He stepped back, and she barged into the living room. "Well sure, please, come in."
 She spun around and shouted, "Do you know what you've done?"
 "Uh, no."
 "You filled my mother's head with a bunch a BS."
 "I'm guessing this is about the article she wrote."
 "Now she's mad at me just for sayin' somethin'. But she's gonna piss off the whole damn town!" Alex walked across the room and grabbed a T-shirt draped across the couch. He motioned for her to follow him to the kitchen.

He pulled a pitcher of tea from the refrigerator while she continued.

"You're actin' like everything's fine, but you don't understand what's gonna happen."

Any response from Alex would be gas on the fire, so he quietly continued fixing himself a cold drink, giving Toni time to vent.

"She's gonna to be a laughin' stock thanks to you." When he offered no response, Toni snapped, "So, you're not gonna say anything? You're fine with turnin' my elderly mother into an outcast? Is that who you are?"

Alex had seen Toni wound up before and thought she simply needed someone to listen, so he played it cool.

"No, of course not. Do you want some tea?" he nonchalantly offered.

Toni's thundering response nearly tore the roof off. "No! I don't want a damn thing from you. How could you?"

She turned to leave, and he immediately realized that playing it cool was the wrong approach.

"Wait," he said. "Please." He offered her a chair.

"I ain't gonna sit 'cause there ain't nothin' to talk about." She folded her arms, fuming. "I can't believe this." He poured her a glass and set it on the kitchen table, then calmly sat. She remained standing, alternating between folded arms and hands on hips. "You don't get it, do you?"

He shook his head and sincerely said, "I'm sorry. I guess I don't. Help me out."

She plopped down in the chair and exhaled heavily. "God, I'm so angry with you, Alex. Hamilton's a tiny little town, and Mom's a fixture around here. Everyone turns to her 'cause she's the rock that never budges."

"She is tough."

"She is, but you're clueless about what goes on here. Do you know how bad it's been for me 'cause a Andy?" Alex shook his head, appearing curious but concerned. "I've lived most my life here, and everyone knows me, but they didn't think twice about turnin' on me. Accordin' to them, I was cheatin' on Andy with you! They accused me of endin' things with Andy, but he was the one who got mad and started actin' like a fool. But that's not the story anyone told. They heard a bunch a BS and now they believe I'm the cheater who broke up with Andy, and he did nothin' wrong." She stopped for a moment to gain control over her heavy breathing and unclench her jaw. "And that's just some of it."

"I had no idea."

"That's why I keep tellin' you, Alex. And now you talk Mom into writin' this BS that's gonna make her look like a kook."

"I didn't talk her into anything. And I don't think she's going to look bad at all. She said no one reads the paper."

"Normally they don't, but when Larry puts that crap on the front page—like he said he would—and they find out what she wrote, they'll all read it."

"So?"

She slapped the table. "So! Everyone's gonna read that bullshit you sold her. It'll spread like wildfire."

"I understand people here are incredibly conservative, but she wrote about going to Heaven. That's hardly controversial."

"She said it's okay to believe in reincarnation! That ain't what Christians believe. They're gonna think she lost her marbles."

"Darlene's a big girl."

"She's an old woman. What's she gonna do without friends, or worse, if her friends mock her?"

Alex scoffed. "I pity the first person who mocks Darlene."

Toni took a deep breath, still angry, but pausing as the reality of Alex's words struck her. "Yeah, she can take care of herself, but it's gonna be sad when everyone thinks she's lost it."

"But she hasn't lost it."

"That don't matter. Folks are gonna talk. And like I told you, they'll believe what they hear, 'specially if it's the only thing they hear all day. Just like some of 'em'll always believe I cheated on Andy… with you."

He rose to refill his drink. "Listen, I'm sorry about what happened to you because of Andy, but it sounds like there's nothing you could've done to change things. I mean, if the truth is being ignored, what can you do?"

"Exactly!" she barked. "You don't give 'em anything to talk about. If the gossipmongers don't know nothin' they ain't got nothin' to spread."

He shook his head. "They're going to talk no matter what. If you hide the truth, they'll just make something up. I say ignore the BS and be who you are. Your mom can take care of herself." He chuckled and continued. "Every time I think I've outsmarted her, she responds with something I've never thought of, or she shows me how I'm wrong. Like my career. She made me realize my problems are self-inflicted, but more importantly, they're fixable. Listen, I read the article and there's no doubt in my mind she can defend every word. She thought things out, read books, went to see her pastor, and even found the scriptures that support what she's saying."

"She shouldn't have to defend herself. You shouldn't a started it."

He smiled. "I think she'll enjoy defending herself and, like I said, the article wasn't my idea. I didn't start this. Hell, when I read it, I was just as surprised as you. But seriously, your mom's one of the greatest people I've ever met. I'd never do anything to hurt her. And I don't think she going to get near the backlash you think."

Toni's anger was waning. "I just wanna protect her. I worry about her."

"I know, but you can't predict how people are going to react. They might love what she wrote."

Toni shook her head. "I know exactly how they'll react. I ain't the only one who's been lied about. And it ain't really about the lies." She paused, wanting Alex to understand where she was coming from, but apprehensive about revealing more of her past. "Remember when we first met?"

"At Gibson's."

"I said I don't know why anyone'd wanna live in Hamiton."

He nodded.

"When I started datin' Virgil, my ex-husband, I heard all kinds a crap like he could do better, I was just lookin' for a meal ticket, and a bunch a other BS about how he was good and I was trash. I ignored it, but when we got engaged, folks started sayin' I was pregnant, which I wasn't. They said I was cheatin' on him, which I wasn't, and a bunch a total BS."

Alex tilted his head. "Why? I mean, I haven't known you long, but I can't imagine people having that kind of opinion of you."

"It's what I keep tellin' you. They believe the lies. And for me it goes back to high school. I started datin' this guy after he broke up with a girl named Laura. She was beautiful and popular. She told everyone I stole her boyfriend and was sleepin' with him."

"In high school?"

She nodded. "Everyone believed Laura, the perfect princess. I barely dated after that because every guy thought I was a slut or a cheater or both."

"Man, that's terrible."

"It was. After high school things got better, but when I met Virgil, it all started back up. I was a cheater, I was a slut, and Virgil oughta get away from me."

"Obviously he didn't listen."

"No. Virgil knew there were liars who liked spreadin' BS. He couldn't wait to leave Hamilton either." She again paused before saying, "It ain't nobody's business, but Virgil was… I'd never been with anyone before him."

Her confession surprised Alex, but her story struck him deeply.

"So, you see, it don't matter what the truth is. A couple a jerks decide to spread BS and before you know it, the whole town hates you. It happened to me and I've seen it happen to others."

"Man, I understand why you wanted to leave. I'm sorry you went through that, but I'm glad you told me. I see why you've been so reluctant about things like having lunch together."

She felt better that Alex knew more about her, but also felt vulnerable. "I wouldn't mind goin' to lunch or somethin' but I don't wanna make things worse with people talkin' and stuff."

He nodded. "I get it. Someday we'll make it happen, but it's your call."

"Someday."

Both felt a connection, but a lull in the conversation made the moment uncomfortable.

"So, your mom said you moved back because this is home to you."

"It is, and the BS ain't as bad, probably because I'm older and enough people found out the truth about Virgil cheatin' on me. But I know they're gonna say Mom's crazy and spread BS." She shook her head. "I know it 'cause I've seen it."

"I hope you're wrong about your mom."

She shook her head. "They'll spread crap about anything."

"Surely Darlene knew the risk. Maybe she wanted to stir up some controversy."

"That's stupid. Why would she want people makin' fun of her?"

"I don't know. Maybe because she's right and wants to challenge the status quo."

"She ain't never done that before."

He shook his head. "From what you've told me, she's done it lots of times. She's always stood her ground when challenged."

Toni thought for a second. "Yeah, maybe, but I don't think she realizes what she's gettin' into this time."

"Let's see what happens before you make yourself sick worrying."

"Too late for that."

The distant sound of the doorbell caught both of their attention.

"Pizza delivery?" she asked.

"No." Puzzled, he walked inside the house. Following close behind, Toni froze when Alex opened the front door and came face to face with Baneta.

"Alex!" Baneta cheerfully called out.

Toni's eyes lit up and her lips tightened, thoroughly appalled.

Alex was shocked.

"What are you doing here? And how do you know where I live?"

"When I want something, I get it." She flashed a cutesy smile.

Toni glowered at Baneta, then at Alex. Having just opened up to Alex, she felt betrayed. "Why am I not surprised?" she said, marching past Baneta and out the front door.

Alex tried to catch her. "No! You've got it all wrong," he called out, but Toni never looked back. She walked straight to her truck and drove away.

Alex stood in the front yard, shaking his head, dumbfounded. He fired a disapproving smirk at Baneta standing in the doorway. "Thanks," he remarked, believing Baneta had just destroyed a trust he'd been hoping to build with Toni.

"Is this a bad time?" Baneta thoughtlessly asked.

"Very. How did you find me?"

"Easy. I asked a guy at the gas station if he knew where Alex the musician lived."

Although Baneta was stunningly beautiful, Alex was angry and could only see her as having damaged his fragile relationship with Toni.

"You have to leave."

She stepped closer, put her hand on his arm, and spoke in a seductive voice. "Are you sure?"

He sensed she was going to kiss his neck and stepped back. "Yeah, I'm sure. I'm sorry if I gave you the wrong impression at the fair, but you can't be here."

Baneta left and Alex immediately texted Toni, asking for a chance to explain. She didn't respond. He considered calling her, but decided to give her some time.

Chapter 24

The following day, Alex still found no success at the piano. In the afternoon, exhausted from his efforts, he opted for a breath of fresh air. He went to the front yard in search of a project, like mowing the lawn. When he saw Darlene at the mailbox, he waved and walked over.

"So I guess you heard about Toni being mad at me," Alex said.

"That's alright, Alex. I was a little miffed at her after she drove me to Larry's to drop off my article."

"What did Larry think?"

"He liked it better 'n Toni and Ruthie."

Alex smiled. "Toni gave me an earful. She thinks everyone will think you're crazy."

"Pfft. She and Ruthie like bein' mother hens. I told both of 'em I can take care of myself."

"That's what I said to Toni, but man, after she told me about high school and how they treated her, I understand why she's that way."

Darlene looked surprised. "She told you all that?"

Alex nodded. "But then she got mad when that young girl from the fair showed up out of nowhere."

Darlene raised her eyebrows. "That young number sellin' books?"

Alex nodded.

"I can see why Antoinette left in a huff."

"That's an understatement. She probably thought about shooting me."

Darlene chuckled. "She might a thought about it but she ain't likely to follow through."

"I hate that she was starting to trust me and this happens."

"I'm surprised she told you 'bout Virgil. He really done a number on her, but she's tough."

"I know, but I hate that I opened the wound."

"Give it time." Alex nodded but Darlene could tell he was bothered. "You wanna snort?" she offered. "Help take your mind off your troubles."

Alex looked at his watch. "It's a little early."

Darlene waved a hand. "It's Saturday."

"What the hell."

Inside Darlene's kitchen, they ran into Ruth Ann. "Hello Alex," Her tone was a little cooler than normal.

"Good morning, or I guess it's actually afternoon."

"Hmm, yes I suppose."

"Where are you goin'?" Darlene asked, noticing Ruth Ann was carrying a purse.

Ruth Ann hesitated. "I'm going shopping."

"With who?"

"That's my business."

Darlene waved her away and started for the cupboard. "I don't care what you and Antoinette do."

"No one said anything about Toni," Ruth Ann corrected.

"Okay, then who you goin' shoppin' with?"

Before Ruth Ann could respond, Darlene heard Toni's truck pull into the driveway. She gave her sister a knowing look.

"Hmph," Ruth Ann snorted and hurried out the door.

With Toni's help, Ruth Ann climbed in the truck and they left.

"So I guess we're both in the doghouse?" Alex remarked, taking a seat at the table as Darlene set two glasses and a bottle of whiskey down.

"I ain't in the doghouse. The hens decided I was wrong 'bout the article so they got their dander up."

"I'm sure Toni told Ruth Ann about what happened yesterday, so she's mad at me, too."

"Alex, them two's the first to complain 'bout gossip but I can guarantee you this, they're gossipin' right now. And it ain't no big mystery what they're talkin' about."

"You and me?"

She nodded and they clinked glasses.

* * *

Before reaching the end of the street, Toni said, "I guess Mom's hell-bent on publishin' that stupid article."

Ruth Ann nodded. "Sometimes I don't understand my sister."

"She and Alex are in for some serious BS."

"I ain't worried about Alex, but I hate to see my sister being ridiculed."

"And that's exactly what's gonna happen. You can bet Cynthia's gonna toss gas on the fire the moment she finds out about the article."

"I begged Darlene not to do it, but you know my sister, stubborn as an old mule."

"Alex thinks Mom'll ignore everyone, but he just don't know."

"I told everyone to watch out for anyone from California."

"And you were right. And him seein' that young girl from the fair…"

Ruth Ann nodded, sharing Toni's disgust. "I knew he was an operator from the day we met him, especially when that… that woman answered the door."

Toni sighed, punishing herself for showing vulnerability. "I shoulda listened to you."

"Dear, none of us knew for sure. But now we do."

"I can't believe I opened up to him."

Ruth Ann misinterpreted her remark. "What? While you was seein' Andy?"

Toni chuckled. "No, not that. I mean when I told him about the jerks in high school and how folks treated me with Virgil. I thought Alex was different."

"Oh. Sorry, dear. But I'm glad you found out before you really did open yourself up to Alex."

Toni smiled at Ruth Ann's implication. "Well, that wasn't gonna happen anyway, not anytime soon."

"Maybe you and Andy can work things out."

"No way. I need some time alone." Despite knowing it was the right thing to say, she immediately felt lonely. She reflected on her easy and open conversation with Alex. She liked him. He was different; kind and sensitive, and honest, she'd thought. *Was he tellin' the truth?* she wondered. *There's nothin' going on. That little slut just showed up?*

They pulled into the market and shifted their conversation away from Darlene and Alex.

The following week was quiet, with Alex out of town, Toni catching up at work, and the sisters following their normal routine; Wednesday church and Friday shopping.

Before Sunday morning church, Darlene ordered Ruth Ann to keep her mouth shut about the article.

"They ain't gonna like it," Ruth Ann said.

"I don't care, but I don't want you tellin' 'em what's comin'. Let 'em find out Thursday."

"You're afraid I'm right."

Darlene chuckled. "You ain't, but even if you was, I wouldn't care. I just don't want ever'one talkin' 'bout somethin' they ain't read. So you just hush for now."

The Sunday school meeting went like most; drinks and gossip.

It wasn't long before Cynthia started making wisecracks.

"We all know Andy tried his best, but it wasn't good enough for Toni."

Darlene took a deep breath, ready to unload but Sarah jumped in ahead of her. "Now, you know as well as anyone that every couple fights and says things they shouldn't. That doesn't mean Toni did somethin' wrong."

Cynthia righteously said, "She wouldn't even give him a chance to explain why he was with another girl, who, by the way, was just a friend."

Irma fired off the next rebuttal for Cynthia. "Would you let your husband spend time alone with Victoria Olsen?"

Cynthia snorted. "She's half his age. My husband wouldn't even look at Victoria Olsen."

"You sure about that?" Darlene quipped.

"Listen," Cynthia hissed. "Don't you dare accuse Hudson of bein' unfaithful."

"I ain't accusin' no one," Darlene said, pleased with Cynthia's reaction. "But it ain't so nice when the shoes on the other foot."

"Hmph," Cynthia grunted, folding her arms. "All I know is Toni wouldn't listen to a word Andy had to say."

"Why would she?" Darlene asked. "If it was over between 'em, what's it matter what he says?"

"Well," Cynthia said. "It's just common courtesy."

"Would you listen to Hudson if he'd been kissin' Victoria?" Darlene taunted.

Cynthia's eyes lit up. Ready to spew hate, she held her tongue. "I won't even dignify that with a response."

"I wish you'd use some of that *common courtesy* on my daughter. You know it ain't right spreadin' nonsense you know ain't true."

"I only repeated what I heard," Cynthia defended.

"C'mon," Sarah argued. "You repeated what Madelyn Pharris got from Andy."

"And who knows how many glasses of wine she'd had by then," Irma added.

"Bottles," Dorothy piled on, drawing laughs.

Darlene smiled but said, "Now y'all quit. I like a good story too, but y'all know Madelyn ain't like that. That's what I'm talkin' about. It's alright for us makin' fun in here, but when it gets passed on as true... well, that ain't right..." she turned to Cynthia. "Is it?"

"Don't look at me."

Dorothy scoffed at Cynthia's remark. "You're the first person to twist a story into something that's not true."

"And spread it around," Sarah added.

"Okay, so sometimes I embellish, but y'all do it too."

"Not like you."

"She's right," Darlene said, surprising everyone. "Cynthia ain't the only one to stretch the truth. Sometimes Ruthie tells a whopper."

"What!" Ruth Ann shrieked. "I never."

Everyone laughed at Darlene's teasing, which released the tension in the room. The gossip persisted, but the ladies made an effort to be more truthful.

* * *

Darlene's column came out Thursday morning. Sarah was the first to call.

"Hey Dar, I love what you wrote."

Darlene snapped her fingers. "I forgot. It's Thursday."

"Hon, you really outdone yourself this time. I read it three times."

Darlene smiled. "Well, thank ya. I was worried y'all might think I was a little off."

"Not a chance. You know, I never thought about anything but goin' to Heaven after dyin', but you really got me thinkin'."

"Well, thank ya. I never thought about it either till I started talkin' to Alex."

"I knew he was who you was talkin' about in the article."

"He gave me the idea, then I talked to Pastor Brown."

"Preacher agreed?"

"Not about the comin' back part but he didn't say we go straight to Heaven. So I decided he don't know any more about that than anyone else. That's why I wrote what I wrote."

"Well, it makes me wonder what's goin' on when we die. I mean, I ain't worried about not going to Heaven, but that time in between… ain't never thought about it."

After they hung up, Ruth Ann, having overheard Darlene's side said, "What'd Sarah say?"

"She liked what I wrote."

"Well," Ruth Ann said incredulously. "Sarah's your friend. She ain't gonna say nothin' bad to your face. Wait till the likes of Cynthia read it."

"Sarah ain't never pulled punches with me. And I don't give a hoot about what Cynthia says."

Ruth Ann rummaged through the mail on the kitchen table and found the newspaper. "Oh lord," she remarked, afraid the frontpage placement would hasten the inevitable trouble. "That's not where it normally is."

Darlene took the paper from her and smiled proudly. "Well how 'bout that?"

"Wait till Preacher reads it. He'll have somethin'—" The phone rang, cutting her off.

It was Irma. She and most of the inner circle had similar comments to Sarah's, leaving Darlene feeling proud. In fact, none of the callers had anything negative to say, surprising Ruth Ann, who reiterated her belief that Darlene's friends were reluctant to challenge her.

Chapter 25

Toni received the first call from Cynthia Coker.

"Have you read what your mother wrote?" she said contemptuously.

"I know, and before you start spreadin' it all over town, remember Mom's been hangin' out with Alex. I think that's where she got the whole idea." Toni didn't fully believe Alex was responsible, but she wanted to deflect some of the imminent backlash away from her mother.

"I'm not surprised," Cynthia said. "He's been nothing but trouble since he got here."

Toni ignored the remark, knowing not to feed into Cynthia's gossip.

"Mom's article is just her way of sayin' somethin' new. It doesn't really mean anything."

"She's calling herself a Hindu."

"Seriously?" Toni protested. "Mom said *maybe* people get reincarnated. She certainly didn't say the Bible's wrong or that she ain't a Christian, and she did *not* say she's a Hindu."

"Not in those words, but listen, Toni, I know she's your mother and you love her, but she's getting old and maybe her mind's not the same."

"Cynthia, stop!" Toni shouted, startling Cynthia. "I don't want you makin' up stuff that could hurt my mom."

Cynthia feigned sincerity saying, "Oh no, Toni. I'm not trying to hurt anyone. I'm just talking about what your mother wrote. I don't have to make up anything. It's all there in black and white for everyone to read."

Toni knew Cynthia was being deliberately provocative and contained her outrage. "Just let everyone form their own opinions," she calmly requested. "You don't need to add things like callin' her a Hindu or sayin' her mind's goin'. You know that ain't so and it's just mean."

Getting a rise out of Toni brought a smile to Cynthia's face.

"You know I'm just kidding. I didn't mean to upset you."

"I'm fine," Toni lied. "But I also heard a bunch a BS goin' around about me and Andy."

"I was so sorry to hear about you two."

Toni nearly gagged at Cynthia's disingenuity. "Thanks, but it's for the better. But since I can't stop folks from talkin', I wanna set the record straight."

"Well, I didn't believe it, but I heard you cheated on him."

"That's total—!"

"Not my words," Cynthia interrupted.

Toni gritted her teeth, certain that it was Cynthia who had been spreading the lies. "Well, just so you know, I never cheated on any man, ever! And if the truth be told…" She suddenly reconsidered dragging Andy through the mud. "It wasn't about cheatin' or anything like that. I told Andy I wasn't ready to get married. He wants to get married, so we broke up. We both said some stuff, but all this BS about cheatin' is total crap."

"I understand," Cynthia said insincerely. "Breakups are hard."

Toni was ready to scream at Cynthia's patronizing, but held her tongue and delivered a convincing performance. "They are. But next time you hear someone talkin' about it, please tell them what really happened."

"Of course. You know we all like to talk, but I'll make sure they hear what you told me."

"I appreciate it. Listen, I gotta run."

"See you Sunday," Cynthia said with a lilting tone that further irritated Toni.

"Talk to you then," Toni signed off sounding completely unaffected by Cynthia.

* * *

On Friday afternoon, Toni drove the sisters to the market for the weekly shopping.

Almost immediately, they heard whispers as they walked up and down the aisles. The remarks were inaudible until they reached the checkout line. Janice Weatherly, a young mother whose family had lived in Hamilton for generations, pulled up behind them.

"Darlene, I heard about what you wrote in the paper."

"Oh?" Darlene inquired, anticipating her first negative review.

"I ain't read it yet but Mom liked it. Said it surprised her."

"Tell her thank ya."

Toni and Ruth Ann started unloading the groceries onto the conveyor for checkout, keeping a close eye out for trouble.

"I will. And I'll make sure I read it too. Mom said it was about gettin' a second chance or somethin'?"

Darlene nodded. "I don't wanna spoil it for you. Give it a read and let me know what you think."

On the way home, Ruth Ann said, "You ain't gonna get nothing but trouble."

"What're you babblin' about?"

"I told you not to write that nonsense. Now, everywhere we go, folks are gonna go makin' a scene."

"She's right, Mom."

"Pfft. One person—who, by the way, liked it—ain't exactly a mob."

Ruth Ann grimaced. "You heard all those whispers. I told you, most folks ain't willin' to confront you."

"This could be the tip of the iceberg," Toni said.

"Y'all are puttin' the cart before the horse." Darlene wore a defiant face, but the whispers gave her pause.

* * *

Word of Darlene's article continued spreading quickly around Hamilton. And while the negative comments still weren't reaching Darlene or Ruth Ann, a few friends confided in Toni with remarks like, "I can't believe she wrote that," and "She's been spending too much time with that guy from California." Toni never shared those or the ones made by Cynthia Coker with her mother, hoping they were outliers.

Larry Westin called Darlene Saturday morning—two days after publication—in a frenzy. "I've only got a second," he said. "But can you stop by my office later today?"

"I gotta ask Toni to drive me. Is ever'thing alright?"

"Everything's great. I'll see you this afternoon." He hung up.

Toni set aside her disapproval of her mother's actions, despite still feeling miffed. *What's done is done,* she concluded.

Darlene and Toni found Larry on the phone working madly in his office. He pulled the phone away from his ear and smiled while extending his hand, saying, "Please have a seat."

Settling in the chairs across from the desk, Larry hung up the phone and silenced the ringer. He took a few seconds to catch his breath before focusing focused on the ladies. "Wow. Darlene, I could kiss you."

Surprised, Darlene grinned. "Well, no thank you. What's this about?"

Larry was nearly manic. "Life is good!" He leaned back, exhaling deeply. "Darlene, your article has ignited a firestorm." He lunged forward and rolled his chair over to a credenza where he lifted a stack of papers. "This is why I asked you to stop by. This is a small portion of the responses I've gotten today. I printed them out for you since I know you don't have email."

"That's nice."

"You don't understand. CNN.com picked up your article and posted it on their website. That means national, perhaps international exposure. Thousands, maybe *millions* of people will read your article. You're going viral!" His wide eyes resembled a child on Christmas morning.

Darlene slapped Toni on the leg. "Well, how 'bout that!"

Toni felt foolish for disagreeing with her mother. Her opinion of Darlene's article made a complete about-face. "Outta all them people, how many liked Mom's article?" Toni asked.

Larry stood. "Almost everyone." He spun his computer screen around. "We've received over eight *thousand* emails. Maybe two didn't like it." He again lifted the enormous stack of papers. "The website has crashed three times."

"Because of Mom's article?"

"And that's just the beginning. CNN, among others, want a follow-up article."

"'Bout what?" Darlene asked.

"It doesn't matter. They just want to hear from you. If you read some of the emails, you'll find lots of questions, along with lots of praise." He pulled several pages from the stack and began reading aloud, "Judith Evans from Portland, Oregon wrote: 'Darlene, I'm not a religious person, but after reading your article, I dug out my Bible and started studying.'" He flipped the page. "Terrance Brooks from Chicago said: 'I lost my faith years ago because of all the greedy TV preachers, but when you said no one really knows where we go when we die, I realized it's between me and God.'" He looked at Darlene. "These go on and on." He read one more. "'You woke something in me. Thank you.'"

"All them people wrote in 'cause a what I wrote?"

Toni rose and started skimming the replies. She'd never been happier about being wrong.

"I've never seen anything like it," Larry said.

Amazed, Toni began reading from the stack of papers. "Simple words that speak to me." She flipped through several more. "Thank you… Inspiring… Well written… Thought provoking." She glanced at Larry. "Where did all these come from?"

"Everywhere. All over the world. Darlene, you started something incredible. Now I need you to follow it up."

"It ain't my turn. I think Irma's after me?"

"That doesn't matter. The public wants to hear more from you."

Darlene waved her hand. "That ain't right. 'Sides, I had my say."

"But there are countless people who want more from you."

Darlene let the reality sink in while Toni continued thumbing through the responses. "Some of these are amazin'. This guy wrote: 'Darlene, I've always believed John 3:13. No one has ascended into Heaven but He who descended from Heaven, the Son of Man. But I never considered what happens between leavin' the body and enterin' Heaven. I'm intrigued.'" She continued reading, then laughed. "At breakfast this mornin', God told me you weren't wrong." She set the papers down and looked at Larry. "How many people wrote in?"

"I lost count, but over eight thousand."

"And those are just the folks who wrote back?" Toni asked.

Larry nodded. "The website has had thousands of hits. Facebook, Twitter and other social media channels have also received thousands of likes, shares, and comments. I can't really tell with CNN. Their comments go on endlessly, but the numbers are unbelievable. And, there are a ton of comments saying they're looking forward to your next article."

"Man, Mom, folks really like what you said."

Larry settled down and faced Darlene. "You've started something very special. Now it's time to push it forward."

Darlene pointed at the stack of papers in Toni's hand. "I ain't gonna read all them."

Larry chuckled. "Read some of 'em to understand people's thoughts, then write a general response. I'd like to publish a follow-up article in a couple of weeks. We can tease them with the next issue on Thursday, then publish a new article the following week. Maybe do a special edition."

"I don't know," Darlene said, looking at the thick stack of responses.

Toni sat down and put an encouraging arm around her mother. "Why not, Mom?"

"'Cause I already had my say."

Toni smiled. "When've you ever run outta things to say?"

"They wanna know more 'bout dyin' and goin' to Heaven, and I already wrote ever'thing I know."

Larry said, "You might think you've said it all, but after reading the emails, you'll have a lot more to say."

"I guess I can give it a try," Darlene said apprehensively.

Larry turned the phone back on and it immediately started ringing. Before answering it, he loaded a folder full of papers. "Here are some emails I printed. Call me when you have a first draft."

Darlene started thumbing through the responses during the drive home. "I can't answer all these."

"You don't have to, Mom. That's not what he wants."

Darlene continued reading. "These folks are askin' things I can't answer. Like this fella askin', why does God let babies die?"

"That ain't for you to answer. Larry wants you to figure out what they liked about your article."

The ride was quiet until they pulled into the driveway and Darlene said, "I'll get Alex to help."

The hair on the back of Toni's neck stood up at the mere mention of his name. She was still mad about Baneta. "He's already done his part by givin' you the idea."

Darlene ignored Toni. "If Alex'll help me, that's the ticket."

Toni hurried around the truck to help her mother out. "You don't need him. Remember, it was your words that started all this."

"Sweetheart, I know you're mad at him, but I want him to help." Darlene paused, wearing a pensive expression. The overwhelming reality was catching up with her. "It don't seem real." She quickly broke the trance and stood taller. As they started for the door, Alex pulled into his driveway. Toni tried to hurry her mother inside, but Darlene had already caught sight of Alex.

"I gotta tell Alex," she said, bolting—as well as she could—across the lawn toward his house. Toni stayed behind. Alex spotted Darlene coming and met her in the middle of the quiet street.

She relayed everything Larry had told her and that he wanted her to write a follow up. She showed him the stack of responses. "So, can you help me?"

"This is fantastic! Congratulations."

She blushed and waved him away. "Quit it. They was your words to begin with… So you'll help me?"

"I'd be honored."

"How 'bout you come over and we'll sit around the kitchen table?"

Alex was all smiles until he noticed Toni standing by her truck with her arms folded. "I'm guessing Toni won't be joining us."

Darlene glanced at her daughter. "Nah, she's still mad 'bout that young lady showin' up at your house."

"When do you want me?"

"I need time to read all these. You should read 'em too. I'll bring some over later."

"Works for me."

"Then, I need a couple a days 'fore I'm ready to start writin'."

"I've got lots of time. Just let me know."

"Count on it. Thank ya, Alex."

Chapter 26

On the first Sunday after Darlene's article came out, Sarah stood behind the bar at the Superbowl taking drink orders. She soon noticed Darlene hadn't raised her fingers to request a glass.

Sarah delivered the drinks while Irma set the snacks out.

"You sure you don't want nothing?" Sarah asked Darlene. "Water?"

Darlene shook her head no, surprising Ruth Ann. "Hon, you feel alright?"

"I'm fine. Just a little tired."

"You've been working late," Ruth Ann commented.

"Converting from Hindu to Islam?" Cynthia sniped.

Sarah glared at Cynthia. "What're you talkin' about?"

"She said reincarnation's okay, like Hindus. Now she's quittin' drinkin' like a Muslim? So, which is it? Are you a Hindu or a Muslim?" She stood in her customary spot a few steps away from the group because she was special.

Darlene turned to respond but Ruth Ann, knowing her sister didn't feel well, stood and said, "You got somethin' to say, missy? Say it."

With Ruth Ann not advancing, Cynthia shifted her posture onto one leg and folded her arms. "I think Darlene's column is blasphemous and she should be ashamed. And I'm not the only one who thinks that."

Uncharacteristically, Ruth Ann abruptly stepped forward, startling Cynthia enough to step back. "Listen, my sister's got every right to believe whatever she wants. And it ain't up to you to judge." She stared down Cynthia for a heated moment before sitting.

"I'm with Ruth Ann," Irma said. "I don't have to agree with what Darlene or anyone says, but they got a right to say and believe whatever they want."

"It ain't just me," Cynthia fired back. "Why do you think Miss Virgina and Bertha ain't here? They agree with me that Darlene shouldn't a taken liberties with the scripture and written what she wrote."

Darlene responded with a less thunderous voice than usual. "Well, that's on them. 'Sides, who put you in charge of what I can say or write? Maybe you oughta talk to Pastor Brown 'bout what I wrote, and while you're at it, ask him 'bout that scripture that says he who has no sin shall cast the first stone."

"Don't you dare quote scripture to me," warned Cynthia. "You're the one who threw the Bible out the window and gave a ringing endorsement of paganism. Ain't nothin' you can say to defend that."

Darlene chuckled, then winced slightly from a sharp pain. "And I ain't gonna try. If you wanna run around town tellin' folks I'm crazy, I ain't gonna stop ya. But maybe you oughta read what I wrote first."

"Oh, I know what you wrote."

"It don't sound like it."

Sarah said, "When the article first came out, Me and Irma talked about it, and we both said the same thing."

Irma chimed in, finishing Sarah's thought. "We never thought about there bein' time between dyin' and goin' to Heaven. Then I read John 3:13 'No one has ascended into Heaven 'cept he who descended from Heaven, the Son of Man.' That made me wonder about what Darlene wrote."

"And it didn't seem so crazy," Sarah said.

Cynthia wasn't ready to back down. She glared at Darlene. "How can you call yourself a good Christian tellin' the entire world you agree with some third-world pagan religion?"

"I don't think that's what she was saying," Dorothy defended. "I looked up lots of scripture and I agree with everyone else. God's plan might give everyone more than one chance to know Him."

Darlene shook her head at Cynthia. "You're just stirrin' the pot 'cause you ain't listened to what I said. 'Sides, what I believe's 'tween me and God."

"You, God, and now the entire world. *You* put the words out there. Don't try hiding behind God now." Cynthia was in her element, believing she had Darlene on the ropes.

"I ain't hidin' behind nothin'. Why're you so all fired up 'bout it anyway?"

"Because you criticize everything I say as if you never say anything wrong."

"That's 'cause you make up stuff and say so many ignorant things. I ain't pretendin' to be perfect, but I ain't the one spreadin' nonsense just to rile ever'one up."

"Hmph," Cynthia grunted. "Well, people outside of Hamilton are gonna think we're a bunch of godless heathens."

"Pfft. You don't know what folks are thinkin'. And just 'cause I wrote a few words in the newspaper ain't gonna turn Hamilton into Sodom and Gomorrah."

Several ladies chuckled, but Dorothy cautiously said, "I understand what Cynthia's sayin'. I mean, to me there's nothin' wrong with Darlene's article, but Larry said folks all over the country are readin' it, and I don't want 'em comin' here thinkin' we all believe in reincarnation."

Darlene snickered. "That's nonsense. Ain't no one comin' here 'cept for the fair, and certainly not 'cause a what I wrote."

"And even if they showed up lookin' for a temple or somethin' like that," Sarah said. "They ain't gonna find one."

"They'd find us just as we are," noted Ruth Ann. "A small town of God-fearin' Christians."

Darlene looked at her watch and said, "We gotta go." She stood, motioning for Ruth Ann to join her.

"Dar?" Sarah said. "You don't have to leave."

"Don't let Cynthia run you off," Irma added.

Darlene chuckled. "Pigs'll fly 'fore Cynthia Coker's mouth runs me off. Larry asked me to write another article so I gotta get started. And I've been feelin' a little pekid lately, so Toni's pickin' us up a little early."

"You alright?" Sarah asked.

"I'm fine. Y'all go on. Sarah, call me later and catch me up on anything I miss."

* * *

Pastor Brown called Darlene on Monday. "Miss Darlene, I was hoping to catch you after the service yesterday. I must say, your article in the Hamilton Gazette has created quite a stir."

Darlene wasn't sure if he was praising or scolding her, but his tone was pleasant. "I tried to tell it like I see it, Pastor."

"Oh, no. I was pleased with what you said and impressed with how you said it."

"Well, thank ya."

"I called to thank you."

"For what? I didn't think you'd approve of what I wrote, it not all bein' in the Bible and all."

"Ah, yes, but to paraphrase your own words, no one has all the answers. As Christians, we like to believe ours is the only truth. But the learned man realizes there is more that he does *not* know than he knows."

"Amen."

"And that has been my response to the faithful, and to those questioning their faith who have sought my opinion of your article. While they may not agree with everything you wrote, they are all seeking answers for their own lives. Your article has inspired many not to question their faith, but to explore it further. Your words are a blessing for our church and for everyone. That's why I called to thank you."

"I'm kinda taken aback, Preacher."

"Miss Darlene, rejoice in what you have done. Your voice is His voice, and He is proud of you."

"Thank you kindly."

"I will see you on Wednesday and God bless you."

After they hung up, Darlene stared at the phone for a minute, feeling choked up. The pastor's words were the push she needed to work on the follow-up article.

* * *

Darlene's article was the talk of the town. At Whitman's, patrons overheard comments like, "I hope Darlene's right 'cause there's a couple of things I'd like to do over," and "It's pretty wild for an old church lady like Darlene to write somethin' that ain't strictly spelled out in the Bible." Most echoed the sentiment that the article made them reconsider what they already knew or thought they believed. One young man said, "I never enjoyed bein' around churchies 'cause they expect me to believe what they believe, but Darlene pretty much put 'em all in their place when she wrote, no one knows for sure."

Sitting at the dinner table, Buford McCaleb said to Ada, "I don't know that I'd wanna come back."

Ada shook her head. "I'm too wore out. Unless I got a recharge, I couldn't make it again."

Buford chuckled. "That ain't what I was worried about. Imagine tryin' to live like young folks today."

"Lord, if I gotta act like that, take me once and call it a day."

* * *

The article sparked numerous discussions around Hamilton, but very few found her words disturbing or offensive. Everyone assumed they would reach Heaven, and saw no harm in adding a few extra steps. The idea of starting over and fixing past mistakes intrigued some while providing comfort and hope to others as they imagined the possibilities it could bring to their lives.

* * *

Throughout the week, Darlene read through stacks of responses, jotting down notes, then taking them across the street to Alex in batches.

Between searching for inspiration at the piano, Alex read through the responses.

I believe in the Bible, but in church they always want to tell me what it means. Your article made me realize I should read the Bible and think for myself. ~Gary, Stillwater, Ok

Losing my big brother in 1990 at such a young age (thirty-five) was devastating, but I smile at the idea that his spirit is back on Earth. We can never have enough people like him. Thank you for putting the possibility in my heart and mind. ~Andrew, Midland, Tx

Alex placed his hands on the piano and closed his eyes, immersing himself in the stories of those who had written to Darlene. He briefly escaped the confines of his own thoughts. It was encouraging but short-lived.

Darlene also found inspiration sitting at the kitchen table, poring over responses.

You made my day. My (so called) friends like to pick on me for having my own opinions. I like wearing vintage clothes but they call me names and make fun of me. Your article reminds me it's okay to have an opinion and my own style. Thank you. ~Lizette, Des Moine, IA

Can bad people still enter Heaven? What if I don't get a do-over because of all the bad things I did when I was young? I know the Bible says God will forgive me, but he can't forgive everyone, can he? I'm nicer than I used to be but I can't fix what

I did unless I get to go back. Any response would help. ~LT, Victorville, CA

Some messages were hard for Darlene to address. She was comfortable being a sounding board for her local circle of friends because their problems seemed manageable; abusive husbands, broken hearts, health problems, etc... But some of what she was reading tugged at her heart in ways she'd never imagined. She prayed for wisdom, not to solve their problems, but to give her insight into the questions that had no simple answer, hoping she could offer *some* comfort.

* * *

By Sunday, the excitement about Darlene's article was still high, especially with the senior ladies. The weekly meeting at the Superbowl got underway with a round of drinks.

"Dar," Sarah started, setting a glass of whiskey in front of her. "That article of yours is all I hear about. Folks are askin' if you're gonna write another."

Darlene pushed the whiskey away. "Y'all know Larry wants me to write another."

Sitting next to her sister, Ruth Ann noticed Darlene abstaining from liquor. "Hon, you feel alright?" she softly asked.

Darlene subtly waved her off but quietly replied, "I'm fine."

"How's that Alex doin'?" Irma asked.

"He's fine," Darlene said.

Worried, Ruth Ann leaned over to Darlene and said, "Let's you and me go home and you can get some rest."

"I'm fine," Darlene reiterated, but she wasn't. She'd been working hard and had slept little.

At the end of their hour, the ladies downed their drinks, put their shoes on and filed out.

At home, Darlene continued moving slowly, concerning Ruth Ann. "Hon, you want me to make you some tea?"

"Nah, I'm gonna take a short nap. Then I gotta lotta emails to get through."

Ruth Ann wanted to express her concern, but pressing Darlene about her health would only irritate her.

Darlene's short nap turned into several hours of restful sleep, giving Ruth Ann a sense of relief.

Chapter 27

Alex and Darlene waited through the weekend to get a fresh start on Monday afternoon.

They bounced ideas back and forth for hours at Darlene's kitchen table, both with a drink, paper and pencil. Ruth Ann tried her best not to disturb them, but she remained nearby out of concern for Darlene's health.

"We got a few ideas here," Darlene said, reviewing her notes. "But I don't know if it's what folks are lookin' for."

Alex shuffled through the stack of responses. "A lot of these people sound like me."

"How's that?"

He pulled out a single response. "Like this guy; 'I messed up every relationship I had. I gave up long ago, but you've made me reconsider fixing things.'"

"That don't sound like you. You said you was quittin'."

"Exactly. This guy quit, but he's thinking about trying again."

"You sayin' you're gonna try again?"

"No. I'm saying I can relate. He messed up every relationship. I messed up my opportunities at success."

"Listen, Babe Ruth struck out over a thousand times 'cause he kept swingin' for the fences."

Alex turned sharply. "I didn't know you like baseball."

"I don't, and don't try changin' the subject."

He smiled. "You want a refill?"

"Alex," she warned him.

"Okay. Babe Ruth could afford to strike out because he had what it takes to hit a home run. I repeatedly swung for the fences but missed every time."

"Considerin' what you been doin' with playin' and all, failin' to hit the big time in music ain't what I'd call a major failure."

"It is to me. I've spent my whole life working toward it."

"I spent five years tryin' to get pregnant. Then when I did…" she paused to choose her words. "I didn't exactly get what I wanted."

Hesitantly, Alex said, "The son you lost."

"Joey passed when he was eleven."

Alex hated resurrecting her pain. "I'm sorry. Was he older than Toni?"

"He passed the year she was born."

"Man, that had to be a tough year."

She nodded somberly. "You talk about missin' your callin' and gettin' a do-over and all that… I've seen how life is. Joey was just the sweetest thing. Broke my heart watchin' him suffer. Then, when God called him home, I felt guilty 'bout feelin' better."

"Because the suffering was over?"

She took a long drink. "See, Alex, I got a second chance with Antoinette, and now with writin', I'm gettin' another chance at doin' somethin' that helps folks. I never set out to be a writer but I'm willin' to do whatever God calls me to do. Whatever comes next, it's up to Him. You just keep prayin' and movin' on."

"I'm sorry you had to go through that. I feel foolish complaining about my life compared to what you went through."

"It ain't the same. But part of who you are is what you do. A mother don't have a career in motherin' but that's who she is. You're a musician 'cause that's who you are, good or bad. And I understand what it feels like to lose who you are…" She paused to again organize her thoughts. "But that ain't all you are, just like a mother ain't just a mother. You been livin' each day doin' what you believed was right, but so far it ain't turned out exactly like you wanted. Now you wanna look back and say you done it wrong—failed—and quit? That ain't right and you know it. You pick yourself up and move on, just like I done when Joey passed. Most folks aren't as fortunate as you. They struggle ever day tryin' to pay the bills, fightin' with their loved ones, sick children, and lotsa other things you ain't had to fuss with."

Alex humbly nodded. "I'm very fortunate. Of course, I've had setbacks—one big one in particular—but I've spent most of my life having a blast. I always wanted to give something back. I guess that's why I feel like I messed up. I was busy having fun and blowing off the future when I should have been planting some seeds, so to speak. You raised a child, helped your friends, and now you're writing.

I have nothing like that; something that will outlive me, like a great song or children."

"That ain't why you're here. You've been givin' back by sharin' the gift that God gave you. And you got a lotta years left. Ain't nothin' stoppin' you from givin' back even more, startin' today."

"I'd like nothing more, but the older I get, the more it seems like my creativity and inspiration have dried up."

"Alex, them are just excuses, and I don't buy 'em for one second. Grandma Moses didn't even *start* paintin' till she was my age. And Julia Child didn't write her first cookbook till she was fifty. Nothin' goes down till you die, 'cept the body. The soul never changes."

Her words gave him pause. "What makes you say that? People evolve and change every day."

"Folks learn to be better or worse, but inside, they're the same. A bad young'un grows up to be a bad person."

"But there's lots of bad people who've changed their evil ways."

"Then they wasn't bad to begin with. 'Member, lotsa kids ain't been raised proper. They ain't always taught right from wrong. That don't mean they're bad, just means they wasn't raised right. Them are the ones that change their ways when they grow up."

"I guess it's the difference between what everyone sees and what's actually inside."

"Only God knows what's in your heart. That don't change. We ain't no different now than we ever was, only what we're doin' is."

The conversation paused when Ruth Ann wandered in to fix herself a glass of tea. "I don't wanna bother y'all," she said.

Alex noticed her pouring from a pitcher she'd pulled from the refrigerator. "Is that my friend's secret recipe tea?"

"I can't get enough of it. I wish my sister'd drink more of it and less whiskey."

"Pfft," Darlene said, putting a hand on her drink.

"I know," Ruth Ann continued. "I ain't your keeper." She gripped her glass and started for her room but paused, bothered by Darlene's tired look. "I do wish you'd take it easy."

"Alright, mother hen."

Ruth Ann looked at Alex pleadingly, hoping he would also suggest that Darlene get some rest. Alex noted Ruth Ann's concern, but didn't feel it was his place to comment.

After Ruth Ann left, they studied their notes before Alex said, "You know, we've got a few good ideas, but I like what you said a minute ago for an article."

"Okay, I'm an old lady, so remind me what I said." She tapped her glass on the table. "And get me a tiny refill. Also, bring me them pills in the top kitchen drawer."

He responded while completing the chore. "You said the soul never changes. Even though we're the same inside, people like me feel defeated by our self-inflicted failures. There are so many things I should've done differently, and maybe God will forgive us for our mistakes, but it's too late to start over. We still want what we've been working towards—for me success—but it's passed us by. *My unchanging soul is stuck with failure.*"

Darlene downed a pill with a glass of water, followed by a small sip of whiskey. "I'm not sure about that self-inflicted part, but I agree that God forgives sins. But, some folks can't get over the sins of others, and they can't forgive themselves, like you. You're twistin' this whole thing up into somethin' it ain't. You ain't defeated. You just got it in your head. You hit a dry spell and think you're a failure, and the more you dwell on it, the worse it gets until you can't do nothin' at all."

He tuned out for a moment as Darlene's words echoed through his mind. *They can't forgive themselves. You just got it in your head.* "I think I understand."

"Understand what?" she asked, noticing the preoccupied look on Alex's face.

"Once you cross that line and give yourself a label—failure, loser, defeated, whatever—you stop questioning it. Once I decided my career was a series of failures, that's all I saw."

Darlene smiled. "Exactly. You get an idea in your head, and even if it's wrong you believe it's true. And it goes beyond what you're thinkin'. Folks say hurtful things and never speak again. They're still good people but they can't forgive one another or themselves. They'd rather go on bein' miserable than puttin' it behind 'em and movin' on."

"But how does that relate to the unchanging soul?"

"Like you said, you ain't no different inside today than you was when you thought you was full of ideas. And neither is someone who said somethin' unkind they shouldn't a. God knows your heart, but folks let pride and stubbornness get in the way. Or in your case, you just decide you ain't gonna keep tryin'. Life gives what it gives, but it's up to you to make somethin' out of it. But when you decide to give up 'cause you got a bum steer, that don't mean somethin' inside's changed. The soul never changes." She paused and closed her eyes, clearly experiencing some discomfort. She slowly exhaled. "Now, help me get it on paper 'fore I forget."

After she tweaked and dictated the words to him, they looked over the finished copy together.

The Good in All of Us (Shed the Labels)
by Darlene Viriglio

After my last article, folks wrote in asking a lot of questions like, How does God decide who gets into Heaven? Who, if anyone, gets a do-over? Can I still go to Heaven if I don't go to church, pray, or even if I'm not sure I believe in God? The answer to these is, I don't know. But I'll tell you what I believe.

I believe we are all sinners and unworthy of God's rewards. But I also believe He forgives us and wants us to grow in our relationship with Him because he sees the good in all of us. Proverbs 27:19 says, 'As water reflects the face, so one's life reflects the heart.' While good people make mistakes that God forgives, people don't always forgive themselves, though they should. We remember our failures, our shortcomings, and most of all, we carry the discouraging labels we've accepted throughout our lives. Some of those labels we gave to ourselves, while others were given to us. We hear words like failure, stupid, loser, and jerk echoing through our minds day after day, year after year, and we allow those words to hold us back. I think we should be more like the Lord and learn to forgive ourselves.

    Proverbs 15:4 says, 'A gentle tongue is a tree of life, but perverseness in it breaks the spirit.' I have a friend who wants to give up his career because he thinks he's failed. I remind him of a legendary guitarist who could barely read and write, a man many would call ignorant, but also a man who wasn't defined by his inability to read and write. He was beloved worldwide for the way his life reflected his heart through sharing his God-given talent as a musician. Had that man given in and allowed others to define him solely as being illiterate or dumb, the world may never have been blessed with his music. I told my friend that just like this guitar player, he should never label himself a failure, nor should he give up on what he loves. He should be more hopeful. Romans 12:12 says, 'Rejoice in hope, be patient in tribulation, be constant in prayer.' Everyone makes mistakes and everyone has shortcomings. We all have bad days and do dumb things but that doesn't make us bad or dumb. It makes us unique and interesting.

    My friends, shed the negative labels you've learned to accept, and

```
never allow them to become a
lifetime of self-inflicted wounds.
In this way, you can have a do-over
in this life. Forgive yourself and
move on. Listen as God speaks to your
heart through things like hope,
redemption, forgiveness, and
perseverance. He knows there is a
good soul, a special soul, a one of
a kind soul inside almost everyone.
Let the gifts God has blessed you
with and the good He sees in everyone
be the force that guides you. ~DV
```

Satisfied with the final version, Alex said, "You want me to drop this off at Larry's?"

"You know where he lives?"

"No, but if you write down the address, I'll find it."

She jotted down the address and said, "'Preciate it, Alex."

Chapter 28

The Wednesday church service was shorter and more informal than the Sunday morning worship, with only a few dozen attending.

Darlene was pale, and moving slower than normal, but insisted she was fine. She sat with Ruth Ann, Irma, and Sarah while Pastor Brown delivered the sermon. Ruth Ann kept a close eye on her sister, worried about the declining energy she'd witnessed over the previous several days.

When the congregation lowered their heads for the final prayer, Darlene remained slumped after the final amen.

Ruth Ann knew something was wrong. She nudged Darlene. "Hon?" Darlene lifted her head halfway and stared at Ruth Ann. Her eyes were glassy and unfocused.

"Are you okay?" Ruth Ann asked. Darlene nodded, but struggled to keep her head up. Ruth Ann jumped up. "Someone, help me!"

"I'm fine," Darlene mumbled as several congregants rushed to her aid.

"Get her some water!" Irma called out. "Dar, honey, what's wrong?"

"She can barely hold her head up," Ruth Ann said.

Darlene was pale and lethargic but still managed to wave her hand. "Quit your fussin'," she said. "I'm just a little…" Her word trailed off as her eyes closed and she started to fall forward.

Irma caught her before she fell out of the pew and shouted, "Call 911!"

While Sarah made the call, Ruth Ann tried to revive her sister.

"Hon," Ruth Ann said, first patting Darlene's hand then her face. "Darlene, wake up." When Darlene barely moved, Ruth Ann began panicking. "Darlene!" she shouted, shaking her sister.

A young man arrived with a glass of water. Irma put her fingers in the glass and splashed water on Darlene's face. "Darlene," Irma called. "Wake up."

"What're we gonna do?" Ruth Ann cried out.

"Give her some air," Irma said, motioning for everyone to step back.

Ruth Ann remained seated next to her sister while Irma again splashed water on Darlene's face and stretched her out on the pew with her head in Ruth Ann's lap.

"Somebody do something," Ruth Ann begged.

Sarah took a seat next to Ruth Ann and calmly said, "The ambulance'll be here any minute."

Darlene was in and out of consciousness, her eyes slowly opening and closing but never focusing on anything.

For Ruth Ann, an eternity passed before the ambulance arrived. Once the paramedics took over, Ruth Ann stood nearby saying, "Hang in there, hon." She was on the verge of collapse but the surrealness of the situation kept her from breaking down.

The paramedics assessed Darlene's condition, checking her blood pressure, heart rate, and respiration. All three were low. They quickly hooked up an IV.

Darlene's condition improved; her eyes were open and she was looking around, but her color was poor, and she was very still and quiet.

"We need to transport her immediately," the paramedic said as they lifted Darlene onto the stretcher.

Ruth Ann held her sister's hand as they wheeled Darlene out of the church. When they got to the ambulance, the paramedic gently motioned for Ruth Ann to step back. "She's in good hands," he said.

Ruth Ann was nearly paralyzed with fear but still demanded, "I'm goin' with her."

Without hesitation, the paramedic assisted Ruth Ann into the ambulance where she regripped her sister's hand.

With Darlene on her way to Hamilton General Hospital, Irma called Toni with the news.

"Oh my God!" Toni shrieked. She had a million questions, but simply said, "I'm on my way." She hung up and raced out the door.

* * *

Not long after Toni arrived at the hospital, the doctor appeared in the waiting room.

Toni jumped up and said, "How is she?"

"She's resting," the doctor replied.

"What's wrong with her? Can we see her?" Toni anxiously asked.

Sarah, Irma, and Ruth Ann all stood, hoping to see Darlene.

The doctor put up a cautionary hand. "Not at this time. We ran a few tests, and we suspect Ms. Viriglio may have contracted viral pneumonia."

"May have?" Toni repeated.

"Although she doesn't exhibit the typical symptoms of coughing and lung congestion, it is likely that she was exposed given her advanced age and the recent viral outbreak."

"What's that mean?" Toni asked.

"We will run more tests, but right now bed rest is the most important thing."

"So we can take her home?" Ruth asked.

The doctor shook his head. "Her condition is very serious. She will need to be here for several days, at least."

Ruth Ann began tearing up. "When can I see my sister?"

"She resting comfortably now. Let's see how she's doing in the morning."

Ruth Ann was overwhelmed by stress as she took a seat, completely drained of energy. Sarah took the seat next to her and said, "She's gonna be fine."

Ruth Ann suddenly stood up and said, "I wanna see her."

The doctor reassured, "She won't know you're there. We are keeping a close eye on her, so my advice to you is to go home and get some rest."

"No! I wanna see my sister."

The doctor studied Ruth Ann for a moment before giving a nod. "They're transferring her to a room now, but I'll come get you as soon as she's settled."

* * *

Darlene lay on her back, peacefully asleep in a room partitioned by a curtain to accommodate another patient. She had an IV in her arm, while a few machines hummed softly nearby.

Ruth Ann stared at her sister while a nurse stood nearby.

"We should let her sleep," the nurse whispered.

Ruth Ann disregarded the nurse and proceeded to move a chair beside the bed. She sat down and gently held Darlene's hand.

The nurse departed, only to reappear few minutes later. "Ma'am, I'm sorry, but she needs to rest," she stated as she extended her hand towards Ruth Ann.

"I ain't leavin'."

The nurse started to object, but instead left. Upon her return, she drew back the curtain, revealing a second bed.

"They said you can stay, as long as you let Ms. Viriglio sleep."

"I promise."

The nurse gently placed her arm around Ruth Ann's shoulder and said, "You also have to promise me that you'll lay down and get some rest. You must be exhausted from all this."

Ruth Ann glanced at the bed but didn't rise from the chair. "I'm alright, but thank you. I'll try."

Darlene slept for most of the next day and a half.

* * *

Unaware of Darlene's illness, Larry published the second article on Thursday morning, the day after she was admitted to the hospital.

After the first article, several news outlets, along with a few social media influencers, had asked Larry to notify them when the next article was released. He emailed those who'd requested notification then sat back and waited for the mayhem to begin.

The influencers wasted no time initiating lively discussions on major platforms. Darlene's simple but empowering call to shed the labels that were holding people back resonated with a large audience. Several major media websites linked to the new article, and within the first few hours the responses overflowed the comments section of the *Hamilton Gazette*. By the end of the second day, Darlene and her articles were considered viral sensations.

"The Good in All of Us" peaked on day three, but traffic remained high. Message boards, social media, and direct emails to Larry all begged for more articles from Darlene.

The volume of requests and the public's appetite for all things Darlene was more than Larry could handle, so he set up a blog-type page for Darlene to pen a daily or weekly column. He also created an email address for her and placed it on the *Gazette's* website so the public could email her directly.

Larry was busier than he'd ever been, thanks to Darlene's column, which also kept him unaware she was ill. It wasn't until late Thursday that he learned Darlene was in the hospital in serious condition. He stopped by on Friday to check on her, but Toni and Ruth Ann intercepted him in the hall.

"How's she doing?" Larry asked.

"Not good," answered Toni.

"She's sleepin'," Ruth Ann added. "And I don't want no one upsettin' her."

"I came to share the good news about the article."

"It'll have to wait."

Disappointed, Larry asked, "Is there anything I can do?"

While Toni was happy about her mother's success, she blamed Larry for enticing Darlene into working too hard. Seeing her mother seriously ill and fearing the worst, Toni unleashed her emotions on Larry. "You can say what you're thinkin'; that you need her to write another article and her bein' sick's gettin' in the way."

"That's not fair."

"Whatever," Toni said, rolling her eyes. "It's true. I'll tell her you're circlin'."

"Please don't be like that."

"I told my sister to slow down," Ruth Ann remarked.

"She's barely slept since you started all this," Toni added. "Do you know how stressful it's been for her; readin' all them emails and havin' deadlines, all 'cause a that stupid article?"

Larry immediately realized arguing would do no good. "I'll come back later."

"Don't bother," Ruth Ann said. "She ain't seein' no one till she's outta the hospital."

"No one?"

"No one 'cept family."

"But I need to talk to her."

Sternly, Ruth Ann said, "Look, she ain't gonna be workin' on nothin' but gettin' better. The doctor said if she doesn't rest and take it easy, she could get worse. And I ain't gonna let that happen."

"Please let her know I was here and that we need to talk as soon as she's up to it."

"I'll tell her, but I ain't makin' no promises she's gonna call."

"You might have to do without her," Toni suggested.

Larry nodded and walked away. He ran into Alex coming from the opposite direction.

"How's she doing?" Alex asked.

"They wouldn't let me see her."

"I guess she's still out of it."

"I wanted to update her on how well the article did, but Ruth Ann wouldn't even consider it."

Alex smiled at the thought of Ruth Ann denying Larry access.

"She's pretty tough, too."

"She is," Larry agreed. "But surely Darlene could use some good news."

Alex smiled and held up a folded piece of paper. "I brought her a printout of some of the responses posted online. From what I saw, the second article is doing well."

"Better than the first," Larry said, glancing at his watch. "I'm sure by the time I get back to my computer, my inbox will be overflowing."

"That's a high-class problem," Alex joked.

"What? Oh, yeah. It's a problem." He pulled out his cellphone. "Emails are pouring in and my phone is blowing up. I really need to talk to Darlene."

Alex tilted his head. "About what? She doesn't have anything to do with email or the website."

"Not yet, but I'm setting up an email account for her so she can handle the readers and their comments. I'm also thinking about adding a blog for her."

"You know she doesn't have a computer."

"I know, but one of us can get her a laptop or something simple just for email and posting to the blog."

Alex nodded. "I can handle that, but it's really up to her if she wants to answer email and do a blog."

"That's why I need to talk to her. I'm sure she's gonna want to do it, especially after she hears how great the second article is going." He looked at his watch. "I gotta run. Will you talk to her for me?"

"I don't know if they'll let me in," Alex said. "But if they do, I'll tell her." Alex wasn't a big fan of Larry's, but he knew the articles were very important to Darlene. He was also eager to share several responses posted on the website.

Alex approached Darlene's room but stopped when Ruth Ann and Toni blocked the door.

"You can't go in," Ruth Ann stated. "Doctor said she's gotta rest."

"Not even for a minute?"

Ruth Ann shook her head.

"Not even to bring her good news about how well her article's doing?"

"'Specially not for that. I don't want her gettin' all excited. You need to let her be for now."

"I understand," he said, respecting Ruth Ann's authority. He turned to Toni. "Will you call me when she's able to receive visitors?"

Toni nodded and motioned for Alex to escort her to the elevator.

"Look Alex, she's really sick and we're all worried. I didn't wanna talk in front of Aunt Ruthie."

"Anything I can do; check on the house, bring you guys some food or something?"

"Thanks, no. We got it covered."

"Okay, but please don't hesitate to call me. Even if you just want someone to talk to."

They exchanged a quick hug before he left.

* * *

The following day, Darlene's condition worsened, pushing Ruth Ann close to a breakdown. She remained by her sister's side twenty-four hours a day, allowing only Toni and the hospital staff in the room. Darlene mostly slept through the day but the following day she bounced back. She was awake, hungry, and somewhat back to her old self, surprising everyone, including the doctors.

Toni relayed the good news to Alex but suggested giving her another day before visiting.

Alex stopped by on Monday but Ruth Ann again intercepted him outside Darlene's door. However, when Darlene heard Alex's voice in the hall, she insisted they let him in. Ruth Ann gave Alex a stern look. "Don't rile her up. I mean it."

"I promise," Alex said, adding a reassuring nod.

Darlene was seated upright on a tilted bed, her head on the pillow looking tired and gaunt. Alex put on a smile to hide his shock and concern.

"Hey slacker," he joked.

"Very funny. Good to see you."

"How are you feeling?"

"Been better."

"Well, with Ruthie out there running blocker, you should get plenty of quiet time."

"Quiet time, hell. I'm bored silly." She started a deep, guttural cough but took a sip of water, which calmed the cough.

"Has anyone told you about the response to the second article?"

"I asked my sister and Antoinette but they won't tell me nothin'. Did folks like it?"

Alex smiled and shook his head. "You're lying in a hospital bed, coughing up a lung, and you're worried about your public?"

She chuckled, but it turned into another nasty coughing fit. Alex chastised himself for making her laugh. He started refilling her water when Ruth Ann stormed in and took over.

"I told you not to rile her," Ruth Ann chided, wedging Alex out of the way so she could help Darlene with the cup, and to fluff her pillow.

"I'm fine. Let me be," Darlene said, before clearing her scratchy voice. Ruth Ann reluctantly returned to her post outside the door.

"I talked with Larry and I read some of the online responses." Darlene's expression lightened, waiting for Alex to finish. He gave her a sly grin but said nothing.

Darlene sneered at him. "Don't play with me, Alex."

"It was a hit."

"Really?" Her burst of enthusiasm started another coughing fit, but she fought it back enough to keep Ruthie away.

Alex continued while she sipped some water. "I ran into him in the hall on Friday and he said it did a lot better than the first one. I saw it on his website and I found a link to it on CNN's website. It's a big success."

Darlene smiled. "Find out how big."

Alex laughed. "You enjoy being famous, don't you?"

"I ain't famous, but I like that folks like my... well, our stories."

"We've been through that."

"Either way, see if you can get me some of them responses from Larry, like before."

"Will do. Now, will you do me one favor?"

She gave him a skeptical squint. "Maybe."

"Do whatever the doctor says so you can hurry up and get the hell outta here."

"Amen, brother."

Alex ran into Toni just outside Darlene's room.

"How'd she seem to you?" Toni asked.

"She sounds good, except for that nasty cough."

Toni looked concerned. "Yeah, that's what I thought." She noticed Ruth Ann nearby and said, "I'm on my way to the cafeteria. Why don't you come with me?" Alex nodded and they walked toward the elevator. "Mom's cough sounds bad but I think they're gonna release her, anyway."

"As long as she takes whatever drugs they give her, that's probably a good idea."

They stepped into the elevator and Toni said, "It's not a good idea. She's sick!"

"She's safer at home, away from the germs in this place."

"This is a hospital. It's gotta be cleaner than Mom's house."

"Cleaner, maybe, but think about it. The medical staff moves from room to room. They might wash their hands, but they still carry germs on their clothes, hair, and in the air. It's pretty common knowledge that hospitals might be clean, but there's no way for the staff to avoid spreading germs."

"I never thought about that, but Mom's not gonna stay in bed at home."

"She will with Officer Ruthie posted at the door."

Toni chuckled, but quickly returned to a serious tone. "She's worn out. Aunt Ruthie, I mean. She's gotta get some sleep, or she's gonna get sick, too. She can't watch Mom and sleep at the same time, which means I gotta babysit both of 'em."

"So?"

"So, I got things to do, like work."

"Get some of her friends to stay with her."

Toni stopped to think as the elevator door opened. "I thought about that, but you gotta help, too."

"I can't stay with her."

"No, not that. I need you to leave her alone. She's gonna want you to come over and drink with her."

"You want me to drink alone?"

"I'm serious, Alex. She needs to rest. And if you come over and get her talkin' and drinkin', she's gonna end up back here."

"Does that mean you're going to come drink with me so I don't have to drink alone?"

She smirked.

They entered the cafeteria and placed an order to go. "Listen," he said. "I joke around, but you know I'm available for whatever. If you need me to sit with Darlene, just call or stop by."

"I'll call first. I don't wanna interrupt one of your harem meetings."

"We meet at the library, so come on by."

She shook her head. "Smart ass."

"Seriously," he said. "I'm available anytime."

"I'll let you know." She turned to walk to the elevator.

"How about lunch tomorrow?" Alex asked.

"Probably not."

"Why not? They're not going to release her tomorrow."

"I know," Toni said. "But I should be here in case they need me."

"It's a hospital. They've got it covered."

She thought for a moment, then softly said, "Listen, I still ain't interested in seein' anyone right now."

"Perfect. Neither am I." His pleasant tone confused her.

"But you just said—"

"I said let's have lunch. I didn't say let's have sex."

She laughed. "Well, that's good. 'Cause I might a said yes."

"Really?"

"No, jackass."

Both smiled and Alex said, "Look. I like spending time with you, like I said. Let's just have lunch, hang out, and talk. Nothing more."

She was still apprehensive but said, "Maybe. I still don't want people talkin'."

"Okay, so some place out of view. How about Waco?"

She smirked.

"I'll text you?" he said.

She nodded. "Okay."

"Jeez. I've never worked so hard to get a non-date lunch."

"See ya, Alex."

"Later," he said, walking away.

She smiled, knowing he couldn't see her face.

Chapter 29

Alex returned to the hospital on Tuesday with a stack of responses to the second article. Ruth Ann and Toni objected, believing the responses would unnecessarily excite Darlene. However, Alex changed their minds, saying, "I only brought the positive, uplifting ones. They should help her feel better." He wasn't lying.

As Darlene lay in bed reading responses, she couldn't help but feel moved, saying, "Listen to what Trisha in St. Louis wrote: 'People always told me I was too negative. But those same people call me when they're looking for an honest opinion. I'm not negative. I just don't substitute approval for opinion.' I like that." She searched for a pencil to jot it down. "You want my opinion or my approval? I like that a lot. I'm gonna use it." Each response gave her ideas for a new column. She read from another page. "This is from Walter Neweland in Miami; 'It's surprisin' how the words in your head come from other people. Thanks to you, I started listenin' to my own voice.' Well shoot, that's nice to hear."

Many of the correspondents thanked Darlene for opening their eyes to something they'd never realized. Many felt freed from long-standing burdens caused by something beyond their control, and often untrue. Darlene read what a woman from Enid, Oklahoma, wrote, 'I told my husband I was as smart as anyone. He laughed until we took an online IQ test and I beat him. He always believed men were smarter than women until this morning. Maybe I'll get a job and let him take care of the house. He's not too happy I read your article, but you made my day.' Darlene smiled. As happy as she was at the outpouring of positive comments, it was also bittersweet. She felt a sense of regret, wishing she would have started writing at a younger age. For a moment, she understood what Alex had been saying about missing his calling. Still, she couldn't help but feel blessed.

When Ruth Ann wasn't hovering—pretending to read or watch the television—Darlene read and made notes for her next article. She tried to rest but the better she felt, the more restless she became. It wasn't long before she was asking to go home.

Her disposition improved once Ruth Ann started allowing visitors. Among the first was Esma Beth, the church organist.

"Hello there, Miss Darlene." Darlene stacked her papers and set them to one side.

"Howdy, Esma Beth."

"You look wonderful."

"Well, thank ya."

"I hear you're getting out of here soon."

"Ain't soon enough. I was ready to go yesterday."

Esma Beth laughed. "I'm sure you were. I'm surprised they held you for even one day."

"If it was up to me, they wouldn't a."

She patted Darlene on the leg. "Listen, it'll all be over before you know it. Is there anything I can bring you? Something to read?"

"Nah, but thank ya. I just gotta lay here till someone who don't know more about me than I do says I can go."

"I'll pray that it's soon. Listen, while I'm here, I want to say what a wonderful column you wrote for the Hamilton Gazette. It's all anyone can talk about."

"Thank ya, hon." She held up a few pages on the nightstand. "Lotta folks been writin' in."

"It must be so rewarding."

"It'd be better if I wasn't stuck here in this bed."

"You might feel held down right now, but God has elevated us all through you."

"That's mighty kind a you to say."

"Well, it's the truth. Listen, I don't want to overstay my welcome. You hang in there and we'll see you in church, hopefully this Sunday."

"With the good Lord willin'."

Esma Beth left and later Irma stopped by.

"Hey Dar. Ruth Ann said I can only stay a minute."

"Stay as long as you like. She ain't in charge."

"How're you feelin'?"

"I'm fine. Tired of bein' here."

"No one likes bein' in the hospital. But you'll be glad to hear ol' Cynthia Coker's been stewin' 'bout all the good things folks are sayin' about your article."

Darlene smiled. "I'm glad folks like what I wrote. And Cynthia…" her smile grew. "Well, that's just extra."

Irma chucked. "Everyone's been askin' about you."

"Well tell 'em I'm fine. 'Course ain't many come by to see me."

"Muriel Franklin said Ruth Ann wouldn't let her in."

Darlene shook her head. "Tell her I'm sorry 'bout that. Ruthie means well."

Ruth Ann peered in the door, perhaps having heard her name, or it was time for Irma to leave. "Listen, you get well," Irma said. "And, oh, I forgot to mention, even my husband, who don't hardly read, actually said he liked your article."

"Now that's worth somethin' if Otis read it. You tell him thank ya."

"We'll see you Sunday."

"I'll be there," Darlene called out as Ruth Ann hustled Irma out.

Ruth Ann returned to Darlene's bedside. "It's time for you to get some rest."

Darlene wasn't in the mood to argue with her sister so she laid back and closed her eyes. She knew Ruth Ann would leave, and as soon as she did, Darlene picked up the stack of responses and resumed her reading and making notes.

* * *

By Wednesday morning, Darlene was demanding her release. Despite Ruth Ann and Toni lobbying against her, the doctor sent her home, but only after she agreed to limit her activities.

Toni took Thursday and Friday off work to give Ruth Ann a break. Their time was mostly devoted to making sure Darlene stayed in bed while they tended to her every need. Their incessant scrutiny and refusal to bring her liquor—her only request—drove Darlene crazy. They even removed the phone from her bedroom.

By Saturday, Darlene had had enough. "Y'all let me be!" she snapped. "I'm goin' to sleep." Once they left, she snuck into the hall and called Alex. "I'm comin' over."

"You just got out of the hospital. How about I come over there?"

"You won't get past the hens."

Alex chuckled. "Tell them we need to talk, and I won't stay long."

"I'll try. C'mon over."

By the time Alex reached the front door carrying a laptop, Toni was standing out front wearing an uncompromising expression. "Go home, Alex."

"I promise I won't stay long."

Toni shook her head. "She's gotta rest."

"She needs interaction after being cooped up for so long."

"She barely slept in the hospital, and she's only been home three days. Right now, she's in there arguin' with Aunt Ruthie, which is the last thing either of 'em needs."

"When she called me, she was ready to sneak over to my house."

Toni's eyes lit up. "She better not!"

"You can't treat her like a child. The more you try, the more she'll rebel. Let me have five minutes with her. She'll feel like she got her way, then maybe she'll do what you want."

Toni thought for a moment, then opened the front door. "Five minutes. No more. And you tell her she *has* to rest like the doctor said."

"Agreed."

Toni led Alex to the hallway outside Darlene's bedroom. Ruth Ann and Darlene were still bickering so Alex waited in the hall while Toni entered.

"You don't get to tell me what to do," Darlene stated.

"I'm askin' you to do what the doctor ordered," Ruth Ann pleaded. "And I'm tired of repeating myself."

"Good, 'cause I'm tired a hearin' it."

"Mom," Toni said. "Alex agreed to only stay for five minutes."

"No!" Ruth Ann ordered.

"Hush," Darlene barked. "Let him in."

"Hon," Ruth Ann said with a kinder, more concerned voice. "I wish you wouldn't."

Darlene also backed off her harsh tone. "If I start feelin' bad, I'll stop."

Ruth Ann knew there was no changing her sister's mind. "Five minutes. No more."

Toni stuck her head into the hall and waved Alex in. As he entered the room Ruth Ann firmly warned, "Do not rile her."

"I promise."

"You got five minutes."

Toni and Ruth Ann left, leaving Alex alone with Darlene.

He smiled. "I hope I have half your resolve when I'm your age."

"Did you bring the whiskey?"

Alex chuckled. "Sorry, no. I couldn't risk a strip search by the guards."

Darlene shook her head in disgust. "Ever'one thinks they know what's best for poor ol' decrepit Darlene."

"Well, before they return, let's get to it."

"I called Larry but Ruthie snatched the phone away 'fore I was done. He said somethin' 'bout email and blogs and some other nonsense I didn't understand."

"Larry told me what the plan is. You sure you're up for it?"

"If one more person asks me that, I'm gonna cut me a switch and start tannin' some hides."

Alex opened his laptop and connected to the Internet through his phone. "You'll need an Internet connection in your house, but I can help with that. Also, you'll need a laptop but you can borrow mine. Larry is setting up a blog where you type in a message, hit a button and everyone can see it."

"I don't understand any a this stuff, but I'm gonna do whatever you say."

"He's also setting you up an email account so you'll get messages on the computer—like the ones Larry's been printing out for you—and you can answer people back."

"I like that."

"Good. It's really easy and I think it'll work well for you."

"Why can't we keep doin' what we've been doin'?"

"We are. You'll just be getting the responses directly. You and I are going to write the way we've always done. The only difference is we'll type the final version into the computer and send it to Larry."

She wasn't sure she could do it, but was eager to try. "When am I s'posed to start?"

He hesitated, cognizant of his agreement with Toni to give Darlene time to rest. "Well, we need to get your Internet set up, which usually takes a few days, maybe longer in Hamilton. I'll check on that. I can set up the computer on the same day. Larry didn't expect you to get out of the hospital for a few more days and he wants you to get better." Alex privately questioned Larry's concern for Darlene's health. "So he's not expecting anything immediately. I told him you'd need at least a week after you got home. So I'm thinking maybe Wednesday or Thursday."

Alex refilled her water from a pitcher on the nightstand. Darlene drained the glass and

tapped it on the table. "Wish you'd a brought me a little whiskey, but top me off."

Alex smiled. "You got any idea what you'll write next?"

"I got a few, but I figured we'd do what we did last time—read what folks wrote, sip on a few fingers, and figure it out."

He laughed. "You still need to take it easy, but I'm in. I'm working on a few new songs, but I've got a lot of free time."

"New songs?"

"Believe it or not, I've actually come up with a few new ideas."

"You gonna let me hear 'em?"

"Someday. I've got a long way to go but the fact that I'm writing anything is a miracle."

"Ain't a miracle, but I'm glad you quit runnin' away from it."

He nodded. "I'm trying."

"Good for you."

"Now, like I said, you need to take it easy, but I'm ready to start anytime you are."

"I'll take it easy when I start my next life."

"Maybe that's your next article."

Toni knocked on the door and entered with Ruth Ann. "Times up."

"We'll be done in a jiff."

"Mom, the doctor said you've gotta rest. Do you wanna end up in the hospital again?"

Darlene looked at Alex. "Mother hen number two." Toni gripped Alex by the arm and started leading him out. "Leave him be," Darlene said but Toni ignored her.

Ruth Ann fluffed Darlene's pillow and tucked the covers around her.

"Go on!" Darlene barked, shooing Ruth Ann.

Everyone left, expecting Darlene to rest.

A few minutes later, Darlene snuck into the hall and called Alex.

"Listen, I only got a second. Thanks for comin' over. Sorry they run you off. Let's start writin' day after tomorrow."

"That's too soon. We agreed to wait a week. You got out of the hospital Wednesday, today's Saturday, so let's wait three more days and start bright and early Wednesday morning."

"Alex, I feel fine, but alright. I guess that gives me plenty a time to get the hens off my back." She heard footsteps coming. "Uh oh, gotta go." She hung up.

Alex stood at his kitchen counter wearing a contented grin. Darlene's resilience and tenacity had energized him. He sat at the piano and started playing with a renewed spirit. His mind cleared, allowing him to play without thinking about anything—something he'd been trying to do for longer than he could remember.

It didn't last long but as Alex returned to reality, he remembered Darlene's comment about failure; *The more you dwell on it, the worse it gets until you can't do nothin' at all.* Her words and their discussions were slowly breaking his fixation on failure and the past.

Chapter 30

It was raining on Wednesday afternoon when Alex arrived at Darlene's with the laptop tucked under his shirt to keep it dry. Toni met him at the door.

"Hey Alex. I pulled a couple a strings and got the Internet hooked up this mornin'."

"That's cool, thanks. You going to join us?"

Toni chuckled. "Not a chance. I just came by to relieve Aunt Ruthie."

"Does that mean you're on guard duty?" he kidded.

She nodded with a stern but playful look. "Watch out."

She left Alex with Darlene seated at the kitchen table.

Toni convinced Ruth Ann to relax in her room while she kept an eye on Darlene. She busied herself with chores—vacuuming, laundry, dusting—while keeping tabs on her mother.

As Darlene flipped through a few printed emails, Alex said, "I'd ask how you're doing but I don't want you cuttin' a switch."

She grinned while he opened the laptop and connected to the new Internet connection.

"You wanna beer?" Darlene asked.

Alex glanced at the doorway, keenly aware of Toni surveilling from nearby, but out of sight. "Maybe later."

Darlene raised her yellow tablet. "I got a few ideas."

"Alright. Hit me."

"I saw one of them award shows the other day where ever'one was all dolled up. I started thinkin' about how folks think what they see out there on TV and all is better. Truth is, ain't no one better 'n anyone else, even if they are gettin' awards or bein' put up on a pedestal."

"There's a lot of unsung heroes out there. You said Buford McCaleb makes anonymous gifts to the school, and that organist, Esma Beth, donates her free time. I doubt anyone's giving them awards. I think you're onto something."

As the conversation in the kitchen picked up, Ruth Ann soon nodded off while Toni—intrigued by what Alex had to say—wasn't comfortable hanging out just to eavesdrop. Having decided her mother was fine, she quietly left. Neither exit escaped Alex and Darlene's notice. Before Toni's truck reached the end of the street, Darlene said, "You ready for a snort?"

"Aren't you on medication?"

"That ain't no one's business but mine."

"I know, but mixing alcohol with prescriptions is dangerous."

"Nothin' happened yesterday."

She knocked back one quick shot and Alex opened a beer, saying, "Only one. I promised I'd keep an eye on you."

"Pfft. They ain't got a say in what I do."

"I know, but I don't want you making a liar out of me."

"Next time don't promise nothin'."

Darlene returned to her notes. "Okay, here's what I'm thinkin'. Folks listen to famous people like they got all the answers."

"But they're wrong?"

"I didn't say they was wrong. Alex, what kinda piana player would you be without a piana?"

"Obviously, I wouldn't be one at all."

"And if no one tuned your piana or helped you move it?"

"I see where you're going. Successful people don't do it alone."

"It ain't just the successful ones. Is the fella who works ever day to feed his family less important? He buys food, raises kids, supports his family, helps his friends, and whatever else he does."

"That applies to just about everything—the guy who drives the truck that brings food to the stores, gas to the stations, supplies, furniture, clothing, medicine, and everything. Without the simple truck driver, the world would grind to a screeching halt."

"And that's the message. Folks are always makin' a big fuss about some famous athlete or some person on television as if they was better 'n ever'one. And, they ain't."

"But part of that is paying respect, like when a firefighter saves someone, or a teacher inspires kids. Don't you think that's appropriate?"

"Well sure, but is a babysitter takin' care of a young'un so his momma can go to work or school any less important, or is their job any easier?"

Alex chuckled. "Listen, I wouldn't change diapers and listen to crying babies for all the money in the world, so in my book, their job is a lot tougher and somewhat thankless."

"That's where we start."

Alex made notes on the computer, keeping track of their discussion while Darlene continued scribbling her ideas on paper.

Alex finished his beer and rose to toss the empty can in the trash. "Listen, you sound good. How're you feeling?"

"Don't start with me, Alex."

He laughed. "I'm not starting with you. I'm just saying you look good and seem like you're running on all cylinders." He stopped at the refrigerator for a fresh beer but remembered he was limiting himself in solidarity with Darlene. He returned to the table.

"You givin' up drinkin'?"

"No, but I'm not ready for another one."

"Well, I am." She tapped her glass on the table. "'Bout three fingers, please."

"I promised Toni," he pleaded, but she again tapped the glass. "She's gonna have my butt." Alex retrieved the bottle of Jack Daniel's and stopped at the refrigerator for a beer.

He poured Darlene a small refill and sat. She downed the entire shot. "Pace yourself," he asked.

"Now don't you start actin' like my sister and Antoinette."

Alex raised his hands in mock surrender. "But they're right. I need you around to listen to my *nonsense*. They need you, and your fans online need you." Alex expected a pfft or some other dismissive sound, but Darlene silently stared at the floor. "What's wrong?" She raised her head and looked him in the eye.

"Alex," she said in an uneasy voice he'd never heard before. "I gotta tell you somethin' but you gotta promise like you ain't never promised before not to tell a soul. And I mean no one."

"What is it?"

"I mean it. Not Ruthie. Not Antoinette. No one."

Alex felt a wave of fear pass through him as he wondered, what could be so secret that she wouldn't tell her own daughter or her closest friends?

"I promise."

She studied him through a long silence then tapped her empty glass on the table. He reticently poured another shot. She took a sip then gave Alex another hard stare.

"I ain't got long."

"Till what?"

"I'm dyin'."

Alex's froze, his mind reeling. "What?"

"Doc said I got a heart condition that ain't gonna get better."

"I don't know what to say," he said incredulously, but feeling a heavy sadness looming.

"Say you ain't gonna tell no one. I don't want folks treatin' me differently. You've seen how my daughter and Ruthie try to run my life. I'll tell 'em in time."

Tears began pooling. "I'm sorry."

Darlene took another sip and set the glass down, gazing thoughtfully into the distance. "Alex, the way I see it, it's outta my hands, and there ain't no need to cry."

She suddenly stood up, took Alex by the hand, and led him to the back door. They stared out at the steady, gentle rain. She opened the door and walked Alex to the middle of the yard. She released Alex's hand, spread her arms out, and spun around like a child on a playground. "Tell me, Alex," she called out. "Would you waste this day if it was all you had left?"

Fearing she'd lost her mind or was perhaps having an adverse reaction to the pills mixing with the whiskey, he took her hand. "C'mon. Before you make yourself sick again."

Alex led her inside to the kitchen table. He retrieved a blanket from the living room sofa and wrapped it around her while she sat with an odd smile on her face.

"You're supposed to take it easy," he scolded.

She suddenly threw the blanket off. "I *been* takin' it easy. I barely been outta bed after bein' stuck in the hospital for a week. How long am I s'posed to wait 'fore I start livin' again? A year goes by and I'm gone."

Rattled, Alex wrestled with indecision through a long silence. "I don't know what to say."

Her expression turned thoughtful. "Alex, no one knows what to say. Folks don't wanna talk about dyin'. You saw their letters. They wanna talk about what ails 'em and goin' to Heaven. That ain't for me."

"Heaven?"

"Don't get smart." She picked up her empty whiskey glass, stared at it thoughtfully before setting it down. "That kind a moanin' ain't for me. I ain't interested in bein' sick or bein' told what I can't do."

"Eventually you may not have a choice."

She gave an affirming nod. "Well, while I do, I'm gonna make sure I'm livin' and not just waitin' to die."

"Now that I understand. Hey, maybe that's your next article."

Her face filled with a warm, glowing smile. "That's why I like you, Alex. You ain't set in one way a thinkin'."

"Thank you."

Although curious about her shocking news, Alex picked up on her change of subject as a signal to let it go. "Are you suggesting we create another article instead of the one we're working on?"

"Let's do both."

"Okay, then we'll pick the best one?"

"Nope. We'll release 'em both."

Alex pulled the laptop in front of him and they started working.

"I wanna write about how folks are always chasin' tomorrow instead a livin' today."

As they worked to the sound of pattering rain, Alex couldn't help thinking about Darlene spinning around in the backyard, as though she'd experienced an epiphany of sorts. He sensed he'd witnessed something profound and magical, and yet he found a stark contrast between her enthusiastic commitment to living each day to the fullest and the sad reality of her declining health disquieting.

After a long day and many revisions, both articles were complete.

"Okay," Alex said, holding up the first article. "'Everyone's a Hero'. I like the title and I think you're right about adding the scripture early in the text."

"I told ya."

"Let me read it out loud and see what you think."

Everyone's a Hero by Darlene Viriglio

I was watching another award show celebrating famous people for their accomplishments, and it made me think that sometimes we lose sight of the importance of everyday people. Romans 2:11 says, *'For God does not show favoritism.'* Consider the sacrifice every mother makes day after day teaching, nurturing, feeding, and clothing her child, along with the countless other tasks that don't come with an award or any sort of recognition.

In the eyes of God, we are all important—equally important. Acts 10:34 says, *'Truly I understand God shows no partiality.'*

Where would we be without the trash collector keeping our streets free of disease-spreading garbage or the scientist who quietly dedicates her entire life to finding cures and treatments for human suffering? Perhaps you're a secretary or a waitress or a mechanic who works every day to feed your family and support your community. You are no less important than a Nobel prize winner. Each one of us is a vital part of life, working together like the parts of a machine. You can't buy food unless a farmer grows it, a worker picks it, a trucker transports it, and a stock boy puts it on the shelf. While we admire those paraded on television for their achievements, let's not overlook the contributions of other professionals that make those accolades possible. Movie stars are made because of well-written stories, directors, producers, cameramen, costume designers, and on and on. We barely notice great actors in bad movies, yet they are still great actors. Just the same, great parents, spouses, friends, employees, and social workers make the world a better place for everyone in ways that are rarely rewarded.

Whatever your contribution; whether it's heartbreaking, backbreaking, or simply supporting the efforts of a loved one, it all means something, something important, something that should never be disregarded.

So, my friends, we talked about shedding labels and not allowing others or our shortcomings to define who we are. Now it is time to remind yourself and everyone that you are just as important as the most important person on earth. Celebrate the great accomplishments of your fellow man but never forget the unseen and equally important contribution of every man, woman and

```
child, for as Proverbs 22:2 says,
'Rich and poor have this in common:
The Lord is the Maker of them all.'
~DV
```

"I like it," Darlen said. "But maybe we oughta focus more on ever'day people like ranchers or strugglin' artists at the fair."

"You mention them in the next article. You want to go through it now?"

She stretched her arms and yawned. "Alex, we been workin' all day, and I think the second one—'At the End of the Day'—is ready, but let's sleep on it 'fore we decide we got it right."

Chapter 31

They reconvened the next morning with fresh eyes and minds. Darlene wanted a change of scenery, as she had barely been out of the house since her release from the hospital, so they met in Alex's kitchen.

She began reviewing the article, saying, "I was thinkin' 'bout changin' the sentence that starts, 'You see, if you enjoy each day,' but it's fine."

Alex set his copy on the table. "I think you nailed it."

"Read it again," she asked.

At the End of the Day, Did it Go Your Way?
by Darlene Viriglio

```
    I've been on this Earth longer
than many of you, and there's one
thing I know for sure. Tomorrow will
be here soon enough—too soon. When
```

you're young, you can't wait for tomorrow, especially if it's Christmas Eve or the eve of any day you're looking forward to. But, I'm here to say stop waiting for tomorrow. Focus on today. Matthew 6:34 says, *'Therefore, do not be anxious about tomorrow, for tomorrow will be anxious for itself. Sufficient for the day is its own trouble.'* This means don't waste today worrying about tomorrow. Live today and let tomorrow take care of itself.

I recently spent some time in the hospital watching the days crawl by. While I was lying there, unable to do much, counting the hours until I could return to my daily activities, I wondered how many times in the past had I sat around waiting to get on with life, even though there was nothing stopping me like being sick? Sometimes I was just putting things off thinking, *I'll do that tomorrow* or *next week when the weather's better*. We all make excuses, but as I was lying in that hospital bed listening to the doctor tell me I had to rest—even after I went home—before I could return to the life I loved, I wondered how many hours, days, and weeks I'm supposed to wait before resuming the life I love?

The answer I came up with is none. Once I got home, I walked into the backyard in the middle of a rainstorm and asked, *What would I do today if this was my last day on Earth?* Now, no one thinks it's their last day, so we all sit inside and waste the day because the weather's bad, or we're tired, or we don't feel like it right now. I started asking myself, *Am I living or waiting to die?*

  You should ask yourself that same question every day. I could repeat clichés like "Don't put off for tomorrow what you can do today," but I'm not telling you to work all the time. I'm saying, get up and listen to your heart, for it knows your wishes and dreams. Don't make excuses or chase someone else's dream. Imagine yourself in the future, smiling as you reflect on the days when you relentlessly pursued the life you desired. Luke 12:34 says, '*For where your treasure is, there will your heart be also.*'

  When I lay down at night, I say, "It's the end of the day, did it go my way?" It brings a smile to my face even on a bad day because I know I gave it my best shot instead of just sitting around wishing for things to change or waiting for tomorrow. You see, if you enjoy each day—making the most of whatever comes your way—you can end each day happy. Of course, you're going to have good

```
days and bad days, but if you're
waiting for the right time to live,
you're waiting to die. Live each day
chasing the life you desire, the
life you're supposed to live.
Whether it's the day, the week, the
month, or the year, it's simple my
friends, no regrets at the end. ~DV
```

"I like it," Darlene said. "And put your name on there, too."

"We've talked about this, and I appreciate it, but I'm fine with it being your name only."

"That ain't right. You helped, and folks oughta know."

"Again, I appreciate it, but everything I've contributed is based on your ideas. And you've been making the final decisions on what goes in. I also think it's better for the public to believe this is your voice, which it is, and not a committee's voice."

"Alright. But if you change your mind, put your name on there."

Alex typed the final formatting adjustments into the laptop and said, "Send it?"

"Send it."

He pressed the final button. "Done. I sent Larry a message asking him to publish both articles. Hopefully, he won't wait too long between releases."

"We done what he wanted, so now it's up to him. Now, let's make it official. But make it small."

"Seriously? It's not even noon."

"That's why I said make 'em small."

Alex fixed two tiny shots of whiskey. They clinked glasses and downed the shots. Alex picked up the empties and started for the sink. "Hold it," she said. "We done two articles. Two shots."

He put a splash of whiskey in each glass and they again toasted.

On his way to the sink with the empties, Alex was struck with a familiar feeling; like when he played for Susanne. "You feel like hearing a little piano music?" he offered.

"Hell yeah. I mean heck yeah, Alex." She smiled, feeling a little embarrassed. They moved to the den, where Alex took his seat at the piano.

"I've been practicing for an upcoming gig but I've also been toying with a few ideas I started long ago."

He launched into a series of songs he'd played with various bands. Most were ballads that featured the piano. Darlene closed her eyes and let the music fill her. Alex did likewise, but occasionally glanced at Darlene's contented expression. He smiled bitter sweetly, remembering Susanne. He let the emotion permeate his playing, resulting in some of the best ideas he'd had in months.

After thirty minutes, he let the final notes ring out, then lifted his hands.

"Alex, that was beautiful."

"Thank you. I used to play stuff like that for the woman who gave me this piano."

"Gave you?"

Alex suddenly realized he couldn't tell Darlene the story of Susanne dying. It was too close to home. "Long story," he lightheartedly remarked before jumping up from the bench. "You want a refill?"

"Nah, I'm alright. But anytime you want an audience, I'm here."

"You're gonna make me blush," he joked, settling back onto the piano bench.

"Shoot, Alex. God gave you a gift and folks ain't ever gonna stop praisin' it."

"I appreciate it, but you know how it is."

"No, Alex I don't. I can't play nothin'."

"Not that. The praise. You understand what it's like when I say things like you're one of the most interesting people I've ever met."

"Pfft."

He chuckled. "That's what I thought you'd say."

"Listen, I got an idea for a fifth—" She stopped with an uncomfortable grimace.

Alex leapt up. "What is it? Are you okay?"

Darlene raised her hand for him to sit him back down. She closed her eyes for a moment. "I'm fine." She took a few shallow breaths before a long exhale.

"You sure? Should I call a doctor?"

She shook her head. "It's passed."

"Let me get you some water."

She waved him off but stood and followed him to the kitchen. She sat at the table while he fixed her a glass.

After a long drink, she continued. "I wanna pull ever'thing together for a fifth article."

"Okay," he said, still worried about her health. "What are you thinking?"

"I ain't got it all worked out yet but I wanna get it done in the next couple a days."

"What's the rush? Larry probably won't release the third article online before Tuesday. That means the fourth article won't come out for almost three weeks. Plus, tomorrow's church for you."

"And for you."

"I don't go to church."

"You do tomorrow."

"Says who?"

"Alex, you and I been talkin' a lot about God and Heaven, and livin'. I know you ain't a heathen."

"I'm not a choirboy either," he joked.

"You ain't been to church since you moved here, and it's time you went."

"I might turn to dust."

She smiled. "I'm willin' to chance it. You can ride with us. Antoinette picks us up at seven forty-five." He shook his head, but she firmly stated, "I won't take no for an answer."

"I guess I'm going."

"Good. You and I'll get together after Sunday school."

"Sunday at the bowling alley? I've heard about that."

She flashed a sly smile. "You ain't heard nothin'."

The laptop dinged. "Larry received both articles and said he'll release 'Everyone's a Hero' online Tuesday." The laptop dinged again. "Oh, he also sent the login information for your new Gazette email address. He posted it below the first two articles, so there should already be some messages in there. Here, let me show you how to log in."

After a few minutes of working on the laptop, he said, "Okay, here we go. Yup. You've got mail!" He chuckled and Darlene looked at him blankly.

"Lemme see."

He pivoted the computer and pointed. "These are email messages people sent directly to you. Wow, there's a lot." The screen held Darlene's attention as she was awestruck. Seeing the message on the screen seemed to add more life to the fans.

"Why don't we set up the laptop at your house so you can read and respond at your own pace?"

"Are you throwin' me out?" she kidded.

"No, not at all, but God may smite me tomorrow at church, so I need to get my suit pressed."

She chuckled, keeping her eyes fixed on the screen. "How do I write back to folks?"

He showed her how to respond, and spent the next half-hour guiding her through the finer points. When she grew tired, they walked across the street and set up the laptop in her bedroom.

Darlene sat at the dresser, clicking and reading like a child with her first toy. It didn't matter that she couldn't type fast. She was communicating with her new friends, so each word was entered with care and thought. For her, the world had suddenly grown exponentially. Every message, name, and opportunity to communicate directly, thrilled her.

Alex watched for a few minutes, smiling. "Call me if you need something."

"Thank ya, Alex." She never looked up but waved her arm. As he started walking away, she called out, "We like to get there early, so be here at 7:45. Don't be late."

"I won't."

Chapter 32

The buzzing 6:30 alarm arrived too soon for Alex. It was a time he'd rarely seen after waking up. He showered, trimmed his scraggly beard, pulled his hair into a ponytail before putting on a dark suit with a white shirt and gray tie. It was the only suit he owned. He glanced in the mirror one final time before crossing the street at 7:42, three minutes ahead of schedule.

Toni stood beside her truck, parked in the sisters' driveway. She snickered at Alex approaching.

"Look at you," she said. "Mom told me you was worried, so is that suit flameproof?"

He chuckled. "I hope so."

"I can't believe you're up this early, and you almost look presentable."

"It wasn't easy," he replied, tugging at the buttoned collar.

"What, gettin' up early or cleanin' yourself up?"

"Both." He stretched his arms out and took in a big yawn.

She smiled. "There ain't no turnin' back now."

Alex had been in Hamilton for over six months and had met many of the townspeople, but was still uncomfortable entering church—not only because he hadn't attended in decades but because he felt like an outsider. Attending church with the sisters helped calm his concerns, but he still expected whispers.

Entering the sanctuary, he felt several sets of eyes following his every move. Those he'd already met smiled and gave him an approving nod. Darlene strolled in ahead of him at a much slower-than-normal pace, but with her head held high. She led Ruth Ann, Toni, and Alex down the aisle to a seat near the front. Alex leaned over to Toni and whispered, "I should sit near the aisle in case I catch fire and need to run out."

"Good idea," she said with a chuckle.

The service began with a prayer followed by a hymn led by the musical director. Alex followed along in the hymnal but didn't sing along.

After a few more songs and prayers, Pastor Brown took the pulpit and delivered a sermon centered on service. While he focused on serving God and your fellow man, Alex was intrigued when the Pastor said, "Now, my friends, we all like being rewarded for our efforts—a paycheck at the end of a hard week's work, a thank you for holding a door open, the smile of appreciation for helping with a task—but we mustn't seek recognition as a reason to serve..." He offered several scriptures about giving of yourself unconditionally, unselfishly, and without any expectations. "And let us not forget that we make sacrifices not because they come with a reward but because God has led us to make those sacrifices. Do you hold the door open for your neighbor so they can thank you? Or is it in your heart to offer assistance unconditionally?" He quoted and expanded on several more scriptures while Alex zoned into his own thoughts. He reflected on how he'd always enjoyed hearing the applause after playing a song, but he smiled, thinking, *But that's not why I play. The applause is like a bonus.* He realized his motivation for performing was to make people happy. He enjoyed earning a living but thought, *Like Darlene said about writing, I'd do it for free.*

When the service let out, the foyer became a beehive of activity. Toni and the sisters introduced Alex to a dozen members of the small congregation.

"Alex," Dorothy said, reaching out her hand to shake, "It's nice to meet you."

Alex smiled and shook her hand. "Thank you…"

"Dorothy McArthur. I saw you at the fair but we haven't been introduced."

"Well, it's nice to meet you."

"What did you think of the sermon?"

"I liked his point about not making sacrifices just to get recognition."

Irma overheard Alex and stepped closer. "I liked that too, Alex," she said, drawing his attention to her. "Irma Buchanan. It's nice to finally meet you."

"You too," Alex said, trying to recall *something* Darlene had told him about either lady so he could add to the conversation. He drew a blank.

"Listen, Alex," Irma continued. "You keep comin' back. Pastor only gets better."

Ada and Buford McCaleb approached Darlene and Ruth Ann. "Ladies, it's nice to see you. Darlene, we're so happy to see you out of the hospital and back at church." Ada made it a point to address Alex. "Mr. Patterson, we haven't seen much of you around town. I'm so glad you joined us today. Will you be joining us again?"

"Maybe. I certainly enjoyed the service."

"The single adults meet in room 104 for Sunday school," Ada said. "I'm sure they'd love to have you attend."

Alex glanced pleadingly at Toni and the sisters.

"We don't want him overdoin' it," Toni said. "Maybe next week."

"He ain't used to bein' up so early," Darlene added. "We're gonna send him home so he can get a nap." She smiled and nudged Alex, drawing laughter from the group. "C'mon Alex. Let's get you home."

Toni led the way to her truck where Alex and the ladies piled in.

"Alex, you done good," Darlene said.

"Because I behaved?" he kidded.

"'Cause you listened to Pastor Brown and probably learnt somethin'."

"He spoke well. And the people were nice."

"They ain't like them California heathens, are they?" Ruth Ann said.

Alex chuckled. "Definitely not."

"You're welcome to ride with us next Sunday," Ruth Ann offered.

"Don't put him on the spot," Darlene chided. "Alex, you're welcome to come with us anytime, but it's up to you."

"I ain't puttin' him on the spot," Ruth Ann shot back. "And look who's tellin' *me* not to call someone out."

Toni drove the block and a half to the bowling alley, prompting the sisters to end their argument. From there, she drove Alex home.

Toni pulled into Alex's driveway and put the truck in park. "Well, you didn't burst into flames."

"Thank God. I mean, yeah, thank God. You want to come in? I was going to order a pizza."

"Aren't you the big spender? But no, thanks. I gotta get back to the bowlin' alley."

"I thought they meet for an hour."

"They do, but since Mom's been sick, I wanna be nearby in case she starts feelin' bad."

Alex suddenly felt conflicted, flashing on what Darlene had confided in him about her health. He desperately wanted to share it with Toni but couldn't. He blocked it out, smiled, and raised his eyebrows enticingly at Toni. "Some other time?"

She grinned. "You're such a hound."

"Woof."

She shook her head. "Call me."

* * *

Darlene entered the bowling alley last. The group had asked Ruth Ann to delay her so they could prepare the room. Sarah and Irma put up two banners that read WELCOME HOME and CONGRATULATIONS. Sarah made a cake and decorated it to look like a newspaper article. The ladies huddled together, shouting "surprise" as Darlene turned the corner. She was startled, but thrilled. It took her an extra moment to reach the group, as she'd been moving much slower since her stay in the hospital.

Darlene crossed the room to her chair while the ladies fawned over her as though she were royalty. "We're so proud of you," Irma said, patting her on the back. "We was gonna throw you a party a few weeks back, but you had to go and get sick. Welcome back and congratulations."

"Thank ya."

"You've been passin' out advice practically all my life," Sarah said. "But I ain't never heard you say things like you wrote."

"That's 'cause Alex helped me find the right words."

"I thought you and Alex just sat around chewin' the fat," Irma said.

"We do. But he's a smart fella who likes to talk."

"'Bout the Bible?" Sarah questioned.

Darlene shook her head. "He don't know much about scripture, but I tell him what I'm tryin' to say and he helps me put it on paper. It don't matter what subject."

Irma patted Darlene's shoulder. "We're all so proud of you."

Cynthia quickly grew tired of being in the shadows. "You know…" she inquisitively remarked. The ladies glanced at her.

"You got somethin' to say?" Darlene started, but Ruth Ann put a hand up to stop her.

"Don't get riled," Ruth Ann said before turning to Cynthia. "Go on ahead and say somethin' ignorant," Ruth Ann challenged.

With everyone's attention on her, Cynthia relished the moment. She couldn't help herself. "Well," she said, looking at her nails, trying to seem aloof. "It sounds like Alex might actually have some talent."

"He's got more talent in his little finger than you do in you that oversized head of yours," Darlene said, drawing a few chuckles. "So go on ahead and take your best shot at knockin' him down."

"Oh no," Cynthia said innocently. "That's not what I'm sayin'."

Irma stepped in front of Cynthia and shook her head. "Not now." She turned to Darlene. "I heard you was gonna do a television interview."

"I don't know nothin' 'bout that," Darlene said, glancing across the room to catch Sarah's attention. Holding up two fingers, she signaled for a small glass of whiskey. Sarah delivered and Darlene took the entire drink in one gulp.

"Steady ol' girl," Ruth Ann said, rubbing her on the back.

Darlene took a deep breath. "I'm fine."

Sarah picked up the empty glass and said, "Dar, I read your second article 'bout three times, and dang if you ain't right about sheddin' labels. Some folks got a low opinion of widows and divorced women, makin' me feel like a second-class citizen. But when you kinda said those were *their* opinions, it dawned on me. There's nothin' wrong with me 'cause I'm single, and that's all that matters."

"I still like the first one about the time between dyin' and goin' to Heaven," Dorothy said.

"Some called it sacrilegious," Cynthia spouted.

"You're sacrilegious," Darlene fired back, drawing a raucous laugh.

"Look," Cynthia defensively said, "I didn't say it, but I was over at Whitman's where I heard Marjorie Collins sayin' what you wrote was unchristian."

"Marjorie Collins?" Darlene questioned. "She'd knock a sunny day."

"Well," Cynthia continued. "I'm just telling you what I heard, and like you said, everyone's entitled to their own opinion."

Darlene raised a single finger. "Let's not forget Matthew chapter 7, 'Judge not lest ye be judged.'" Cynthia made a dismissive snort, but flinched when Darlene added, "But you're right. Marjorie's got a right to her own opinion, just like I'm entitled to believe that folks don't go immediately to Heaven after dyin', and it ain't for you or Marjorie to judge what I believe." Cynthia smirked and looked away, folding her arms.

"Miss Darlene," Virginia said. "At first I wasn't real fond of that first article. I thought you was disrespectin' the Bible by sayin' it was alright to believe in reincarnation. But when that second one came out, and everyone was talkin' 'bout how good it was, I decided to read 'em both again. I didn't realize you was talkin' about lettin' people believe what they believe. I know reincarnation ain't in the Bible, but you wasn't sayin' it was, or that it was real. You was sayin' don't nobody know for sure and it don't hurt nobody to believe it. I was wrong thinkin' you was bein' disrespectful. I gotta thank ya 'cause now I see how puttin' labels on things made me miss somethin' interestin', and it made me a better person."

"Well thank ya, Miss Virginia. That's mighty nice."

Hearing stories of how her writing had woken the women up to ideas they'd never considered made Darlene feel a pride she'd never felt before. She never sought approval or admiration, but it felt good to hear how her words had impacted people she'd known for decades.

"Hon," Ruth Ann said, "You gonna tell us about the next article?"

"Me and Alex sent two new ones over to Larry yesterday mornin', but y'all'll have to wait to read 'em."

"I hate to admit it," Cynthia chimed, surprising everyone. "But my niece said some of her friends read the one about labels and said they'd been judgin' people unfairly. I don't know if I agree, but they liked what you wrote."

Darlene gave Cynthia a genuine smile. "You tell them I said thank ya."

"Listen," Irma said. "I said it before. We don't have to agree or disagree with what you wrote."

"Just start thinkin' for yourself," added Dorothy. "It sounds simple."

"But it took Darlene sayin' it for everyone to realize it," Sarah said.

"We all grew up bein' told what to think, from our fathers and husbands to Pastor Brown," Dorothy remarked.

"Joe didn't do my thinkin'," Darlene stated.

Ruth Ann chuckled. "No one does your thinkin'."

"What about Alex?" Cynthia snidely asked, unable to resist provoking Darlene. "Maybe he doesn't think *for* you but some of that stuff you wrote sounds like someone from California."

Darlene smiled. "He don't think for me, but he sure helps me sort it all out. And, by the way, I wrote the first article—the one y'all keep sayin's 'bout reincarnation—by myself."

"I sure wish you'd tell us what's comin' next." Miss Virginia pleaded.

Before long, Ernie appeared, signaling last call. Irma and Sarah cleaned up while the conversation continued flowing. They took down the banners, gathered their belongings, and started for the door.

"It's a good one Miss Virginia," Darlene said.

Ruth Ann and Irma flanked Darlene, escorting her to Toni's truck.

Chapter 33

The following Tuesday, Larry released the third article—'Everyone's a Hero'—online. The printed version came out on Thursday. Darlene received an overwhelming number of responses and wanted to personally reply to each one. She called Alex over for help.

"Look at 'em all," she said, pointing at the long list of new emails. "You gotta help me. I can't answer 'em all myself."

Alex chuckled. "I don't think you have to."

"It'd be rude not to."

"When people send messages online, they don't always expect a response, especially from someone popular like you."

"Well, that don't sound right."

"Trust me," he said, leaning in to get a closer look at the screen. "Yeah, see, this guy just wanted to say thanks.

You don't need to respond." He took charge of the mouse, sorted the messages, and pointed, saying, "Look. Each of these has a subject that says thanks or thank you or something similar. Let's skip those and see if there're others we can also skip."

"I oughta at least say you're welcome."

"It would take days of working non-stop. When would you write the next article, or eat or sleep, or go to church?"

Darlene resumed control of the mouse and opened one message with the subject line: 'Finding my way'. Alex looked over her shoulder as they read; *After losing my husband, I struggled to get out of bed until I read your article about a do-over. While I'm not a religious person, your words struck something in me that got me out of bed and into a life I had given up on long ago. I can't put into words how you've changed my life and my outlook. All I can say is thank you. ~Joanna, Phoenix AZ*

Darlene looked up and whispered, "Thank you, Lord."

They continued reading messages from people who were struggling with issues like abuse, depression, drug addiction, and illness, but the common thread was that Darlene's words had helped them find a way through.

After several hours of sorting and filing, Alex said, "Listen, I need to do a few things at home. Are you okay without me?"

Without looking up, she said, "I got it." On his way out she said, "Stop by later and we'll have a snort and shoot the bull."

Alex smiled. "See you then."

Darlene continued sorting and reading until she hit a message she had never expected.

Henry Cortez, a twenty-year-old who'd spent two years in a coma followed by a year in rehab learning how to walk and talk again, wrote; *I'm not the same as I was before I got sick. And I missed the best years of my life. I lost the only girl I ever loved. All my friends moved on, and my father died. All I have left is my mother. When you wrote about getting a do-over, I thought I'd get another chance. I was looking forward to leaving this life and starting a new one, as your first article suggested. Then, you started talking about how life is hard and everyone gets labeled. I hate the idea of being remembered as the guy who gave up and killed himself, but I don't want to live having missed out on everything. Dying and starting over still seems like the best thing for me. I'll get the girl, keep my friends and go on with life like everyone else.*

Darlene stopped reading as an icy shiver hit her. She'd never considered someone would use her words to justify suicide. She took a deep breath and read on.

You're probably too busy to write me back, but in your next article I hope you'll say something that will help me follow through with my plan so I can have a do-over.

Horrified, Darlene immediately hit the reply button and began typing.

Henry, you sound like a wonderful young man with a story that others should hear. Working your way back from a coma is something special. This could already be the beginning of your do-over and, there's no doubt in my mind that the world would not be the same if you left early. I'm not gonna write a bunch of nonsense just to make you feel good. I'm gonna tell you like it is. Life can be hard and unfair. But it can also be wonderful. Maybe you missed some good times, but you also met a girl and got to feel what love is like. That's how life is for everyone. Giving up because you're having a run of bad luck, even a long run, isn't the answer. I too lost the love of my life, twice. When I lost my son, I felt like I died too. I don't know how you feel, but I know how it feels when it seems like the world has ended. Don't give up yet. You don't want to miss out on another chance at love. You know what it's like and you know there's nothing better. Stick around with the rest of us and see what happens. ~Darlene.

She clicked 'send,' then stared at the screen, her nerves frazzled. She considered downing a shot of whiskey but took a deep breath and pressed on, fearing there could be another message from someone in crisis.

Unwilling to sleep, Darlene read through a multitude of emails. Despite fatigue and her declining health, she thanked God over and over for rewarding her with what felt like one of the greatest experiences of her life.

* * *

On Thursday afternoon, Alex stopped by and found Darlene taking a break, fixing herself some tea.

"Alex, you wanna beer?"

"Are you making your tea Irish?" he asked with a smile.

"No, I got a lotta emails to write, and the whiskey makes me tired."

"Then I'll skip the beer and join you in a glass of tea."

"You ain't gotta quit on my account."

"I know, but I've also got some practicing to do."

"You goin' back on the road?"

"No. Actually, that's part of why I stopped by." He paused, wearing a grin. "I wondered if you and Ruth Ann wanted to come over tomorrow and listen to some new material I've written."

Darlene's face lit up. "We'd love to. I mean, I can't speak for Ruthie, but I'm sure she'll wanna come."

"Great. Say one o'clock. I'll order a pizza, and you can bring whiskey, unless you're on the wagon. I'll make some tea for Ruth Ann."

"That sounds great."

"I'm also going to invite Toni. She said she only works half-days on Friday. Hopefully, she doesn't already have plans."

Ruth Ann was in her bedroom but picked up on the enthusiastic tone in Darlene's voice and wandered into the kitchen.

"Hello, Alex," Ruth Ann said. "I hope you two aren't drinking this early in the day. Hon, you know you're still supposed to take it easy."

"We ain't drinkin', mother hen. Alex here invited us over to hear him play."

"Oh. That's sounds wonderful, Alex. When do you want us there?"

"I know it's short notice but can you make it tomorrow at one o'clock?"

Ruth Ann smiled. "Yes. I can be there."

"Great. I was thinking about serving boiled mule."

Ruth Ann's smile grew. "Shoot, Alex."

"I'll make some tea and you can munch on pizza. I don't have a lot of new material, but I can probably give you thirty minutes."

"Will you play that song you played last time?" Ruth Ann asked.

"I could be persuaded."

"I love that song," Ruth Ann said as she poured herself a cup of tea and started to leave. "Thank you, Alex. I will see you tomorrow."

Darlene said, "Alex, you oughta get on home."

"Are you throwing me out?" he asked with a smile.

"No. Wisenheimer. But if you been writin' new music, I think you oughta spend ever minute you got doin' it. Ain't that what you been wantin'?"

"It is, but I also like helping you."

"I 'preciate that, but I can handle it. You go on back to practicin'. I expect to hear somethin' special tomorrow, so you better not disappoint."

He grinned at her smile. "Okay, but promise me you won't work too hard. I don't want you nodding off during my performance."

"Shoot, Alex. I'll tape my eyes open if I hafta."

Alex noticed how tired she looked. "Better yet, take a break and get some sleep."

"You turnin' into a hen?"

He laughed and started for the door. "Cluck cluck."

* * *

Back home, Alex played through the list of pieces he would perform for the sisters. Although most were incomplete, he improvised the endings, confident they would sound good. He stopped when he remembered to invite Toni.

He drafted a quick text.

- *Hey, I'm playing for your mom and aunt at 1 tomorrow. I hope you can you join us?*

Her response came within a few minutes.

- *Sounds good. See you then.*

Alex stared at Toni's message while his thoughts ran. He was excited about sharing his new music. He rarely played unfinished pieces for an audience, but the sisters and Toni felt more like family than an audience. *They will like anything I play,* he thought, but then he started practicing again, wanting them to hear his best efforts. He thought of Susanne, remembering how his playing brightened her dark days. Playing for Darlene gave him the same feeling. He wore a bittersweet smile thinking, *there's no better reason to play.*

Chapter 34

On Friday morning, Alex woke up excited about performing. He checked the clock and smiled. *Three hours.* He showered, dressed, and started preparing. After stuffing all the dirty dishes and clothes out of sight, he dug out the paper plates and plastic cups. He set an alarm on his phone, reminding him to order the pizza at 12:30. Having tidied the house, he settled at the piano and loosened up his hands.

It was close to one o'clock when he heard Toni's truck rumble into the sisters' driveway. His heart pounded as it normally did before an important gig.

Before long, everyone was eating pizza and drinking tea.

"I have some bourbon," Alex said to Darlene. "You want a shot?"

"Nah. I got lots to do later."

Alex noticed once again how tired Darlene looked, but she still seemed full of energy.

"Anyone need anything?" Alex asked, glancing at the three ladies all comfortably seated. When they all shook their heads he said, "Then I guess I should take the stage."

The ladies clapped as Alex took his seat on the piano bench. He started softly with a dark, haunting piece he'd written while reflecting on his struggles of the past eighteen months. It had been a difficult piece to compose, requiring him to revisit a time he'd rather forget. Whenever Alex experienced strong emotions—usually love or happiness—he wrote about it. Reliving the most depressing period he'd ever experienced turned out to be healing, although the resulting composition was among the most disquieting he'd ever written. The song ended with an unresolved chord that Alex held until it slowly faded away, leaving everyone unsettled. For a moment, the silence lingered as the ladies weren't sure Alex was finished.

Once Alex released the sustain pedal and lifted his hand from the keys, Darlene said. "Alex, that was beautiful, but it wasn't like what you played last time."

He nodded somberly. "I've never written anything like that. When I couldn't come up with anything inspiring, I decided to dive in to everything I wanted to get away from; the hard times in L.A., endless nights on the road, bad relationships, band breakups, and so on. I quickly figured out there was plenty to bum me out."

"I'm with my sister. It was beautiful but kinda sad," Ruth Ann offered.

"Okay," Alex said, in an uplifting voice. "Now that I've bummed you all out, let me see if I can change that."

He started the second song, which was completely different. The piece was lighter yet intensely powerful. It was a complicated, demanding jazz piece he'd written as an exercise designed to pull his mind away from dwelling on his problems.

He played the next three pieces without stopping. Each one had been composed while reflecting on the encouraging messages Darlene had conveyed with 'The Road to Heaven' and 'Everyone's a Hero'.

What was supposed to be the last piece was Ananya's song, the one Ruth Ann requested. The moment he started playing, he felt the excitement of all three ladies. He played through the piece twice, each time remembering his life with Ananya. But as he was nearing the end, his thoughts unexpectedly shifted to the moment Darlene told him she was dying. He remembered the final few weeks he played for Susanne. It was a great honor to bring joy to her when she needed it most, but he wasn't prepared for her passing. *I can't go through that again*, he thought. It hit him hard, almost causing him to stop. Then, Darlene's words filled his head. *It's outta my hands. There's no need to cry. It's a blessing in disguise.* The sadness was replaced with a sense of purpose. He'd brought happiness to Susanne and was doing the same for Darlene. A warm feeling filled him as he hit the final note of Ananya's song. He closed his eyes and let his hands follow an idea he'd had a few days earlier. He blocked out everything and everyone, and reached deep inside. His mind filled with the story of Darlene's life and her message as the idea transformed into a song. He was close to tears at the thought of Darlene leaving, but it was also bittersweet. Darlene was Alex's gift from God, and losing her would crush him. But, none of that matter in that moment. He was there for a reason; to give back.

He finished the piece but kept his back to them as they applauded. He took a few deep breaths, quietly sniffling back the tears. Before turning around to acknowledge the applause, he wiped his eyes.

"Alex," Darlene said, dabbing a tear of her own. "That ain't the way you played it last time, but I ain't ever heard nothin' as beautiful as that."

Her words filled Alex with more satisfaction than he could contain, nearly causing him to break down. He laughed once to cover up the outcry of joy and said, "Thank you."

"Amen," Ruth Ann added to her sister's praise, choking up.

Alex looked at them, then at Toni. She struggled to speak. "I don't know how you do it." She swallowed and caught her breath. "But that got to me."

In order to regain control over his emotions, and to lighten the mood, Alex launched into a few minutes of some playful blues progressions before ending with a Jerry Lee Lewis style glissando, sliding his hand across all the keys and banging the final chord before jumping up and bowing.

He drew another ovation, but also turned a tear-jerking moment into a festive ending.

"Alex, that was great," Darlene said.

"Maybe I'll make this my weekly gig. How would y'all feel about a cover charge?"

"Hell, I'd pay," Darlene said.

"Now Alex," Ruth Ann said. "I told you I'd buy a copy of that song, the one I like so much, but I don't know about any cover charge." She smiled, believing she'd made a great joke.

"Thank you," Alex said. "I'll get you a free pass."

Both laughed as the sisters rose, sensing it was time to leave.

Toni was quiet, struggling to find the right words. This was the second time Alex had impressed her beyond words.

Just as they reached the door, Toni surprised Alex with a hug. "Thank you," she said, releasing quickly and turning so he couldn't see how overwhelmed she was. "See ya Alex," she called out, hurrying out the door.

The sisters followed, with Darlene being last. She stopped on Alex's porch and said, "I ain't gonna bend your ear right now, but you and me's gonna talk tomorrow."

"You want to work on a new article?"

"Maybe. I still have emails to go through, but come on by."

"Sometime in the afternoon?"

She nodded but before she turned to leave, she looked Alex in the eye and said, "You don't know what it means to hear you play, but I do… Thank you."

Her words felt like the greatest compliment he'd ever received. He choked up, barely able to say, "You are welcome."

She ambled across the street and he stepped inside, wiping the tears he'd held back before sitting at the piano. He reflected on his performance, then smiled and let his satisfaction flow through his fingers into the piano.

* * *

The following afternoon, Darlene had been up for hours answering emails. She'd been working tirelessly for days. The pace had exhausted her. Ruth Ann watched as Darlene sat at the kitchen table—her new office—with her legal tablet filled with notes, and her head buried in the laptop. "Hon, you've gotta take a break. You ain't hardly slept in two days."

Darlene looked up, revealing how run-down she looked. "Just a few more and I'm gonna quit."

"Promise?"

"Don't start with me but I promise. Can you call Alex while I finish this?"

Ruth Ann picked up the phone and started toward the table. Before dialing, she stared long and hard at Darlene. "You look so tired."

"Hush. I got a lotta folks wantin' me to write 'em back, and I got one more column to write."

"You don't have to respond to everyone. Even Ann Landers didn't reply to *everyone*. Please slow down?"

Darlene stopped and glowered at her sister. "I done told you I would. Now stop pesterin' me, you ol' hen."

Ruth Ann smiled and handed her the phone. "*You* call Alex, you ol' bossy."

Darlene took the phone and called Alex.

"Listen, I gotta postpone us gettin' together."

"Is everything alright," Alex asked, hearing fatigue in her voice.

"I still got a lotta emails to go through and I'm beat."

"I understand. When do you want to get together?"

"Let's shoot for tomorrow after church, say one o'clock?"

"Works for me."

"You gonna join us for church?"

"Thanks, but I'm probably going to be up late tonight."

"Alright, but shame on you for skippin' church."

He smiled, knowing she wasn't really scolding him. "I'll say ten hail Mary's."

"We don't do that. But listen, I'll see you tomorrow."

After hanging up, she worked for a few more hours and went to bed. She felt drained, even though it was barely seven o'clock.

Chapter 35

On Sunday afternoon, Darlene sat at the kitchen table while Alex stood at the refrigerator craning left then right, looking for Ruth Ann.

"'Bout three fingers?" he asked, pulling a beer out for himself.

After a good night's sleep, Darlene felt much better but still said, "No, thank you. I wanna get this done first."

Darlene's words sounded odd and ominous, giving Alex an unsettled feeling. He returned the beer to the fridge, grabbed a pitcher of tea, and joined Darlene at the table with two glasses.

"Alex, I've been thinkin' 'bout this whole article thing."

"And?"

"And I always said I didn't have nothin' to say."

"You always have something to say. I mean things people want to hear."

"I've said a lot, but enough's enough."

"Don't wanna beat a dead horse?"

She smiled. "Spoken like a local. The next article's gonna be the last one."

"You want to stop writing?"

She nodded. "I wanna tie all four articles together with one last column."

Alex studied Darlene, hesitant to ask, but his concern and curiosity were too strong. "Is this about what you told me earlier?"

They sat through a long silence before she nodded. "I still ain't told my sister and Antoinette. I don't want 'em fussin' over me and gettin' in the way, and I don't want you or them treatin' me different either."

"I haven't. I won't. But you've got to tell me what you're thinking."

"Alex, before all this writin' stuff, I'd done ever'thing I wanted. I was married, raised Antoinette, went to church, and helped folks when I could. When you get to my age, there ain't much left to do."

"You told me I *ain't* done, and I shouldn't quit."

She smiled. "That's right, and I ain't quittin'. But God gave me this column and I think He expects me to finish it."

"Even though you could keep writing for years?"

She tilted her head with a furrowed brow. "Maybe, but my time's runnin' out. I been thinkin' long and hard 'bout how God wants me to finish my time."

Her words were hard for Alex to hear, so he jokingly said, "Maybe you'll get a do-over and come back."

She grinned but her expression was poignant. "I'm ready to rest and wait for the Lord."

"But not until you write one more column?" They shared a long, silent gaze before she nodded. He picked up a pencil and flipped to a fresh page in his notepad. "Alright. Let's get it done." He read aloud from his notes. "'The Road to Heaven'. 'The Good in All of Us, Shed the Labels'. 'Everyone's a Hero'. 'At the End of the Day Did it Go Your Way?'" He looked up and asked, "What's the common element other than God, except the last one?"

"It all goes back to 'The Road to Heaven'. There's a path we all take that ends in Heaven. Along the way we're given challenges, opportunities, setback, victories, and a whole lotta other things that show us who we are. It ain't what comes our way that's important, it's how we respond to each a them. We learn to walk and talk by fallin' down and makin' mistakes. Same's true for arithmetic, makin' friends, and gettin' to know God. Someday you'll get married and find out you ain't a perfect husband. No one is right off the bat. It takes time and experience, just like walkin', talkin', and all them other things. Just like you done with playin' the piana and writin' songs; it takes practice and makin' mistakes. Ever'one has the potential to get better, to make more of themselves, and to grow, but it ain't gonna happen if you don't face up to the things that come at you ever day; the challenges, opportunities, setback, and even the good things."

"So, each event or challenge, opportunity, setback, etcetera, has value, but adding them together is who we are?"

She nodded. "Sorta. You ain't got control over what happens, but you can decide how you respond. Like I been sayin' 'bout your music. You gotta sit at the piana or wherever and try to write. And sometimes you gotta fail. Most importantly, you gotta keep comin' back and tryin' again and again. To do better takes effort. It don't matter if you succeed. It matters that you tried."

"Like your end-of-the-day article, you can only regret not trying. But how can people *not* have regrets if they can't achieve their desires?"

"'Cause it ain't about what you achieve. It's the journey. You practice the piana and play it beautifully, and so does Esma Beth. Both y'all keep practicin', playin', and tryin' to get better, but do you do it to be rich and famous? Is that what you set out to do?"

"For me, being rich and famous would be like a bonus for writing a hit. So, no, I didn't set out to be rich or famous. But I won't feel successful until I've written something really special."

"But you keep tryin'."

He nodded. "Still, everyone works to achieve a goal. For some it's paying the bills, for others it's wealth. For me it's a great song, and I'm not going to be satisfied with anything less."

She smiled. "Alex, you're makin' my point. Ever'one works toward somethin'. You just said it. Life ain't about the goal, it's about the workin' toward it."

"I'm not sure I agree with that."

"You ain't gotta agree. Let's look at what folks do. How many rich folks quit workin' the day they get rich?"

"Some."

"Some. Not all. Not even most. Rich folks don't stop workin' just 'cause they got rich. Look at all them young guys who have more money 'n they could ever spend. They want more 'cause they like what they do; workin'. Actors and musicians ain't no different. Actors wanna act, musicians wanna write and perform. You see, it ain't about what you achieve, it's about what you *do*."

"Okay. But what about the guy who wants to get rich but fails, just like I failed to write a great song?"

"You ain't failed. That song you played for us is as special as anything out there. I'd say that makes you a success. And the fella who wanted to get rich but didn't make it is probably just as happy as someone who did. There's lots a millionaires out there that made *and* lost fortunes 'cause they kept workin' at it. Just like you'll keep workin' at writin' long after you've written a great song. Maybe you wanna feather in your cap, but bein' known for writin' a great song ain't the same. Think about it, Alex. The journey—the time you spent at the piana practicin', writin', findin' inspiration—*that's* what you do, it's who you are. I hope you write the biggest song in history, but if you don't, you ain't gonna regret it. You'd only regret not tryin' to write one. If it don't happen, you're gonna look back and smile sayin' I gave it my best shot."

He smiled. "Pursuit is better than the capture. Or better yet, effort is its own reward." He pondered for a moment. "I guess that's right. Transforming a good song into greatness isn't easy, but it's the challenge that brings me back, the lure of creating something timeless, the process of getting there, or as you put it, *tryin'*. I never thought about it, but successful people don't stop when they achieve success."

"Nah. They work even harder."

He smiled. "I hope you're right when I get to the end."

"Trust me, Alex. I am."

"So, how does someone relate this to their life?"

"The journey Alex. You go through life with God's gifts. Along the way, you either use 'em like you done with music or you don't. But even when you do use His gifts, you still got challenges, like failin' or goin' through a dry spell and thinkin' you messed up."

"Agreed."

"But look at where you are now. You're writin' again, and you've been playin' again for us ladies."

"It's getting better."

"Alex, your journey through life ain't no different than anyone else's. You did what you liked doin' until it got hard. Then you wanted to quit. You talk to any married person and they'll tell you they loved bein' married till it got tough, and they all thought about quittin'. It's how you respond. When you're given a challenge, you either stand and face it or cut and run. God has given me the challenge of failin' health. I can quit livin' and hide out, or I can push it aside and finish His work. I choose to face it and give it my best shot."

"So, everyone should face the challenges God gives them?"

"I don't know what folks *oughta* do, but it's *what* they do that counts."

"Wow. Okay, so let's work out the wording."

They spent the next few hours writing and completing the fifth and final article. After their requisite whiskey celebration—a small shot—Darlene said, "Alex, there's something I wanna talk to you about."

"Am I in trouble?"

"Sit."

"Can I have a beer?"

She nodded and tapped her glass on the table. "And hit me with a small one."

He poured her a few ounces of Jack and pulled a beer from the refrigerator. "What's on your mind?"

Chapter 36

Alex returned to his seat across from Darlene at the kitchen table. Now, with the fifth and final article finished, Darlene was looking to answer the one question that had eluded her.

"From the day I met you, I never understood why you moved to Hamilton. Here we are good friends and I still don't understand why you won't tell me or anyone why you quit such an excitin' life and moved to Podunk, Hamilton."

"Maybe I'm here to annoy and motivate you to write about getting a do-over?"

Darlene chuckled, but returned to seriousness. "You been makin' jokes and all, but it's time you told me the truth. And I don't wanna hear that same horse manure you been sellin' 'bout failin' and runnin' outta ideas. Ever'one fails but you're a smart, talented man. It don't add up. I wanna know what the straw was that broke the camel's back. I told you about my son Joey, but I got back up. Now it's your turn."

He hesitated before sliding the whiskey bottle over and pouring himself a large shot, downing the entire drink. He took a deep breath and slowly began. "I've never shared this with anyone." He chased the whiskey with a large gulp of beer. "I was in love with a girl named Ananya. She was probably the only woman I ever loved. We lived together for a while in L.A., but being the idiot I was, I pushed her away."

"Ever'one loses girlfriends and boyfriends. That ain't enough reason."

"No," he said slowly. "We got back together several times but always ended up having the same argument that broke us up."

"What was that?"

"I was gone a lot with touring, and she wanted me home more. She'd say, 'How can I plan a future with someone who's never home?' To which I always answered with, 'If I quit traveling, how can you plan a future with someone who doesn't have a job?'"

"She was just lonely, Alex. You can't blame her for that."

"I didn't. In fact, I felt guilty and wanted her to travel with me, but that wasn't possible."

"So you quit playin' so you can get her back?"

Alex sighed deeply, dreading the pain he was about to relive. "I was playing in Denver a year and a half, two years ago when she called to tell me she was getting married."

"Alex, I'm sorry," she said, pouring herself a small shot as she felt his pain and some of her own.

"Yeah. I begged her to reconsider. I told her I'd quit the road and start a normal life with her. We talked for hours that night but I couldn't convince her. She told me she was tired of being alone and wanted to settle down, said she couldn't spend the rest of her life waiting for me. I had told her I'd get off the road before but never did. She'd been dating this guy for about six months and he was really good to her; taking her out a lot, spending a lot of time with her, and always available for her. He was everything I wasn't. Maybe she loved him, but not like me. She wanted security, and that's what she was getting with him. The following week, she married him. Her last words to me were, 'I'll always love you.'" He took another large drink. "Since she still loved me—always loved me—I figured she'd eventually divorce the guy and come back. Her getting married really bummed me out, but again, I thought I'd get another shot someday." He chuckled ironically. "Ha. A do-over." He sighed and trudged over to the window. "When I got home from the road a few weeks later, her brother called." He paused.

"And?"

He began choking up. "She and her new husband were in Costa Rica when they took one of those bus tours. I never got all the details, but the bus slid off the road and rolled." He inhaled deeply and slowly exhaled. "She didn't make it." Darlene's eyes opened wide. "That was November 8, 2016." He stopped, overcome with emotion and unable to speak.

"I'm so sorry, Alex." She waited through a long pause. "I understand that musta broken your heart, but don't you think she'd a wanted you to continue doin' what you loved?"

He nodded and whispered, "I guess."

"You didn't have nothin' to do with her dyin'."

He turned to Darlene, his face twisted with grief. "She married him because I wouldn't get off the road. If I could go back..." His words trailed off. He downed what was left of his beer and fought to regain his composure. "Yeah, she wanted me to do what I loved, and maybe we could've worked it out, but when she died, a part of me died, and my love for playing died. I loved her like I loved music. But after that, playing was an empty, soulless experience, like staring at a blank wall." He slowly shook his head, sullenly gazing at the floor. "Everything I'd done and everything I was doing—playing, writing, traveling—was meaningless. I was dead inside." He looked at Darlene. "There was no point to any of it, so I left L.A."

"But you started playin' again for me, my sister, and my daughter."

He humbly nodded. "Being here and talking with you, and playing for you guys, has helped." Another silence filled the room while Alex recounted the agonizing past. He pulled another beer from the refrigerator and continued. "I kept telling myself it wasn't my fault; she'd want me to move on. Yet, sitting at the piano, there was nothing. I had no reason to play—no inspiration. I saw no joy in the world. I drank a lot, thinking I'd go to the piano and unlock all that sadness in a song, but nothing happened. I felt unbelievable pain and grief. The emptiness was beyond agonizing, but I couldn't express it." He set the unopened beer on the table. "It was a really dark time. My inspiration was gone. I had to change... something... everything... That's when I decided to move. I thought getting away from L.A. and the road would somehow fix me. Although, I never really got off the road, as you know. But I didn't know what else to do. Nothing was working.

And after I got here, I felt no different. You never saw it, but I was seriously depressed."

"You don't seem so depressed now? What changed?"

"You and I started talking and working on these articles. After the first one, and you badgering me…" he paused, giving her a brief smile. "I realized Ananya's death was something time wasn't going to heal, which was hard to accept. But somewhere during our chats I realized it was up to me to work through losing her."

Darlene nodded. "Joey gettin' sick knocked me to my knees. And when he passed, I felt like dyin'. But I had to go on. I had Antoinette to raise, and the rest of my life to live."

"Didn't it feel like you were forgetting about them, or their life didn't matter? I mean, Ananya was the love of my life." He slowly shook his head. "I need a do-over."

"Alex, it was years 'fore a day went by that I didn't constantly think about my sweet little boy. Losin' someone's somethin' that don't ever go away, but life don't stop either. Neither does love. You never forget. But you can't change the past, and you can't go back for that do-over nonsense. The do-over is you pickin' yourself up, movin' on, and honorin' the one you lost by bein' better 'cause of what she gave you. It also means keepin' her memory alive. If you loved her, you still got it in you. I told you long ago love don't ever die."

"But she's gone."

"Do you still love her?"

He wiped a tear from his eye. "Of course."

"There you go. Love don't die. You gotta thank God you found it."

"I'm definitely not there yet, but I'll always love her."

"You're a lucky man, Alex."

He scoffed. "I don't feel lucky."

"Life ain't always 'bout gettin' what you dreamed of. Like we just wrote, it's about the journey. It's about gettin' better and learnin', and havin' experiences. Remember? Each moment adds to the last one, and if you keep chasin' what you love, you finish with no regrets"

"I can't chase Ananya anymore."

"She ain't your only love. You loved music long before you met her."

"But I'll always regret losing her."

"Do you regret fallin' in love?"

"No."

"Do you regret havin' all them memories of her?"

"Of course not, but I regret letting her get away."

"Alex, you didn't *let* her get away. And she ain't really gone." Alex furrowed his brow, confused. "She'll always be a part of you, a part that makes you better. She left you with memories that'll become inspiration and lots of other stuff you'll realize some day."

He nodded. "And love. I get it. She did. And I feel better having told you all this, and admitting it to myself."

They smiled and exchanged a warm hug, silently honoring their most bittersweet memories.

"Our chats have definitely helped me," he said. "Not just with dealing with Ananya and music, but with life. I guess it's the combination of time passing and realizing you might be right."

"Holy cow! Did you just say I was right?" she mocked.

He chuckled, but spoke sincerely. "No, I mean, to get back to your original question of why I moved to Hamilton." He took a deep breath and slowly exhaled. "Ananya was an artist. In fact, she was painting a mural at a Bel Air mansion when the owner decided to get rid of their rosewood grand piano."

Darlene's eyebrows raised. "Your piana?"

Alex nodded. "It's a long story, and I'll tell it to you someday, but Ananya loved to paint and she was incredibly talented. We used to talk about moving somewhere where she could paint all day and I could write music. She hated L.A., but I was there and she was making a pretty good living. But she never stopped dreaming about a simple life somewhere else." He paused, remembering Ananya sharing her vision for their life together. "She grew up outside of Dallas and her mother used to take her to art fairs around the state."

Surprised, Darlene interrupted. "You ain't gonna tell me she came to Hamilton?"

Alex nodded with a grin. "She mentioned Hamilton several times. 'There's this cool little town in the middle of Texas', she used to say, followed by 'It would be so perfect.'" He paused as the memories carried his thoughts away. Again, he sighed. "I'll always remember the look on her face when she talked about the simple life. She didn't care about money or fame, and she knew I was happiest when I was sitting at the piano. I *knew* that was going to be our future… Once I'd found success. Man, I was such an idiot."

"You couldn't a known."

"No, but after she passed, and I lost my inspiration, I decided to follow her… our dream. And here I am."

"Alex, I don't know what to say but there no denyin' God had a plan for both of us. If you hadn't come here, I wouldn't a written that first article."

He grinned. "I told you."

"You was makin' a joke but I'm serious."

"I know. And you're right. My moving here, meeting you, and how things have gone, can't all be coincidental."

"Amen.

"After Ananya died and my playing got worse and my writing completely stopped, I had to change my life. I wasn't thinking it at the time, but Hamilton was going to be my do-over."

Darlene smiled. "It was you who came up with those words—do-over. It was you who gave me the idea for the first article. You see Alex, you ain't outta ideas or inspiration. You'll always have 'em."

"When I first moved here I would've said no way. But in the last few weeks, I'd say, maybe."

"That's progress. It don't have to happen all at once."

"I still stare at keys a lot, but I play a little more each day. Still, it's frustrating because I want to feel the magic like before. Hopefully, those days will return."

"You'll keep tryin'. You got hit with a tough blow, but you ain't done. What happened to that young woman wasn't your fault. Quit usin' it as an excuse to hold you down. Let it be a lesson. You don't know what's gonna happen tomorrow, but you *do* know that God gave you the gift of playin' and writin' music. He put those obstacles in your path to test you and to teach you. Like we wrote today, it's how you respond that matters. It's time for you to respond, to move on, and make more outta your life, not retreat from it." She stopped at the sound of Toni pulling into the driveway with Ruth Ann.

Chapter 37

When Toni and Ruth Ann entered carrying sacks, Alex rose to see if they needed help.

"We got it," Toni said. She noticed the tablet of paper in front of Darlene. "Y'all still workin'?"

Before Darlene could answer, the doorbell rang.

"Now who's that?" Darlene asked, rising. "I ain't expectin' company."

"I got it, Mom." Toni left but quickly returned, excited.

"Mom! There's a woman from CNN here to interview you."

"Aw hell. I forgot all about that. Tell her to go away."

"You knew she was comin'?" Toni asked.

"Some woman called last week sayin' she wanted to interview me. I forgot it was today." She touched her hair and glanced down at her clothes. "I ain't decent."

Alex laughed, drawing a glare from Darlene. "You look fine," he said.

Ruth Ann took her sister by the arm. "C'mon, hon. Let's put you together." Toni joined Ruth Ann as they escorted Darlene to the bedroom.

Toni called out. "Alex, tell 'em we need a few minutes."

Alex escorted the reporter and cameraman to the dining room, and shortly after, the ladies appeared.

After making the proper introductions, Darlene and the reporter, Sherita Carrisales, sat at the dining room table while the cameraman set up across from them. Ruth Ann, Toni, and Alex stood nearby. Sherita sat next to Darlene, explaining how the interview would work. "I'll ask a little about your background; where you grew up, what you did for a living, then we'll talk about your column; why you wrote it, what inspired you, and so on."

Darlene said, "Alex oughta be here too." She waved him over.

"Ms. Viriglio, we'd like to interview you first. We can talk to everyone else later."

"But Alex helped write the articles."

"With all due respect, we want to focus on you, Ms. Viriglio, and we don't need Mr. Patterson for this interview."

"Yes, we do," Darlene insisted. "I want Alex to stay."

Sherita released a frustrated sigh, and relented with a feigned smile. "Mr. Patterson, won't you please join us?" Alex took the seat next to Darlene while Sherita addressed the cameraman. "Let's get everyone mic'd up. We'll shoot an intro scene after we're done here."

When everything was set, Sherita said, "Ready?" Darlene nodded. "Great. Here we go." Sherita turned to the camera and nodded. The red light came on and Sherita switched to her on-camera expression. "Ms. Viriglio—"

"Darlene, please."

"Darlene. Let me first say that all three of your articles blew me away. Tell me, what inspired you to write them?"

"Oh, I don't know. I guess it's just what comes outta sittin' around shootin' the bull."

"I see. Do you have a background in psychology or theology?"

"Nah, but what Christian ain't wondered 'bout dyin' and Heaven, 'specially one my age?"

"Good point. But your writing is not just attracting senior citizens. People of all ages, races, and nationalities have shared their voices with us. Why do you believe your work is so popular?"

"'Cause we're all gonna die someday so folks are interested in it. Alex, what do you think?" She put a hand on Alex's shoulder. "This is Alex. He helps me put ever'thing on paper."

Sherita turned to Alex. "Tell us about the process you and Darlene go through."

Alex grinned, looking charming. "Like she said, we talk through her ideas and then I help her focus those insights into something that makes sense on paper."

"Can you give us an example?"

"Oh," Alex thought. "One time she pressed me about my career. I was going through some setbacks and she pointed out that failure is necessary and people should embrace it. Darlene has a unique ability to look past the extraneous and drill straight into the heart of the matter."

Darlene chuckled and said, "Alex, you're spreadin' it a little thick, ain't ya?" She looked at Sherita. "Sorry."

"That's interesting," Sherita said. "You two seem to have a unique style." She focused on Darlene. "You've generated over a million views in the last few weeks. My producer tells me you have another article coming out in a few days."

"Online Tuesday," Alex offered.

"Care to give us a preview?"

"Well, I don't wanna give too much away but, it's about takin' charge of your life and not havin' regrets."

"I can't wait to read it. Darlene, people are curious about your life; where you're from, what your interests are, who influences you, and so on."

"Well, I grew up here in Hamilton, and I ain't got a lotta interests 'cept goin' to church. I used to read a lotta books, and I like gardenin', but I ain't done much of that in a while cause my old bones don't let me get up and down like they used to. I enjoy writin' but that's just recent. What was the rest of the question?"

"Tell me about growing up in Hamilton? Did you get married, have children, a career?"

"Me and my sister Ruthie grew up 'bout a mile from here. Life back then wasn't like it is today. Ever'one worked, includin' the young'uns."

"You had a job as a child?"

"Me and Ruthie had chores. We was responsible for washin' the clothes, sweepin' the floors, doin' the dishes, and anything else Momma and Daddy told us to do. That's how it was back then. You did whatever your momma and daddy told ya to do. Then, when Momma passed while me and Ruthie was still just girls, we started doin' the grocery shoppin' and the cookin'."

"Sound like a rough upbringing."

"That's just how things were. Then I got a job at the phone company."

"How old were you when you started working?"

"Lemme see, I skipped a couple a grades and finished high school at fifteen, so I guess I was fourteen or fifteen when I started."

"Did you attend college?"

"We didn't have no money, so I just kept workin'."

"What about marriage and children?"

"Me and Joe's first young'un was Joey. You met my daughter Antoinette over there," she pointed at Toni watching nearby. "She came along later. We raised her here till she got married."

"And you continued working for the phone company?"

"I worked till Joey was born. Ain't had a regular job since. I volunteered at the church and hospital while Antoinette was in school."

"There's a lot of Christian influence in your writing. Can I assume you grew up in the church?"

Darlene nodded. "Went ever Sunday, and I still do. Once I learned to read, Momma made sure I read the Bible."

"So you've lived your entire life in Hamilton? What about traveling?"

"Me and Joe'd go Dallas ever now and then, and once we visited New York City, but I'm fine right where I am."

"Where's Joe now?"

"He passed seven, eight years ago. I lived alone till Ruthie's husband passed and she moved in. And my daughter Antoinette. She practically lives here, sometimes."

"Sounds like a wonderful place to be. Tell me—"

Sherita paused when Darlene suddenly motioned to Toni and Ruth Ann. "Can one a y'all fix me 'bout two fingers of whiskey?"

Sherita smiled and made sure the cameraman continued filming.

With Ruth Ann and Toni frozen in fear of the camera, Alex got up and headed to the kitchen. Toni followed closely, saying, "You're not seriously gonna fix her a drink in the middle of an interview?"

Alex shrugged. "You're not seriously going to tell her no?"

Toni relented while Ruth Ann stepped close to her sister, trying to avoid getting in front of the camera.

"Hon, you ought'n be drinkin' liquor while they're filmin'. Everyone's gonna see it."

"Pfft," Darlene said, brushing her off. "Ain't nothin' wrong with a little nip."

Alex returned with Darlene's drink. She took a stiff shot, followed by a deep breath. She looked at Sherita. "My sister'd prefer it if y'all didn't show this part. She don't like me drinkin'—'specially on television."

Sherita smiled. "I'll see what we can do."

"Thank ya." She turned to Alex and tapped the glass on the table. "One more time." She nodded at Sherita and said, "Good for the nerves."

Alex refilled her glass and sat back down.

Darlene looked at Sherita and the cameraman. "Any y'all like a few fingers?" she asked, raising her glass.

Sherita smiled and shook her head, then waited for everyone to settle. "Ready?" Alex and Darlene nodded, and she cued the cameraman.

"Darlene, Alex mentioned how you helped him understand that failure is part of life. Is that part of your next article?"

"I don't think so, but me and Alex been talkin' a lot, and he's been bellyachin' a lot about his career." She turned to Alex. "Sorry, Alex. I ain't tryin' to air your dirty laundry." Alex smiled and nodded. "So," Darlene said to Sherita. "I told him it's easy to do easy things. If you're happy with easy, then alright. But like he said a minute ago, if you want more, you gotta get used to failin' now and then."

"That's interesting. I guess everyone faces failure; whether it's in their pursuit of a job, a relationship, or simply in a competitive sport."

"But if they kept tryin', they got better at it. And maybe didn't get what they was after but they got what they needed."

"Before we finish," Sherita said. "Any parting tips for a happier life?"

"Now, I ain't got all the answers, but I'd tell folks to listen to that voice inside a them. It knows right from wrong, and it knows what makes you happy. Listenin' to the folks around you might help, but that voice inside comes from God. *That's* the one you listen to."

"Words to live by," Sherita said.

"Listen, doll, do you have ever'thing you need? I gotta lie down."

It was obvious the day's activity had exhausted Darlene. Ruth Ann and Toni swooped in and got her to bed while Alex finished up with Sherita and the cameraman, seeing them out.

Once everyone was gone and the sisters were in bed, Alex sat with Toni in the kitchen. "Mom was out like a light. The interview wiped her out. And that drink didn't help."

"Did you see how her face lit up once they got going?"

"Yeah, but she's on medication and shouldn't be drinkin'."

"I know, but she was great. She's so comfortable in every situation. It's like she never feels pressure."

Toni smiled. "She's got a way about her."

"The cameraman cracked up when she asked for a shot of whiskey."

"That was a bad idea, but like you said, she took it in stride. She's always been comfortable in the spotlight."

"When have you seen her in the spotlight?"

"Are you kiddin'? Everywhere she goes she's the center of attention."

"She sure impressed Sherita."

Toni nodded. "I was proud of her."

"Listen," Alex said, rising. "I'd love to stay but it's been a long day."

She started laughing. "What happened to Mr. Up-All-Night? It's barely nine o'clock."

He glanced at his watch. "Man, I must be getting old. Let's make this our little secret. I don't want anyone finding out that I'm no longer a professional night owl."

"Oh, the shame."

"What about you? Aren't you working tomorrow?"

She nodded. "I am, but Monday's usually slow for me. I'll probably go in late."

"So, you're staying here tonight?"

She glanced at her watch. "Probably, but don't get any ideas about sneakin' in my window. Remember, I have a gun and I know how to use it."

He chuckled as he strolled out the door. "Thanks for the reminder."

Chapter 38

Despite feeling tired, Alex couldn't sleep. Confessing to Darlene the real reason he'd moved to Hamilton had awakened his optimism for the future.

Still, thoughts of Ananya, Darlene, and Toni crowded his mind, making him anxious. He wandered from room to room, burning off nervous energy, ending up in the backyard where he gazed at the stars, while mentally replaying recent events. Darlene's words repeated like a song stuck in his head. *Failure is necessary. You're just goin' through a dry spell. Don't you think she'd a wanted you to do what you loved? Failure is necessary.*

As the lessons looped endlessly, he understood the self-fulfilling prophecy he'd created. *I wanted to fall in love again like I did with Ananya. I wanted to write music that came from the way I felt about her.* He let those thoughts percolate for a moment, realizing they were the foundation for the struggles that had plagued him for the past eighteen months. *I dismissed Desiree, Baneta, and all those girls in L.A. because I didn't love them the way I loved Ananya. Just like I dismiss every new song idea that I wasn't excited about sharing with Ananya.* The source of his problem was clear, but a solution seemed impossible. *Ananya's gone, and with her went my inspiration.* For the first time those words sounded different. *I've been telling myself that since she died. I'm not moving on. I'm actually going out of my way <u>not</u> to move on.* It was a cathartic moment.

The reality came flooding in. Inspiration isn't the problem. He remembered Darlene telling him about her son's passing. I had to go on. I had Antoinette to raise, and the rest of my life to live. He smiled hearing her say, You never forget 'em. She left you with memories that'll become inspiration and lots of other stuff you'll realize some day. He nodded at the admission he was finally making to himself. Ananya's gone forever, and I'm still here. I'll never forget her, but I have to move on. He'd said those words to himself before, but now they had meaning. His mind raced. Time to open up to inspiration and love. I love playing. I used to. No, I do! And Desiree, Baneta, and all those other girls weren't 'the one'. Maybe I love Toni, although I barely know her. He thought about Toni and felt the fear of rejection, of pain, of loss, but he also felt his heart pound, like the excitement he felt before an important gig. It was the sound of a waking heart. He lit a cigarette, smiling at the feelings he'd been without for too long. He strolled around the yard while his thoughts wandered.

"The journey through everything," he said aloud. Success, failure, love, loss, L.A., music, moving, Darlene, Toni. He paused when Ananya popped into his head. A nostalgic smile appeared. Her memory <u>will</u> live on. I <u>will</u> finish her song. And I <u>will</u> move on.

He made a beeline for the piano and played through 'Ananya's Song', feeling totally released from the prison of his own making. He jotted down a few lyrics, knowing the rest would come someday soon, but the magic was back.

Alex played into the wee hours of the morning, full of energy and ideas.

He paced around, hoping time would speed up so he could share with Darlene. He lay down, hoping to nod off and skip through time, but his mind continued dancing through the previous few hours. Once it was evident he wouldn't sleep, he got up and opened the laptop to see if Sherita had posted Darlene's interview. It hadn't even been twelve hours since they left Darlene's house, so he expected nothing. His face lit up when he spotted a link near the top of CNN's lifestyle page. 'Interview with Do-Over columnist.'

He clicked the link and watched. Sherita had edited the one-hour interview down to a ninety-second video. There was also a synopsis below the video with links to Darlene's three articles. The video started with Sherita standing in front of Darlene's house.

"I'm here in the tiny Texas town of Hamilton to visit with Darlene Viriglio, the woman behind the wildly popular column commonly referred to as Do-over. For those of you not familiar, Darlene has written articles on various topics, including life after death but before Heaven, shedding labels, and the hero within. Her words have become a viral sensation. We sat down with Darlene, where she offered us not only her insights into how to live a happier life, but also, as she put it, 'bout three fingers of whiskey."

The next scene was Sherita and Darlene at the table.

"Tell us about growing up in Hamilton," Sherita asked. The camera started on Darlene. As she talked, the scene cut to a shot of downtown Hamilton, then faded through a series of images around town and a few rural shots of ranch land. "Me and my sister Ruthie grew up 'bout a mile from here. Life back then wasn't like it is today. Me and Ruthie was responsible for washin' the clothes, sweepin' the floors, doin' the dishes, and anything else Momma and Daddy told us to do." The image returned to Darlene. "That's how it was back then. You did what your momma and daddy told ya to do. Then, when Momma passed while we was still just girls, we started doin' the grocery shoppin' and the cookin'."

Sherita followed up with questions about her religious background.

While Darlene answered, the screen filled with a shot of her church then back to Darlene. "Went to church ever Sunday, and I still do. Once I learned to read, Momma made sure I read the Bible." The video mixed shots of Sherita listening intently and Darlene speaking thoughtfully. "It's easy to do easy things. If you're happy with easy, then alright. But if you want more, you gotta get used to failin' now and then."

Sherita added a voiceover while an image of Alex appeared. "Darlene insisted we include Alex, the man who helps organize her thoughts and get them down on paper."

The camera returned to Sherita when she asked for Darlene's advice on how to live.

"Listenin' to the folks around you might help but that voice inside comes from God. It knows right from wrong, and it knows what makes you happy. *That's* the voice you listen to."

Finally, Sherita added a scene of her sitting at a desk in the studio. "We added this next clip because we believe this inspiring woman is the real deal. She was genuine in every way, gracious, honest, and without an ounce of pretense. She never tried to hide anything or put on any kind of act. We couldn't have been more impressed with Darlene, so we included the one clip that touched us all." The image returned to Darlene's dining room.

"Can one a y'all fix me 'bout two fingers of whiskey?"

While the camera rolled on Darlene holding up a shot glass, Sherita voiced, "To which she also looked at the crew and said, 'Any y'all like a few fingers?'"

The final shot was of Sherita in the studio. "What a wonderful and fascinating woman. Be on the lookout for her next column and maybe next time we sit down with her, we'll join her for a few fingers of whiskey."

Alex replayed the video several times. He was so excited he couldn't sit still.

He sat at the piano and played whatever came out. The ideas came fast, and for a time, he pulled out his legal pad and jotted down a few words as he played through 'Ananya's Song'. He nodded and repeated the hook line he'd been searching for for the last eighteen months. *She's the hero in me.*

No sleep, but still too early to show Darlene the video, he decided to compose himself and begin the day.

As he showered, his mind continued in overdrive—filled with musical ideas and a few lyrics. He slipped on a pair of jeans and rushed back to the piano with wet hair. He tinkered with his newest idea, the one he'd discovered during the last performance for the sisters. It was an emotional ballad, much like 'Ananya's Song'. Suddenly, Darlene's words came thundering into his head—*At the*

End of the Day, Did it Go Your Way?—and he stopped. His scattered thoughts suddenly come into focus. He grabbed a notepad and began writing madly. He set the pad on the music stand and again played the song while the words bounced around his head. *She didn't have long… I'm sorry… You've got it all wrong… Outta my hands… No need to cry… Blessing in disguise.* Slowly, the words fell into place. He played the first verse and chorus over and over, singing the melody softly to himself. "At the end of the day, did it go your way?" He occasionally paused to revise and embrace the renewed inspiration. Gone were the losses, setbacks, and failures, and in their place was a beautiful song. Suddenly, a wave of sadness washed over him, remembering Susanne, and knowing this wonderful song was about an imminent loss; Darlene. Alone, he longed for Ananya's presence to share the moment and listen to the song. With tears in his eyes, he choked up. He played on as the words again flowed. He wrote and wrote—filling up two pages. Later, he would organize and fine tune them. He stared at the paper, cigarette in hand, shocked by his sudden accomplishment. "Wow."

He looked up to see the sun peering through the window and remembered Darlene's interview. He smiled and played the new song—Darlene's Song—one more time.

* * *

At seven a.m. Alex spotted a light coming from Darlene's kitchen window. He sent a text message to Toni.

- *You up?*

She quickly responded,

- *Yep. Couldn't sleep thinking about me?*

Alex smiled, walked across the street with his laptop, and gently tapped on the kitchen door.

Toni answered wearing a robe. "What're you doin' up so early? I knew you couldn't stay away from me."

"Well, yeah. But also they posted the interview online." He held up his laptop.

"No way. Already?" She let him in and both hurried to the kitchen table. Alex loaded the page and watched the video with Toni.

"Wow," she said. "This is great."

"Let's show it to your mom."

"She ain't up yet. But Aunt Ruthie is. I'll grab her." She scurried away and returned with her aunt.

As the trio watched the interview several times, Ruth Ann swelled with pride, saying, "She's gotta see this." She started for Darlene's room.

"Let her sleep," Toni said.

"She can go back to bed later."

Alex started the video again while Ruth Ann left to wake up Darlene.

"They almost cut you out completely," Toni teased.

"I think Sherita wanted to."

Toni smiled and nodded, then playfully leaned against him. They quietly enjoyed the cozy moment until a terrible cry echoed through the house.

They raced into Darlene's room and found Ruth Ann draped across Darlene's body, bellowing.

Toni slowly approached the bed as a thousand thoughts flooded her mind, all trying to make sense of what she was seeing. *This isn't happening, I just saw her.* A part of her expected Darlene to open her eyes and sit up. She continued staring, willing her mother to wake up. *C'mon,* she wished. *Wake up!* She remembered vividly the moment Darlene broke the news to her about her father's passing.

It was a haunting memory Toni rarely visited. Strolling down a lengthy corridor in Hamilton General Hospital, she caught sight of her mother leaning against a wall, one hand firmly pressed against it for support, while her head was buried in her other hand. When Toni approached, Darlene glanced up, displaying a look that Toni had never seen before. The memory of her mother's overwhelming sorrow was possibly the most agonizing recollection Toni held onto. She shook her head to clear the awful image, yet found herself faced with a harsh reality that was quickly becoming too much to handle.

Staring at her deceased mother, Toni's heart and mind filled with fear and grief. She took a reluctant step toward the bed and tears streamed down her face as she crumbled beside Ruth Ann on the bed.

Alex remained standing in the doorway, motionless. *She's gone*, he said to himself, not really believing his own thoughts. It was surreal, but also starkly real. *What am I going to do without her? She the only one who understood what I've been going through.* His self-centered thoughts quickly faded away when he revisited the day she told him this was coming. *I wonder if she knew how close it was?* he thought. Seeing the two heartbroken ladies before him, Alex experienced a sense of déjà vu, having pictured this day every time Toni mentioned her mother's health. It was a sad moment that Darlene had prepared him for, but one he hadn't expected so soon, and without warning.

Chapter 39

Word of Darlene's passing spread rapidly. CNN posted the news below the interview video. Social media picked up on her passing, driving large numbers of followers to view the video; the only public images of Darlene.

Larry released Darlene's fourth article, 'At the End of the Day, Did it Go Your Way?' online the day after her passing.

The comments overflowed the message board, the largest response so far. Many offered condolences, but most commented on the article.

I was waiting for retirement to take a trip to Alaska with my wife. Now it's 'why wait?' Thank you. ~JJ, Newark, NJ

Your article described me perfectly. I always worried about tomorrow and spent years not living today. I've got a long list of things I'm planning to do and I can't wait to get up each day. No regrets. ~CH, Cleveland, OH

* * *

The regulars at Whitman's sat around for hours talking about Darlene.

"I didn't know her like the rest of y'all," Caroline, the counter girl, said. "But one time this jerk from out of town called me an ugly name. Darlene said to me, 'He don't know you. And if he did, he'd know *he* was the donkey.' I never forgot it."

"She was that way," Kirk, a local merchant, said. "She didn't have to confront the jerks. She understood the importance of speaking up for the mistreated person."

"Oh, she could be confrontational," Mary, a high school teacher, said. "I remember one time she saw a freshman boy knock down a young girl in the market. Darlene stepped in front of that boy and said, 'Son, I know your momma didn't raise you to treat young ladies like that. Now you apologize right now and don't let it happen again.' I thought the boy was gonna mouth off, but she was intimidating. That boy apologized and you can bet he didn't do that again." The grouped chuckled.

Over at Nita's Deli, Nita, the owner said, "She was a no-nonsense woman who spoke her mind; just like she did in the paper. When I was thinking about opening this place, she said, 'Nita, you don't mind workin' and I ain't never known you to quit. I think you could make a go of it.' She was all about empowering you to solve your own problems rather than telling you to do things her way. I'm gonna miss her."

* * *

Darlene's inner circle congregated at Darlene and Ruth Ann's house, turning it into the hub for everything related to the funeral, which was eventually scheduled for Saturday.

Toni and Alex drifted around the house—often into the backyard to escape the activity—on their phones making funeral arrangements. Sarah and the Sunday school ladies managed the house as mourners began stopping by Monday afternoon to express their condolences and offering to help. Soon the house was overflowing with food, and the phone rang constantly with local and out-of-town well-wishers.

Alex met up with Toni just outside Ruth Ann's bedroom.

"I talked to Pastor Brown, like you asked," Alex said.

"He's gonna do the service?"

"He said he'd be honored, but the sanctuary won't hold everyone."

"I got a call from Sherita at CNN. I don't know how she got my number, but she said to expect a lotta people. Everybody's askin' when and where the funeral's gonna be."

Alex thought for a moment. "What about that resort just outside town?"

"Circle T?"

"Yeah. You think they'd let us use it?"

Toni said, "I'll call 'em."

"If they say yes, I can cover the deposit."

"Thanks Alex. I think Mom had some money saved so whatever you spend we can probably reimburse."

"I'm not worried about it," Alex said.

Ruth Ann remained hidden, devastated, and unable to help with any of the arrangements.

* * *

Out-of-town visitors began arriving Tuesday, some bringing flowers or gifts, but some simply dropping by to express their sympathy. Additionally, several reporters were spotted around town with cameramen.

Dorothy glanced at the crowd outside Darlene and Ruth Ann's house. "Y'all want me to do something about the people out front?"

The ladies hesitated and exchanged glances until Toni said, "These people mean a lot to Mom." She went outside, stood on the porch, and began greeting visitors.

A few feet from the door, an older woman stepped forward and took hold of Toni's hand. "I am so sorry," the woman said. "My name is Ellen Masters, and I drove here from El Paso the moment I heard about Darlene." Tears began running down her cheek, but she kept talking, struggling to maintain her composure. "I've been trying to get my life back on track after… well, it doesn't really matter why. Everyone around me was being nice and trying to help, but it wasn't until I read Darlene's column and I saw that video that I realized getting my life back was up to me. It was her straight-forward, no nonsense way of dealing with things that saved me… or rather inspired me to save myself."

Toni listened carefully, trying not to breakdown. "Thank you," she said softly, sniffling. "Mom woulda been pleased to hear that?"

Ellen stepped closer and gave her a tight hug. "I am so sorry. I obviously didn't know her, but I feel like I did and I had to come here."

"Thank you."

Ellen politely stepped back as the next visitors stepped forward. It was a young man in uniform with his brother. "Ma'am. I'm Staff Sergeant Timothy Akins and this is my little brother Scott. We lost our older brother in Afghanistan in 2015. We never talked about it or about him because it was just too hard. When I read Darlene's first column, the one about the road to Heaven, something happened. I sent the link to everyone in my family and suddenly we all started talking about what happened. Ma'am," he said, swallowing the lump in his throat. "It was like that article brought our brother back to us. We started sharing stories about him, how he talked, how he laughed, and all the great things he meant to all of us."

Toni nodded. "Mom had a special place in her heart for servicemen."

"Yes, ma'am, and we all have a special place in our hearts for her. She gave us back something that had left us all lost. Perhaps we'll reunite with our brother, but regardless, his presence remains in our hearts and in our conversations when we gather."

Choked up, Toni said, "I'm sorry you lost him, but thank you for reading Mom's words. If she were here she'd be humbled by your story."

"Thank you, ma'am."

Toni listened to a few more stories, but the overwhelming emotions forced her to step inside.

Alex stepped outside to take over. Some recognized him from the video.

* * *

The number of cars passing by—some stopping to leave flowers and gifts—continued to grow. They drove by day and night, some with license plates from far-off places like Oregon and Maine. The front yard quickly become a makeshift shrine.

The volume of visitors created major gridlock in town; far worse than the annual arts fair. People parked miles away and walked to the house, determined to pay their respects. Their walk became a pilgrimage of sorts.

The outpouring swamped Alex and Toni, keeping them far too busy to mourn. Alex reached out to some old friends for help with the funeral, anticipating a very large turnout. Several remarked that they'd been loyal readers of Darlene's column and were thrilled when they saw Alex on the CNN interview. They were eager to help in any way they could. It humbled Alex that so many people he'd thought were just passing acquaintances were actually interested and concerned about him.

* * *

The funeral was set for one o'clock Saturday at the Circle T. Alex worked with the resort to accommodate as many people as possible in their pavilion. The open-air facility could comfortably seat a few hundred, but they were expecting more than a thousand to attend Darlene's funeral. Alex's friends rounded up as many chairs as they could find but many would be left standing.

By Thursday morning, with the arrangements coming together, Alex returned to Darlene's house, where things were chaotic.

Toni paced back and forth, talking on the phone with the funeral director. "If Mom already picked out a casket, then let's stay with that."

"Very good," Mr. Bowman, the funeral director, said. "I assume you're doing a viewing on Friday at the funeral home."

"We hadn't talked about it but I guess so. When do y'all move the casket?"

"Saturday, before the service."

"And then y'all move it to the gravesite after the service?"

"Indeed. We will coordinate with all involved parties and lead the procession from the service to the gravesite."

As they spoke, Toni's phone beeped several times with other callers. She said, "I hate to cut this short, but my phone keeps blowin' up."

"Very good," Mr. Bowman said. "We're very sorry for your loss, and please call us if you remember anything else."

She thanked him, hung up, and sighed, glancing at all the missed calls.

* * *

Friday morning, a large group gathered outside the funeral home, including many out-of-town attendees.

When Alex, Toni, and Ruth Ann pulled into the funeral home parking lot, Ruth Ann absently said, "My, look at all the cars. She sure got to a lotta folks."

Toni climbed out and opened the door, helping Ruth Ann out. She'd been almost catatonic since the day Darlene passed. Toni and Alex flanked her as they entered the building. Despite their apprehension, all three pushed through to see Darlene, knowing it would be their final meeting.

"You sure you wanna do this?" Toni asked Ruth Ann.

"She's my sister. I gotta say goodbye." Hearing her own words, she became teary.

The trio passed through the foyer and entered the chapel. Seeing the casket, both ladies immediately began crying. Alex stoically fought back the tears. They stood over the open casket staring at Darlene.

"Do you want some time alone?" Alex asked Ruth Ann. She never took her eyes off her sister but shook her head no. Sensing they could have stood there indefinitely, at the appointed hour, Alex whispered, "It's time." He escorted them back into the foyer where the mourners were waiting to view the body and pay their respects. Ruth Ann wasn't ready to receive anyone so Toni escorted her to a chair where she sat for a few minutes composing herself.

Toni and Alex stood between her and the crowd as several approached to express their condolences. A few offered soft words of comfort.

Slowly, Ruth Ann rose and stood between Alex and Toni, but rarely spoke. When long-time friends like Buford and Ada McCaleb approached, they hugged her and wept. Others, including Pastor Brown, organist Esma Beth Anderson, and Miss Virginia, hugged Ruth Ann and offered kind words. Ruth Ann mostly nodded, wiping her sniffles with a tissue.

Ruth Ann soon grew tired, so Sarah and Irma drove her home.

Alex and Toni stayed until the funeral director passed the word that the viewing was ending. He closed the casket, followed by closing the chapel. The crowd mingled for a short time until Toni and Alex left.

Chapter 40

Hamilton was gridlocked on the day of the funeral, with cars parked everywhere and traffic limited to one direction at a time. Thankfully, a local police officer cleared the route from Darlene's house to the Circle T.

The limousine dropped Alex, Toni, and Ruth Ann behind the stage, which helped them avoid walking through the crowd. They were led to reserved seats off to one side of the stage where select members of Darlene's inner circle sat.

The attendees spilled out far beyond the covered pavilion onto the undeveloped land. Alex's friends had set up a small stage with a powerful sound system that could reach the masses. They managed to round up 800 chairs; not even enough for half of the crowd. The remaining mourners stood.

Toni glanced out at the crowd then leaned over to Alex. "Wow! Who are all these people?" He nodded and shrugged; his eyes wide with surprise. The crowd wasn't rowdy but large enough that the ground rumbled.

Seated on the aisle, near the front, Toni spotted Andy sitting with his mother and Victoria Olsen. She hadn't seen or talked with him since their final blow up outside her work. For a split second, irritation filled Toni, but the feeling quickly subsided and she felt pleased that Andy had found someone. She smiled hearing Darlene's words; *You'd be marryin' a man you don't love.* "Talk about dodgin' a bullet," she blurted as her thoughts inadvertently leaked out.

"What?" Alex asked.

She smiled and took Alex's hand. "Nothin'."

He smiled, comforted by their interlocked fingers.

Ruth Ann was faring better than expected—distracted by the size of the crowd—until she began weeping at the sight of the casket surrounded by a mountain of flowers. It was near the front of the stage with a lone podium directly behind it.

Esma Beth stepped to the podium and simply said, "Please join me." She sat at the piano and led the congregation in singing 'It Is Well with My Soul', followed by 'Great Is Thy Faithfulness'. Many knew the songs while the rest followed the printed words in the program.

Pastor Brown stepped up to the microphone, intimidated by the largest funeral in Hamilton history, certainly the largest crowd he'd ever addressed, but composed. After delivering the classic scripted funeral service he'd learned in divinity school—quoting the Bible's explanation of life, death, Heaven and Jesus—he personalized his concluding remarks. "Darlene was a friend to many. A faithful friend. A loyal friend. I cannot count the number of parishioners who, over the years, have come to me saying they had confided in Darlene some great tribulation, some great burden, some overwhelming secret. And, in her own special way, Darlene comforted and guided them, never breaking anyone's confidence, never letting it known all the secrets she knew, never betraying her fellow man or woman. And for those who knew her best, knew she always enjoyed a good piece of gossip." The audience chuckled. "She was a wonderful Christian, a true friend, and a trusted confidant who was always there when you needed her. And while she stood tall in the spotlight, fearless and unwavering, she never sought the attention so many crave. Her faith in God was strong and without question. We all witnessed the confident, self-assured woman Darlene was, yet she was never arrogant in her heart. Those close to her and readers of her divine words witnessed her boundless care, compassion, and unwavering conviction to aid those in need. I am sure God is pleased to have her sitting beside Him today. And I am sure she smiled when He welcomed her saying, good job faithful servant. We will always remember her as our beloved sister, mentor, and friend." He paused before bowing his head to say a short prayer. He stepped back and Sarah took the podium. Ruth Ann declined to speak, too overcome with emotion.

Sarah stared at the crowd, fighting back tears. "I've known Darlene most of my life, and there's one thing that never changed. You always knew where you stood with Dar. If she said it, she believed it. No straddlin' the fence, as she'd say. I remember one time when we was in our twenties. I think it was 1969, and we was gonna drive to Dallas to see the Creedence Clearwater Revival. She'd never heard of 'em, but said she'd like goin' to a revival. We didn't tell her it wasn't *exactly* a revival. Well, durin' the drive she found out it was a rock and roll band that played secular music. She ordered me to turn the car around and take her home that instant." The audience laughed. "She wouldn't speak to me the rest of that summer. But that was who she was. Like Pastor Brown said, she was a woman of conviction and principles. But she'd also give you anything she had if you needed it. It wasn't long after that concert when I was gettin' married but didn't have money for a dress. She'd been savin' her money for somethin', I don't remember what, but without a second thought, she handed me more money than I needed to buy my dress and said, 'Get what you want, hon, and don't think nothin' more 'bout it.'" She paused as she choked up. "I don't think she ever knew how much that meant to me. And I can't count the number of times she was there for me. If I needed a place to stay 'cause I was put out, or help when times were lean, or just someone to talk through somethin' that had me tied up, she never hesitated, not one second, and she never held it over me later." She blurted out a sob that was a mixture of laughter and pain. "Sometimes she wasn't even speakin' to me 'cause I made her mad or somethin', but even then, if I needed help, she'd come runnin'. A true, honest friend to the end." She looked up. "We love you." With tears streaming, she walked away from the podium.

Toni stepped up next. "Mom wasn't like most moms." She started choking up, unable to continue. She took a step back and stared at her mother's casket. The crowd broke down as the wailing grew. She briefly glanced at Ruth Ann, then composed herself and returned to the podium. She unfolded her prepared words.

"Mom wasn't like most moms. You couldn't get anything past her." A soft chuckle washed through the room, easing Toni's stress. "I remember bein' in junior high and we skipped class to go swimmin' in the Walker's stock pond. When I got home, the first thing outta Mom's mouth was 'How was the water?'" The crowd laughed. "I learned long ago you couldn't hide nothin' from her. When I had a bad day, she knew it immediately, and she'd find a way to make me feel better. She never let me keep my problems bottled up. As much as I wanted to keep 'em to myself, she'd pry 'em outta me just so we could talk 'em through. When my first boyfriend broke up with me, she said he ain't the last boy on earth and he ain't gonna be the last one to break your heart." She reflected. "Like Sarah said, she gave of herself, no matter how bad her own life was. She cried with me when Daddy died. Oh, she put up a strong front, but she also shared her sadness, showin' me she felt the same pain as I did, even though hers was probably a lot worse. She said 'We'll never forget your daddy 'cause he left us a part of himself. Sometimes you're gonna hear him talkin' to you, and it's gonna make you sad. But that's 'cause he's always with you.'"

She again paused to collect her emotions.

"Mom could drive you nuts. There were times I just wanted her to be on my side, like when I caught my boyfriend cheatin'. I thought for sure she'd load Daddy's shotgun and tell me she goin' to take care of him." The crowd again laughed. "But no, not my mom. She said 'He ain't worth wastin' the shells on.' And as I think back, I understand now how she knew I wasn't all that crazy 'bout that boy, so him cheatin' on me was actually a blessin' 'cause it made it easy to move on. She had a way of seein' things for what they really were, not what I wanted to see at the time. Now…" she took a long deep breath. "Now, like she said about Daddy, she's gonna live on, not just inside those of us who knew her but with everyone she's touched with her writin'." She gazed at the casket. "Mom, I'll miss you every day and I'll love you forever."

She stepped back and Alex met her next to the podium. He gave her a long hug, then took the podium. He'd faced large crowds before, but never as a speaker, and never with this much raw emotion.

"I only knew Darlene for a short time." Alex started, his voice quivering. "But Darlene Viriglio had a greater impact on my life than any other force in nature. Today, we celebrate her life, but I can only share with you how she impacted mine. I met Darlene about a year ago when I was at a low point in life. Almost from the day we met, she started asking about me and why I had moved to Hamilton. For those of you who didn't know her personally, Darlene could see through any smoke screen you put up. I told her I was leaving my chosen career because I'd had a long run of failures. Well, she never accepted that and said I was pushin' manure." The crowd chuckled. "For months, I danced around her questions, trying to keep my struggles private but she wouldn't give up. She wasn't being nosey or trying to run my life. All she wanted was to help. And with me, she did. For months, I sat with her chatting and drinking and listening to her unique outlook on life. As most of you know, her words were powerful; often saying a lot with only a few words." He paused as if to ponder. "Words, interesting and insightful, but still mere words. As days and weeks went by, I not only heard her words in my head, I understood more about what she was saying and soon I started seeing things differently… more clearly. Just hours before she passed, Darlene said to me, 'Alex, the ones you love always leave something special in you that lives on.' I realize now what she was saying. Like Toni's story moments ago about the passing of her father, Darlene's husband, she was telling us that those we lose don't just leave us with love. They leave what they created in us; something truly special, unique, perhaps divine. Whatever it is, it will always live on as a part of us. The people we love change us in ways we don't even realize until after they're gone. They make us better and more complete." He took a deep breath. "As the days pass without Darlene, I still hear her words... Words, but so much more. 'Failure is necessary. No one starts out great at anything. Let the good in all of us that God sees be the force that drives you. No regrets at the end.'" The crowd rumbled with a few claps and 'amens'. "Darlene believed God has a plan but also that life is a journey that we should never give up on. She gave us hope that perhaps some of us will get a do-over."

The crowd started clapping, but he put up a hand to stop them. "Her final words to me... Her final *instructions*." He took a few deep breaths and slowly nodded. "'Alex, it's time for you to respond, to move on, and to make more outta your life and not retreat from it.'" He took a moment to let that sink in. "It won't be easy," he said through a cracking voice. "But she would want everyone to move on. To make more out of your life. To never retreat. Those were her final words to me." He smiled, wiped a tear. "We will miss her every day, and I hope to meet her again, someday, somewhere."

He stepped away from the podium and sat at the piano, adjusting the microphone. The crowd went completely silent. "I call this 'At the End.' He paused and looked up, "Darlene, this is what you inspired in me. I hope you like it." He began playing the song that came to him while playing for the sisters and Toni, and singing the lyrics that flooded his thoughts the night after Darlene's CNN interview.

> When she told me, she didn't have long.
> I said I'm sorry. She said you've got it all wrong.
> It outta my hands. There's no need to cry.
> It's a blessing in disguise.
>
> She took my hand and led me out in the rain.
> She asked me if I would waste this day if it's all that remains?
> How many weeks would pass? A year goes by.
> Am I living or just waiting to die?
>
> At the end of the day, did it go your way?
> At the end of the week, will you look back and smile?
> At the end of the year, will you stand and cheer?
> It's simple my friend, no regrets at the end.
> It's simple my friend, no regrets at the end.
>
> The Father called her home yesterday.
> Her final words trust your heart to find your way.
> 'Cause when you look in the mirror
> Are you living your best life?
> It's simply my friend, now it's your time to fly.
>
> At the end of the day, did it go your way?
> At the end of the week will you look back and smile?
> At the end of the year will you stand and cheer?
> It's simple my friend, no regrets at the end
> It's simple my friend, no regrets at the end

It's simple my friend, no regrets at the end

When he finished, the crowd applauded as he quietly walked off.

Pastor Brown led a prayer, followed by Esma Beth leading the throngs in singing 'Amazing Grace'. Hearts poured out in song, leaving an unforgettable magic in the air. Pastor Brown concluded the service with a final prayer.

The gravesite service was brief with only Toni, Ruth Ann, Alex, and the Sunday ladies attending. Pastor Brown offered a few words and a prayer. Ruth Ann was almost catatonic from fatigue and grief. The ladies rallied around her, helping her into the car and making sure at least one of them was with her for the next several days.

Chapter 41

By Sunday afternoon, the day after the funeral, the frenzy at Darlene's house had slowed, but Toni was still busy with phone calls, visitors, and deliveries.

Alex spotted Toni's truck parked in Ruth Ann's driveway and texted, asking if he could stop by.

She replied:
- *Come in through the garage. I'm taking a break from answering the door.*

He found Toni in Darlene's bedroom looking at her computer, crying.

"You okay?" he asked.

She sniffled and nodded. "I been watchin' the coverage of Mom's funeral."

Alex stood behind Toni as they watched several videos about Darlene's funeral that had been posted.

A young woman faced the reporter, saying, "I stumbled on to Darlene's column and it hit me like a light going on. *I* was the obstacle, and *I* was the problem. But I picked myself up and almost immediately landed a great job. Now I feel like that guy who spoke and sang at the service—failure's no longer a label that keeps me down. It's part of what makes me better."

"Cool," Alex said. "I'm glad they're running these."

Toni nodded. "Theres a bunch more."

They focused on the next video as a man spoke above a caption reading Miguel Rivera, Chicago Il. "I was going nowhere and I wanted more out of life, so I started volunteering at the local food bank. Next month I start college again."

The scene cut to Phyllis from Orlando Fl. "I can't believe she's gone," she started, wiping her eyes. "I read one of her columns and it was like she gave me permission to make the change. Now, rather than counting the days until retirement, I'm starting a new business and can't imagine stopping. I just wish she were here so I could tell her what she did for me."

Toni clicked to another media outlet where they watched Jackson from Colorado Springs, Co., with a big smile. "She made me want to go to church again."

Toni looked at Alex and said, "See, some people *do* start goin' to church again."

He chuckled. "Point taken. Now that I'm pretty sure I won't catch fire."

She laughed, and they watched a few more videos.

"Mom woulda been so proud."

* * *

The press reported on selfless acts in and around Hamilton, mostly rides shared and meals.

The townspeople responded to the large influx of out-of-towners in the same way they handled the annual arts fair; they all worked together, but this time to honor the memory of the Hamilton's most famous citizen.

Since Darlene's passing, the mailman delivered countless letters and packages daily. It wasn't until Monday when Toni and Ruth Ann started opening the cards, letters, and packages together, sharing the tributes to Darlene. While they often cried, reading about Darlene's impact on so many lives, it also helped Ruth Ann begin the process of returning to life again.

"I never thought my sister'd touch so many people. But I'm glad she did. She'd be so proud."

Toni hugged Ruth Ann and said, "Mom made things better for everyone."

While Ruth Ann continued working through the mail, Toni divided her time between helping Ruth Ann and returning phone calls.

On Monday afternoon, Toni hadn't seen Alex all day so she called him.

"Hey," she said. "Where are you?"

"I just pulled into Circle T. They called me about settling-up."

"I thought you already paid that."

"Only the deposit."

"You ain't responsible for payin'. Let me know how much it is and me and Aunt Ruthie'll reimburse you. Hopefully, Mom left some money."

"We'll work it out later. How're you doing?"

She sighed from exhaustion. "Oh, I'm alright. I finally got Aunt Ruthie to lie down."

"How's she doing?"

"Better. Me and her been goin' through some of the letters people sent, but I still got a lotta folks callin' and stoppin' by."

"If it gets too crazy over there, feel free to hide out at my house. I left the door unlocked, like a real Hamiltonian. It's quiet and you can sleep. Just don't wake up my girlfriend."

She again laughed. "That might be funny if I knew it wasn't true."

"It's not. My girlfriend's father won't let her spend the night."

She again laughed. "Stop it. Are you comin' over?"

"Maybe later."

Irma and Sarah came in through the kitchen so Toni said, "I gotta go. I'll see ya later."

Alex entered the business office for the Circle T resort where he was greeted by the Director of Operation, Francine Bostick.

"Good afternoon Mr. Patterson."

"Alex, please."

They shook hands, and both sat. She opened a folder on her desk and pulled out an envelope. She handed it to Alex. "This is your deposit."

Alex reached for the envelope, confused. "I don't understand. Was there a problem with my check?"

She smiled. "No, not at all. Someone paid the entire bill, so we're simply returning your deposit."

"Who?"

"They asked to remain anonymous."

Alex's mind ran wild, wondering who would have paid. It wasn't cheap.

"I'd really like to thank them. Was it someone from out of town? I won't tell anyone."

"I wish I could, but I gave my word not to reveal their identity."

"Man," Alex said. "It could've been anyone."

He thanked Francine and left.

As Alex stepped outside the Circle T office, one car in the parking lot caught his attention. It was the one he'd ridden in when he was looking at houses.

He approached the car, and the driver rolled down her window. "Get in," she said.

Puzzled, Alex got in the front seat of Cynthia Coker's car.

"How are you?" Alex asked. "We haven't talked since you sold me the house. Where are we going?"

Cynthia looked around, making sure no one was watching.

"Nowhere. I just don't want anyone seein' us talkin'."

"Okay?" he suspiciously replied.

"I guess you know someone paid the funeral bill."

With raised eyebrows, Alex pointed at her.

"Look," Cynthia continued. "I'm telling you this because I don't want you asking around about who paid, and I don't want anyone else askin'."

"Okay?"

She again looked around. "I want your word that you'll tell no one."

"Okay."

She stared at him for an uncomfortable moment, glanced around, then shifted sideways in her seat to face him. "I'm sure you know I'm not the most popular person in town, especially with Darlene."

Alex smiled and shrugged. "I'm not exactly the homecoming king."

She smiled. "Well, just like you, I am who I am. But there's something about me and Darlene no one knows." Alex suddenly felt special, like a real Hamiltonian, getting a piece of gossip no one else had. "But if you repeat it, I'll deny it till the day I die."

"I won't."

"Darlene and I been feudin' since I don't remember when. We've always been like oil and vinegar. We disagree even when we agree."

Alex appeared puzzled by her statement.

"It doesn't matter," she said. "But we've never gotten along." She paused, taking in a deep breath. "Several years ago, Darlene was late getting to the bowling alley one Sunday. You know about the Sunday school meeting?"

"I've heard."

"That morning, my husband and I were having the worst fight we'd ever had. Hudson had followed me, yellin' and carryin' on like I'd never seen before. I thought for sure everyone in the bowling alley was gonna hear him and I tried to get him to calm down. Then, I see Darlene coming down the sidewalk and I wanted to die. I just knew she'd relish in seeing Hudson acting a fool. In a panic I grabbed Hudson by arm and shook him, ordering him to shut up." She again paused, reliving the memory. "He'd never been violent with me, but outta nowhere he ripped his arm free and shoved me into the wall, almost knocking me out."

Alex's eyes lit up. "Wow."

"At first I thought it was an accident and I expected Hudson to help me up and apologize, but he just stood there lookin' down at me like a crazy man. I didn't know if he was gonna hit me or kick me or what. In an instant, Darlene jumped between me and Hudson. I thought he was gonna take a swing at her or at least shove her down like he did me, but she stood there eyein' Hudson and pokin' him in the chest. 'Don't you ever treat a lady like that again!' she shouted. She had a look on her face like I'd never seen." Cynthia nervously chuckled. "It startled Hudson, and he took a step back. And after she stared him down, he turned and left."

"Wow. I knew she was tough, but that was brave."

"Whatever it was, I was grateful. You can't image. It wasn't just what Hudson did that shocked me, it was the fact that Darlene had put herself in harm's way *for me*."

"No doubt. What happened after that?"

"Darlene helped me up and made sure I was okay. I had a knot on the back of my head and I'm sure I looked awful, so I certainly couldn't go into the bowling alley. She looked me in the eye and said, 'You shouldn't go home till Hudson cools down, and even then, I'd wait a while.' I didn't know what to do. Back then, Hudson controlled all the money, so I had nowhere to go. Darlene reached into her purse and dug out a hundred-dollar bill. 'Here,' she said. 'This is my mad money. Put yourself up in a hotel for a few days while you figure out what to do.' I was in such a daze, I took the cash, but I just stood there. She walked me to my car and said, 'Look, ain't no one allowed to treat a lady like that, and you know it. You tell Hudson he can't ever do that again or you'll leave him for good. And if you start changin' your mind, call me, and I'll give him an earful.'"

"Man, that had to be the most surreal moment of your life. Your sworn enemy coming to the rescue."

Cynthia chuckled, hearing Alex put it like that. "To say the least. But to make a long story short, Hudson begged me to forgive him. He took an anger management class and since then he's apologized more times than I can count, and never again even raised his voice to me."

"That's great. I understand why you don't want anyone knowing about your husband."

"I don't care about that. Hell, half the women in this town have been pushed around by their husbands at one time or another. I don't want anyone to know what Darlene did."

"Why? She's a hero."

"Yes, she is. She knows it and I know it, but we never spoke about it and I'm pretty sure she never told a soul."

"Okay?" Alex said, clearly not understanding.

"You see, Alex, Darlene never did anything for recognition. She's exactly what everyone described at her funeral. She always did the right thing because it was the right thing. I'm forever indebted to her for that day."

Alex smiled. "So you paid for the funeral."

Cynthia nodded. "And no one can ever know."

"They'll never hear it from me, but I'm glad you told me."

Cynthia's eyes welled up. "I hated her, but I loved her," she said, choking up.

Alex felt a lump forming in his throat. "Don't make me start." He opened the car door and stepped out.

"I envy you Alex."

"Me?"

"You got to be close to her."

He nodded. "We're both fortunate."

She smiled and nodded as he closed the car door.

As Alex started for home, he smiled and looked up at the sky.

Chapter 42

By Wednesday, the out-of-town crowd was mostly gone and Hamilton was returning to normal. Alex and Toni sat on the couch, finally relaxing after days of exhaustion.

Toni went to the refrigerator and grabbed a beer for Alex. She also grabbed the bottle and a glass for a few fingers of Darlene's whiskey. "Shall we toast Mom?"

Alex's sleepy eyes came to life. "Sure."

Toni wasn't much of a drinker but poured herself a small glass of Jack Daniel's.

Alex opened the beer and held up the can. "To Darlene."

"To Mom."

"What a week. I think I talked to every person in this town. Pastor Brown said he was going to use some of her articles for his next sermon."

"That's pretty cool," Toni said, pouring herself a second shot. "I heard a lotta people say they was readin' the Bible again."

"That's funny. I heard people say they didn't know where theirs was so they were going to buy a new one."

"Me and Aunt Ruthie got Mom's will tomorrow. She didn't have much but Ruthie'll get the house and I'll probably get the rest. We're her only blood."

"That's sounds about right. Then I assume you'll get the house when Ruth Ann passes."

"Probably. Let's hope that's not anytime soon. I wish Mom had time to put something in her will for you."

"What? No, I'm not family and I barely knew her."

"No, I mean somethin' meaningful to her, like if she had a lucky pen or somethin' like that."

"I don't need anything to remember her by. Her words inspired a great song and a lot of new ideas, which I haven't had in a long time. I've also gotten a few calls from music publishers who heard the song at the funeral because someone posted it on social media. They want to talk."

She smiled and punched him in the shoulder. "Well, son of a bitch. How 'bout that? Congratulations. What're you gonna do?"

"First, I'm gonna do this." He leaned in and kissed her. "I've wanted to do that for a long time."

She smiled. "'Course you have."

Alex draped his arm around her.

Both were exhausted and sat quietly, relaxing and content.

"This doesn't mean you can have your way with me," he said.

She giggled. "From the day we met at the market, I knew Mom would like you."

"Why's that?"

"I told you this before. You always got a smart answer, and I don't mean like IQ."

"She was an excellent judge of character."

Toni suddenly felt vulnerable and alone; her mother gone, her aunt dispirited, and Alex getting an upgrade in life. "So, are you gonna leave Hamilton?"

He waited to answer.

She gave him a peck on the cheek but looked worried. "Are you?"

"Not right away."

"But soon?"

"I don't know. I'm not moving back to Los Angeles, and I don't want to spend my life on the road, but I'm a musician. I have to do something."

"If I was you, I'd a left long time ago," she said, sounding depressed.

"I may travel for a gig here and there, but I like it here."

"Seriously?"

He leaned over and kissed her again. "Seriously. I'm not leaving anytime soon. Especially since I've met the entire town. I like it here and I like the people. I like you and I… and I want to see where *this* goes."

She smiled and leaned in for another long kiss until a knock at the door interrupted them.

Alex and Toni were greeted by a woman named Sylvia Cortez who asked if they would meet her son. "He read Darlene's articles and insisted we come here. We couldn't get here for the funeral, but he heard about Darlene's daughter and wanted to meet you and share his story."

Toni and Alex stepped onto the porch where a thin, twenty-year-old man took a deep breath and said, "Hi. I'm Henry Cortez."

"Nice to meet you Henry," Toni said as she and Alex shook his hand.

"Go ahead," Sylvia prodded.

"Last year I woke up from a coma. I didn't know what had happened but I couldn't walk or talk."

"I'm so sorry," Toni said.

"Thank you. But that was the easy part. After two years, I woke up to a completely different world. My friends had all left for college, my dad died, and my girlfriend got married."

"Mercy," Toni whispered.

Henry humbly nodded and took a deep breath as his emotions were surfacing. "Everything was gone except my mom." He glanced at her as she held back the tears. "I… I wanted to die." The words choked him up but he continued. "They said I was depressed and gave me some pills, said it would help, but I didn't take any. I had a plan. I crushed all the pills so I could put them in a glass of water and end my life."

Stunned, Alex and Toni remained motionless.

"Then I read Darlene's first article about getting a do-over… and I couldn't wait to start over."

Toni steadied herself gripping Alex's hand. Alex was riveted but disquieted, having encouraged Darlene to publish the column.

"I was ready to go, but then I saw Darlene was going to write a follow-up article. I decided to wait to see what she said. I read her next article, about shedding labels, which kinda made me mad. I didn't want everyone remembering me as the guy who gave up, but nothing had changed and I still wanted a do-over. But, since Darlene gave me the idea of getting a do-over, I waited to see what she'd say next. Then I read the one called 'Everyone's a Hero.' He released a deep sigh. "I definitely didn't feel like a hero... and after the first article, I thought Darlene was telling me that a do-over was the answer, but the other articles made me keep thinking about it. I *wanted* to go, so I wrote Darlene an email asking her to give me the strength to follow through." The quiver in Henry's voice increased. "I never expected her to write back, so as soon as I sent her the message, I dumped the crushed pills into the water. I was sitting at my desk staring at my computer, ready to die; looking forward to it. Then, almost immediately, my computer dinged with Darlene's reply." He pulled a piece of paper from his pocket, unfolded it, and handed it to Toni. "I carry this with me. It's what Darlene wrote me."

Alex looked over her shoulder as Toni quickly read her mother's email to Henry. She looked up and fixed her teary eyes on Henry.

Henry smiled through tears of his own. Overwhelmed, he could only utter, "She told me to stick around."

Toni threw her arms around Henry for the tightest hug she'd ever given.

Alex reached out and hugged Sylvia. Soon, Toni was hugging Sylvia and Alex was doing that handshake hug that guys do, with Henry.

"Thank you," Toni said to Henry. She could barely speak, but she'd never felt prouder of her mother than she did at that moment.

Toni invited them in for tea, and after an hour of chatting, it was time for Henry and Sylvia to go home. They spent several emotional minutes saying goodbye but everyone promised to keep in touch, agreeing that Henry's story should be told over and over as a testament to his victory over illness and depression, and a fitting tribute to Darlene's memory.

* * *

On the day after the funeral, the Sunday ladies were occupied helping out-of-town guests, and thus skipped Sunday school. However, on the second Sunday after the funeral, they returned to Superbowl. It was the first one since Darlene's passing. Ruth Ann attended church but wasn't ready for the bowling alley.

The group fell into their normal routine, with Sarah tending bar while Irma and Dorothy set up the snacks. The mood was initially somber, but before long, things started returning to normal, especially as the liquor flowed.

"Did y'all see that fella at the funeral with the blue hair?" Irma remarked.

"I thought it was a wig," Dorothy said.

"Well, we all know he ain't from around here," Sarah added. "And he wasn't the only one."

"I kinda liked it," Cynthia said from her position a few feet from everyone.

"You would," Irma said, drawing laughs.

The light mood continued despite the dark cloud of Darlene's absence that hovered over them. No one wanted to kill the moment, so they continued deriding the out-of-town oddballs; laughing, drinking, and praising Darlene for giving them a show even after she passed.

In the middle of all the fun, Sarah stepped to the center and raised her glass. "I don't know about y'all but it makes me laugh when I think about everything Darlene woulda said about the last two weeks."

Some laughed, and some said amen, but everyone smiled, thinking about all the colorful ways Darlene would have made her presence known. They ended the meeting with a toast to Darlene and a vow to carry her memory with them, always.

Epilogue

Alex recorded a simple demo of the funeral song at his home studio and sent the low-budget recording to a publisher who'd expressed interest after hearing the live funeral version. After one listen, the publisher handed it to a veteran producer who was in the studio working on a new album for a gifted singer named Lyla Page. They immediately added it to her upcoming release.

The funeral song, titled "No Regrets at the End," was the first single released before Lyla's full album. The song was a tremendous success and opened several doors for Alex with publishers, bands, and agents. He played a few select dates around the country with The Lyla Page Band, then returned to Hamilton to continue writing.

Larry Westin periodically republished all of Darlene's articles on the home page of the *Hamilton Gazette*, even though they were archived on the website. On the anniversary of her death, he ran a special edition, paying tribute to Darlene, which included memorial tributes from friends and other locals.

Sarah and Irma penned an editorial together in memory of their friend. They wrote:

It has been a year since we said farewell to our beloved sister, Darlene Viriglio. We have missed her every day of this mournful year, but feel her presence regularly, especially when we hear stories about how she impacted so many lives. We wanted to share some of the stories of how Darlene has forever changed our tiny town.

Pastor Brown of the First Christian Church reported that attendance has nearly doubled over the past year, forcing him to add a second service on Sunday. He said, "It is humbling to see how God works through those like Miss Darlene, who open their hearts and minds to His will."

This year's fair brought a new artist who truly embodied Darlene's inspiration. Joanna Travers traveled to Hamilton for Darlene's funeral, and shared her story of how Darlene's writing helped her overcome tragedy, hardship, and loss, and ultimately led her to re-discover her love of painting. Since then, her work has received national attention. Vowing to never stop sharing Darlene's message, Joanna still hands out cards with quotes from Darlene every chance she gets. She told us, "Darlene's essays not only pulled me from the darkness, but they lift me higher every day." We couldn't have said it better. Dar, we'll always miss you, but thank you for leaving a little piece of you with all of us.

Ruth Ann continued struggling with the loss of her sister, and might have given up on life, if Toni hadn't moved in to help with the house and nurture her through the quiet, lonely nights. As time passed, Ruth Ann began reminiscing about her sister, sharing stories from their childhood to their final years of living together. Surprisingly, she started spending time with Ernie, owner of the Superbowl bowling alley. He had lost his wife many years earlier and, like Ruth Ann, needed a companion who could share the memories of a simpler time. They enjoyed car rides and picnics and quiet time together. With Ernie and her support system always nearby, Ruth Ann found comfort in the memories of her sister and the legacy she left behind.

Toni and Alex's relationship continued to grow as they spent many nights having dinner with Ruth Ann; with Ernie occasionally joining in. The trio went to church, shopped for groceries, and, of course, attended the annual fair.

Alex and Toni both pursued their passions: songwriting for Alex and a new career in nursing for Toni. They found in one another the partner they'd always sought; Alex sharing his life with Toni, occasionally taking her on the road while Toni blossomed in her own way, finding the foundation and support of someone she loved and trusted. Their lives were busy, but they never stopped living the lessons Darlene left them—live each day to its fullest and never have regrets.

The Journey Home by Darlene Viriglio

```
     Life is a journey, not just of
age and time, but of experience. No
one starts out great at anything.
Artist learns to paint, musicians to
```

play, scholars to think, and men and women learn how to relate to one another. In my past columns, I've talked about life after death, shedding the labels that hold you back, the importance of recognizing that everyone matters, and that you should try to live your life without regret. All these things are part of your journey through life. Your job, your relationships, your health, your faith, and all the seemingly insignificant events in your life are filled with challenges that are also opportunities. How you respond to these moments determines how your journey will progress or end. Learning to play a musical instrument comes with the challenge of practicing. You must practice *and* make mistakes or you will never get better. The same is true for relationships. You *must* learn to compromise, among other things, and you *will* make mistakes. And while you may not always notice it, success happens quietly—day by day—as you progress, whether it's relating to your spouse, your career, or your relationship with God. 1 Corinthians 13:11 says, '*When I was a child, I spoke like a child, I thought like a child, I reasoned like a child. When I became a man, I gave up childish ways.*'

From learning to walk, talk, and read, to navigating relationships, careers, and raising children, we all gain a lifetime of experiences and failures. Each obstacle, task, challenge, and opportunity shapes our entire life. It is easy to see what years of practice do for a concert pianist, but what a pianist does is no different from what you and I do every day in our jobs, our family life, how we handle setbacks and disappointment, and just about everything we do, no matter how insignificant it may seem. And, while at times it feels like we're losing—like my friend who wanted to quit his 'failing' career—I remind you that Babe Ruth struck out thousands of times *because* he continued stepping up to the plate and swinging for the fences. Failure is just another experience, and experience is the lifeblood of our time on earth. I believe you should embrace it and enjoy every hour, every day, every week, every person, and event that comes your way, as it is all part of the journey through life that makes you who you are.

And finally, maybe we all get a do-over, but if you learn from the successes and failures of your journey through life, you won't need one. **~DV**

Acknowledgments

A very special thanks to Joelle Yudin. Her tireless editing helped me discover the wonderful characters that make this story come alive.

About the Author

Gordon Amick is a long-time resident of Austin, Texas. He spends his days writing novels and songs as well as reading anything he can get his hands on. He's had careers in music, design, and business, but is happiest chasing anything creative, and spending time with his beloved dogs. He even, on rare occasions, picks up a gig playing piano with a local band.

The song portrayed in the story has been recorded and will soon be released!

No Regrets At The End, the song this book inspired, will soon be available on all the popular streaming services, as well as for download.

You can hear a preview at 319press.com/authors

Thank you for your interest and feel free to send us an email letting us know your thoughts, opinions, criticisms, or anything thing you'd like to say. We'd love to hear it. contact@319press.com

Milton Keynes UK
Ingram Content Group UK Ltd.
UKHW021505310824
447642UK00011B/279/J